Gerald's War

Based on the tragic tale of one man's life in peace and war.

(1918 - 1941)

Nigel Davies-Williams

From The Author

The glory pilots of the Second World War are those who flew Spitfires and Hurricanes. The Blenheim Bomber and its crews are the unsung heroes of the war. The Blenheim was the first British aircraft to cross the German coast at the outbreak of war on 3 September 1939 and a Blenheim sank the first U-Boat of the war on 11 March 1940. This is the story of some of the men of 211 Squadron of the RAF who flew the out-of-date Bristol Blenheim bombers and who died way before their time, so we can all live the lives we do now.

My considerable research has ensured that events described in the book are historically accurate.
The characters in this novel existed, of that there is no doubt, but some of the circumstances and conversations between the characters, as described in this work, are dramatised and may or may not have taken place at the time, we will never know for sure. What we do know is that the brave men who lost their lives during the conflict should never be forgotten and tribute should be paid for the sacrifices they made for us all.
This is one man's story, Gerald's War. My uncle who never came home and a family never gave up hope.

This book is in recognition of all of those heroes of war - combatants and families alike.

In Corfu

Kostas Kavvadias

Papa Spiro Monasterios
Without these people I never would have retrieved many documents and never would have been able to visit the exact site where L8511 crashed.

In Australia

Don Clark
Without Don, I would never have got in touch with many other people I spoke to and from whom I learned so much to write my book. Don is the mastermind behind the 211 Squadron website and his efforts have helped so many families over the years.

Others
There are others mentioned in this book. All served their country - many paid the ultimate sacrifice. Many went quietly to their graves and now remain only as inscriptions on walls and tombstones.
Long dead but not forgotten, in the hearts and souls of the world forever.

This Book is Dedicated to the Blenheim Boys of World War Two

Particularly those of 211 Squadron who lost their lives on
Easter Sunday, 13 April 1941

L8478 - Squadron Leader Antony Thorburn Irvine (27 years), Pilot Officer Gerald (Gerry) Davies (23 years),
Pilot Officer Arthur Geary - DFC (31 years)

L4819 - Flying Officer Richard Vivian Herbert (Herby) (21 years), Wing Commander Patric (Paddy) Bernard Coote (31 years),
Sergeant William Neilson Young (Jock) (26 years)

L1434 - Flight Lieutenant Lindsay Basil Buchanan (Buck) - DFC (24 years)*,
Squadron Leader Leslie Edward Cryer - DFC (28 years)*, Sergeant George Pattison - DFM (26 years)*

L8449 - Sergeant James (Peggy) Benjamin Thomas O'Neil, Flight Sergeant Jack Wainhouse (21 years)

L8664 - Flying Officer Charles Edward Vasey Thompson (Tommy) - DFC (23 years)*, Pilot Officer Peter Hogarth (26 years)*,
Sergeant Wilfred Arscott (38 years)*

L1539 - Sergeant Andrew (Andy) Bryce (24 years), Sergeant Arthur James Waring (Pongo) (24 years)*

Also, to survivors of the 13th April whose lives were lost shortly afterwards in other aircraft losses or accidents:

L1539 - Sergeant Arthur Graham James (Jimmy) (22 years) died 15th April 1941

L8449 - Flight Lieutenant Alan Clement Godfrey - DFC (26 years) died 7th August 1946 (Memorialised at Golders Green Crem)

All buried/memorialised at Phaleron War Cemetery, Athens, Greece unless stated.
*Memorialised on the Alamein Memorial, North Africa

*

320 men from 211 Squadron lost their lives between 1939 and 1945.

211 Squadron RAF

'Toujours a Propos'

Always To The Purpose

During the Second World War:
57,205 Bomber Command were killed (46% death rate) - a vast number of
them Blenheim Boys
8,403 were Wounded in Action
9,838 became PoWs
60% on operations were killed, wounded or taken prisoner.
Gerald Davies was just one of them.

FOREWORD FROM SIR DAVID JASON
'GERALD'S WAR'

It is a sad fact of life that so many accounts have been committed to paper of the stories of hundreds of young men and women involved in our two World Wars. Each and every one of them deserves to be heard as little did these service personnel know that their commitment to protecting our country would lead to such life-changing experiences, never to be forgotten. In this particular account of Gerald's War, Pilot Officer Gerald Davies joined the RAF as an Aircraftsman in 1936 but was called away to war all too soon. His journey ended in Greece on 13th April 1941 at just 23 years old but his story and that of his Squadron, the ill-fated 211 Squadron, lives on through this book and in the RAF records in perpetuity. There are moments of levity and camaraderie in the book as Gerald was an ordinary, young man like so many of his fallen comrades.

As always, we acknowledge these accounts lest we forget.

Sir David Jason

211 Squadron in Greece 1940 -1941

Gerald's War
Map of 211 Squadron
Locations, Targets and Other Sites
Nigel Davies-Williams

Map: Nigel Davies-Williams 2021

Chapter One

'The Blenheim Boys'

'The devotion and gallantry... are beyond all praise. The Charge of the Light Brigade at Balaclava is eclipsed in brightness by these almost daily deeds of fame.'

Winston Churchill on the Blenheim Crews - Prime Minister's Personal Minute, M.852/1, 30 August 1941

Lazy tendrils of smoke swirled around the man as he waded through the crystal-clear shallows towards the beach. As he shook himself down, he recalled childhood days when a pack of ragamuffins ran, shrieking with laughter through the backstreets jumping over glowing remains of Guy Fawkes' night bonfires, phoenix-like, emerging unscathed on the other side. Just a minute before, the Royal Air Force Pilot Officer had slid back the plexiglass covering the smoke-filled cockpit of his aircraft and slid down the fuselage into the shallow waters of the Ionian Sea.

He looked to the sky. He'd escaped being burned alive by the skin of his teeth. Burning to death was HIS, no, THE worst nightmare of all his comrades in the RAF. As he wafted the smoke away, he checked himself over. <'No injuries. No burns. That's a miracle! Thank God!'>

The officer sighed with relief, pulled open his smoke drenched tunic to reveal striped pyjamas which he wore under his uniform to keep himself warm at altitude in his cold outdated plane. Only a day before he'd been fighting in the Western Desert, in the heat of Egypt. No one had expected Greece to be colder and the cosy RAF Irvin jackets had

3

yet to be issued. So, as he'd readied himself for his first flight over Albania, he'd improvised and thrown his RAF uniform straight over his pyjamas. Surprisingly, at sea-level, it wasn't that cold considering it was November and as he waded around the front of the aircraft and onto the narrowest piece of beach imaginable; he opened his tunic a bit more. The beach had looked narrow from the sky but now he was on the ground it looked narrower than ever, dwarfed by the Blenheim, skewed on impact, sitting facing out to sea, its nose pointing towards the olive-green mountains of the coast across the water which they'd been following south.

The sun peeped from behind heavy rain clouds, offering welcome warmth as the officer walked down the narrow strip of beach, like a latter-day Robinson Crusoe, marooned on a desert island after disaster had struck his ship. This was no desert island, but it was a disaster, a disaster that still may not be over. As he mulled over his situation, thoughts crowded his head of the girlfriend he'd left behind in Henley-on-Thames. He had crash landed onto an island, but this was no desert island, this was Corfu in the Ionian Sea.

The RAF officer walked away from the wreck of the Bristol Blenheim Mark 1, number L8511, smoke still pouring from a huge hole in, what remained of the port engine cowling, now with little engine inside. The starboard engine, what was left of it, exuded thick black smoke, and the entire plane looked like a piece of Greek Graviera cheese, shrapnel and bullet holes littering its entire surface.

The air was heavy with aviation fuel and beautiful coloured patterns swirled on the crystal clear sea around the aircraft. The pilot officer breathed a sigh of relief to be walking away in one piece as he glanced at the battle-battered piece of machinery behind him. That was at least one of his nine lives used up and he knew it. He had stared death in the face several times in the past few minutes, and it wasn't over yet. He might be safely on terra firma on this Sunday morning, but this wasn't any ordinary Sabbath, this was the 24th of November 1940 and the Greco-Italian War was in full swing. Straying too far from the aircraft might be a problem, but the young man had no option. He had to find help and hoped this was a friendly place. He shaded his eyes with his hand as he took in his surroundings. He could see no one, but he could see a little building with a red roof sat neatly amongst a small grove of Eucalyptus and Olive trees and he made his way slowly towards it. As he got nearer, he could see the dirty, white-washed walls and two large mahogany doors. Now he could see red roof tiles laid in neat rows and at the far end of the roof on the gable, sat a wooden cross nailed on precariously.

<'A church in the middle of nowhere? Jesus. Bloody God, getting me shot shown.'> Gerald looked to the sky shaking his head remembering the strict Pastor, Herbert Barrow at Rivertown Congregational Church in his hometown of Shotton, who was always quoting the third of the Ten Commandments in Exodus: Verse 7 of Chapter 20.   He could remember it verbatim. 'Thou shalt not take the name of the Lord thy God in vain; for the LORD will not hold him guiltless that taketh his name in vain.'

It was a favourite of his dad Frank too, who was always harping on to all and sundry about 'taking the Lord's name in vain,' but who often fell at the first hurdle himself. He hoped that God would forgive him this once, given the current circumstances.

<'Doesn't look much like a church.'>

Not a soul in sight, although they had seen the odd peasant dotted in the fields as they had made their undignified approach.

He touched the beige canvas holster holding his standard service .38 Enfield revolver, which he'd quickly stuffed into his tunic, as he'd exited the stricken plane and he nervously walked on slowly along a beach no more than two or three yards wide, less than that in places.

His boots squelched with salty water from his impromptu paddle in the cold Ionian Sea. The water wasn't freezing though and the air was pleasantly mild considering it was November. He looked down at his sodden boots, peppered with grains of filthy looking sand from the narrow beach. He took a deep breath and shook his head with disbelief as he considered what might have been.

<'All in a days' work!' > He comforted himself with that thought.

He fumbled through his pockets as he walked, searching frantically.

<'Where the hell is that photo?'>

Despite not finding what he was looking for, he was glad to be alive. They had escaped by the skin of their teeth; their hydraulics had been shot away and there was no option but to pancake it down onto the narrowest of shorelines.

There came a shout from the aircraft behind him. "Come on, Gerry lad. Get some help. Stop fidgeting for that damn photo. She'll be shagging someone else by now anyhow, ol' man."

There were hoots of laugher from two RAF officers who were standing with their heads poking through the glass hatch Gerald had just popped out of, despite the plane's precarious landing position half

5

in and half out of the gently lapping waves.

"Hilarious, gentlemen. Shame one of those Macchi bullets didn't get one of you two blighters on the tongue."

Gerald carried on walking, still checking his pockets and thinking of Sue, his girl back in Henley-on-Thames. His two comrades strived to douse the billowing smoke coming from the starboard engine in an attempt to prevent the entire plane exploding in a ball of fire.

Nine aircraft took off that day at ten-fifteen in the morning, in groups of three. Pilot Officers Gerald 'Gerry' Davies and Arthur Geary were with Squadron Leader 'The Bish,' James Gordon-Finlayson or 'G-F' as they sometimes called him, as usual, L8511 led the three Blenheims of 211 Squadron's 'A' flight. The squadron's commanding officer, The Bish, led by example and chose a crew he knew he could trust and even at Gerald's tender age, he had a plethora of experience under their belt, Arthur too.

The Mission: Raid Durazzo. And they had.

Twenty-two-year-old Gerald was the navigator and bomb aimer of the crew of three. He'd done an outstanding job over Durazzo. He was a trainee pilot and would soon be flying as the rate of losses of pilots was high but for now, he was the best bomb-aimer and navigator 211 Squadron had and that's why The Bish had chosen him. Gerald had plotted their course to precision. They'd come at Durazzo from the north on what was quite a fine day, although they'd experienced heavy cloud over the mountains of northern Albania. They clung to the cumulus clouds which hung over the coast of the Adriatic; it was safer this way. Any sign of fighters and they had a hiding place. This raid by 211 Squadron would be the opening shots of their campaign to join the Battle for Greece, which was now starting to take hold like a wildfire in the region. Durazzo had a value to all sides as a strategic seaport. This was where the Italians were bringing in supplies for their ever-growing army in the area. They'd first landed here on 7th April 1939 and had attempted to invade Greece but had failed. They were reinforcing once again and had to be stopped at all costs.

As they approached their target, the temperature monitor had recorded a chilly four degrees. The Bish had shivered, bashing his gloved hands together to get some warmth shouting, "Bloody freezing boys! Let's do the business and head for home lads." Gerald agreed, shivering both with cold and fright, as he looked down through the bomb aimer. "We've only been here a day and winter's kicked in good style, sir."

"It's Europe m'boy, not Africa! Wouldn't be here young Gerry boy, but for those damned Itis. Can't leave their greasy hands off anything."

The target was imminent. All went quiet in the aircraft as concentration kicked in. The only words spoken now were those necessary to do what they had to do. Their bomb load had been securely placed on board from the fusing-shed at Menidi, their base on the Greek mainland. 'A' flight had refuelled at Larissa but now their base was over 350 miles away and they were, but three aircraft ahead of six more some minutes behind them.

There were several ships anchored in the harbour, which was Durazzo Bay. Gerald carefully gripped 'the tit' - the thingamabob that released the bomb load as it was creatively called by anyone who worked it.

"Bombs Gone!" Gerald had called in a matter-of-fact way, as below two cargo ships took direct hits. Fire and oily black smoke billowed from the successful hit. Little two-legged ants could be seen running away from the scene along the dock. Gerald hated the cruelty of it all but knew it had to be done. This was war, and this was what he had trained to do for many months. He had no idea how many people he'd killed below, but he knew he had. The little ants running were the lucky ones who'd escaped the carnage he'd delivered on them. Despite inner feelings, they cheered as their plane sped up and away towards the clouds, but their cheering was premature, as fierce anti-aircraft fire burst from the ground. There was little they could do in such a slow-moving bomber to take evasive action, such was the intensity of the ground fire and two ack-ack shells hit their Blenheim, cartwheeling it right over. An enormous hole was torn in the cowling of the port engine and at once oil poured out, but the engine still chugged away, keeping the undamaged propeller working. The same couldn't be said for the starboard engine, which was also hit.

Plumes of smoke billowed out from the damaged engines and traced the movement of the plane in the sky as it continued to tumble, out of control.

"Bloody hell. We're in for it, boys," shouted The Bish, as he pushed his stick with some force, trying to regain control of the Blenheim. Gerald hung on, gripping whatever he could. Geary was thrown to the top of his glass turret and then back into his seat.

The Bish felt his rudder engage and throttled back the Blenheim.

"We're in business, gentlemen!" he coughed wildly as he shouted. A mixture of petrol fumes and smoke were now filling the cockpit as the Blenheim levelled up from its sharp descent. "I have her back. God knows for how long though chaps."

Gerald pushed his nose to the plexiglass and looked out. It wasn't good.

They were on their own. Their formation was nowhere to be seen, but both engines seemed to still be working, although the damage to the Blenheim was enormous with oil pouring from the port engine, a hole he could fit through in the port wing and fuel leaking from shrapnel holes peppering the plane.

"We ARE airborne? I mean STILL in the air, G-F? Are we sir?" he joked, as he involuntarily wretched from the heavy fumes filling the cabin.

"There's oil and petrol streaming into the turret chaps," Arthur Geary coughed, "Shite, I'm struggling to breathe here. I know you don't like me chaps but trying to poison me with fumes to get rid of me is a bit much."

All three occupants of the Blenheim fiddled furiously in an attempt to open a hatch or anything which would let in some fresh air, despite the cold outside. Fumes and laughter pervaded the aircraft and several thumbs up followed.

The Bish knew the plane could catch fire or break apart at any moment, and they would need more than luck to make it. He had no option but to close down the port engine, its pressure fallen to zero.

The Bish and Gerald, watery eyed, exchanged a glance through the thick fumes and smiled amidst the surrounding chaos. Their battle for survival was about to get a whole lot worse.

"Fighters! Beam attack lads." Geary squealed, sounding like a choirboy striving for the highest note.

Rain now fell heavily across the windows of the Bristol Blenheim, as a Macchi 200 settled in behind. It mattered not whether they'd seen the plane coming; they were no match for the superior Italian aircraft, even without all the damage they had sustained. The Italian could reach speeds of up to 270 mph, and their survival was looking more unlikely by the second.

A single burst of half inch machine-gun bullets ripped holes in the tail and some of the fuselage of the ever-slowing Bristol Blenheim. Luckily the damage was limited and the plane flew on with its crew of Blenheim Boys.

"Christ's sake, chaps, that was close! We're a sitting bird for the Itis!"

the Bish sang out as he tried to take evasive action in a plane which had lost almost all of its manoeuvrability.

"Fuck sake Bish, a bit too close for me..." Geary coughed and laughed nervously in his cramped air-gunner position in the dorsal turret of the plane. The Macchi had peppered his space with holes, but he was still alive. He felt like a wick in an oil lamp, such was the amount of fuel and oil which had sprayed onto him. His biggest worry had been catching fire, but he had been lucky this time. Then he looked down to see his notebook shredded in his knee trouser pocket.

"I've been hit!" he shouted forward, but there was no blood on his leg, just a slight trickle from a tiny wound on his left cheek. He sighed with relief. He'd been the width of some deadly piece of shrapnel from death.

"False alarm! I'm okay," shouted the old head of Geary, an experienced 31-year-old from Edmonton in Middlesex. He got to grips with his machine gun. "Have it!" He gritted his teeth as the gun rattled away. "Have it fucker," he repeated as he did his best to get the Macchi into the sights of his .303 Vickers K Machine Gun.

"You all right back there? Keep those damned shells going," Gerald shouted down to Arthur Geary.

"Couldn't be better 'ol boys... er... unless this piece of metal we're now in falls apart any more. They like to give us a parting gift hey?" Geary wiped the blood away from the minor wound on his cheek.

The bullets hitting the beleaguered Blenheim were too close for comfort for The Bish. It was now possible to smell the unpleasant odour of the explosive bullets, such was the proximity of their attacker. The Bish put the plane into a nosedive to build up speed to escape the Macchi 200. Arthur Geary clung on inside his turret, as the plane lurched violently from side to side, but the Italian fighter didn't fire another shot. He watched it peel away. "He's buggered off boys. No ammo or short on fuel, hey?"

They heaved a sigh of relief and looked at each other when suddenly a blinding beam of sunlight pierced the heavy clouds shining onto the Bristol Blenheim as it levelled out. Their relief was short-lived. A Fiat G50 Freccia, using the cover of the sun, had been watching his comrade and now saw his opportunity to attack.

Luckily for them all, Geary spotted the plane on its dive of death towards them and shouted a warning not a moment too soon.

"Shit, bandits at two... "

The Bish sprung into action with an evasive s-manoeuvre as streams of tracer bullets whisked by the Blenheim. Geary fired off over 900 rounds, but without hitting their pursuer. A profanity accompanying every bullet. Something he did to calm his nerves.

Arthur Geary, had a dual role as wireless operator and air gunner, but using the wireless was not an option. His full concentration was firing his machine gun from the powered gun turret part way down the fuselage of the aircraft, but he was a second slower than the Italian ace who's burst of fire once again hit the engine of the Bristol Blenheim. More oil and smoke spewed out of the port engine.

They hit cloud cover, and the Italian lost sight of the Blenheim as it headed deeper into the clouds. He recorded it as a firm kill and headed back to base.

The relief on the faces of the crew of the Blenheim was palpable. No longer were they under attack, but now their primary worry was keeping in the air.

"We'll never make it back over the mountains and any rate, we'll all die of suffocation if we don't sort something out and soon," The Bish shouted as the fumes and smoke in the cockpit became thicker. "We'll have to ditch or bail out. If you want to take your chances, I don't mind. Let me know."

"Not a chance Skip, I'm not brollying it for anyone. If you're staying, we're staying with you. We all leave together, or we all go down together skip," shouted Gerald, as he still searched for THAT photo which he had no intention of leaving on the Blenheim if they abandoned it. "Besides, I've dropped my pic of Sue somewhere and I'm not leaving this damned heap of shit without it. Anyway, as I said, if we're going down, I'm going with you. How about you Geary ol' man, you fit for bailing?"

Nothing.

"Hey!" he shouted louder. "You still alive and kicking?"

The shout came from the back of the aircraft. "Alive an' AOK skipper. No chance of me jumping. I hate heights! Take my chances with you pair of buggers."

They barely kept a speed of 120 mph and headed south-south-east down the Adriatic coast, trailing thick black smoke, struggling to keep an altitude of 1,500 feet.

Leaden skies and a worsening rain storm intensified their plight, although they were thankful this was, in its own way, a significant benefit, as low cloud kept them pretty much invisible, despite the beacon of smoke trailing behind.

After two hours of precarious flying with all windows and hatches open to stop them suffocating, Gerald spotted land. "Corfu skip. We can put her down there for sure."

They knew they had only a few minutes before their plane crashed into the sea or worse still, plummeted into the unforgiving rocky terrain of Corfu.

Only a minute or so ago he'd been frantically checking the charts against the compass on the plane, whilst from time to time scanning the terrain below looking for a safe place to land.

"Down there skip, starboard. Looks like salt flats and a field... yes, a field, with a narrow beach."

The plane was a wing and a prayer away from disaster and if they didn't put down soon the plane would decide their fate for them.

The Bish looked down. "Bloody hell, Gerry boy, that's one hell of a narrow beach. He took a deep breath, "Running out of options here. Those gremlins are running riot around this damn plane and pulling it to pieces."

"There's a red roof just ahead of it. A building."

"Gotcha Gerry. Let's give it a shot."

With the Blenheim flying in ever decreasing circles, Gerald fired off the colours of the day flare, the primary purpose of which was to let people on the ground know they were a friendly aircraft. They didn't want shooting at again. One more bullet would surely see the aircraft disintegrate mid-air.

There seemed to be nowhere to land. There was one flat field but it looked boggy and other flat patches of ground were obstructed with what looked like barrels of tar plainly put there to stop any Italian or German invasion.

Gerald was ever watchful for a landing spot. Then he saw it. "Look Bish, a beach. Looks flat enough... erm... if a little narrow! Can we do that?"

"Possibly so 'ol boy. Get the gear down."

Gerald did his best to work the hydraulic selection lever, but it was useless and wouldn't budge.

"Gonna have to pancake it skip," he shouted. "Those gremlins have done their worst on the landing gear. It just won't budge."

Suddenly, without warning, the Blenheim shook violently. There was an explosion and the terrible shriek of grinding metal. The port engine, more or less in its entirety, fell away from the plane, dropping to the sea below, luckily leaving the wing intact. More fuel spilled out and the tanks were now empty. There was just enough fuel in the pipes to keep the starboard engine running, albeit poorly. With the one remaining engine slowly stuttering to a halt, the plane was going down whether they liked it or not. They had one chance to make the narrow landing strip on the beach, which they were luckily on course for.

"Here we go boys, we're gonna pancake it down," The Bish shouted. "Gonna be a rough one. It'll be part sea and part sand. Probably mostly sea!" He suppressed a nervous half-laugh. "If you're religious, get your payer book out now."

Gerald was a Congregationalist but hadn't gone to his church much and Geary was a church on Sunday man, mainly because everyone else in his family went and he felt obliged. Both felt God would do them no good at this stage, but looked to the heavens anyway, praying they would make it. Without landing gear and one engine missing, this would be a touch and go affair.

The jumbled mass of metal, the barely aerodynamic Blenheim gracefully glided into the shallow waves lapping the shore, trailing thick black smoke, which had been its companion since Durazzo. The first part of the aircraft to touch the water was one wheel, which had come down on the port wing. Neither The Bish nor Gerald had any inclination the wheel had come down and by some miracle The Bish was landing with the port wing into deeper water. Had it been the other side the shallower water may have ripped the wing off and the plane would have gone up in smoke. Crew and all. As it was, the wheel caused the Blenheim skew sideways and as the body of the aircraft touched the water, spray covered the entire plane and within seconds it had come to a halt, sinking down two or three feet into the shallow water.

The three Blenheim Boys let out a cheer of delight. Gerald, closest to The Bish, patted him gratefully on the back. "Great job skip. Great job!"

Geary shouted in agreement as he crawled from the gun turret down the body of the Blenheim. The three men shook hands in the confines of their metal coffin. Each said their own personal prayer of thanks. They were safely on the ground and thanked God they'd made it.

Smoke still poured from the starboard engine and from the remains of where the port engine had sat. The plane drifted with the gentle lap of the Ionian Sea and now felt more like a boat. Water had poured in, but to no more than a couple of feet. There was an overwhelming silence now the roar of the broken engine had died away apart from the welcoming sounds of raindrops on the metal of the fuselage and the occasional bigger wave crashing on the outside. The smell of the seashore was now permeating the fumes and smoke. Gerald had been to Brighton many times and the smell reminded him of holidays spent there. His dreams of times in Brighton were rudely shattered when The Bish shouted, "Right, Pilot Officer Davies. You're the youngest and fittest of us all. Go find us some help, lad."

"G-F, on my way."

"Geary, get on the radio and tell them what the situation is. You know the drill."

"G-F, sir. I've tried contact a few times and nothing."

Author's Note

As the Second World War began in 1939, the Blenheim was the plane of choice for the RAF and they had more of this plane than any other. Used as 24/7 bomber and a long-range fighter in multi-combat roles. So hazardous were the missions flown by the crews of the Blenheims that the 'Blenheim Boys' earned the respect of everyone else in the RAF.

A remarkable aircraft flown by remarkable people.

Chapter Two

'A Meeting in Chester'

Just after two in the afternoon, the black LNWR steam locomotive noisily hissed its way into Chester Railway Station. First to alight from the train was an army officer of the Cheshire Regiment, who quickly grabbed a copy of the day's paper from the busy newsstand on the platform. The Chester Chronicle was dated Saturday 6th October 1917. It was pleasantly warm for the time of year. The summer had been a wet one all round and everyone was enjoying the October sunshine. The soldier stood, relaxed, unlit pipe hanging from his mouth, flicking through the pages of the broadsheet, leaning against the newsstand.

The train had been full of soldiers, as was the railway station itself. The air hung heavy with pungent blue-grey tobacco smoke drifting slowly through the still air. Almost everyone was smoking. Men in uniform and old men in flat caps smoked pipes or rolled their own from leather pouches they pulled from their pockets. The sound of striking Swan Vestas reverberated around the platform and men cupped their hands around their mouths or pipe-bowls to make the flame last as long as possible. One or two threw the match down with a shake of their hand as the flame scorched their nicotine'd skin. The atmosphere was somewhat melancholy, but occasional jocularity and someone, who'd had one too many of a rum-ration, was jollily singing "Carry me back to Blighty... drop me anywhere... I don't care... " with the words all jumbled and in the wrong order, broke the atmosphere.

These weren't the best of times, but people made the most of what they had. Women, some with children, some crying, some flinging their arms wide open with joy, greeted a loved one they hadn't seen since the last grant of leave. World-weary soldiers walked by, some on their way home from the front line. You tell these soldiers easily, as the mud from the trenches still clung to their thick woollen uniforms and puttees, often caked and thick. Many appeared tired and emotionally traumatised, their souls left behind on a French or Belgian battlefield, but all weathered their personal storm, some better than others. Either way, no one dared mention how they felt, for fear of being called a malingerer or worse. They had trench gnarled and windswept faces; faces which had stared into a cold and unforgiving hell which no one who hadn't been there could begin to imagine. They all held secrets which most would take to their graves either when they went back to the front or many years later, when they died a thankful-peaceful death in the comfort of home, not in some foreign trench.

Many were the walking-wounded on their way home. Patches over eyes, arms in slings and walking sticks or crutches for the one limbed, were a common sight. The Chester Chronicle being read that day declared this was the 166th week of *The War* and held gripping stories of glory and of death to local soldiers. This was right in the middle of the third battle of Ypres or Passchendaele, as the history books would recall it, in dispassionate black and white, with no hint of the pain and suffering of the men who were there. 300,000 more would die following Arras earlier in the year which had killed men in numbers beyond belief. There was no hope the war, which had been raging for over three years, would end soon. What ghosts accompanied the soldiers on the platforms of Chester Railway Station that day?

Francis Davies had diligently been respectful to his elders and so was the very last passenger to leave the train. He hopped off the smoky train with a skip in his step. The sixteen-year-old had been coming to Chester every other Saturday for a few months now and was dressed smartly in his dark brown suit and matching plain brown tie. He'd been working at the local ironworks for two years now and gave the best part of his weekly wages to his parents, but he could still afford to look a little dapper, especially when meeting the girl of his dreams. He loved coming to Chester. The city bustled with activity, even during the war, and it was just a quick hop on the train from his home in Shotton, just over the border in Wales.

It was in Chester, just a few short months ago, he'd met Lizzie Sumner. She lived on the other side of Chester close to Waverton Railway Station and she was also a regular visitor to the city. She was fifteen, almost sixteen, and had paid twopence for the privilege of

15

travelling one stop to Chester.

The two had agreed to meet by the newsstand, where the officer stood reading his paper. Francis approached the stand and stood next to the smart officer, reading the reverse side of his paper whilst he waited for Lizzie to arrive.

The officer, who was no more than twenty-four or twenty-five years old, peeked around his paper, aware of the staring eyes from the other side.

"Young man, are you reading my paper?" demanded the officer haughtily, with a wry smile on his face.

"Sorry, sir. Was just waiting for my girlfriend and saw the headlines about the war."

"You were, were you? I ought to charge you half the cost of the paper." The captain placed his tongue in his cheek and looked at Francis with a grin.

Francis, not understanding the joke, changed the subject. "I wanted to join up, but I was too young. I work in the ironworks... er the steelworks now, but the army is far more exciting. I mean, your uniform, it's lovely sir."

The officer stopped reading for a moment.

"Captain Gerald Sidebotham 4th Battalion, Cheshires. *[1]* Pleased to meet you, young man."

"Francis Edward Griffiths Davies, sir. Pleased to meet you."

"That's some name, Francis. Yes, the damned war... and don't be in such a great hurry to join up young man."

"Sir. Why, sir?"

"See all these heroes in the paper here. They're someone's son or husband, and they're never coming home again. EVER. Their bodies are fertiliser in France or somewhere else. Look here at this one." He pointed to one article on the back page of the paper showing a blurred picture of a soldier in uniform. "It says here... *'One of the Cheshire's Missing'* One from my own regiment young man '... *Private James Anderton, Cheshire Regiment, has been missing since August 10th. His mother who lives at Upton Heys Cottage, Upton, Chester, is very anxious concerning her son's fate, and will be obliged if any comrade can give information about him.'* Poor bugger will be dead and his mother hasn't got a clue what's happened. The Hun will have given him a metal sandwich. His mother knows he's dead really, but we all hang on to hope when someone goes missing."

Francis nodded with a worried look as he looked at the picture.

"A few more pictures on this page. Second-Lieutenant E. Douglas Howard...er...killed in action in France on 20th September. Er...says here, he was at the Battle of the Somme and had been invalided home with Trench Fever. He'd have been covered in lice and riddled with disease. Poor bugger."

He puffed heavily on his pipe to re-ignite the tobacco.

"Got him recovered, then they sent him back. Now he's dead. Twenty-three it says here."

Francis' face looked grim.

"Lost my older brother February last year and been wounded myself twice, last time at Sulva Bay just over a year ago. Grim business was Gallipoli, but we mustn't think of my war. No."

The Captain looked at his newspaper again, shaking his head and squinting his eyes as if thrown into the fight again. He regained his composure, breathing heavily and tapping his pipe against his teeth. He looked to the newspaper for a way out.

"Here's another... Gunner Harold Herbert Walley... son of a Chester Magistrate. Gone in his prime. Not a great deal older than you, lad. Twenty. Says here he was a member of Waverton Presbyterian Church, well he's not going to be saying any more prayers there lad. They'll be saying the prayers for him more like."

The officer shook his head derisively.

"My Lizzie is from Waverton way."

"That who you meeting, lad? A lady acquaintance."

"Yes, sir."

"Nice. Well, look after her by not joining up. Want me to read you about more men dying... the paper's full of them. Do me a favour and don't be one of them... and do you know what lad?"

"No sir, what, sir?"

"Once you're there, you belong to the army no matter what you think of it. Some have tried to run away, I've heard them shouting for their mother but our own army, would you believe it, our own lot, have shot them for doing so. Stood them at a post at dawn and BANG! No Hun bullet killed them. Cowardice they call it, but these men were suffering from the constant noise of shells. Boom, boom, all the time and they had to get away." He made a final loud. "BOOM!"

Francis jumped with fright for the second time.

"Sorry lad but it's the truth." The Captain looked up and saw a young girl approaching. "This her?"

Francis looked toward the bottom of the stairs at the throng of people approaching from a train just in at another platform, to see Lizzie heading his way in a calf length beige cotton dress. Most of the surrounding people were soldiers, so Lizzie, in her Sunday best, stood out.

"Pretty girl."

"She is, sir."

Lizzie walked up to the two. She looked up at the Captain.

"Hello, sir." She directed her greeting first to Captain Sidebotham, who touched his forage cap to signal hello, still clinging to his newspaper. "Sorry I'm late Francis. Train was late for some reason."

"Just been telling your young man not to join up," Captain Sidebotham informed her before Francis could say anything.

Lizzie nodded in agreement. "He's too young, anyway."

"So are many others but they're not checking how old they are. If they're old enough to hold the weight of a Lee-Enfield, then they're in. Watch who gives you the King's shilling I would advise."

"This is Captain Gerald Sidebotham," Francis introduced the army officer formally. "He's been showing me the paper and all the people killed in the war."

"Lizzie Sumner, sir." Lizzie almost curtsied before the officer. "Yes sir, it's very tragic. Who would want a son or father or anyone to be in such a nasty war, sir?"

Captain Sidebotham lit his pipe, folded the newspaper under his arm, moved closer to Francis and gripped his arm. "You wouldn't want to be dead, would you now, dear boy? Not with a beautiful girl on your arm like this."

"No, sir. No."

"And you, pretty lady, don't let him go. Look after each other, there's no marrying a photograph of a loved one."

"I agree, sir."

With an immense noise amidst a haze of steam and smoke, a train pulled alongside the platform not ten yards from the newsstand where they were stood.

"My train! Duty calls." The officer took a last long look at Francis. "Mark my words and do me a favour. Stay working at the factory lad." The Captain then looked directly at Lizzie. "I'm going now, but remember the words of Captain Gerald Sidebotham will you both? Stay away from the war."

The Captain walked away, not looking back, and headed for the train. The clouds of his own pipe smoke blending neatly with the smoke from the train.

"Nice man" said Lizzie.

"Yes, nice man."

Gerald he was wasn't he?"

"Yes, Gerald."

"I like that name. Anyway, YOUNG MAN... " Lizzie smiled. "We have to talk, but not here. There's something I need to tell you. Let's go to Grosvenor Park. You like it there."

The couple walked away from the railway station and headed for the park, over the canal, hand in hand. Something was troubling Lizzie, and it wasn't what she'd heard from Captain Gerald Sidebotham. Francis wondered all the way to the park what the matter could be, but all Lizzie could do was talk about how wet the summer had been and how much she had enjoyed their previous outings to Chester since they'd met.

It was a good fifteen-minute walk to the park, and the young couple soon found a bench on which they could sit and talk.

"So what's up, Lizzie? You've been strange since we met. Are you going to stop our courting? I know we're young, but this is the war and things are odd. It'll get better."

"I know it will... the war, I mean."

"You think we won't?"

"Stop putting words into my mouth. I wasn't saying anything about us..."

He didn't let her finish. "This park is where we met those few short months ago. I dashed under a tree when the rain pelted down and someone else dashed in a few seconds later. Soaked to the skin."

"I'd have frozen without your coat."

"Ha ha, yes, and we'd have not met if the rain hadn't poured down. Fate at work, I'd say."

"Fate or what I'm not sure, but we met a few times since and I like us meeting but... "

"But you've had enough of me."

"You think so? No, of course not. It's worse than that... "

"Worse than what?"

"Worse is a bad way of describing this. Oh God. I just don't know how to say what I want to say, you idiot. I just don't know how to say it."

"I can't stand this. You're telling me you don't want to see me any more? Well, I'm going before I hear things I don't want to hear."

Francis stood up from the bench they'd been sitting on.

"Francis. Listen."

Lizzie stood up.

Francis began walking away.

She shouted, looking around at the people who were walking in the park. "Francis, come back."

Francis walked on. Lizzie ran after him. "Wait!"

"Don't want to hear it." He shook his head several times.

Lizzie had no option.

She shouted, "I'm up the... YOU KNOW... the..." She stopped in her tracks, biting her lip, nodding and furtively pointing at the pattern on the front of her dress. It seemed the whole of the park had its eyes on her now. There was great anticipation as to the next word.

Francis, now thirty yards away, stopped and looked around.

"What?"

Lizzie whispered and tried to mouth the words. "I'm with child."

"Ay?"

She shouted. "With child! I'm having a baby for God's sake, cloth ears." She added as an afterthought, "... er ... darling."

Now the whole park focussed their gaze on Lizzie. There was a flurry of disapproving, shaking heads as people walked by.

"Give you a good five-minutes gossip ay?" Lizzie tearfully said to a couple who looked most disgusted as they scurried away, holding their heads high and scattering several squirrels busy on the pathway.

Lizzie walked towards Francis ignoring the frowns and gestures of the surrounding people. This was the business of her and Francis alone. Besides, no one knew who they were, anyway. Francis had remained frozen to the spot. This was not the news he was expecting. Lizzie waked straight to him. "It's true."

They hugged. Francis was shaking with fear. Lizzie was now crying openly.

"Let's go somewhere else and talk."

They headed for the canal side, ten minutes' walk away, and on the way talked about anything but being in the family way. Lizzie spoke of women having the right to vote, about which there was much being written in the newspapers. This was a grand distraction from thinking about what was to come in a few months' time.

"If women have ever proved themselves entitled to the right to vote," she began, "then they have doubled and probably trebled this right, since this damned war broke out!" If Lizzie have been from a more eminent and educated background, she would have been wearing purple, white and green. As it was, she was the daughter of farm labourers who worked every hour God sent to keep a roof over their heads. "We are the silence behind the men and take some of the heaviest blows of life during war. Oh, yes."

Francis nodded. His mind was elsewhere.

"Wives and mothers all over the place, as Captain Gerald Sidebot... whatever his name was... Gerald, I'll remember him as Gerald... has shown us, are mourning the loss of fathers, husbands, brothers and sons and it is the wives and sweethearts who have to bear this burden for evermore. And now we have the hardships of men's work too. All without the vote. Your ironworks Francis... are there many women doing the work of men there now?"

Francis nodded as if to say yes.

'You're not listening, Francis."

"Sorry, sorry. Yes, there are." He hadn't really paid attention to what Lizzie was saying and he hadn't seen many women in his works, but he didn't want to argue. Babies, and what his parents might say, was uppermost in his mind. He worked in the rolling mill of the ironworks and yes, there were an increasing amount of women working there whilst the men were away.

Lizzie persisted. "So what do you think about women and the vote?"

He had to answer. He knew women were doing men's work everywhere. Anyone could see that. "Neither of us has the vote anyway, and there's loads of reasons why. We're too young for a start and even my dad, who's forty-eight, hasn't got a vote because he doesn't own his house."

"We'll get the vote after the war for sure. You wait and see."

1917 was a time when all women and 40% of adult males were still without the vote, but this couple had more pressing things to worry about.

They found a secluded spot.

"It's secluded spots like his which got us into trouble. ME into trouble." Lizzie said, touching her stomach.

"Do you know for sure?... AND it is mine?"

"I should slap you for that right now. What do you think I am AND yes, I'm as sure as I can be. Everything is different. My body feels like it's getting owned by someone else. Something else! Plus, I've felt so sick for enough mornings in the past few weeks to know it's real enough."

"So you knew last time you saw me? When is it... you know... due?"

"Questions Francis. Questions. No, I wasn't sure last time I saw you and, if all goes well, it will be February, perhaps March... next year."

"Oh Lord! What are my parents going to say?"

"What are mine going to say more like? They don't have a clue yet, and they'll flip their lids once they know. They'll kill me or send me away. I'm really frightened, Francis. More frightened than I've ever been in my life."

Francis eyed her up and down. She looked as lovely as ever and unchanged in any way. "... But you look as slim as ever."

Lizzie grabbed Francis' hand. "Feel that belly. It's not bigger, but it's firm like a soldier's drum. It can only start moving out from now onwards. Someone will spot my condition, eventually. My mother, for sure. She's not the worry though, but my dad will be mad..."

"But we can... er ... you can hide it for now, yes? AND your dad's a big bloke."

They both laughed together. They had no idea why.

*

Lizzie Sumner had lived most of her life in the Cheshire countryside and her family wouldn't take too kindly to her arriving home with the news she was with child. Not a soul would discuss the subject openly in 1917, least of all her family, and she would bring shame on them as far as she was concerned. These thoughts plagued Lizzie and presented her with a dilemma she could not handle at her tender age. How would she even tell her family and how would she approach the subject, if she approached it at all!

It crossed her mind not to tell anyone and get rid of the incumbency now growing inside her, but abortion was not an option for several reasons. It was a dangerous and highly illegal procedure during the 1900s. Back street abortionists and the purchase of supposedly natural abortifacients were rife. Without the aid of modern contraception, young women, in desperation, would often seek to do anything to ease themselves of the burden of a pregnancy. Lizzie, despite what might be said at home, would not go down this route and she had told Francis this, the very day she had told him she was expecting.

Francis hadn't got a clue what his parents, Elizabeth and Francis, might say, and he would not be having the conversation with them anytime soon.

*

Francis' dad was also called Francis and his mother was called Elizabeth, the same name as his girlfriend Lizzie. Luckily Francis' father was known at the steelworks as Frank, so after Francis was born, Francis senior became known as Frank to everyone. Frank and Francis worked together at the steelworks, one of the biggest iron and steel works in Britain - John Summers' at Shotton in Flintshire. Surrounded by white-hot pieces of metal one day in early November 1917, the two had a chance conversation about Lizzie.

"Why doesn't she come to live with us?" Frank had suggested, not knowing at all that Lizzie was expecting a baby.

"Erm… because she works in-service at some hall near her home, so she would have to give that up."

"Well, that's the reason I'm saying," Frank had gone on, "have you seen the ad on the noticeboard?"

"For?"

"For a canteen worker here. It would suit her down to the ground and she could live with us if she gets the job. She can pay for her keep and so we'll have more coming into the house, especially with having young Berty around. Youngsters cost so much to feed and clothe. You'll get to know one day lad if you knock the young girl up."

Francis took fright at the words. <'Surely he couldn't know?'>

"Hilarious dad."

"Well, you young un's, hey. One day it's fun and frolics and the next it's our life mapped out. Yes… What was I saying… yes… Lizzie can have your room. Berty's in with us, you know we have to have him there with his fitting 'an all. We've nearly lost him a few times now, poor bugger has been through the mill but he seems to pull through each time. We'll find somewhere for you to sleep don't fret. Save you going to Chester every other Saturday, hey? No funny business lad, we have a reputation at church to uphold."

<'So he doesn't know!'>

There was a method in Frank's madness. He wasn't concerned for the wellbeing of Francis or Lizzie, but for his own pocket. These were hard times, and the money they got from working at the steelworks was a pittance.

Frank had ruminated on his thoughts for a while. <*'Lizzie paying for her keep and contributing to the household budget will be a bonus. All the more money in my pocket.'*>

For Francis, this was manna sent from heaven, and he set about ensuring Frank's idea came to fruition. Within a few days Lizzie had applied for the job at the steelworks and was deemed as ideal to work in the canteen. Her waiting on, cooking and cleaning AND being a general dogsbody in-service, made her the best candidate by far.

This was fate intervening for the better in Francis' life. Now Lizzie could live away from her parents and her ever-expanding waistline could be hidden from them. Luckily for Lizzie, she was very slim and could hide her state easily under her loose fitting dresses. How long she could continue do this concerned her greatly.

Francis' mother Elizabeth was a kindly soul and adopted Lizzie as her own daughter. Elizabeth always ensured she had clean clothes and was well fed. Then one day a couple of weeks later, when Francis and Frank were out at work, the two women were sat having a cup of tea together in the backroom of 31 Ash Grove in Shotton. Their conversation would change things. Little Herbert 'Berty' Davies, who was now almost two and a half, was playing quietly on a thread-bare tatty mat, with a top and whip, which he hadn't a clue what to do with, but was keeping him quiet.

"I've been looking at you for a few weeks now Lizzie," Elizabeth Davies had moved closer, gently touching Lizzie's dress by her stomach with the back of her hand.

"You have?"

"You're altering in so many ways, growing up I suppose you might call it, but you're growing up because you have to. Am I right?"
Lizzie hadn't a clue what to say. She looked across at her surrogate mother embarrassed. She knew she'd been rumbled. "Please don't throw me out Mrs Davies, please!" she cried. Holding onto her secret for so long had been one of the most difficult things she had ever done. She wondered where it would all lead. Now it had come to a head. Someone else knew, and now her entire life was at risk.

"No one is going to kick you out, Lizzie. I am right though? You are with child?"

Lizzie nodded coyly, a worried look spreading across her pretty face.

"When will it be born?"

Lizzie breathed heavily. "February or March for sure."

"I have to ask this question. It is my boy's isn't it?"

"What's in here is the baby of Francis, yes. No doubt. He's the only boy…"

"Yes, yes, I know." Elizabeth smiled. "Then we can deal with this in an excellent way, my girl."

"We can?"

"Oh, yes, we can. I've seen your secret blossoming for weeks now. Us women know." She touched her index finger to the side of her temple and patted it several times. "I've seen the subtle changes. I know. I've got two children of my own." She looked down at Berty playing quietly. "Doesn't do your body much good though. Frank hates small children. I suppose you've seen him."

Lizzie didn't know how to react but started to nod.

"It's all right. You don't have to say. You've seen the clip around the ear here and there though, for as much as a small cry or for doing something slight, which all children do."

"Even for Francis. More than a clip, I'd say. I saw him get a proper whacking a few days ago for coming in, without removing his muddy boots."

"He stands for no nonsense, does Frank. He's got a good heart though, but is too handy with his knuckles and he doesn't care who with."

"You, you mean?"

It was Elizabeth's turn to nod now.

"Does Mr. Davies know about me? I mean, you know, my state."

"He doesn't and he shall never know. I have a plan young lady that'll make us all happy if you agree to it."

"Try me, Mrs. Davies. Try me. I have nothing to lose. My parents will disown me if I go home like this, I know. Dad is a little like Mr. Davies and he wouldn't take kindly to my stupidity."

"It's not stupidity, dear. We are all human. We are all human and we make the same mistakes generation after generation. That I know. He who is without sin, cast the first stone and all that, hey? Frank Davies is not without sin, that is certain."

"And that plan, Mrs. Davies, what is it? How shall I get out of this predicament I have put myself into?"

"Frank takes no notice of anyone but himself. He can be guided and I intend to guide him the way I want him to go."

"How so?"

"You are slim and hide your state well. I have the look already of someone who might be child bearing…"

The two women smiled.

"You're fine Mrs. Davies."

"I know what I am and what I look like dear. So, if you agree, we tell Frank…   er … I tell Frank I am to have a baby again. We hide your state from him until the end and I make it look like I'm getting bigger. When the time comes, he won't want to be near me, I know from previous experience."

"Yes, but how can we do this? It is me who will have the child… "

"I have a maternal supporter here, which you can wear whilst you work for as long as you can. Give up your work, when you can no longer do it, but you should be all right almost to the end. We can deal with matters as and when they arise.   We don't have to think of everything now. Frank will have to put up with whatever happens. My friend, old Mrs Boswell [2] has been a midwife all her life AND she can keep a secret."

"And what about Francis?"

"Leave him to me. I'll talk with him."

"So the baby will become yours."

"Only if you agree?"

"I'm too young to be a mother."

"But you will be around all the time anyway, so it's not as if the child will be taken away, which it might, if people find out."

"My own father would give it away for sure."

"Then he won't know. He doesn't have to know. Ever. So are you in agreement?"

"I am… with one little thing to ask. As the baby will then be yours, can I… can I name it after it is born?"

"That's a deal. Frank will want a say, but he won't get one then. This shall be our secret to take to the grave with us and we shall succeed."

The two laughed, clinked their cups together and the deal was done.

Author's Note

[1] Captain Gerald Sidebotham was killed in action on the 9th March 1918. Final resting place: Jerusalem War Cemetery. Along with Gerald Sidebotham, 5 Privates if the 1/4th Battalion were killed in action on the 9th March 1918. All now lie in Jerusalem War Cemetery. Two days after this, Gerald Davies was born.

'While this attack was in progress, the rest of the Battalion, crowded behind the summit of Munatir, came under fire from 77mm guns to the north and enfilade fire from a machine gun on the other side of the wadi, on the right or eastern flank. As it was quite impossible to get across the wadi to the high ground on which the enemy gun was posted, a couple of Lewis guns were told to deal with it. This Turkish machine gun inflicted many casualties, among whom was Captain G Sidebotham.'

Source: The History of the Cheshire Regiment in the Great War by Col Arthur Crookenden

[2] Mary Jane Boswell, (1843 - 1927) 1911 Census: Midwife

Chapter Three

'A Child is Born'

Wednesday 6th March 1918 was the day it all began. Fine rain fell and mixed with the thick fumes belching out of the nearby iron and steel works forming pernicious smog, making the entire area an unhealthy place to be outdoors. Elizabeth Davies was used to the smog, and venturing out into it was an everyday occurrence. This day she had been going about her business as usual and in the morning had gone 'up the road,' as Shottonites termed the line of shops on the main Chester Road in Shotton, to get some butter, bread and eggs. She'd then returned home, boiled the eggs hard and made Frank and Francis their snapping - egg mashed onto a good slab of bread from the 2lb tin loaf, which she'd toasted on one side to give it a more appealing look as it was getting to the point of being stale when she'd bought it. The two were on the afternoon shift and by one thirty had left the house for work.

Elizabeth managed the house like a military operation whilst Frank wandered in and out from work, oblivious to how it all ran so orderly. Within ten minutes of the two men leaving Elizabeth had taken delivery of the coal ration, moaning at the price of the hundredweight bag to Edward Bithell the local coal and coke merchant. She'd paid one shilling and thruppence (1s3d) last time, now the bag was one and fivepence (1s5d) and the quality of house coal these days wasn't half as good as before the war. She couldn't complain about the quality under these circumstances, but the price she could. Bithell's response was to blame the local war committee who set the prices locally.

The winter of 1917 through to 1918 wasn't over yet by any means, and keeping the house warm was a genuine dilemma. Everything revolved around the fire in the main back room and the Yorkshire black grate was the oven, the water heater, the toaster (with a toasting fork) and central heating appliance. Winter had been long, and the cold had prevailed for many a month without respite, so the cost of everyday living had gone up.   Elizabeth Davies had even taken the step of buying the new wonder Rinso to wash clothes in cold water instead of boil washing which had been the practise in years gone past. Lord Rhondda, who was now in charge of food supplies for the nation, was creating all sorts of havoc for people in the cities up and down the land but the more rural areas fared better. Elizabeth did her best to ration the house needs of coal between heat and cooking. Getting coal had been a problem since war broke out as many miners saw the outbreak of war as an opportunity, if you could call it that, to get themselves out of the mine by joining up.   This meant fewer miners digging up the coal and so coal production hit a new low.   The government hadn't worried too much in the first months of the war believing, like everyone else, the war would be over by Christmas but the football games on the western front that first Christmas of 1914 would be the last. Here in 1918, nothing had changed with war still raging in Europe and most men still away. In fact as the war progressed more miners had joined up and low coal production became a national coal crisis.   Luckily, for the ironworkers of the area they were allowed some supplies of the coke used to fire the furnaces just across the River Dee a few hundred yards away. Besides this, Edward Bithell, the coal merchant, had a soft spot for Elizabeth and always ensured the household had its regular delivery of coal or coke. Many others in the area found themselves queuing at the coal yards with prams, soap carts or anything with wheels they could lay their hands on to get their supply of heat.

These were hard times and worse was to come. There had been a local rationing of sorts of many foods. Shopkeepers couldn't get hold of many of the usual things, so took decisions unilaterally to ration their locals. On top of this, since 25th February of 1918, butter, margarine and meat were rationed with a forecast the same would happen with coal, gas and electricity from 20th March, so Elizabeth Davies did her best to manage the household with an ever-deceasing amount of means.

To add to the worry, a baby was imminent and Elizabeth had been pretending for months now she would be the one who produced it. Frank hadn't been too happy when he'd found out she was 'up the duff' but he'd accepted it all the same. Elizabeth made sure she was never caught in a compromising position half dressed, and Frank only ever saw Lizzie in her loose fitting dress or in her baggy pinny at the canteen. Francis had been told never to discuss the subject with Lizzie anywhere near the house, and he didn't. Lizzie respected this. Frank had accused her of having too much to eat and putting on weight, but this was as far as his observations went and was more to do with his selfish concern about who was getting what at mealtimes in the house.

Elizabeth had been protecting Lizzie in so many ways for months now. If Frank had had his way, he'd have had her filling the coal scuttle and heading along the main line with Francis to collect the fragments of coal falling from the many trains travelling between Holyhead and Chester. He'd shouted at her several times for being lazy and once had tried to kick her in the rear for not getting him his cup of Ovaltine before he went to bed, only to be stopped by Elizabeth who'd intervened, calling him a bully. He'd clipped her around the head instead and headed off to bed early slamming doors in his wake, followed by a whispered "good riddance" from his wife who'd looked at Lizzie, winked and smiled.

Frank was a demanding character in the house and various strategies had to be deployed by Elizabeth to ensure he felt his rule was obeyed when in fact sometimes the opposite was true. Frank was the breadwinner as far as he was concerned, and so what he said was law and bugger everyone else. He gave orders for the fire not to be lit until just before he got home and expected his meals on the table at a certain time, berating Elizabeth if the biggest and best portions weren't his. Elizabeth's way around this was to partially feed others in the house either when Frank was in work or when he disappeared to the dirt toilet at the back of the terraced house, where he spent an inordinate amount of time, sometimes in the pitch dark reading the contents of the toilet paper, cut up newspapers containing the news from previous weeks and months. Elizabeth also used the phrase 'fire not to be lit until just before Frank gets home' to her advantage and often lit the fire throughout the day, telling him it had been lit just half an hour before his arrival home.

Luckily for the house finances Frank never smoked, so no money was wasted on choking up his lungs - that was the reserve of the filth and soot of the ironworks which saw many a man off before his time. If they weren't killed in the meantime by the lack of health and safety in the place which saw many a man scalded or crushed to death.

Elizabeth prayed every Sunday in church that her sins of lying about having a baby would not be exposed to anyone, most of all Frank. By early March 1918, she was believing God had granted her wishes as he had never suspected thing. All the same, she wanted Lizzie to have the baby and the sooner the better.

It was mid-afternoon when the knock came on the front door. It was Lizzie stood in the wet. She looked distressed. Elizabeth knew what it was.

"There's no one in. Go inside. Quickly!" She looked up and down the street. It was a cold day. Not a soul was about, but curtains twitched everywhere in those days and you couldn't sneeze without someone knowing it had happened. Elizabeth shut the front door. "Put the water on the grate. I'll be back in a minute."

Elizabeth ran down the street, holding onto her linen stuffed dress. It wouldn't be good if it fell out at this stage. She'd been 'growing' her stomach for months now, adding a tea-towel or a pillow case every now and then for effect. She now had a full floral patterned chintz comforter under her dress tied with string into the shape of a belly fit to burst.

The pretence was working; she looked full-term, but mimicking pregnancy hadn't been easy, especially with the nosey neighbours who occupied the street, many of whom had asked to touch her bump from time to time, but all had been given short-shrift. Mrs Sprake, the elderly neighbourhood busy-body from number 17, had once said she could, 'recognise a pregnant woman just by looking her in the eye.' Well, Mrs Sprake hadn't managed to spot Elizabeth's deception so far, despite looking her in the eye in Jeffs' shop at the bottom of the railway bridge, at least two or three times a week since December. In fact, only that morning the two had met in the shop.

"You'll have another mouth to feed in a few days by the looks of you girl," Mrs Sprake had commented with some glee in her voice, as if Elizabeth should know the pain of having lots of children. "Had seven myself, bless 'em. Lost two before they were one. Got three in France at the front. One in the Navy. Jim was at Jutland, you know."

"Yes I know. Brave lad"

"… and our Ethel is up the road working in Johnson's the hardware. They're all involved in the war effort."

"Oh, yes, have said hello to Ethel. Nice girl."

"There's a lot who could've gone to war but didn't you know. Cowards."

Elizabeth knew it was the likes of Mrs Sprake who'd given white feathers to young lads in the area.

"My two are both working for the war effort at the works."

"But not fighting for their country…"

"If you're tying to insinuate… "

"Just saying about people."

"Well, don't say. Keep your nose out!"

"Charming Mrs Davies, I'm sure,"

"Look let's not fall out Mrs Sprake hey?" Elizabeth rubbed her spine with the back of her hand and held the bump of linen tight under her coat. "Be glad when it's here," she'd replied. "Back's killing me!"

"Well, I hope it all goes well for you then Mrs Davies."

The two had parted and thankfully Mrs Sprake was none the wiser.

Even better, not one neighbour had suspected Lizzie was the person who was expecting and it had to stay that way. The talk of the street was of 48-year-old Elizabeth *'expecting at her age.'* Neighbours whispered and gossip abounded. 'She should know better.' 'It'll never be born alive at her age.' 'Do you think it's Frank's?' She'd heard all the whispers a thousand times about anyone and everyone in the back streets of Shotton. None ever bothered her. There wasn't one whisper that the baby was Lizzie's and not hers. That meant no one knew the secret.

It would be more bother if anyone ever found out the truth of her pregnancy, especially Frank. Deceiving Frank was the worst crime she was committing. She was sure, at best, he would throw her out of the house if he ever found out. Frank had a temper which Elizabeth had seen at first hand many times, so at worst she feared he might kill her.

Elizabeth hobbled as if she had come into labour and shouted, "Mrs. Boswell," before she arrived at her house. The curtains twitched and her job was done. The neighbours would now know and the gossip would be spread that she was in labour.

No more than two minutes later Elizabeth arrived back with a heavyset woman in a pale green woollen coat tied with a thick woollen belt. The woman's grey hair was covered by a headscarf which had been tied hastily over unbrushed hair.

Lizzie, now bent over with labour pains, was ushered upstairs to Frank and Elizabeth's bedroom and little Berty was dragged along too, pushed into one corner and told to play and be quiet. He was used to occupying himself and played noisily with teaspoons he'd been given, whilst the ladies went about their secret business.

Lizzie had come into labour when the men were out at work, which was fortuitous. The secret remained under wraps.

By early evening, Francis and Frank had arrived home. Mrs. Boswell had been looking out for them and at once had greeted them with the news of Elizabeth's confinement…plus Berty, whom she had carried downstairs.

"Yours, I believe," she had said. "You stay here with him whilst the women do their work upstairs. I DO NOT want to see either of you two near us. Got it."

Frank and Francis had nodded. The fact they were met by old Mrs. Boswell meant women's business was afoot, and they knew instinctively to keep out of the way. She needn't have said a word. They now had charge of Berty, but this was no great hardship. He had his spoons and now had some glass beads, which originally belonged to Francis.

The men sat down to the sound of muffled voices and the occasional high-pitched yelp of pain from upstairs.

"You'll have a new brother or sister soon, lad from the sounds of those shrieks!" He screwed his face up and turned an ear to listen more carefully. "Sounds a bit like your Lizzie, lad!" Frank hadn't an inkling how close he was to the truth.

Frank continued. "Sounds like your girl can't cope with watching another woman pop a sprog. She'll get used to it. Be doing it herself one day." Frank winked and nudged Francis with his elbow. "Plumps 'em like marbles does your mother lad, so she's no need to worry about anything."

"No need to worry. No need to worry. Yes."

Concern filled Francis' eyes, which almost gave the game away.

He paced up and down and repeated, "Hope she's all right?"

"Sit down, lad. You'd think it was Lizzie having the kid from the looks of you."

Francis so wanted to tell the truth, but kept his lips firmly sealed. He kept nodding inanely to the odd comments being made by Frank about whether it would be a boy or a girl. Of course he knew the answer was, <*'I'll have a new son or daughter and you'll have a grandson or granddaughter.'*>

*

* * *

Through all of this Berty played away with the spoons and beads on the mat in front of the Yorkshire grate. The fire was in and everyone was warm. Too warm at times. They boiled water for whatever was going on upstairs, and now and then old Mrs. Boswell would puff her way downstairs to refill a jug with boiling water.

Through all the turmoil going on in the house, no one had thought to take off Berty's heavy woollen cardigan as he got hotter and hotter.

Then it happened. Berty keeled over on the mat and jerked like he'd touched a live electric wire. His body went rigid as his eyelids flickered violently, showing the white in his eyes which flickered orange in the fire's light.

"Dad, dad!" shouted Francis. "What's wrong with Berty?"

"Jesus lad. I don't know."

Berty went completely still and then there was nothing.

"What do we do?"

Francis rushed to the stairs. "Mrs Boswell, Mrs Boswell!"

Mary Jane Boswell appeared in the gloomy light at the top of the steep stairs of the terraced house.

"I told you not to disturb us."

"He's dead, he's dead."

"Who's dead."

"Berty's dead."

"What?"

Elizabeth's head appeared around the door, only to be pushed back by Mrs. Boswell's hand. "Get back in there. I'll sort this."

Francis headed back into the living room with old Mrs. Boswell going at a pace, faster than she'd walked in many a year. Frank now had hold of Berty and was shaking him violently. "He's dead! He's gone!"

"Stop it, man!" shouted Mrs. Boswell. "Stop it now! Let me see."

Mary Jane Boswell was well into her seventies and had seen death in all its forms, from the stillborn to people she'd help layout on the back of spench doors, removed from their hinges, until the coffin arrived from the undertakers. Despite her great age, she was a strong woman and instantly grabbed Berty from Frank and laid him on the floor. She began stripping his clothing off. She put her ear to his chest and listened. "He's alive. He's breathing."

"Shout them upstairs, Francis. Tell them he's okay. Tell them to stay where they are."

Frank began to head towards the stairs. "Not you, Frank! Not you! I need you here."

Francis headed for the bottom of the stairs and shouted up. "Berty's okay, I think. He's okay."

"He's been too hot, Frank. Far too bloody hot. Weren't you bloody watching him, you stupid man?"

Frank wasn't used to a woman calling the shots, but Mary Jane Boswell was well capable of dealing with Frank.

"Right, you hold him. He's coming 'round now. He's had a bloody fit or a seizure. I've seen it before…"

"Do I get a doctor?"

"Who's going to come now?"

As Berty came around, he started to cry."

"What's the matter with him, Mrs. Boswell?"

"Shock… he's had a shock. He's frightened. Well bloody frightened."

"What do I do now?"

"Are you that stupid, Frank? Just hold him. Talk to him. Bloody talk to him."

Truth was, Frank had had little to do with his children when they were small. Babies and toddlers were a woman's work. He earned the money and 'the wife' looked after the children. It was as clear cut as that. Frank was a fish out of water when it came to dealing with young children.

"And you, young Francis. Make us all a cup of tea."

"Is he all right?" shouted Elizabeth from upstairs.

"Yes he's fine" Mrs. Boswell shouted back, whispering to Frank, "she must be between contractions."

The comment was lost on Frank, who just sighed and took a deep breath.

"Bring the tea to the top of the stairs, Francis and leave it there. If you need me again Frank, I'm just a shout away, but he seems to be a little better now."

Mary Jane Boswell epitomised someone in complete control as she collected more hot water and some towels from the pulley line over the Yorkshire grate. Before she headed back upstairs, she warned Frank again, pointing her index finger threateningly into his nose. "Stay away! Look after little Herbert. He might fit again, so watch him." She then went all calm. "Sorry for the swearing before but there we are… there we are and it is what it is." Frank had NO intention of going upstairs.

Both Francis and Frank felt comforted by the fact there was someone there who knew what they were doing. Francis had delivered the cups of tea and within the hour Berty had fallen asleep, as had the men. All sat in armchairs downstairs. The noises of labour continued unheard until the early hours of the morning from what was now the delivery room at 31 Ash Grove, Shotton.

It was eleven minutes past two on Thursday 7th March 1918 when Lizzie's baby was born.

A boy.

Half an hour later Mrs. Boswell quietly left the house, creeping past the snoring men downstairs. The women had decided it was best to leave the men to sleep as the pair had work in the morning. It also gave Lizzie time with her baby.

The issue now was how would they get away with Lizzie feeding the baby and how would they get away with Lizzie returning to work at the canteen. Elizabeth had already investigated the price of Nestlé's baby milk and found out it was 1s 1½d for a tin. This was doable, even with Lizzie not working, if they could get away with it. Francis would have to pull his weight and get more overtime, provided he wasn't called up, which was a distinct prospect now with the war in its fourth year and so many men having been killed.

He'd already been given a white feather in the street just a few days ago by two nasty women in their forties, one of whom had shouted, "Why ain't you doin' your bit lad. My Harry's not coming back and he didn't go to support lazy cowards like you."

She'd spat at Francis and had pushed into his hand a poster from the government which he showed to his mother when he'd arrived home in tears saying he wanted to sign up but a good conversation with his mother about Lizzie and the baby had made him change his mind. For now.

FOUR QUESTIONS

TO WOMEN.

1. You have read what the Germans have done in Belgium. Have you thought what they would do if they invaded this country **?**

2. Do you realise that the safety of your home and children depends on our getting more men <u>now</u> **?**

3. Do you realise that the one word "Go" from you may send another man to fight for our King and Country = - = **?**

4. When the War is over and your husband or your son is asked "What did you do in the great War?" is he to hang his head because you would not let him go **?**

Won't you help and send a man to join the Army to-day?

Published by the PARLIAMENTARY RECRUITING COMMITTEE, 12, Downing Street, London, S.W., and Printed by HARELL, WATSON & VINEY, LD., 52, Long Acre, London, W.C.

W 10853—362 20,000 1.15 (T) **Leaflet No. 31.**

First World War Government Propaganda Poster/Leaflet

Conscription of a lad of Francis' age wasn't compulsory. He had to be 18 according to the Military Service Act which had been passed in January 1916 and he was in the ironworks making much needed metal for the war effort. He and his father were in reserved occupations, but people out there were nasty, especially when they'd lost loved ones themselves. They wanted other families to feel their hurt.

"So what you going to call him them Lizzie?"

"I've had a name in my mind since the day I told Francis I was caught."

Lizzie told her the story of the soldier on the railway station and said she'd like to name the baby after him.

"Gerald. He's called Gerald."

'Two eleven,' the time of Gerald's birth would be a significant number in his life, but this was all to come in his future.

Much to Frank's annoyance, Lizzie never went back to her job at the canteen and helped Elizabeth look after Gerald. Elizabeth needed all the help she could get as Berty's fits were getting worse. Lizzie and Elizabeth became close, their secret safe for now.

Author's Note

Gerald Davies was born on 7th March 1918 and his parents did indeed become Elizabeth and Frank Davies - who were his actual grandparents.

Chapter Four

'Another Meeting in Chester'

"Aunt Lizzie!" shouted Gerald as he knocked on the door of 6 Ashfield Road in Shotton. "Only me!"

"I know it's only you. It's always *only you* at this time, Gerald."

"Your jam butty's ready. Lot's of blackcurrant jam, just like you like it."

Gerald smacked his lips loudly, "Mmm... can't wait." His fingers reached eagerly for the sandwich as he bounced down into Francis' chair, wiggling his bum to make himself more comfortable.

"Good job he's not in Gerald. He'd have your guts for garters, sitting in his throne."

"What time's he in Aunt Lizzie?"

"After seven as usual."

"Can I stay till then? Mum and dad won't mind."

The words mum and dad grated on Lizzie, but she stuck with it. Gerald was eight now and it wouldn't be fair to burden him with telling him his parents weren't who he thought they were.

"I'm like a mum to you anyway... " was Lizzie's way of saying the truth. "And... seven is late enough. You're only eight and you've got school again in the morning."

Gerald, butty in hands, dashed up and gave Lizzie a hug. "I wish you were sometimes. Dad is miserable and just isn't nice to mum sometimes."

"He isn't? Why?"

Gerald shook his head, shrugged his shoulders and raised his eyes to the ceiling. "Shouldn't say. I'll get in trouble."

"But you can tell Aunt Lizzie. Secret'll be safe with me. Promise."
"Pinky promise?"
The two linked little fingers.
"Okay... I hear them rowing at night. Dad's got a proper temper you know. I think he hits her."
"He does?" Shock shaded Lizzie's face. "How do you know?"
Gerald took another bite of his tasty jam butty and chewed away. "I've heard her crying and shouting *'stop it Frank!'*, then he shouts *'I'll give you another one if you don't shut up you stupid bitch.'* He's just not nice."
"Does he hit you?"
Gerald looked even more coy and didn't want to answer. He said nothing. A tear came to his eye as he swallowed heavily.
"He does! Wait till I... "
Gerald burst out crying. "You can't say anything, Aunt Lizzie. Please! Please! He'll kill me or mum. You promised. A pinky promise is a secret we have to keep. Our secret? Promise?"
"Okay. Okay. Promise. Just one last question... does he hit Berty as well?"
Gerald nodded fearfully. "Yep, hit him and caused him to shake mad as heck once."
"What, he hit him and he had a turn? He's only 11 for God's sake and you're only 8. He's a bully that man."
Gerald said nothing. His face said it all.
Lizzie stayed quiet and slowly shook her head.
She hugged him tighter against her mauve flowery pinny, which she wore very day without fail.
It was Gerald who broke the silence. "You're like a mum to me anyway, Aunt Lizzie."
Lizzie grasped Gerald's head and kissed his hair. "You can always come and live here, you know... "
Gerald sniffed his tears away and nibbled away again at the jam butty, as both held each other tight.
"You got no room Aunt Lizzie and all my things are at home."
"We can make room for you. I can chat with your mum." She hated saying the word mum when talking to Gerald.
"There's one secret mum has told me to keep... "
"What? Besides the fact Frank... er ... your dad *<why am I calling him that!>* hits your mum and Berty... AND you?"
Gerald nodded again. His watery puppy eyes looked up.

Lizzie held him by his upper-arms, with her arms outstretched.

Gerald put the last piece of his jam butty into his mouth and chewed.

"Well, go on then Gerald, you just can't tell me that. There's only you and me here right now. What is it? What's going on?"

"She said not to tell. I can't tell… "

"We've known each other since you were born. Before you were born even! Pinky promises count for something in this place." She smiled warmly. The comment was lost in Gerald. "There's no secrets between you and me. Hey?"

Gerald shrugged and nodded.

"You CAN tell me. You know that."

Gerald's eyes wondered about the room. He was ready to say, but not just yet.

"I'll make you your favourite lime cordial and then you can tell me, hey?"

The two wandered to the Belfast sink.

"So, what's that secret, hey Gerald?"

"Promise you won't say?"

"Cross my heart and hope to die."

"It's mum. I've seen her having those horrible turns like Berty. She starts shaking and falls on the ground. Her eyes roll up into her head. It's frightening. She's sick sometimes."

"Sick?"

"Yes, yukky sick, everywhere. If she knows the turn is coming, she'll lie down and tells me not to worry, but, oh, Aunt Lizzie it's so worrying to see. I think she's going to die." Gerald hugged Lizzie. "Will she die Aunt Lizzie? Will she?"

"Now you don't worry, young man. You just don't worry your little head about this. You concentrate on your school and let me do the worrying."

"You can't speak to her about it. She'll know it's me."

"I'll find a way. I'll find a way young man." Gerald took a last bite of his sandwich and nodded. "You can trust me like your own mother, Gerald. You can trust me."

*

Three days later, Lizzie walked the few short yards to Elizabeth's house. A game of Russian roulette for the lungs. The roaring twenties had a different meaning here in Shotton, as every house belched its own flavour of smoke adding to the acrid smell of the nearby works. If this wasn't bad enough, thick smoke clouded the air from a recent goods train, passing noisily on its way to Holyhead. This was the day after Valentine's Day of 1927 and rain threatened the already damp cobbles, on which could be heard the eerie clop, clop of hooves and shouts of "any'ol'ion." The horse completely hidden somewhere in the smoke further up the street. Lizzie knew it was the rag and bone man shouting for *any old iron* as she'd seen the tired-looking horse dragging its flat backed cart full of people's cast-offs many times before.

Before she caught sight of the cart, she arrived at the wooden name plate painted lime green with 'Dee View' written on it. Elizabeth and Frank's place had a grand name, despite the fact the house was a two up two down terrace which overlooked the railway line and not the River Dee.

Lizzie had been intent on a deep and meaningful conversation with Elizabeth about what was happening behind the closed doors of Dee View, but events had overtaken everyone. Something awful had happened and Lizzie had been summoned to her mother-in-law's *'once the coast was clear,'* and it was. Frank had gone to work with Francis. Gerald had headed off to school with Berty. The only thing which altered the normality of the look of Dee View from the outside were the drawn curtains both upstairs and downstairs in the front. This was the signal everyone knew. Someone had died.

Lizzie knocked the green 'steelworks' door and waited.

Elizabeth answered and looked around the street. No one was about, but behind every door were the gossipers who would think nothing of holding onto a secret they could tell someone else.

Lizzie was soon behind a closed door and walked through the darkness of the front of the house to the small back room where a warm coal fire comforted a room where ragged looking clothes sat airing over a wooden clothes horse.

"Thanks for coming, love. Tea?"

Elizabeth, who didn't wait for an answer, went straight to a green tin on the side marked tea. The old tin, now bared silver to the metal in places, had been around for as long as Lizzie could remember. Its top was pitted with rust, but no one cared as everyone got a great cuppa from the loose Horniman's tea grounds inside. Elizabeth's favourite blend of tea. Two spoons were soon inside the china teapot and boiling water from the black iron kettle on the range, hidden by the washing, soon filled the pot.

Lizzie had seen it all before, many times. The tea making was almost a ritual for the two when the men had headed off to the steelworks.

They sat down at the ancient gate-leg dark mahogany table covered with a white lace tablecloth with tea-pot burn marks, which washing had failed to remove.

"Do you know, yes... " began Elizabeth, "this very tea service was a wedding present from my parents." She picked up an empty cup and inspected it closely. "... this cup is older than you. They were temperance people, you know. The lot of them. Old Aunt Jane, on my dad's side, ran the Coach and Dogs and the Bailey Head Temperance Hotels, in Oswestry at the turn of the century. Hated drink and did her best to stop anyone else drinking. Cos' of her brother you know... my dad."

"You don't drink either, Mrs Davies? I mean alcohol."

"I've told you to call me Elizabeth," she smiled, knowing how difficult she'd found it as a young person to call adults by their first names. Elders were to be respected, and that was the bottom line. "No, just never got into the habit. As I said, no one in the family did, they were... they ARE such a religious lot and seems it's passed on to us these days. Anyway, tea's so much better for you. Drink causes trouble and it did in our family - I'll come to that. Anyway, all Griffiths' don't touch the stuff. Proper Welsh chapel an' all that. But there's just one black sheep. All families have got one." She looked back at the cup. "I'm digressing, but that's me." She examined the cup more closely. "China. It's so fragile, it's like life... one false move or an unlucky break and it's gone." She mused on her words and stared into thin air, then looked back at the cup again, with its intricately painted flowers in yellow, blue and pink. She ran a finger thoughtfully along the gold leaf edging the rim of the cup. "It's a wonder it's lasted till now. Pretty pattern though. All hand painted."

She turned the cup over and looked at the bottom "... in ... er ... Old Country Roses...Royal Albert... made in The Potteries I suppose. Was expensive at the time. Dad was a stonemason, so I was lucky. In the early days we had some money to spare and I was the first to be married, so I got this beautiful tea-service. The best gift ever. We've looked after it well."

"YOU certainly have... I presume it's like that because Frank hasn't washed a cup in his life?"

Giggles filled the room.

"I shouldn't laugh, not at this time. I've just had a telegram to say Herbert's died in the hospital in Shelton not two days ago." She pointed to the telegram, still propped up on the windowsill against the nets.

"Shelton?"

"Shrewsbury… the dreaded damn asylum. It's got a hold on our family has that place."

"Your brother! Herbert. Sorry to hear that… er… Mrs Davies." Lizzie didn't think it appropriate to use Elizabeth this time and Elizabeth didn't notice.

"Thank you, yes, my brother. Telegram's from his wife, Marge. Poor soul. She's on her own now with two boys. History repeating itself in the Griffiths'. Mind you, she's been on her own for a bit. They can't be no more than eight and three, I think. He had turns you know. Runs in the family. Mam and Dad had it… have been gone twenty-odd years and I… I… can't believe I'm saying this. Mind you, the war saw him off more than anything."

Lizzie listened intently as Elizabeth talked, yet stared at the net curtains through which came the poorest of dismal light reflecting the mood within.

"He wasn't right before he went away and was a hundred times worse after the war." Elizabeth paused and took a deep breath. "You see, he had these awful fits on and off as a child. Epilepsy it was; the scourge of the family. Mam and dad had the same - they were both Griffiths'- cousins married they were, from small villages in the borders of Wales. I mean, where did you go in those days to meet someone?"

The two women smiled nervously at each other.

"I'm named after my mam, only she's the other way around to me… well her name is. Mary Elizabeth [1] as opposed to Elizabeth Mary…" Elizabeth cackled loudly, shaking her head, "not much imagination there Lizzie dear… well she died first in '89 and dad [2] went next in '95, but he was in the asylum not long after mam died, he took to the demon drink you see, which is where the problems got worse. The drink took the very food from his children's mouths. No one could stop him. He fell into the bottomless pit of moral degradation which drink causes. What with that and his epilepsy, he was doomed and I'm afraid he was sent mad. It's why I hate drink so much! Herbert was only four when his mother died and within months his father was gone to the asylum, dying there four years later, just like his wife. They say she died of Phth... Phth... Phthisis, yes that's it.   With another word Pulmo something." She stuttered the words out.   "I can't even say it see. It's like TB I think but the asylum caused that. Dad officially died of paralysis of the brain but I knew what that meant.   The drink and the epilepsy as I said but the asylum medical jargon just shows he was mad I suppose."

"You were young when that happened?"

"I was lucky, believe you me! I was old enough to look after myself when mam died.   Working age I was, but my younger brother and sisters weren't. Dear God..." She looked up to the ceiling and clasped her hands together as if in prayer. "... three children; the youngest was 6, had no parents. Thank God for Aunty Jane. She moved into Greenfield Cottage... that's where they lived. Albert Road, Oswestry, yes... and she looked after them, lock stock and barrel."

"So did they have epilepsy then, I mean your mum and dad?"

"Look, I know what the death certificates say but for sure, it was what they had. Epilepsy is a nasty beast in the mind, which for no known reason creeps up and just throttles your head leaving you helpless. Makes you do things you don't want to do and makes other people see you, at best as having an affliction and at worst as being mad."

"So, it was epilepsy what did for your mum and dad really, is that what you're saying Mrs. Davies?"

"You've done it again. Elizabeth, dear.   Elizabeth! I would say it contributed to their deaths. Look,   I know from my on experience, there's nothing wrong with me, but when I have a turn, everyone would see me as mad and incapable of looking after myself. It's only temporary is that, so MAD I am not."

"Of course you're not Elizabeth."

"You can't tell people who haven't got epilepsy that though. They see you as DIFFERENT! So for mam and dad, yes they had epilepsy, but once THEY get you in the asylum there's no coming out. No one comes out." She repeated "NO ONE!"

Lizzie nodded, biting her bottom lip as she listened intently.

"Once you're there, they pump you full of God knows what. Even if you're not a loony, they'll turn you into one. I've seen it with my own eyes. People go into the asylum looking not too bad and within weeks they're frothing at the mouth. Proper imbeciles they look and then, worse than that, the asylum turns people from into cabbages!"

"Cabbages?" Lizzie looked perplexed.

"Yeh, CABBAGES. Sat there dribbling food down their faces they are. Piddling themselves and unable to speak, like slugs with salt on them in the garden. What they give them to make them like this, heaven knows."

"Did your mum and dad both go to the same asylum then?"

"It's now Shelton Asylum, but it was Bicton... that's why I was horrified when Herbert went there. An inhumane, cold and cruel place, so I suppose they had to give it a different name to freshen up its image but believe you me, it's the same God-awful place, you can be rest-assured of that. It's a fair distance from here but nearer to where I come from originally."

"I don't really understand Elizabeth. Epilepsy... that's TURNS isn't it? I mean fits of the body like."

"Epilepsy, what can I say. People in the country used to believe it was catching. Like a pox or something."

"Catching?"

"You know, contagious, like a cold. Some ignorant people still say it is, but it's not. Worse thing is that people isolate epileptics and say we are possessed or violent or are religious zealots to be avoided. Epilepsy they say is the demon in the Griffiths family. That's what us Griffiths' say about ourselves too and now the demons are after me."

"No, surely not Mrs. Davies. That's not true. You mustn't give in to the thoughts of others. You are so fit and well."

"Frank already has a low opinion of me and tells me I have demons in my head! The death of poor Herbert will make Frank think worse of me."

"How can the death of your brother make Frank think that way?"

"He's told me I'm next to the loony bin. He's told me he wants rid of me and it'll happen, you mark my words. He says I've caught the demons from the Griffiths'. To make matters worse, Frank's started seeing a gir... "

She stopped in her tracks.

"Seeing someone?"

Elizabeth looked completely flustered.

"I never said that. Yes, where was I... what? Yes. Herbert. Herbert is dead. The war... well the war happened and..." She shook her head sadly. "He was in France from 1914 right through to 1920 coming home on leave every now and then."

"We saw them on the station in Chester. Me and Francis, we saw them. Mud on their trousers and empty eyes. That's why we wanted him called Gerald, you know, that's why, after the officer Gerald on the platform."

"… when he finally came home, yes, he was never the same but at least he came home… but… "

Elizabeth went quiet and went about her business making the tea. She opened a smaller green tin. "Sugar?"

"Just one as usual, thank you. But… what were you saying, Mrs D..? Er, yes… Elizabeth."

"Herbert was in a mess. My little baby-brother in a hell of a mess. Excuse my language. Talked to himself at night. Any loud noise and he hid under the bed. God knows what he saw in France."

"No one speaks of it, do they?"

"No one! It's ruined lives. Anyway, the turns just got worse and he couldn't control his inner demons. After his second son, another Herbert…" she laughed. "… was born he coped less and less, and Marge called the doctor. He was put away like mam and dad were. Away!"

Silence overcame the room and tear-filled eyes observed the surroundings. Elizabeth poured the brewed tea and pushed the cup across to Lizzie.

"And… are you all right, Mrs Davies. Are you?"

"You have to be. What else can I do?"

"You can talk to me. Look, it was something Gerald said… " she added in quickly, "… he told me not to say. I promised I wouldn't, then I thought. I thought… I had to check you were okay… then you asked to see me, so here we are."

"I did because Herbert's died and I fear Frank may use it to… " Elizabeth burst into tears. "Oh, Lizzie I'm frightened I'm losing it all. I'll lose my children."

"There's more as well." Lizzie looked nervous. She waited, taking a sip of her tea. "Lovely tea, Mrs. Davies." She looked across at Elizabeth over the steaming golden rim. "Elizabeth… Gerald says Frank is handy, you know, with his hands… and your turns worry him."

Elizabeth turned away, putting her hand across her face.

"He's worried about you that's all."

Elizabeth stood up. She looked anxious and was fidgeting into the front pockets of her apron. She drew out a cloth which served as a handkerchief and wiped her face several times even though it didn't need wiping at all. She paced the room giving the odd glance across to Lizzie. Lizzie sat and watched. Anxiety etched deep into her face.

"You… you… you can't divulge this to anyone." She raised her voice. "Your hear?"

This was the first time Lizzie had heard Elizabeth raise her voice. She nodded vigorously. "I hear. Cross my heart and hope to die."

"I don't want you to die… but you must keep this a secret like you have kept the secret of… " she went into a complete whisper and looked around as if the room was one big ear. "…Gerald."

"You can rely on me, that's for sure."

"The story of mam and dad shows you what they do to people who have fits like me. God, Lizzie I only have to look at Herbert. The County Loony Bin in Shropshire killed him. He went downhill from the day he went in a couple of years ago. He could walk when he went in and within weeks it was like his soul had been taken from his body. There was nothing behind his eyes. Nothing! He was dead inside."

"So how are you?"

"You don't worry about me. You just get on with your life. There's only one thing I would ask, and that's this… " Elizabeth held Lizzie firmly on both shoulders. "You promise me you will make sure Gerald and Berty are all right if anything happens to me. Promise me!" She added sternly.

"I promise."

*

The mid-morning LMS train from Holyhead squealed and clanked its way slowly into a busy Chester General railway station, pushing heavy clouds of steam and smoke into the waiting throng on Platform 4. The same journey made by generations of Welsh into Chester since an 1844 Act of Parliament granted over £2 million to create the 85 mile link from Holyhead to Chester.

It was Saturday 5th March 1927 and Frank Davies adjusted his chocolate coloured trilby, as he stepped off the train, dressed in his best dark blue suit. He'd made this trip a hundred times before, always in his Sunday best, and headed in the direction of the city centre on the tram which dropped him off minutes later at The Cross. Chester was a favourite place for the Welsh and the arrival of the railway had seen a significant expansion of the city including several Welsh-speaking areas. Some people getting off the train that morning were here to do business of some sort, but most had come to Chester for its market to the side of the great Town Hall built in 1863, a Town Hall with a clock on three sides only, such was the rivalry with Wales that the side facing Wales had no clock. Rumour had it the good men of Chester had said they wouldn't want to give the time of day to Wales.

None of this of course bothered most people, and as Frank looked up at the Town Hall clock, he checked it against his watch. Frank altered his slow running timepiece by two minutes so both clocks tallied. It was now forty-two minutes before noon and he was in good time. He headed off into the market hall for a quick perusal of what was on offer. The smell was divine. Cheeses galore, apples from across the land, and so many other things filled the various stalls. The railway had done its job, and now there was so much more on offer in Chester than any of his ancestors would have ever seen. He quickly made a purchase of a good slice of Cheshire cheese, neatly cut off a huge roundel with a wire on a marble slab. A quarter pound of best ham followed and then he headed off to buy loose peppermint humbugs and the new Black Jacks, which he loved, despite them making your mouth black.

In early 1927 there were some signs of the Great Depression on the horizon, but most people in the Chester area were lucky to have some form of work and so they had money in their pocket. Not being a drinker helped Frank and he always had a few shillings to spare from his wages, the total sum of which he kept a well-guarded secret from Elizabeth who managed the house in Shotton on a meagre sum when Frank could easily have given her more but he felt in more control when he arrived home from Chester with goodies from the market which she always looked so grateful for.

A flu epidemic was killing a thousand people a week across Britain and Frank was keenly aware of this, so whilst in Chester, he avoided getting too close to people he didn't know, if he could help it. Mostly though, people hadn't a clue about the epidemic and even if they knew, they'd not long been through a devastating war, so their concerns were for living life for the day they were in. No one worried about dying; after all, everyone died at some stage, so why worry about it.

Frank constantly checked his watch as he wandered through the market. The canvas bag he'd carried to Chester in his large woollen overcoat pocket was now full to the brim with an assortment of vegetables, groceries and two jars of blackcurrant jam which he adored. It was two minutes before noon before he knew it and he raced out to the square in front of the Town Hall and just stood there with his bag set down on the ancient-looking sandstone slabs.

People busied themselves heading in and out of the market hall and cyclists rang their bells constantly to warn of their approach. Frank paid no attention to anyone. He observed his timepiece almost by the second and looked frantically around the milling crowd. It was soon almost ten-past noon and Frank had a more concerned look across his face. He picked up his bag and was about to leave when there was a shout.

"Frank! Frank! Over here."

Frank looked across to a slim girl heading in his direction and waving her hands frantically over the many Chester shoppers. She was dressed in a dark terracotta shaded coat which was unbuttoned revealing a drop waist blue cotton checked dress. A black felt cloche with a matching black bow gripped her head and hid most of her mousy hair. The relief on Frank's face was plain for the woman to see and was only matched by her own face.

"Thought I'd missed you, Frank," said the girl as she came right up to Frank, kissing him lightly on the cheek. "Thought I'd missed you," she repeated with a sigh, as she wiped the perspiration from her brow.

"Me too. I was about to head off. I thought you weren't coming. Thought you'd fallen out with me?"

The girl took hold of Frank's hand and pulled him closer. "Never, why would I do that?"

"Because I'm an old bloke Ede and you're a pretty young girl who could get anyone."

"Why would I want anyone when I've got you?" She kissed him on the cheek again.

"Careful Edith, er … Ede, we don't want the whole world to see."

"Why not? I could be your daughter anyway, kissing her dad on the cheek after he's been away for the week and anyway you have been away for the week… and I'm young enough to be your daughter after all."

Frank shook his head. "Less of the father-daughter stuff, Ede, young lady dear."

"Well, I am twenty years younger… "

She sidled in closer.

"You like that, don't you? A young woman by your side. Makes you feel good?"

"I like the fact you're you Ede. It's not your age. Now watch out people might be watching."

"Let them." She kissed him on the cheek again, and this time he smiled as he kissed her on the cheek back. Frank then grabbed his shopping and grasped Edith by the hand.

"We should go hey. Let's go for a walk down by the river shall we? It's quieter there."

"Whatever pleases the master. What's in the bag, Frank? Anything nice we can picnic on?"

"Just a few bits and pieces and a jar of jam our Gerald likes. It's his 9th birthday on Monday."

"Do I get an invite?"

"Now don't make me laugh too much Ede."

"How's his mother doing too?"

"She's same old same old."

"The madness you mean?"

"The madness, yes."

The couple walked on briskly, heading down Northgate Street, around by The Cross and into Bridge Street, where the tram bells sounded and new fangled noisy lorries spewing out filthy fumes beeped their horns to keep people from walking under them, which they did from time to time. The pair headed down towards the Old Dee Bridge, which had stood there since Roman times but which had seen a huge reconstruction in 1387. All the same, it was the oldest bridge in Chester and Frank and Edith had stood on it many times together since they'd met watching life and the river flow by over the nearby weir.

As they walked, both did their best to avoid heaps of horse muck from the horses and carts laden with goods for the businesses in the city. Both were soon stood on the bridge in the first carved out niche they had come to with a brisk westerly flowing into their faces. A usual spot for them. It was too cold a day for most people to stop, so the couple could embrace and talk as most people hurried by into Chester or back across to Handbridge.

"Cuddle me closer, Frank. She won't be any good to have around with that madness, you know, especially for that young lad Gerald. You have Berty to cope with as well, and that can't be easy. I remember the first time we met."

"Me as well. The football club do before Christmas."

"Being director of the football club has its compensations Frank?"

"And your dad John bringing you along. Not only is he a work and football mate, but he's got a beautiful daughter."

"And poor old Elizabeth had to stay home, hey."

They both smiled and looked into each other's eyes.

"Good job, we'd have never met." Frank added gently kissing Edith on her lips.

"You taste nice. Glad you were there."

"Me too."

"Do you love me, Frank?"

Frank pulled Edith in closer. "You know I do."

"Then we will be together some day won't we.?"

"We will. I'm sorting it, you know. I am."

Author's Note

[1] The author's maternal great great Grandmother was Elizabeth Mary Griffiths (1847 -1889) Died aged 42 years on 11th December 1889. Described as Bricklayer's Wife on death certificate. Cause of death: Phthisis Pulmonalis - Tubercolosis was certified by Arthur Strange MD who was famously of Bicton Asylum on the outskirts of Shrewsbury, England.

[2] The author's maternal great great Grandfather was Edward Griffiths, a Bricklayer (1849 -1895) Died aged 46 years on 23rd March 1895. His address was given as Greenfield Cottage, Albert Road, Oswestry, Shropshire. Cause of Death: Paralysis from disease of brain. Also certified by Dr. Arthur Strange.

* * *

Superintendent Registrar's District *Atcham*

Registrar's Sub-District *Saint Chad Shrewsbury*

18*95* DEATHS in the Sub-District of *Saint Chad Shrewsbury* in the County of *Salop*

Columns:— 1.	2.	3.	4.	5.	6.	7.	8.	9.
No.	When and Where Died.	Name and Surname.	Sex.	Age.	Rank or Profession.	Cause of Death.	Signature, Description, and Residence of Informant.	When registered.	Signature of Registrar
465	Twenty ninth March 1895 County Asylum Bicton R.D.	Edward Griffiths	Male	46 Years	Bricklayer from Greenfield cottage Albert Road Oswestry	Paralysis from disease of brain Certified by Arthur Strange M.D.	Jane Griffiths Sister Greenfield cottage Albert Road Oswestry	Twenty sixth March 1895	Thos Morgan Registrar

Chapter Five

'The Birthday Party'

It was Gerald's ninth birthday.

Lizzie and Francis had come around and they'd all sat in front of the fire toasting bread and singing happy birthday. Berty lay on the floor doing an old jigsaw whilst Gerald had opened his present wrapped in brown paper and tied with string from the steelworks. Inside was a box.

"New shoes, mum!"

Gerald read the box. "Gibson Shoes. You knew what I wanted. Thank you so much, mum." He dashed over to Elizabeth and hugged her tightly. Lizzie looked on as she clung on to a brown paper parcel in her lap.

"They should fit you, our Gerald. Size 3. I got over to Blacklers in Liverpool last week after you saw them in the paper."

Gerald was now sat on the floor pulling them on. "They fit so snug. Can't believe I've got these shoes. Wait 'til my mates see 'em in school."

Elizabeth whispered to Lizzie. " See, it was worth going. Six 'n eleven. A bargain. Wait till he sees what you bought when we were there for two bob."

"Shhh! Mrs. Davies. He'll hear."

Gerald wasn't paying any attention to the women, he was too overcome with delight at his new shoes, which he'd now fully laced up.

"Well, go on then Gerald... walk up there, show them off. They do fit proper, don't they?"

Gerald walked two paces, which was as far as he could get in the tiny back room and one of those was striding across the jigsaw engrossed Berty who took no notice at all.

"They fit."

"They don't rub?"

"Na." Gerald turned his attention to Berty in an effort to make him pay attention to his new footwear. He nudged Berty in the side with his foot.

"Ow Gez! Get off."

"Look at these Berty! Like 'em?"

"Fantastic."

Berty resumed his jigsaw.

"We're not finished yet either, Gerald. Look what Aunt Lizzie and Uncle Francis have for you." Elizabeth nodded toward Lizzie.

"Another parcel? For me?"

Of course, Gerald had already seen the parcel and was eagerly waiting to open it.

"Just for you from us," Lizzie smiled warmly.

"Happy birthday Gerald lad" Francis said shaking his hand as if Gerald was someone he was meeting for the first time.

Lizzie handed the parcel over.

"Thank you so much."

"You don't know what it is yet. You might hate it."

Everyone laughed. Gerald stood there holding the parcel. Francis nudged him from the side.

"Well go on then, open it."

Gerald pulled at the string bow and unravelled the brown paper. He held up the contents. "A brown jersey. Just what I wanted too."

He ran over to Lizzie and hugged her.

"You're welcome. You're welcome. Try it on then. Go on!"

The brown woollen jersey with its polo collar was soon on and once again Gerald was parading around the tiny back room of Dee View, but this time without being asked.

"It's like a fashion show," commented Elizabeth.

"Yes, suits you lad," added Francis.

"We're very proud of you, you know Gerald, like you were our own son."

The comment was lost on Gerald, but Elizabeth looked over at Lizzie and Francis nodding to acknowledge their secret deal all those years ago. Smiles of love were exchanged between the three.

Lizzie turned back to watch Gerald. She loved to see his face and saw in him everything she was. A kind, caring soul who loved life.

"Thanks Aunt Lizzie. Love it. Love it."

The back door opened.

"Is that the time already, Lizzie?" Elizabeth jumped up nervously.

The mood changed the second Frank walked in through the door.

"Oh, lots of you here when I get in from work. Didn't expect that." The disapproval of more people in the house than expected showed across Frank's face. "Anyway, evening all. Full house, I see. Is there an occasion?"

"You know, Frank. You know. Don't be a miserable so and so."

"Just teasing you all. Just teasing. The lad's birthday. Happy birthday lad."

"Thanks dad."

"What are those on your feet, lad?" Frank's face had changed as he pointed at the new shoes.

Gerald looked at Elizabeth for the answer. "This is the first pair of new shoes he's had in a long time. His old ones are second hand clogs. Gerald's been coming home with sores on his toes, but you wouldn't see that. His shoes are not fit to wear, but you probably hadn't noticed. It was me who promised Gerald new shoes for his birthday, so don't shout at the lad Frank for having shoes."

He raised his voice. "Who's shouting at the lad!"

"I'm happy for you to take them back mum," a bewildered Gerald uttered as he took the shoes off and held them out to Frank.

Lizzie had stood up, grabbing Francis by the hand. "It's time we went!"

Gerald got a kiss on top of his head with a whispered. "Happy birthday, love. Love the shoes."

"Thanks Aunt Lizzie. Jersey is the best ever."

Lizzie looked at Elizabeth. She reflected on being Gerald's mother. Then, with some concern, she reached out and touched Elizabeth's arm. "You be all right?"

Elizabeth nodded and wiped the newly welled tears away from her face. She walked Lizzie and Francis to the front door and said goodbye. Lizzie gave her a parting hug at the door.

"If you need us, we're only a couple of minutes away."

Elizabeth nodded as she surveyed the street outside. "Go on, get home, you two. I'll be fine."

Elizabeth found a new determination as she entered the back room.

"Put those shoes back on, Gerald. They're your birthday present." She smiled and pulled Gerald in close.

"You two lads head off upstairs. You can come back down in a bit. I've got something for you, Gerald, but I need a chat with mum first."

Gerald looked at Elizabeth and she nodded as she caressed his face. "It'll be okay. It's not bedtime. It's your birthday, so there's more fun to come."

Gerald wasn't sure, but headed out of the room to follow Berty, who'd already left. Berty knew not to anger his dad and both boys were well versed in keeping out of the way.

Frank closed the door to the stairs, something he never did.

Things were looking serious.

"Those clogs he's got would have lasted months yet. I'm not made of money, woman."

"I dunno what you're on about Frank love," a conciliatory Elizabeth began. "Gerald's done so well in school and at Sunday school. You know he has. It's only a few weeks since he got the scholar's first prize at Rivertown Church from Mr Williams of Hawarden. Have you forgotten how clever our lad is, Frank? Have you?" There was some anger in Elizabeth's intonation. "I was so happy with his prize, but so ashamed of his shoes."

"So you decided to buy him new ones all on your own! Without as much as a mention to me? You knew I'd got him his favourite jam and you had to upstage me."

"This isn't about you Frank dear…"

"Don't dear me."

"… he needed them and it was my money, anyway. Besides, you are busy with the football club. I know you live for that. It was a pleasure to go to Liverpool with Lizzie to get him the shoes. They're from us, he knows that."

"From us?" He shook his head mockingly and sneered. "From us?" Frank uttered under his breath with a scowl. "… and you couldn't tell me?"

"Yes, from us."

"Oh, you have money of your own now, do you? The housekeeping money I give you more like… and you waste it on shoes."

"It's my money from my parents. Herbert left me an envelope with some money as well. His wife gave it to me at the funeral last month… so, it's not yours. No!" she said with a nervous confidence in her voice. "There's more to this, isn't there Frank?

"No idea what you mean, woman."

"I mean, you're always at me nowadays. What happened to the Frank I met all those years ago?" Elizabeth walked straight up to Frank and stood facing him. He was still in his dirty work clothes. She straightened his jacket collar, which his canvas work bag had ruffled over in the wrong direction.

"You might be filthy from work, but I still care about you and this family." Frank's gaze was towards the net curtains. "Look at me, Frank!" Elizabeth's frustration showed. "Why are you so off with me nowadays?"

"There's nothing wrong. Nowt!" he shouted. "Keep your nose out of my business."

"Oh, so you DO have business I don't know about?"

"What you on about woman? I'm the boss of this house and I'll come and go as I please. If you don't like it, you know what you can do. "

"Hey Frank, there's no need for that."

"Oh, and he's my son, so what I say goes and if I don't want him to have shoes, that's my say so."

"Your son, hey! Your son. He bloody well isn't!"

Elizabeth realised what she'd said in fury and immediately turned away to look into the brightly lit fire burning in the grate.

"What woman? What did you say?"

"Nothing."

Elizabeth felt Frank's hand on her shoulders. He pulled her around roughly, jerking her head. Spittle fell from the side of his mouth and he wiped it away with his dirty sleeve, making a black streak across his face.

"What! I damn well heard you. You said HE ISN'T. So what's the truth, woman?"

Elizabeth was shaking. "I said it in temper."

Frank launched himself into the dark parlour and arrived back with the family bible, a big tome which was Elizabeth's family bible. She'd been the eldest when her parents had died in the asylum and the bible was now hers. Frank thrust the bible onto her lap.

"Swear and tell me the truth."

"Frank, no!"

Frank squeezed hard on Elizabeth's shoulder, his muscular fingers digging in deep. "I swear on this bible..." he spat, "... Gerald is our child. DO IT!"

Elizabeth had been brought up in a deeply religious Mid-Wales family with puritanical views. Frank was the same. She looked at the brown leather cover of the bible with 'Y Bibl Cyssegrlan' in gold lettering adorning the front. The whole bible was in Welsh; naturally, of course, as the Griffiths family were Welsh speakers and this was their treasured possession. An Act of Parliament of 1563 had allowed for the translation of the Bible into Welsh, yet it took until 1588 for Bishop Morgan of Llandaff and St Asaph to complete the task. Welsh had no official status as a language in Britain despite it being the original language of the ancient peoples of the land, so all law and administration was conducted in English or Latin, or even French in earlier times. Law also decreed the Bible be read in every church in the land, in English. The Welsh Bible became the foundation stone on which modern Welsh books were moulded, and the importance of this family Bible to Elizabeth was immense. For the first time, the Griffiths family had been able to read and listen to the scriptures in their own language.

Now the very bible was under her nose. How could she lie on it?

"Answer me!" shouted Frank.

Elizabeth stared at the book.

"Swear on God's book, Gerald is ours. Swear!"

Elizabeth shook her head and still said nothing.

Frank took hold of her and shook her violently. "Speak, woman!" He pushed her hand down to the cold leather. "Who's child is Gerald?"

Elizabeth's tears fell across the leather. "I can say this on the good book… " she fell into a whisper, "Gerald knows nothing of this and he must not."

"Go on, I'm all ears."

"Do you recall the night he was born when old Mrs. Boswell came around?"

"Of course I do."

"Berty had a turn, didn't he? Not long before Gerald was born."

"Yes, go on."

"And Mrs. Boswell came to see him and check he was fine."

"She did."

"And I was going to come down to check myself."

"But you couldn't because you were full in labour. I heard you."

"You heard Lizzie."

"Lizzie?"

"Yes, Lizzie. You heard Lizzie. Gerald is Lizzie's."

Frank paced the room in deep thought, repeating quietly, "Lizzie, Gerald is Lizzie's. I... I... don't understand... Lizzie the baby's mother? No, no, no. It can't be. He can't be."

"It's true. I still have my hand on the good book. As God is my witness."

There was fury in Frank's eyes. He looked livid.

"You deceitful whore! You deceitful cow!"

Elizabeth cowered back. Frank's muscles in his arms tensed and the veins in his neck were like a poorly wired house, sticking out everywhere. He punched the wall of the back room and leant his head against it, moving his head angrily from side to side like come caged polar bear. Then he whispered, "Tell me more. I need to know. TELL ME!"

"Don't be angry, Frank. We did it for the right reasons."

"You did?"

"Yes, Lizzie got pregnant..."

"So she's a slut as well?"

"No, no, it's nothing like that. Gerald is our grandson. He is your son's child."

"You know that?"

"Yes."

"Does Francis know that?"

"Yes, he does."

"Nine years to this day and the three of you have been laughing at me. Behind my back!"

"No, Frank, no. Not laughing. Admiring you for being a good father. You are Gerald's father. Lizzie couldn't have managed on her own and well... her and Francis, they were too young..."

"And stupid.... How could I have been so stupid?"

"You weren't stupid."

"I got Lizzie the job in the canteen and she was always in that horrid baggy blue flowery pinny. Hiding her fat belly. I can see it now. How was I so blind?"

"We did it... "

"YOU did it... "

"I did it with Lizzie and Francis to protect them. You know what people are like... "

"Mary Jane Boswell, God rest her soul, was in on it as well. Sly old bitch. Never said a word to me once an' I spoke to her God knows how many times after Gerald was born. But you got ... BIGGER Elizabeth. YOUR belly grew bigger. Are you lying to me?"

"Part of the plan, I'm afraid. Bed sheets and other stuffing made me look pregnant."

"An' I suppose half the damn street knows now, hey? Laughingstock Frank, football club director, outstanding member of his community, goes to Rivertown Church every week and his wife is an out-and-out liar. I have a reputation to uphold."

"No one knows. Mrs. Boswell has gone, so now it's just you, me, Lizzie and Francis. No one else."

"I can't get my head around this." Frank breathed in heavily and deliberately, still shaking his head, then he started nodding, "I'll never be ale to face Lizzie or Francis again, will I?"

"They don't know, you know. Leave it that way. I shouldn't have said."

"But you did. Oh, yes, you did! I'll bet you've been waiting to get that off your chest for years. Feel better, hey?"

Elizabeth pulled the Bible up to her chin and shook her head. "No. Has made me feel so much worse."

"Good. I hope God never forgives you." He snatched the bible from her. "You don't deserve to hold this woman!"

Frank took the book back to its home in the parlour, returning a few seconds later.

"Right, let's start again shall we?"

"Are you okay Frank? Are we okay?"

"Time will tell, time will tell."

"No need either for us to row, especially on Gerald... OUR SON's birthday."

Frank once again took several deep breaths and raised his chin, snorting heavily from his nose. His skin glistened with steel dust in the artificial light of the room and he looked like he was the devil himself on a visit to earth from Hades' inferno. He placed his soot laden face towards Elizabeth. He began wagging his index finger as he spoke, keeping his voice quiet, so the children upstairs wouldn't hear, but the menace in his voice was more than clear to Elizabeth.

"Hear me now, woman. If I want to row. I'll row."

His face was closer to her than it had been in months, and Elizabeth caught the unmistakable smell of the steelworks. A burning acrid smell which sometimes pervaded the air when the blast furnace lit the skies of Shotton and the wind blew the dust over the houses.

"Where do you get to, when you head off in your nice suit on the train?" Elizabeth drew the courage from somewhere within to ask the question. It took Frank aback, and she could see he was shaken. He wasn't used to facing questions, especially from his wife. For the first time, the wind had been taken from his sails.

"Chester, you know I go straight to Chester. To the market. You saw the shopping I brought back the other day."

"Market my... hmm. And once I removed what looked like girl's face powder from you collar... "

"I told you about that. I spoke to an older woman I knew from years ago. She gave me a hug in the market. She was with her husband."

Elizabeth nodded. "And who's Edith?"

"Ede... E... Edith... who?"

"Don't lie to me, Frank."

"Hark, who's the liar in this house after what you've just told me."

"I know what you're up to. You can't get the same train back from Chester on the bottom line with a girl and expect no one to see you."

Frank's face showed he'd been caught, but he still had to bluff.

"Ha, yes, that Edith. Are you stupid woman? That's Edith, John's daughter. I work with him. She was just heading in the same direction as me, that's all. I know her dad."

"She's years younger than you. Cuddling on the train like a teenager. Twenty years, bar a few months she is. You forgive me and I'll forgive you, if you stop this nonsense now."

"Right woman, I'm going to get changed. It's the lad's birthday. It's time we got Gerald back down, don't you think? Him and Berty's been up there long enough now."

He shouted at the top of his voice. "Gerald! Bert lad! Come down!"

Gerald and Berty watched their dad wash quickly in the sink and he headed upstairs to change as Elizabeth grabbed the loaf from the side. By the time Frank had changed, Elizabeth had cut a few slices from the loaf. Frank arrived back in the room with the jar of blackcurrant jam from Chester and a look on his face as if nothing had happened that evening.

"Present for you, lad. Your favourite!"

Gerald looked at Elizabeth as he said, "Thanks dad. That's a great present. We can all have some."

The knife used to slice the tin loaf on Gerald's ninth birthday wouldn't have been sharp enough to cut the atmosphere which prevailed within the walls of Dee View that 7th March 1927. Elizabeth spread the blackcurrant jam on the bread as Frank watched on in silence.

"Happy birthday, dear!" Elizabeth proclaimed with an intonation meant for Frank's ears.

He whispered, "Am I keeping the shoes?"

Frank heard Gerald but never looked up. He'd come home early from work as he said he would to Gerald not two days before, to help him celebrate his birthday before bed time arrived.

Berty chipped in, "Happy birthday, Gerald. Second party today."

"Party?" grumbled Frank.

"He means Lizzie and Francis who were here earlier, don't you Berty?"

Berty smiled apprehensively.

"You'll have us all a nervous wreck, Frank dear, lighten up," Elizabeth beseeched Frank.

Frank still said nothing. His veins and scrunched up red face did the talking.

Gerald chewed on his piece of bread and licked his lips to clear the blackcurrant jam away. Frank went into the dark of the front room and arrived back with a small parcel which looked like a book in a white paper bag. Frank handed it to Gerald.

"It's yours, lad, from ME," he added with a hint of sarcasm.

Gerald pulled the book from the bag. It was a Boys Own annual with a front picture in all in blue, of what looked like an Australian woodcutter reading a letter, whilst stood over a boiling billy can on an open campfire. Gerald flicked through the heavy book, looking for the pictures scattered here and there through the pages. He could read really well, so the lack of pictures in the book didn't bother him too much. He found a story he settled on and sat reading quietly whilst Berty stared over, wishing he could flick the pages back to the colour illustrations he'd seen.

The entire room remained quiet, just the odd smack of lips broke the silence as bread and jam flowed down the throats of all the people in the room. All ate, apart from Elizabeth, who couldn't stomach any food. She was feeling decidedly nauseous from everything which had gone on from the point Frank had arrived home. She felt stuck in a relationship she now didn't want to be in, and a river of thoughts cascaded through her head.

No one said anything for a good twenty minutes.

"Tea Frank?" Elizabeth enquired, trying to break the atmosphere and make Gerald's birthday more pleasant.

"Don't think so," was the curt reply.

"Well, I'm making one, anyway."

Elizabeth filled the fire scorched kettle and headed to the York grate to place it on the boil.

She never made it.

Everyone's eyes were concentrated elsewhere when the clatter came. A kettle full of cold water hit the threadbare mat of the back room of Dee View and bounced its contents everywhere.

"Watch it woman!" was Frank's first response, as cold water splashed up on him from the floor, but Elizabeth knew little of his heartless utterance. A seizure had gripped her and this time it came upon her so fast, she had no time to react.

She'd fallen, as if caught under a strobing light, and everything happened in ultra-slow motion for her. The others in the room didn't see anything until it was too late. Elizabeth had succumbed to the worst grand-mal seizure she had ever experienced. As she smashed to the floor, her head twisted grotesquely to one side and then arched back violently as if the guillotine had fallen across her neck. Elizabeth stared white to the plaster flaking ceiling, as her left arm contorted itself under a now viciously trembling frame. Her legs stiffened like some corpse on a battlefield, but then kicked into life aggressively, as if she was trying to escape some devil in the blackest of nightmares.

"Mum! Mum!" Gerald sprang from his chair, the Boys' Own Annual falling to the floor next to Elizabeth. Gerald grabbed her shoulders, doing his best to stop her shaking. "Mum!" He was crying uncontrollably now. He looked back to Frank, who had sat forward from his reclined position. "Do something, dad. Do something!"

"She'll come to lad, she'll come to. She always does."

Berty sat where he was, crying.

"She doesn't need you wailing, lad. You'll have something to cry about, if you don't stop that nonsense now."

Gerald looked down helplessly at Elizabeth and watched as her eyes closed and then popped open repeatedly, rolling back to reveal just white, as her whole body thrashed about the floor. A gruesome rictus settled across her face and foam spattered relentlessly from her mouth.

"Dad, we have to do something. We have to. She's worse than I've ever seen her," cried Gerald.

Gerald wasn't wrong, this was the worst Frank had even seen Elizabeth, and he looked white with fright himself, which frightened

Gerald even more.

"What do I do?" shouted Gerald. Berty cried even louder. Frank grabbed him by the collar and thrust him towards the stairs. "Out lad! Don't come down 'til I tell you."

Frank looked down at the frightened Gerald and the convulsing body of Elizabeth.

"Get Lizzie then. GET Lizzie!"

*

"How is she? How is she?" were the cries of Lizzie, as she came dashing into Dee View no more than three minutes after Gerald had gone for her.

Frank was now standing somewhat cold-bloodedly over Elizabeth, who'd now entered the postictal state of her seizure. The fitting was easing away and Elizabeth looked completely calm on the floor. Then it changed. Elizabeth sat up quickly and vomited.

Frank turned his back, shouting, "Oh God. I can't stomach this."

"It's all right Mrs Davies, it's all right, I'm here now." Lizzie looked at Frank, who was stood facing away from her. "Get me a cloth and some water, man."

"Gerald. Do as Lizzie says. Do it."

"You lazy… "

"What did you say Lizzie?"

"Nothing."

"I'll leave you to it then. This is woman's stuff and I'm going for a walk." With that Frank headed through the front with its closed curtains and Lizzie was almost saddened by his departure as she heard the door close behind him with a loud thud.

Gerald arrived with water in a tin bowl and a couple of towels."

"Will mum be all right Aunt Lizzie? Will she?"

"She will. She will. You don't worry. She's coming round now, you'll see."

Elizabeth groaned and looked completely drowsy. Her breathing was sounding more normal, then she pushed at Lizzie shouting "No, no, no, Off! Off! Get lost! No!… no. Frank no!"

"What the matter with her? Mum! Mum! It's us." Gerald shouted.

"She's disorientated. She'll be okay in a minute, you see m'lad. She will be. She's had a fright, that's all. A big fright! I'm sure the loss of her brother has something to do with this. She'll be fine soon, though. We'll get her cleaned up now before your dad gets back. Can't be nice for you to see though, Gerald, hey?"

Gerald shook his head and looked more concerned than Lizzie had ever seen him.

"All on your birthday, lad. All on your birthday."

*

Outside Frank was stood on the metal railway bridge, as the 8.50pm to Chester steamed away from Shotton station. Frank disappeared in the smoke as the train passed under the bridge, but Frank didn't even see or hear the train pass. He had other plans and he meant to enact them soon.

Chapter Six

'Denbigh Asylum'

Frank left the house without saying a word and headed off to work at the steelworks, canvas bag, with blackcurrant on bread, cut like the step to his house, being his self-prepared lunch. He usually called on Francis, who lived at 6 Ashfield Road, but this was the day after Gerald's ninth birthday and things had altered. Frank had slept in the chair downstairs when he'd arrived home late after parking himself in front of the lit fire at Shotton railway station to keep warm and staying there for many hours to worry Elizabeth even further. Elizabeth of course was in no fit state to worry about Frank and had been put to bed by Lizzie, who'd left the house mess free and spotless.

Frank hadn't bothered to check on Elizabeth or even the two boys when he'd crept in and left earlier than usual the following morning without as much as saying one goodbye to anyone.

Elizabeth woke up on hearing the door pulled to, and glimpsed Frank as he headed around the corner towards the railway bridge. She used the rest of the savaged loaf to cut thin slices of bread for Berty and Gerald for their lunch, and had sent the two lads walking the short distance to their school earlier than usual.

Elizabeth didn't wait a minute after the lads had gone to head out herself and rushed, still with a muzzy head, the short distance to Lizzie's house. She headed around the back and found Lizzie already pegging washing out in the small backyard.

"Mrs. Davies. Are you all right today? I was worried about you. Come in and I'll get the kettle on. Fire's hot already."

Elizabeth welcomed the warm reception and the two women were soon sipping a cup of tea, chatting about the events of yesterday.

"Frank didn't call for Francis this morning. Was odd. First time in years."

"Something happened yesterday. Something very serious and I had to tell you as soon as I could."

"What Mrs. Davies? What?"

"He knows."

"Knows?"

"I had to tell the truth."

"Had to?"

"He got the family bible. MY FAMILY BIBLE and made me. Faced with God, I told him the truth… that Gerald is not his or mine."

"Oh, my God. My God."

"I know. I'm sorry, Lizzie, I'm sorry."

"Don't you be sorry, Mrs. Davies. Perhaps it's time he knew. It's been on my mind for a long time."

"On your mind?"

"I chatted with Francis once and we both thought, as Gerald got older, we should tell him the truth. I so hate him calling me aunt or aunty now. I know you're mum to him and always will be, after all, he's gone nine years calling you that, well at least since he could talk he has."

Elizabeth smiled. "Yes, I remember his first words and he called me mama. I was delighted but thought about you, even then."

"So what do we do now?"

"I honestly do not know," answered Elizabeth. "What I do know is Frank is capable of anything now he knows this. I am frightened for my future and for Gerald's future and I…"

The front door letter box rattled.

"It'll be the post, I'll go and get it."

Lizzie went through the front of the house, but there was no post on the mat. The letter box went again. "Just coming now," shouted Lizzie as she pulled the door open, moving the old pairs of stuffed stockings, acting as a draft excluder. "Is the letter too big to fit through the letter bo… "

It wasn't the postman. It was Frank.

"Aren't you going to let me in then?" He didn't wait and walked past Lizzie. Lizzie hurriedly closed the door and followed Frank through to the back room.

"Thought I'd find you two ladies gassing."

Elizabeth stood up, startled to the core. "Frank, you're in work."

"Obviously not. I've got a few minutes before they see I'm gone, so I'll say what I have to say and I'll out of your way."

"I have no idea what you two have chittle-chattled about this morning, but our Gerald will have been part of the conversation." He looked at Lizzie. "I know everything you know."

"I know, dear Mrs. Davies has told me." Lizzie was trying her best to be as respectful as possible to her elders, despite the fact she felt she ought not to be deep inside.

"I don't know what exact plans you two conjured up all those years ago and my head still finds it hard to believe what is the reality of this matter but the truth I DO know is that Gerald is MY son... "

His voice was tinted with anger and seething rage was forcing its way from his face through his quivering bottom lip. He continued on.

"... no one knows anything and they shall know NOTHING henceforth, other than what they know now. This is a neighbourhood in which I have a reputation to uphold and, God forgive me for saying this, but I will do anything to make sure that remains the case."

Lizzie was shaking her head slowly and squeezed her tongue tightly between her teeth as he spoke, but she felt unable to keep quiet any longer.

"How dare you, Mr. Davies, how dare you! He is my son. He is your son's son and he shall know when he is of the right age."

"Oh, yes? Is that right, hey?"

Frank was nodding away, breathing heavily and his eyes and mouth twitching like a cornered rabid dog.

Elizabeth remained silent.

"In fact, I have a mind to tell him today and bring him to live with me. I have heard of the vile way you are at home."

"Don't Lizzie, don't!" shouted Elizabeth.

"Yes, you can be oh, so nasty and you don't deserve a nice family, especially one who doesn't even belong to you."

Frank's rage exploded. He raised his hand and looked as if he was about to hit Lizzie. Elizabeth jumped in between the two.

"Frank! No!"

Frank pushed Elizabeth to the side with some force. "You little cheeky bitch. You gave up any rights to Gerald the night he was born, when you, and this pathetic thing of a wife of mine, hatched your nasty plan to deceive me. Well, by God, your deception will now work for me. I'll see to that."

"Not if I tell Gerald and he comes here."

"You tell Gerald and you will never see him again. EVER! Worse still, I'll make sure he hates you forever if you as much as mention one word of your sick and demented plan. You have been warned. Right!"

Lizzie took a deep breath and said nothing.

"I'll see myself out!" He looked at Elizabeth. "Time you went home I think."

Frank nodded to Elizabeth to head to the door and the two left.

*

Shotton was sat on the western side of Britain and its people were used to westerly and southerly winds blowing constantly. March 1927 was no different. And the month brought unsettled but mainly mild weather, although through Gerald's birthday there had been bitter light winds from the north with overnight frosts and awful wintry showers. For Elizabeth, the third week of March had seen the return of milder conditions and she even believed Frank was thawing as he'd been icy cold since that birthday.

Saturday 26th March 1927 was a stormy day, with a deep Atlantic low setting across most of western Britain. It was 2pm sharp when there was a loud bang on the front door of Dee View. Two police officers were at the door and just behind them a man was turning off the ignition to his shiny new 490cc black Norton 16H. The bike made clinking noises as the raindrops hit the hot parts of the engine and exhaust. Its rider was thoroughly wet from the journey.

Frank wasn't in the least surprised by their arrival and ushered them in.

"She's in the back."

Hello Mrs Davies, I'm Dr Joseph Dobson from Buckley and these are two local bobbies. Look, I'll get straight to the point, Frank here tells me you are suffering from delusions. You are saying you never gave birth to your son and you are also suffering from fits. He says he cannot control you and you have fits of awful temper, so bad that you hurt your husband and your son. He says you have been trying to poison him." He added condescendingly, "that's just not good, is it dear?"

"Why are you doing this to me, Frank? Why?"

The police officers moved closer.

"You've never been responsible as a mother to our boy?"

"He's not our boy. He's Lizzie's."

"See Doctor, she's losing her mind AND she's been seeing someone else."

"What Frank!" <'*What in heaven's name... '*>

Frank looked at Elizabeth. "What you've done is against God."

"You are right Mr. Davies, her mind is dislocated from reality, she is obviously delusional and dangerous to others, including her own children. The papers have been signed accordingly."

He nodded approvingly to the police officers.

The police officers took hold of Elizabeth. Handcuffs came out.

"Stop it, stop it!" shouted Elizabeth. "What are you doing? You can't do this."

"Stop struggling, Mrs. Davies. You will have to come with us."

Elizabeth struggled violently to get away, but she was held fast. She kicked out at Frank. Frank jumped back. "See! She's violent in the extreme! Frightens me she does."

"You bastard! You don't know what you are doing. Gerald is Lizzie's baby. He's Lizzie's."

"Come quietly, madam!" shouted one officer as he put an armlock around her neck. Elizabeth screamed.

"Let go!"

"Don't fight it Mrs. Davies, you'll only cause yourself more problems."

Elizabeth struggled to her utmost strength but was now subdued by both burly bobbies who held her tightly.

"Convey Mrs Davies to the asylum at Denbigh. I've already been in contact with them. They know she is coming. "

"You knew before you came into my house? Frank, you bastard."

Frank turned away and said nothing.

"Frank! FRANK!"

She was dragged away screaming through the rain to a waiting ambulance outside. Curtains twitched in the street, but not a soul came out. One police officer got into the ambulance with Elizabeth and the doors closed. Screams from inside could still be heard as the ambulance made its way down Ash Grove in Shotton, followed by a police car and the doctor's motor bike.

Frank watched the tiny convoy head away down the road, then closed the closed the door and made himself a cup of cocoa. He'd sent both boys up to Rivertown Church to help the pastor sort a book sale out, so neither ever knew the exact happenings of that day.

*

* * *

It was almost one hour before they got to Denbigh and, the hour of the day, combined with the heavy hanging rain clouds, saw dark and foreboding skies, when the ambulance, still closely followed by the police car, pulled through the huge entrance gates of the notorious Denbigh Asylum. The Gothic hospital facade matched the foul mood of the weather.

There'd been two men already in the ambulance, one driving and the other who looked like a young trainee full of nerves, seemed ready to plunge a hypodermic needle into Elizabeth, if as much as she said one word. The police officer never said another word to her all journey, and both were looking at Elizabeth as if she was completely deranged. No one understood mental health, least of all the police.

The ambulance came to a stop outside a grand entrance at the top of some steps.

"No, no, no, you've got it wrong. I'm not supposed to be here. Leave me go."

"Now, now… " said the older ambulance man as he firmly grabbed her around her waist. "You're going in."

"Please, please! It's my husband's doing this is. There's nothing wrong with me. He's trying to get rid of me. Can't you see? My husband is lying. Please!"

She panicked even more at the sight of the group of nurses close by and her eyes moved wildly observing them all wondering what they were about to do to her. One or two moved nearer.

Elizabeth shouted, "Stay away from me."

In the background banging, screaming and whoops of extraordinarily horrible sounds filled the pale blue painted corridor she was now stood in.

"It's my son, well he's not my son. Gerald. Yes. Frank found out he's Lizzie's son. So he's flipped his lid. Yes, he's the one who's flipped his lid. Not me. He thought Gerald was his son, now I've told him he's not. That's what this is about. He's the one who wants me put away."

She sweated profusely and could hear the incoherence in her own voice. It didn't sound good, but what else could she react like.

"Yes, he's the one who's mad. Not me! He's plotted to have me put away. He's the one who's mad."

One nurse, a small lady with a face as hard and as round and as lined as a walnut spoke with the police. They gave her some papers, which she read as the police spoke.

Elizabeth had heard some whisperings.

"Lost her senses."

"Violent."

"Seeing someone else. Moral insanity! Imbecility."

"For her own safety."

The police officers turned their backs and walked away, as did the people from the ambulance. The group of nurses in the corridor gathered closer to Elizabeth and two of the male nurses stepped forward at the nod of nurse walnut and took hold of her arms with a tight grip.

"Let me go!" she shouted angrily as she tried to pull herself away. The two nurses gripped her even tighter and two others stood closer in. One held what looked like a straitjacket, it's leather buckles hanging inertly towards the black and yellow smartly tiled floor.

Elizabeth had heard of straitjackets and her eyes flashed wide at its sight.

Nurse 'walnut' spoke. "I'm Sister Lamb. Now Elizabeth, we fully understand. Yes, we understand dear. You do know why you are here, don't you dear?"

Elizabeth was looking at everyone. Shocked. "Please listen! Please!" She put her hands together as if in prayer. "I'm not mad. I shouldn't be here. I'm not violent.

No one was listening.

"Elizabeth Mary Davies, is it deary?"

Elizabeth's eyes were full of tears. "Let me go!" She shouted. "Let me go!"

Nurse Lamb was no lamb at all and her wrinkled face showed scant empathy. Nurse Lamb checked the clips holding her hat firmly to her grey hair. "Now, now dear, do you want that on?" She said grabbing the limp straitjacket covered in vile looking filthy stains.

Elizabeth was horrified at the thought. She shook her head. "NO!"

"Right then, we need to get your reception orders completed. You know where you are then don't you deary."

Elizabeth nodded. The two nurses gripping her released their tight grip but still held onto her by her flowery pinny, which Elizabeth had had no time to take off before being taken away from her house.

"You'll have to lose those clothes, deary. Take her over to Gwynfryn to the Useful Female Patients' block for cleansing and do the necessary."

<'Cleansing? The necessary?'>

The form was headed *North Wales Counties Lunatic Asylum* but the latter two words had been crossed out and replaced with the typed words *'Mental Hospital.'*

Part 3 of the form said:

I formed this conclusion on the following grounds, viz. : —

(a.) Facts indicating Insanity observed by myself at the time of examination (g), viz. :

She is very much depressed and continually cries. She was crying when I visited her this very morning and the same for yesterday when admitted. When asked what she was crying for, she gave such a ludicrously incoherent and a very silly answer, something about her son not being her son and her daughter-in-law being the mother. As such, I deemed her conversation to be totally incoherent and she is insane. I cannot see there will be an improvement of her lunacy and imbecility, unless drastic measures are taken.

The County Asylums Act of 1808 meant that all areas of Britain had to provide some form of care for the mentally ill. By 1840, the poor rural communities of Wales couldn't afford to build such a place. Joseph Ablett of Llanbedr Hall donated 20 acres of land in Denbigh for this purpose, and Queen Victoria joined in donating £50 of her own money to help the *'insane of Wales.'* So the lunatic asylum, as many knew it, commenced building in 1844 from local stone quarries and was opened officially on 14 November 1848. The hospital serving as a refuge for Welsh-speaking mental patients, originally designed to accommodate about 200 patients, was expanded to ease overcrowding in 1899 and eventually was home for up to 1500 patients.

Male nurses in white coats removed Elizabeth along the longest corridor she'd ever been along in her life. All tiled neatly in white with lines of hideous brown tiles and ceramic window ledges as far as the eye could see. The floor became blue and yellow tiles in large rectangles with squares of yellow between. Eventually she was taken into a small room lined from floor to ceiling in white clinical looking tiles. The two women nurses in the room had obviously been expecting her.

"Remove your clothes, er ..." one of the nurses looked down at the papers. "... Mrs. Davies."

"My clothes?"

"All of them."

"I don't want to. I've never removed my clothes in front of anyone, except Frank."

"Do you want me to call in the women who've just brought you here, hey?" There was threat in the voice. "They can remove them for you. It won't be nice. We'll make sure of that, Mrs. Davies. Now you know what we can be like when we want, don't you?"

Elizabeth knew only too well what they could be like. There seemed no choice. She removed her clothes.

"In there, please," came the prompt with a nod towards a cold side room, with what looked like shower facilities around the sides and a drain at the centre of the floor.

Elizabeth shivered and walked in alone. She had never felt so alone and isolated in all her life. One nurse turned on a tap and cold water shot from the shower heads.

Elizabeth screamed at the shock of the water hitting her body. She turned to face the wall.

"Don't be a baby!" a nurse called back and Elizabeth heard sniggering in the background. The water slowly became slightly warmer but was then followed by a sharp blast of freezing cold water from a hose held by one nurse, who was now dressed in a huge black rubber apron and wellingtons, as if she was ready to dip sheep, not deal with a human being. Elizabeth screamed with all her might and scrunched herself into the corner, as yet more cold water hit her body from every angle.

The showering stopped and Elizabeth made for a towel she could see on the side.

"Not yet." Shouted the nurse with the rubber apron, as the other nurse donned rubber gloves. "We have to check you have nothing which might harm you OR US. Spread your legs, dear."

"I don't want to."

The cold water dripped from Elizabeth as she shivered in the freezing room.

The two nurses moved forward swiftly and the larger of the two slapped Elizabeth forcefully across the face, shocking Elizabeth to the core.

"You'll do as you're told. Right?"

Elizabeth looked at the two nurses shaking her head. Then the shake fell to a nod. "Right," she whispered.

"That's an excellent, well-behaved lady. We like patients who do as they are told. Don't we, Jean?"

"We do. We most certainly do, Carys."

The most intrusive and awful medical examination Elizabeth had ever undergone in her life followed. She pushed her face into the cold tiles and thought of better days in her life.

Meanwhile, the two nurses chatted about what they'd had for tea and what they were preparing for tomorrow's main meal at home. They laughed and smiled, paying no attention to the patient in their charge.

It was the 26 March 1927 and Elizabeth shook her head in disbelief. <'Home! I want to go home.'>

She couldn't believe what was happening to her. Silent tears drifted down her face, lost in the water still dripping from her head. She thought back to a day, a Monday almost three weeks ago, and Gerald's smiling face on his birthday when he'd seen those shoes. She wandered what he might be doing right there and then.

It wasn't long before Elizabeth was off again. She was led down another endless dark corridor and through an open courtyard area and then into a dark grey building.

"Our quarters, Mrs. Davies," the nurse said as if she was resident there too.

"I need to speak with a doctor or something. I need to tell him just what is wrong."

The nurse looked down at the notes she was holding. "Seems you have a terrible malady, Mrs. Davies and we are here to help you. The doctors will see you when they can."

Elizabeth was placed into a small room which looked more like a police cell than a hospital room. "Inside please, Mrs. Davies. Inside!"

"I… I… don't want to."

"Now, now Mrs. Davies. You have to do as you're told. We know you haven't been sleeping well and have said you want to die. You are here for your own good. You are not at home now… this is a hospital and you are in our custody."

"Custody? Isn't that for prisoners?"

"Good Lord, Mrs. Davies, it seems you have a false belief you might be a voluntary patient. Where on earth did you get that idea? Now, now Mrs. Davies we can't have you thinking like that can we? There is a difference… prisoners go to prison for doing wrong and patients come into our care for their own good."

"So if I am a patient, then I am free to leave then."

"It doesn't work like that. We have a duty of care to you and doctors who know better than any of us have deemed you need custodial care here for… as I've said before… for your own good."

"I want to go home."

The nurse became more aggressive. The debate ended there. "I'm afraid you cannot go home. This is your home now!"

The nurse pushed Elizabeth into the room and slammed the door behind her.

Yellow walls abounded, and two awful metal beds were at right angles to each other.

One bed was made up tidily with fresh sheets and on the other was an old lady with grey hair and one tooth in her head. She gripped her knees as if she was hugging a child and she rocked up and down.

"It's been thundering. It's been thundering," she repeated endlessly as she occasionally looked up whilst still maintaining the rock forward.

The old lady who could have easily passed for the witch in Snow White, took no notice of Elizabeth's presence in the room. Elizabeth crept forward to the empty bed and sat on it, putting her shaking hands over her head. She had never felt so alone in all her life and cried until she fell asleep, but her sleep didn't last long. Within the darkness of the room, there were terrible screams and shouts.

"Mummy, there's thunder!" screamed the old lady, as she jumped fully against Elizabeth, who shot bolt upright in fright. "Help me, mummy. Thunder. Thunder!" shouted the old lady, who smelled of urine as she clung onto Elizabeth's night gown.

This was Elizabeth's reality and the night became the next day… and the next day.

*

Elizabeth found she'd been admitted to the 'Epileptic and Suicidal Dormitory' at Denbigh. There was one large ward with side rooms for newly admitted patients. The patients on this ward were all regarded as high risk and were put together so they could be better observed.

It was three days before Elizabeth saw a doctor. She was taken to a side room and sat before Mr. Morris, an old doctor who looked like he should have retired many years ago.

She sat there as he read through some notes, but no longer could stomach the silence.

"There's nothing wrong with me, doctor. Yes, I have turns now and then but I'm fit and healthy otherwise. I'm normal. I'm not like the thunder woman… "

Mr. Morris, as everyone called him, looked up over his thick round-rimmed glasses.

"Ah, you are with Maisie Roberts. She is harmless, although she has her moments when she wants to end it all… and there is no such thing as normal. Everyone who comes here says they are normal, but I can assure you they are not."

He flicked through the papers before him. "Now you have these turns… "

"I'm not insane, you know."

Patients who were admitted with epilepsy, were housed separately in the Epileptic and Suicidal dormitory. This dormitory was shared with patients who were a high suicide risk, presumably so they could be better observed.

"Everyone who comes here says that. It is clear from studying your case file, that your primary diagnosis is imbecility with epilepsy as an aggravating factor."

"I have fits, but I'm not an imbecile."

"Yes, yes, Mrs. Davies," said Mr. Morris as he busily scrawled notes without once looking up. "Don't get angry and upset."

"I'm not angry or upset, well yes, I'm upset. Why are you keeping me here?"

"Yes, yes, wait a moment," he whispered as he wrote. "Memory loss, aggressive, confusion… yes… yes… epilepsy… hmm."

At last he looked up. "Now these fits you have and your delusions about your child. How long have you had these?"

"I'm not deluded. Gerald was born to my prospective daughter-in-law. Her names's Lizzie. Yes… and to save her embarrassment, and to save her from being cast out for having a child out of wedlock, we agreed to conceal the fact the child… er … Gerald was mine… but Lizzie gave birth."

"Prospective, that's a grand word." Mr Morris nodded away. "Yes, dear, fascinating story. Absolutely fascinating! How long have you thought this to be true?"

"It is true. I'll swear on a bible if you want."

He looked at the notes again. "I see you have had the Wassermann blood test for syphilis."

"Wassermann?" Elizabeth looked puzzled. "Syphilis? How dare y… I'm a woman of clean virtue doctor. There was no need for any tests."

"We can't be too careful, Mrs. Davies. Syphilis deranges people more than you know."

"Well, you won't find it in me."

"As I said, we can't be too careful, so the test is standard for all people coming here. Protects us as well as our patients and tells us how we might proceed."

"And how are you to proceed?"

Mr. Morris ignored Elizabeth's sensible question completely as he read the notes, speaking and nodding to his own thoughts.

"Yes, yes, ah ha. Yes. Right…dear. Says here you are prone to these fits very often and that you then lose self-control where you are a danger to yourself and others."

"It's not true."

"Insanity comes in all forms Mrs. Davies, and when we are in one of these fits, we cannot always know what we are doing. Don't you see. I mean, you wouldn't know you were a danger when you are having a fit because you are not in control of your senses." He looked back at the notes. "For example, it seems your husband, He is your husband… Mr. Frank Davies… "

"Yes."

"He says you have tried to hurt your children and… "

"Not true. He is lying."

"And you have tried to poison him to get rid of him. Is that not true?"

"He is lying. He is the one who is trying to get rid of me. I want to go home."

But you see Mrs. Davies, you wouldn't know, would you? Don't you see, you just wouldn't know what you are like hey?"

"And your son… er … Gerald?"

"Yes, Gerald."

"Just tell me again… you believe he is now not your son?"

"He is my son in name, but not my son by birth. That's true."

"So, what you are telling me is that your son is not your son?"

"Yes, I am. Lizzie gave birth to him."

"And who is this Lizzie?"

"My son's wife."

"So your son, who is not your son, is your son's wife's?"

"No, that's a different son. My son, who I said was my son, is my actual grandson and he is my son Francis' son."

Mr. Morris shook his head with derision.

"Insanity… insanity!" he quietly uttered through almost closed lips.

He looked at Elizabeth. "But that's all a bit odd isn't it, hey, don't you think? You are a very troubled woman, aren't you Mrs. Davies? Reality and fantasy are the same in your head, so it appears Mrs. Davies. You have some very complex issues, don't you?. More complex than even your notes suggest."

"I don't have any issues other than I have the odd turn or two."

Yes, yes, that's where I think we have to begin… to understand what your issues are. We are very forward thinking here at Denbigh and we have some modern ways of tackling your problem. Have you heard of William Aldren Turner?" [1]

"No."

"He's a foremost expert in the field of epilepsy, which I do believe you suffer from, besides several other things, perhaps."

"Epilepsy, yes, it's not such a bad thing is it?" She thought about Berty and her brother. Then her parents. She dared not mention it ran in the family. Mr. Morris did though.

"I believe you have a recently deceased brother at an asylum in Shropshire and your parents died in asylums too. It's here in your notes."

<'Frank how could you betray me so!'> Elizabeth nodded, it seemed Frank hadn't mentioned Berty so saying nothing was the next best thing.

"Yes, Mr. Turner is an eminent epileptologist - that means he knows about epilepsy to the n'th degree you see."

"Yes, I understood what that means."

"Good, then we are agreed. We shall follow some of his guidelines but we have our own long established routines for epilepsy too. We will treat you accordingly."

"I can be treated at home, surely?"

Mr. Morris shook his head. "I rather think not for all the safety reasons we have already talked about. You will stay here until we decide you are fit to return to your home AND you are no longer a danger to others. Don't want you poisoning anyone, do we?" A hint of a sarcastic smile came across his face.

Elizabeth looked around. A group of nurses, one of whom was Nurse Lamb, had appeared in the open doorway. They said nothing but looked threatening.

"We still use bromides to treat this condition though, so you will be prescribed a course of this treatment." He whispered to himself as he wrote…

"110 grains Bromide per day - mixed with syrup of prune. Borax. Yes, we'll start her on that as well. 30 grains per day. Yes. Erm and er... yes, Belladonna tincture for the spasms I see you have. 10 minims."

Elizabeth listened intently. "Belladonna. That's a poison, isn't it?"

"Not in small doses, dear. Not in small doses. Will stop your spasms."

"I'm not having any spasms right now."

"But you have done." He became stern and distant. "Right you, be quiet for a second. This is for your own good."

"Opium, yes." He wrote in an almost illegible scrawl with his fountain pen, which he constantly wiped on the desk blotting paper to clear the nib of ink blobs which stayed with the nib as it was extracted from the inkwell on the desk. He looked up. "Help you sleep and stop any pain, hey Mrs. Davies."

He wrote more.

"Phenobarbitol after the first seizure here. Dose as dependant of severity of seizure."

As he wrote more notes, he nodded to nurse Lamb and the nurses came in. "Take her back to her room. Begin her treatment."

"No, no," screamed Elizabeth. "You have to let me go home. My children need me. I'm not going back to my room here."

Mr. Morris looked down and never looked up again. Elizabeth was dragged screaming back to her room and locked in with Thunder Maisie as everyone knew her in Denbigh.

*

Routines developed and time moved inexorably forward. Each morning the door would be unlocked and Elizabeth became acclimatised to the routine at Denbigh Asylum. Screams, crying, awful howls, hollering noises, breakfast in a canteen with people who sometimes threw their white enamel cups and plates to the floor in pure frustration. Women would shuffle to her and ask her what was wrong, others would shuffle to her and just scream obscenities. Most of all, she noticed the women seemed to have lost the ability to walk. They all shuffled like they were suffering from some form of dementia.

The chemical restraints were working well on all the patients.

Elizabeth wondered when she might shuffle and what would cause it.

Author's Note
[1] Turner described the dangers of bromism (the syndrome of toxicity) if

the use was prolonged and injudicious in graphic terms: "This condition [bromism] is characterised by a blunting of the intellectual faculties, impairment of the memory, and the production of a dull and apathetic state. The speech is slow, the tongue tremulous, and saliva may flow from the mouth. The gait is staggering, and the movements of the limbs feeble and infirm. The mucous membranes suffer, so that the palatal sensibility may be abolished, and nausea, flatulence, and diarrhoea supervene. The action of the heart is low and feeble, the respiration shallow and imperfect, and the extremities blue and cold. An eruption of acne frequently covers the skin of the face and back."

Chapter Seven

'Palm Sunday'

It was now Palm Sunday, 10th April 1927 and Lizzie and Francis dressed in their Sunday best to head for the service at Rivertown Church. Lizzie hadn't seen Elizabeth, Frank or the children since Frank had arrived unexpectedly at the house to make his demands the day after Gerald's birthday. Francis had seen his dad at the steelworks every day, but Frank had refused to talk about anything to do with home.

Lizzie wanted to understand what was going on, but most of all she wanted to see Gerald. Both had hoped to meet together as they headed up Ash Grove towards Chester Road where the church was, but there was no sight of them anywhere.

Francis and Lizzie walked in and, as usual, were handed the blue ancient and modern hymn book and the red common prayer book. This day they were handed a palm cross, as was habitual in the church every Palm Sunday. They made their way to their usual seats, as was their habit in the church. Lizzie continuously looked around, but they could not see Elizabeth and her family anywhere. The spaces next to them were filled by an unknown family but would have normally been seats reserved for the Davies family.

Pastor Barrow came in and the crowded congregation, mainly comprising steelworkers and their families, stood up spontaneously.

"We shall begin our service today with hymn number 306, *At The Name of Jesus.*"

The organ sprang into action, and the whole was filled with hearty singing. Lizzie was still looking around and then the main door to the church slowly opened at the back and in waked Frank, taking his trilby off as he entered. He was followed by Gerald and Berty in their best brown Sunday suits. Lizzie expected to see Elizabeth walking in next, but instead she saw Edith Clarkson.

Francis was at the top of his voice, starting the second verse. *"At His voice creation…"* Francis was so engrossed singing the hymn, the hard dig in his side from Lizzie's elbow made him flinch. "Ooof!" he exclaimed, as one or two of the congregation nearby gave him dirty looks.

Lizzie whispered in his ear, "Look, look Francis. Behind. LOOK!"

"Who is she?"

"Are you that blind. It's John's daughter, Edith."

"Where's mum? It's not like her to miss the Palm Sunday service."

"More than that, what's Edith doing here, coming in with your dad? So much for having a reputation to uphold."

Frank and the others sat down somewhere at the back of the church.

*

The chapel service at Denbigh asylum was a welcome break for Elizabeth from her small room with the screaming Thunder Maisie, but she found she was increasingly struggling to walk as easily as she did just two weeks before. She was better than most though but still found the short distance to the asylum chapel an arduous feat. Nurse Lamb had informed Elizabeth just over one hour ago she would attend a church service, a complete surprise for Elizabeth. Even more of a surprise would be the fact that this was the first time Elizabeth had been outside since being at the asylum.

As she left the main building and entered the asylum grounds, she took in the air as if this was the first time she had drawn breath in her life. Her breath was taken away completely though when she arrived at the asylum chapel. The chapel at the asylum had been designed by local architects Williams and Underwood and completed in 1862, some 18 years after the building of the main asylum had begun. Elizabeth had not expected such a grand building to be part of such a vile place. [1]

"Inside ladies, inside. Palm Sunday service awaits us all," the ever present Nurse Lamb had insisted as Elizabeth had stopped to look at the building in all its glory.

Inside the chapel was quite plain, but coming from a Welsh chapel background this was almost home from home for Elizabeth, but she felt sad this was not home and her family were nowhere to be seen. She'd almost lost track of what day it was, but Nurse Lamb had told her this was Palm Sunday. She knew her own family would be at Rivertown and a tear came to her eye. Noticed by Nurse Lamb.

"Come on now, Mrs. Davies. These are happy and carefree days. No need for tears. Tears tell of unhappiness and this is a cheerful place."

Nurse Lamb repeated loudly to the file of shuffling ladies "This is our happy place. What is it?"

No one responded, but she hadn't expected them to.

Louder. "What are we ladies? We are HAPPY. HAPPY."

One or two mumbled 'Happy,' through palsy mouths as they filed in.

The elderly asylum chaplain before the congregation was a dead ringer for Mahatma Ghandi and sported the same minimalist round optical spectacles, which he kept to the end of his Ghandiesque nose. As he peered over his glasses, he saw what he'd seen a hundred times before; at least two dozen expressionless women patients before him in he chapel, some with mouths hanging and drooling like Saint Bernards looking at an unobtainable piece of kibble; others grunted, ticked, tapped, or just shook as they sat in their hospital gowns. The chaplain's routine for Palm Sunday was the same service as it had been for thirty years or more at the asylum and he spoke quietly about Jesus' triumphal entry into Jerusalem, interrupted by the odd scream and high-pitched whoop, which kept him on his toes. He had never got used to this and spasmed with fright each time a noise came forth.

He was comforted by the thought this was a harmless sea of empty souls before him who posed little or no danger to his personal safety, despite the animalistic racket which surrounded him. Amongst the congregation that morning were one or two new arrivals, which the chaplain had noticed. This included Elizabeth and the chaplain welcomed the new people to the service whilst at the same time he remained wary. Newcomers were an unknown quantity and could present unknown difficulties. These patients had usually not been on their medication long enough for their bodies and minds to succumb to the usual devastating effects. The chaplain was heartened by the number of nursing staff who stood to the sides of the congregation.

More than usual. This was the run up to Easter after all.

As they sang the last hymn of the service, Elizabeth grasped the dried palm in her hand shaped into the sign of the cross and thought of nothing else but home. She had seen no one and had nothing from home since she had been incarcerated there just over two weeks ago.

She kept mouthing to herself, <*'Must get out. Must get out. Ask the chaplain. Ask the chaplain. He'll help. He'll help. Ask him. Ask him.'*>

The chaplain had asked everyone to go on their knees to say a quiet prayer.

<*'Dear God, I beseech you in you in your kind mercy to help me get away from here. I pray to you to help me see my family. Please God, please.'*>

Then it happened. Elizabeth stood up.

"Please, Mr. Chaplain. I'm not supposed to be here. Help me. I am a prisoner. These nurses and my husband are keeping me prisoner here. You must help me escape. Help me, please. Help me." She started screaming, "Help me! PLEASE!" continuously and began walking towards the elderly chaplain who looked horrified and he backed away as chants and screams filled the chapel at the asylum

"Help us, help us!" filled the room.

The nursing staff were quick off the mark and made directly for Elizabeth.

Nurse Lamb directed the staff with a ruthless efficiency and the women were ushered out of the chapel, whilst Elizabeth shuffled her way towards the chaplain who'd now fallen backwards into his nearby seat.

Elizabeth got to within two yards of the chaplain who'd put his hands out to stop her coming near but before she could take another shuffle, a sharp slap hit the side of her face. It was Nurse Lamb.

Nurse Lamb slapped Elizabeth again twice. "You stupid woman. What the hell are you doing?" Two other male nurses arrived and pulled Elizabeth down to the floor, whereupon she began shaking and convulsing violently. Foam frothing from her mouth.

*

The last hymn of the Palm Sunday service at Rivertown was sung, and Pastor Barrow waited at the back of the church to greet the congregation as they left for their terraced homes on the banks of the Dee.

Lizzie and Francis had stood up quickly but were delayed by the queue of people funnelling through the narrow entrance to the church. Francis could see his dad shaking hands with the pastor, and then the four were gone.

Lizzie couldn't stand it any longer and, dragging Francis by the hand, made her way through the congregation unceremoniously. Francis, ever polite, constantly saying, *'sorry, sorry,'* as she barged her way forward, with a flurry of *'excuse-me please's'* and necessary jostling, which one or two times was met with *'how rude!'* There was a quick handshake with Pastor Barrow, who looked confused, and they were into Chester Road. Frank, Edith and the boys were a couple of hundred yards ahead, just under the railway bridge which crossed the main road.

"Gerald, Gerald! Wait."

Gerald turned around and, seeing Lizzie, he stopped.

"Come on, lad" shouted Frank but Gerald ran back to Lizzie.

He hugged her as he reached her. "Aunt Lizzie. Thought I saw you."

"You look smart as ever, look at you!"

Francis nodded and touched Gerald's arm.

"Dad said you weren't in church, but I was right. We were late… er, waiting for Edith to arrive."

They carried on walking towards Frank, Berty and Edith.

"Edith?" Lizzie pretended she didn't know her.

"Yes. She looks after us when dad is in work… and has tea with us sometimes."

"She does? Where's your mum?"

"She's not well dad says."

"No one had told me."

Dad said not to bother you as you'd not been well yourself, so I hadn't called around. So glad to see you now though."

"Are you looking after your mum?"

"She… she's… dad said not to say."

"Say what?"

They were now near to Frank, and Gerald said nothing.

"How are you, Frank?" Lizzie never waited for an answer and bent over to Berty. "You okay, m'lad?"

Berty nodded.

"Hello Lizzie. Francis lad. Hello. I'm all right Lizzie, thank you for asking. This is Edith. You know her already don't you?"

"Hello," said an embarrassed-looking Edith.

It was Lizzie's turn to nod now.

"No, Mrs Davies today?"

As if to reinforce it, Francis asked, "Where's mum?"

"She's been poorly," Frank added. "You mustn't worry about her."

"We haven't seen her in a few weeks." Concern filled Lizzie's face. "Is she okay. She must be very unwell to have Edith about looking after the boys. I would have done it. I will do it you know. Anything to help… look I know we've had our differences but I want things to be right… you know especially after we talked."

"Talked?"

Francis interrupted. "He knows what you mean, don't you dad?"

Frank ruminated on what words he might choose when Gerald spoke out. "Mum's in hospital. She's not at home."

"Gerald lad!" Frank shouted out with a furious face.

"She's where!" exclaimed Lizzie.

"Hospital somewhere."

"She's not at home then Frank?"

"She's not, I'm afraid. You two lads run along ahead of us now. There's good boys." Gerald and Bert did as they were told. "I didn't want to worry you," a lying Frank rasped, as he started off towards home, ushering Edith in the same direction.

Everyone followed.

"She's my mum, dad. Why couldn't you tell me? Why wouldn't you tell me?"

"Same reason, same reason lad."

"So where is she dad?"

"She's safe and being treated."

"Treated for what?"

Frank stopped in his tracks. "You know what she was like on Gerald's birthday." He sought confirmation from Lizzie. "Lizzie, you know." He raised his eyebrows. "You had to rush to the house. She's very ill lad. Very ill."

"Then we must see her," Lizzie pleaded.

"She's allowed no visitors at the moment."

Lizzie looked concerned. "None? Why?"

"She's in a state and the doctors have said she must have complete rest. People she knows will only worsen her mental plight."

"Mental plight?" Lizzie shrieked. "Where is she, Frank?"

Frank put his finger to his lips. "Shhh. This conversation is not for the street and neither is it for the ears of young lads."

"Then we'll come back to yours." Francis insisted.

Frank looked uneasy. "If you must!" He walked ahead at a pace with Edith at his side.

* * *
*

Elizabeth squirmed round the floor, her body spasming in frightful contortions. The church was emptied by a mass of staff who seemed to appear from everywhere. Soon there was only Elizabeth and five nurses in the building, even the chaplain had disappeared at a pace Eric Liddell would have been proud of, considering he must have been eighty if a day.

It was Nurse Lamb who gave the instruction. "Straitjacket and back to her room for contemplation. Teach the bitch a lesson."

Elizabeth was claustrophobic at the best of times and being put into this torture contraption would ordinarily have been a hell on earth, but in her semi-conscious state her awareness of what was going on around her, and to her was limited. That was until she came to in her room being prodded by the one-toothed Thunder Maisie.

"Thought you was dead. Thought the thunder had got you. It's bad out there. BAD. It gets you in the end. All thunder does."

Elizabeth slowly opened her eyes and went to wipe away the horrible stickiness which she could feel around her mouth and nose. The realisation settled in and Elizabeth squealed with terror as she violently rocked her body to free it of its canvas manacle.

"You'll never get that off, love," shouted Thunder Maisie as she backed away in horror at Elizabeth's contortions. "You keep away from me. You keep away. You've got thunder in you I can see it." She started screaming. "Nurse. Nurse. Thunder. Thunder, it's in the room. She's caught it. Get me out. Get me out."

Elizabeth shouted "No. No. Not this. I'll be good. I'll be good now." But it was too late. No one was listening. The nearest nursing staff were within earshot but were too busy having their afternoon break and people shouting was a normal occurrence. A normal occurrence which was best ignored by anyone who considered themselves a member of staff at the asylum.

*

Francis and Lizzie followed the others into Dee View.

"Would you be a good thing and make a cup of tea for us all, Edith?"

Edith set to making a pot of team using all the things which

Elizabeth herself would have used, even down to the old green tea and sugar tins which she was already well acquainted with.

Frank, Gerald and Berty had gone upstairs to change out of their Sunday best and Lizzie watched her some fury in her eyes, but had said nothing.

"So, how come, you're here, Edith. I don't mean to pry, but it's a bit odd."

"Oh, don't worry, ask as many questions as you want. I'm here because Frank asked me to look after Bert and Gerald after their mother was taken to hospital."

"Oh, I will ask questions, but first where was she taken?" enquired Lizzie, thinking she might get a response from her which she could later question Frank on.

"It's not for me to say. It's for Frank."

"Do you know where she is?"

Edith nervously poured teas. "No sugar for you Francis and you Lizzie?"

"I can sort my own sugar, thank you. So Elizabeth is in Chester hospital and why did Frank call you to look after the children?"

The clumps down the stairs were Frank's. He'd heard the questioning and had rushed to intervene.

"Ede… er, Edith doesn't know. I do. I'll tell you, but there are some conditions. By the way, I've told the lads to stay upstairs so we must talk quietly. They must not know." He closed the door to the stairs quietly and pulled cross the heavy draft excluding curtain, which usually was only closed at night.

"Your tea's there, Frank." Edith pointed to the tea near his green leather armchair. Frank sat down and took a sip. "Nice cup of char Edith. Thank you."

"So Frank, where is Elizabeth? We are so worried."

"We are," concurred Francis. "Where's mum and how is she?"

He whispered and could hardly be heard. "Right, as I was saying…" Everyone moved closer to hear. "… she is extremely poorly and can't be disturbed. I will tell you the hospital she is in, but you must promise me these things Lizzie and our Francis. One. If I tell you, your will not go there unless I say you have permission. Two, you must not tell the boys where she is."

Lizzie and Francis nodded and looked at each other. "Yes, we will."

"Furthermore, if you break these rules, I will ensure you get no access to Gerald… er… and Berty. I am fully aware of the conversation between Elizabeth and you, Lizzie about the boy. That conversation must never pass anyone's lips again. Got it?"

Lizzie wasn't sure what to say to this and once again looked at Francis. "But he's our…" She stopped as she looked at Edith, who was listening.

"Edith knows. I have told her. She will say nothing… "

Edith nodded and smiled.

"… but if you say something, once again, you will not be seeing Gerald. That's not a threat it's a solid promise."

Lizzie was shocked to the core. She was being left with no options and had to agree. "Yes, okay Frank. You have made your point. We agree, don't we Francis."

Francis nodded. <'Is this my dad?'>

"Elizabeth has gone to the asylum in Denbigh. That's where she is and where she shall remain for the time being."

Tears dripped from Lizzie's face at this news. Francis hugged her tight.

Not another word was spoken.

Author's Note

[1] *The North Wales Lunatic Asylum was the first psychiatric institution built in Wales; construction began in 1844 and was completed in 1848 in the town of Denbigh. It was originally called The North Wales Counties of Caernarvonshire, Denbighshire, Flintshire, Merionethshire and Anglesey Asylum.*

The U-shaped style hospital was built because of the spreading word of mistreatment of Welsh people in English asylums; The North Wales Hospital would be a haven for welsh speaking residents to seek treatment without prejudice or a language barrier.

Renovations and extensions were made at the hospital from 1867 until 1956, when the hospital reached its maximum capacity of 1,500 patients living inside her walls and 1,000 staff at hand. Physical treatments such as Cardiazol, malarial treatment, insulin shock treatment, and sulphur based drugs were used and developed in the 1920s and 1930s, and 1941-1942 saw electro convulsive therapy (ECT) and pre-frontal leucotomy (lobotomy) treatments.

In 1960, Enoch Powell visited the North Wales Hospital, and later announced the 'Hospital Plan' for England and Wales, which proposed that psychiatric care facilities be attached to general hospitals and favoured community care over institutional settings. This was the beginning of the end for the North Wales Hospital and others like it; in 1987, a ten-year strategy to close the hospital was formed. The North Wales Hospital was closed in sections from 1991 to 2002; most notable was the closure of the main hospital building in 1995.

Chapter Eight

'A Letter from Elizabeth'

It was the following day when Nurse Lamb opened the room and released Elizabeth from her straitjacket. Too late to stop her from wetting her clothes, but soon enough to prevent her from anything worse. The episode was duly noted down on her personal record.

Everyone in the area knew what *'you'll end up in Denbigh'* meant. There were lots of euphemisms in North Wales. *'The Yellow Van will come to take you away.'* *'The men in white coats will come for you.'* Sat at the heart of its eponymous county, the town of Denbigh, sat in the pretty Vale of Clwyd had for centuries been known for its strategic location and a beautiful castle was constructed there in the 13th Century at the behest of King Edward I, as part of his policy to bring the Welsh to heel.

Then in the mid-1840s, a local landowner and philanthropist by the name of Joseph Ablett donated 20 acres of land in fields to the south of the town, on the edge of the beautiful Ystrad Valley. All overlooked by the castle, less than a third of a mile away. The North Wales Chronicle, in reporting the death of Joseph Ablett on 18th January 1848, stated *'he has left a far more distinguishing memorial of himself in the magnificent pile of building, so soon to be opened for the reception of Lunatics in the Principality which owes its existence to his philanthropy and magnificence. He had long regretted the want of such an institution for the poor Welsh who were thus afflicted - who even when sent to asylums in England, surrounded by English keepers, nurse, etc, unacquainted with the language, were almost precluded from the hopes of recovery.'*

Joseph Ablett died on 7th January 1848 from the flu epidemic

93

ravaging the country that year and never lived to see the asylum opened. The asylum, designed by architect Thomas Fulljames, was initially intended to accommodate 200 patients with psychiatric illnesses, but by the time Elizabeth was there, it housed well over 1200 patients. The initial good intentions of Joseph Ablett were short-lived and following the 1890 Lunacy Act, the welfare and treatment of patients within its walls became less and less important with the hospital being run along similar lines to the workhouse which people dreaded. The majority of people who entered Denbigh in its early days would languish there, often forgotten by their families and stigmatised by the world for their mental health issues. Denbigh Asylum wasn't so much a hospital but a prison for the mentally ill, most of whom would die there.

So, the castle in Denbigh was overshadowed by an even greater construction and the word Denbigh became synonymous with being the place where 'the nuthouse' or 'the loony bin' was.

This where Elizabeth Mary Davies found herself, alone and with no hope of getting out following her incarceration there on 26th March 1927.

Another month passed and Elizabeth had been unable to come to terms with her enforced incarceration at the asylum, but it was Thunder Maisie singing which implanted an idea in her head. It was breakfast time and everyone trundled down to the dining room together. Elizabeth was now trusted by Thunder Maisie, who constantly held onto Elizabeth's arm for moral comfort. She always sang the same song as they walked. She laughed her way through it. Sometimes she sang loudly and other times softly.

"I was outside a lunatic asylum one day, busy picking up stones
When along came a lunatic and said to me, "Good morning Mrs. Roberts,
Oh, how much a week do you get for doing that", "Thirty bob I cried"
"What! Thirty bob a week, with a wife and kids to keep?
Come inside, you silly bugger come inside..."
"... Come inside you silly bugger come inside, you ought to have a bit more
sense.
Working for your living, take my tip, act a little screwy and become a
lunatic.
Oh, you get your meals most regular and a brand new suit besides.
What's thirty bob a week with a husband and kids to keep.
Come inside you silly bugger come inside."

"You sing that song so well, Maisie. I've never heard that before. Who taught you that?"

"Why, Elizabeth dear, my brother sent me the words in a letter."

Maisie went into the front of her breakfast tabard and brought out a tatty old piece of paper. The date was several years before.

"Your brother sent you that?"

"Yes, dear, he did. The only letter he ever sent me. I don't know what's happened to him. Is there thunder today?"

"I think that there will be no thunder for sometime."

"I was a nurse, you know. During the Great War, there was thunder all the time."

"I know there was dear…"

"I saw some awful things. Thunder, then young boys blown apart, burned and dying…. Dying everywhere. Crying with pictures of their young lasses or shouting for their mums. Screaming at night, they were. And then there was thunder… again and again and again."

Maisie pulled away and sat against the brown tiles in the corridor. "No one can help when the thunder comes. It comes and people are gone. Gone. They're gone forever. Nurses gone too. `My tent, where's my tent. He's on fire! She's on fire!" Maisie was screaming.

"You're all right Maisie, you're all right. You're with me now. With me."

Two nurses arrived.

"We can sort her now," said one of them.

"She's fine now" replied Elizabeth as she pulled Maisie up from the side. "She's fine."

Elizabeth hugged Maisie and they carried on walking to breakfast. "You've got me Maisie." She slapped her chest to reinforce what she had said. "I'll make sure the thunder doesn't get you. That's a promise."

"Will you?"

"Promise."

*

It was now six weeks since Lizzie had seen Elizabeth and she thought of nothing else each day, as she went about raking and clearing the fire of cinders from the previous day's burning. The fire was the first task of the day. Without the fire, there would be no hot water and no cup of tea.

Out on the streets of Shotton in the early morning sunshine, Brian Johnson the local postman in his smart bobby-like uniform pushed his post laden bike from house to house, bidding the same message of 'Good Morning' to the constant flow of flat-capped men heading in the direction of the iron and steelworks for the early shift. They would all have to cross the Railway Swing-Bridge [1] over the River Dee, with its narrow walkway along the side of the rail tracks leading to the Hawarden Bridge Works of John Summers & Sons. In the early days called the ironworks, then a mixture of both, but later it was solely known as the steelworks.

The morning for all was no different to the routine of any other morning. Bells and 'oi's' rang out, as the workers from further afield arrived on bicycles and dangerously veered in and out of the men with their canvas snapping bags. There was one distinct thing about this day though as this was the first day Frank had called for Francis in a long time and now the two walked into work again as if they'd never had a cross word between them. Lizzie hadn't been happy, but for the sake of Gerald and Berty had agreed things must get back to some sense of normality.

The postman had nothing for 6 Ashfield Road but dropped a more official-looking letter through Frank's letterbox, which Edith Clarkson had picked up from the mat. She looked at the envelope and placed it centre-sideboard, ready for Frank to see as soon as he came in from work later in the day. At the same time, Gerald had come down. "Can we go and see Aunt Lizzie now things are right between us all?"

Edith looked as if she was about to say no.

"Please!" Both Bert and Gerald had appealed with the look of two King Charles Spaniels.

"It'll save you doing us breakfast," Gerald implored.

A nod followed and the two lads ran from the house down to Lizzie's back door, which they banged excitedly.

"Boys! So nice to see you... " The lads both hugged Lizzie tightly. "Careful you'll squeeze the life out of me," she chuckled with a delighted face. "You'd better go in and make yourselves at home. Have you had breakfast?" she shouted as the two charged their way through to the back room, both squeezing onto Francis' favourite armchair next to the now roaring fire. Gerald grabbed the toasting fork and rubbed his stomach with a nod of his head.

"I'll take that as a no then and cut some bread. Good job I went up the road late yesterday. I had a feeling you'd be here after me and

Uncle Francis chatted with your dad yesterday about getting things straight between us all."

"So glad you did Aunt Lizzie," shouted back Gerald as he patiently waited for the bread with the empty toasting fork, wrapping a towel around his hand, as he knew, from the many times he'd toasted bread, the fire would be too hot for his hand to stand the searing heat once he began to toast the bread."

"Me too" Lizzie said, as she walked back into the room with the freshly cut slices of bread.

"Am all ready to be toast-master," laughed Gerald holding up his freshly towel wrapped hand.

"Don't burn yourself… or the bread too much."

Berty stared, mesmerised by the flames, and never said a word.

"Have you heard anything about your mum?"

"Not a sausage. Dad says she's in there for her own good. FOR GOOD, he said." Gerald looked sad. "I miss her."

"So do I," added Berty, in his fire induced hypnotic state. "Gerald cries at night about it. I've heard him."

"Berty!"

"I'm sure she's not there for good, Gerald. Anyway, there's no point in upsetting yourself. You've got your whole life ahead of you, eh? I'm sure she'll be home soon, just as soon as she's better."

Both boys nodded. The toast was now smoking heavily and a small flame had ignited to one side. Lizzie grabbed the toasting fork. "Watch the toast, Gerald, you'll have the place on fire." Everyone blew on the toast to douse the flame.

Lizzie rotated the toast on the fork. She smiled at Gerald. "We'd like toast we can eat, eh?" She winked.

"So has Fra… your dad been to see her?"

"Don't think so, he hasn't had time what with work and what not," Gerald riposted without looking around, his eyes now fixed on a partially blackened piece of bread, now quickly toasting on the other side.

Lizzie nodded as she pulled the fork away from the fire and replaced the well toasted piece of bread with a fresh slice. She buttered the burnt offering and gave it to Berty.

"Do you want me to speak to your dad about going to see mum?"

Gerald gazed into the fire and nodded.

"Right, we'll do that then."

* * *

*

It was early afternoon when Frank arrived home. Today had been a short eight-hour shift. He was greeted by Edith at the back door with a kiss and a hug.

"Careful, Ede love. We don't want to be seen, eh?"

"Who's gonna see us in the backs?" She hugged him more and pulled him into the house. "Do you forgive me Frank for being a naughty girl then?"

"I take it the boys are still in school?"

"Yes, we've got an hour or so, if you get what I mean?"

"Don't be daft, woman. I'm filthy… and knackered."

"That's what you get for having a young bit of stuff on the side then, hey?"

Edith kissed him and pulled his dirty work jacket off.

"Is that a letter for me?" Frank declared, pulling away towards the sideboard, throwing his cap onto the chair at the same time.

"Came this morning. Looks important. I'll make you a tea while you look at it."

Frank opened the letter, grabbed his glasses from the side and sat down to read."

"Anything important, Frank?"

"It's the asylum about Elizabeth?"

"Saying?"

"Er… it says here… *'Dear Mr. Davies, I desire to inform you of the reception Order for Mrs. Elizabeth Mary Davies to the Asylum for the Counties of North Wales at Denbigh, dated 26th March 1927. Upon your petition, Mrs Davies was admitted by Dr Joseph Dobson, a duly qualified medical practitioner of Buckley, being satisfied that Mrs. Davies posed a danger to herself and those around her, she is therefore now detained at this place until further notice. You may petition for Mrs. Davies' to be discharged and then and only then will such consideration be made.'* That's what it says."

"So she won't be coming home any time soon then Frank."

"I doubt it, unless I… "

"But you won't will you Frank?"

"Erm… no. The letter says more."

"Go on then, read it."

"Well, it says underneath *'It is desired that the patient is not visited by her friends or relatives too soon after admission, but inquiries in person or by letter as to her condition will be answered with pleasure. Such letters about health should be addressed to...* ' blah, blah... it goes on about change of address and stuff so they can notify us of any emergencies... "

"Sounds as if she's in the right place. Trying to poison you and all that."

"Well, we had to make sure, didn't we?" Frank winked.

"Anything else in the letter?"

"Something about visiting... *'The visiting days of the hospital are Mondays, Tuesdays and Wednesdays from 10am to 11.45am and from 2 to 3.45pm, during which times only visits to patients can be made, however, being permitted where serious illness occurs. No patient can, however, be visited should the Medical Superintendent consider it likely to be injurious to her condition.'* There's a bit more... *'I will feel much obliged if you will write and give me any full and accurate particulars you may know as to the causes of the onset of Mrs. Davies' illness and you furnish this information by return of post. I remain, yours faithfully. Medical Superintendent.'* That's it."

"Well, we'd better get a letter together to make sure they know everything about her then hadn't we?"

Frank nodded as the back door burst open. It was Gerald and Berty home from school. Frank quickly put the letter back into the envelope, safe in the knowledge neither boy would dare look at it. "Settle down, lads. Upstairs and changed right now." Frank looked at Edith. "We'll sort a reply later."

*

Elizabeth's world was now a bed in an open ward of eight other women under a strict regime of work and more work. Elizabeth was now trusted to help look after Thunder Maisie, who had accompanied her to Gwynfryn.

Elizabeth had no option but to settle for the daily routine, which started at 7am when breakfast began. Elizabeth, through years of living with Frank, whose preferred drink was cocoa, was happy to be provided with a cup of cocoa every day. Occasionally she would have tea, but never coffee. Each morning Ethel Parry, who'd been in Denbigh for many years, would make an enormous cauldron of porridge which was breakfast for every single person at the asylum. Next to her stood Jemima Owens, who cut a thick slice of bread to go alongside the porridge. This was an unalterable routine, so if you didn't like bread or porridge, then starving until lunchtime was the alternative. Once breakfast had been cleared away, those with allocated duties, regarded and the 'good patients' would head off to their daily work routine. For Elizabeth this was in the asylum laundry at the rear of the main hospital not far from where the hospital mortuary was and she now walked there each morning after breakfast with Thunder Maisie who, because she behaved better with Elizabeth around, now found herself with a role for the first time in years at the asylum. The Grim Reaper was a frequent visitor to the asylum and in the short time Elizabeth had headed off to the laundry for her daily chores, she had seen enough staff wheeling the dead of the place on the archaic looking wooden bier with what looked like large pram wheels attached.

Working at the laundry was not for the feint hearted. Soiled clothing and bedding arrived by the hour. Elizabeth knew some sheets received would have lain over freshly laid out corpses heading for the mortuary. She'd heard of people at the end of their tether, unable to cope with asylum life, so affected by being away from all they knew or just plain had enough of life, who'd taken their own life to be out of their misery for good. Only two days ago a patient in the next ward had throttled themselves with two knotted pillow cases. She'd heard the screams at daylight when the body was found. Sad thing was for Elizabeth, she'd been talking to this nice girl in her twenties just the day before.

<'She wasn't insane. Not even a little mad. Told me she'd been sent here because she was feeling down after the birth of her second baby. Then she'd had a row with her husband over things. He'd slapped her and then and her father-in-law had become involved. Got her sent to this place. She was far from mad. Far from mad.'>

The thought haunted her. <'A new mother sent here because someone in her family took a dislike to the way she behaved.> The thought sent a shiver down Elizabeth's spine. <'That's me. Only it's my husband who's done this to me.'>.

As she filled the metal tubs with boiling water, the myriad of thoughts cascading through her head as to why she'd ended up in this godforsaken place, were only interrupted by the noise of Thunder Maisie singing "Come inside you silly bugger come inside..." as she scraped sheets clean of larger pieces of filth. Vomit, faeces, food flotsam and god knows what, lay caked onto some sheets. Thoughts were interrupted again, as Thunder Maisie threw the sheets across to Elizabeth who dunked them straight into the boiling water using an old wooden brush stale, whitened though being dipped continuously into water which many before Elizabeth had shredded soap pieces into.

It was a filthy, hot and demanding physical job. Elizabeth would pull sheets out of the water with the stale and rub persistent stains with soap across a wooden washboard. The laundry work was a relief though from the day-to-day boredom of sitting on the ward. Once again Elizabeth thought about what was going through a person's mind when they decided to terminate their own life. Elizabeth shook her hard and concentrated hard not to think of the ruinous situation she was in. The potential of never going home was all too real and almost too hard to bear. These were bad thoughts, which wouldn't go away, no matter what good things she tried to think about. Good things of course always brought on bad thoughts. She would think of Gerald and Berty happy at school, then realise she would might never see either again. She would think about walking 'up the road' to the shops and could feel the smell of the air and the river, then she would think she might never smell home again. Even smoke from a passing train, which caused the odd black mark on clothing on the washing line, would be welcome now. She looked at the washing before her and longed to see a sooty mark. She hung her head low and could understand why people ended it all. After all, if you lived in a strange environment and you thought you may never see your family again, then what was the point of living?

It was soon time for lunch, which was always served on the dot from 12:30pm. The lunch menu wasn't too bad usually and comprised food produced on the asylum farm. The belief of the asylum was this should be the main meal of the day.

Bread and a small slab of fruit cake followed in the early evening, but there was nothing after which led some patients to complain of hunger at night. None of this washed with Nurse Lamb, who would always say, "Ladies, listen up!" She clapped her hands. "Hunger at night means you'll eat your morning bite. Eat more in the day and that hunger will stay away. Complaining would do no good, particularly when there were staff shortages. Staff could then tolerate less from the patients and would dose-up complainers and anyone they deemed to be causing a fuss, with a mixture of the sedative paradehyde and vegetable oil. Sleeping patients eased the load.

There were infrequent visits by doctors and Elizabeth learned quickly the power of any member of nursing staff was absolute. If nursing staff wanted a peaceful life, they would dose you up with whatever sedative came to hand and if you resisted, as Elizabeth found out once to her cost, they would strap you to the punishment chair, hands and feet bound with leather straps and then forcefully feed you the medicine. It was only when you woke up the following morning feeling groggy; you realised you had been given something strong which put you out. Most patients soon learned not to grumble too much about how they felt or to argue back with any treatments dealt out, as this could lead to heavier doses of drugs and other barbaric treatments which were supposed to relieve the soul of its afflictions, but which mainly caused other problems such as slurred speech and incontinence from time to time.

Elizabeth was fully aware of her turns and she knew they could be brought on in stressful situations, so she did her best to avoid getting involved in any rows ongoing at the asylum AND these were frequent. The noises and the passions in the place were endless, regardless of the time of day or night. People lost their minds, even when they entered the place with nothing more than persistent headaches or because of a fallout with a boyfriend. All respectability was lost, and many lost their souls or had their entire lives compromised by what a doctor might write on their personal health note.

According to the asylum doctors, Thunder Maisie was 'in need of a change of life' as she 'dislikes and mistrusts people.' These two phrases were enough to keep her held at the asylum without another question being asked. Elizabeth wanted to avoid the same, but avoiding such comments by a doctor was difficult.

*

In charge of Elizabeth's case was Dr Eustace Hutton.

On a visit he asked, "So, Mrs. Davies, tell me why you are here? I just want to remind myself." He was ever so friendly, but his friendly disposition belied his actual intentions. This was the 1920s... the era when 'problem people' could be placed into colonies for the mentally deficient.

1859 saw the publication of Charles Darwin's Origin of Species, a tome which gave substance to the theory of evolution through natural selection. Following release of the book, it was only a matter of time before the scientists and politicians saw an application of the theory and began applying it to humans. This was the birth of eugenics, and the birth of this pseudo-science would have a great impact on Elizabeth Davies and her life as an epileptic sufferer. Anyone with something different about them (epileptics were perceived as different) was viewed as a threat to social progress. Eugenics meant if you were even a bit odd in the late nineteenth and early twentieth century, you were 'put away.' Then in 1871 Darwin released The Descent of Man. His thoughts on the subject being very clear.

'With savages, the weak in body or mind are soon eliminated; and those that survive commonly exhibit a vigorous state of health. We civilised men, on the other hand, do our utmost to check the process of elimination; we build asylums for the imbecile, the maimed, and the sick; we institute poor-laws; and our medical men exert their utmost skill to save the life of every one to the last moment. There is reason to believe that vaccination has preserved thousands, who from a weak constitution would formerly have succumbed to small-pox. Thus the weak members of civilised societies propagate their kind.'

Darwin refers to Francis Galton, as the 'father of eugenics,' but he would, as they shared the same grandfather, so were cousins. In an 1865 treatise on the inheritance of talent where he said, *'I find that talent is transmitted by inheritance in a very remarkable degree... '* the juxtaposition being that 'imbeciles,' a term widely used in that time, breed and produce the opposite. The theories on eugenics of Francis Galton were greatly admired by Adolf Hitler and many other early 20th century leaders. These theories led to untold heartache, death and incarceration for the peoples of Europe in the first half of the twentieth century.

The celebrated urban planner Ebenezer Howard formulated his plans for 'Garden Cities' in 1902 along the lines of so called slumless and smokeless areas, but hidden within the plans were his ideas on eugenics and how the country should deal with epileptics. These utopian ideals were nothing more than an excuse to build depressing new towns. Towns which incorporated the ideals of eugenics with specific areas for the insane, waifs, inebriates and specifically 'farms for epileptics.'

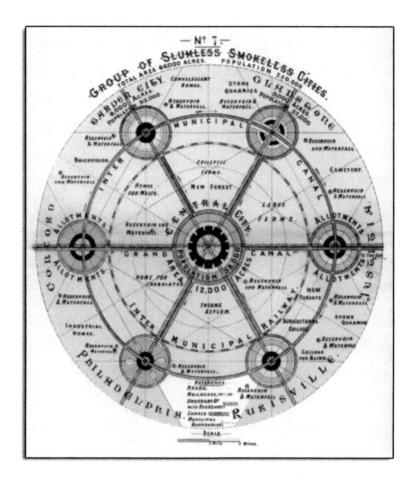

Ebenezer Howard - 'Garden Cities of Tomorrow' (1902)

This was the world Elizabeth Davies now found herself in. A depressing and funless world where, as an epileptic, there were different gradations of being 'put away,' so people the medical profession at the time considered to be reasonably well behaved (and with some mental ability) were often admitted to what they called colonies as in Howard's idealistic world. These were places where the 'male colonists' would complete manual and skilled labour on the land and women colonists would undertake domestic chores. Six days a week, none stop.

Elizabeth Davies didn't fit into this category and was deemed not well behaved enough to enter a colony. The lunatic asylum was for people like her and, if you were particularly bad, then Denbigh had seclusion cells. Something Elizabeth was yet to experience. Safe to say, once in the system and once regarded as a mental defective, then always regarded as such. Unknown to Elizabeth was, besides her freedom being taken away at the say-so of her husband, her hopes would also be removed as she could never get out.

*

The conversation between Elizabeth and Dr. Hutton continued.

"You are in your fifties now, I see Mrs. Davies."

"Yes."

"And you have no more women's issues."

"If you mean I don't, well you know… "

"Don't what Mrs. Davies?"

"I don't like to talk about things like that. It's not our way. I am from a good and proper family."

"So are a lot of people… from good families , I mean. Doesn't stop them coming here to be treated though. Menopause, I mean. You know what that means?"

"I do."

Dr. Hutton wrote <'*Menopause.*'>

"We haven't answered the question have we?"

"I forgot what the question was."

<'*Forgetful and can't remember things.*'>

"Why are you here was the question?"

"Because my husband had me…." She thought about what she was about to say then stopped. "I am here because I suffer from the odd turn which you call Epilepsy," she smiled, at pain to sound as normal as possible.

"And how do you think your treatment is going?"

"Yes, it is going well. I have suffered fewer turns in recent weeks than ever."

"Good, then you are better with us than at home," had been the response Elizabeth had not expected or wanted. Dr. Hutton had turned her reply against her, and he would do worse. "In your notes here…" he looked down quizzically, "… it says your husband, a Mr. Frank Davies, told the doctor that you denied giving birth to your son." Dr. Hutton's face screwed up with disbelief and he stared back at

Elizabeth with a slow shake of his head.

Elizabeth sat and thought about what Dr. Hutton might want to hear. She breathed in deeply, as she thought on her response, and her eyes flickered back and forwards to Dr. Hutton's notes, which he had written, despite her saying nothing.

She felt compelled to speak.

"Yes, he was right," she lied, "… I… I was under some stress and felt I should say that my child Gerald was not my child but I am over that now."

"So you agree you were telling untruths?"

"I do."

Dr. Hutton wrote on the notes.

'To say Mrs. Davies is completely insane is difficult to fathom right now, but imbecility is present. She is unsure of her own mind and doesn't fully understand the concept of telling the truth. She must therefore be considered to be a danger to herself and others. It seems her mind has become deranged in ways yet to be tested. This is no doubt partly owing to her intemperate husband's ill-treatment of her and additionally the epileptic episodes have compounded this. Treatment to continue with increased of doses.'

He scribbled underneath.

Potassium Bromide - 15 grains

Belladonna tincture 15 minims

Phenobarbitone - 100mg. Morning. 200mg. Night.'

As Dr. Hutton flicked through the file he was careful to hide a letter. An unposted letter.

Denbigh Asylum
May 1927

My Dearest Lizzie and Francis,

I haven't heard or seen anyone since I have been here. I am not sure you even know I am here, knowing our Frank, so I decided to write this letter. I shall say though, you must not show the letter to Frank or say you have had this letter. How are you all getting on at Church? How are the boys doing in school? I miss you all.

I'd like to say I am happier, but I am very sad and at my wits' end here in this place, but there's some hope. There's a new part of the hospital opening *soon called Gwynfryn House. I'll be moving over there in a day or two, so if you can come to see me and I sincerely hope you can find the time, then that is the place to find me. I hope Maisie comes with me. Who is Maisie I hear you ask? I have made good friends with a Mrs Maisie Roberts, who is known as Thunder Maisie, as she was in the war and is greatly affected by it. Poor woman, she is a mess. The bombs and shells have done for her, so I feel lucky. She is older than me and has one tooth in her head, which makes her look scary especially after dark, when she creeps up and gets into my bed for comfort. The medicines they give you here are supposed to make you better, but I fear I get more doddery on my feet by the day. Perhaps I am getting old too.*

Anyway, I have only this piece of paper and I don't get that much peace to write, so I'll finish now by sending my good wishes to you. I am in your hands, as Frank seems to be in no hurry to take me from here for what reason I don't know. All of this awful situation must seem strange to you. I feel inclined to cry very much and I do cry constantly.

Please do write back, if you can do nothing else.

Will you get this letter, I wonder?

Yours,

Elizabeth

Denbigh Asylum
May 27

My Dearest Lizzie and Frances,

I haven't heard or seen anyone since I have been here. I am not sure you even know I am here, knowing our Frank, so I decided to write this letter. I shall say though, you must not show this letter to Frank or say you have had this letter. How are you all getting on at Church? How are the boys doing in school? I miss you all.

I'd like to say I am happier, but I am very sad and at my wit's end here in this place, but there's some hope. There's a new part of the hospital opening soon called Gwynfryn House. I'll be moving over there in a day or two, so if you can come to see me and I sincerely hope you can find the time, then that is the place to find me. I hope Maisie comes with me. Who is Maisie I hear you ask? I have made good friends with a Mrs Maisie Roberts, who is known as Thunder Maisie, as she was in the war and is greatly affected by it. Poor woman, she is a mess. The bombs and shells have done for her, so I feel lucky. She is older than me and has one tooth in her head, which makes her look scary especially after dark, when she creeps up and gets into my bed for comfort. The medicines they give you here are supposed to make you better, but I fear I get more doddery on my feet by the day. Perhaps I am getting old too.

Anyway, I have only this piece of paper and I don't get that much peace to write, so I'll finish now by sending my good wishes to you. I am in your hands, as Frank seems to be in no hurry to take me from here for what reason I do not know. All of this awful situation must seem strange to you. I feel inclined to cry very much and I do cry constantly.

Please do write back, if you can do nothing else.

Will you get this letter I wonder?

Yours

Elizabeth.

Author's Note

[1] *The bridge at Shotton had begun its construction on August 16th 1887 when MP William Ewart Gladstone, already the British Prime Minister on three occasions, ceremonially laid the first pillar of the bridge upon which the*

railway line which would connect North Wales with the ports of Birkenhead and Liverpool, would cross. The location of the bridge was afterwards known as Hawarden Bridge as an acknowledgement to Gladstone's home estate, Hawarden Castle, some three miles away. The bridge was constructed as a 'swing bridge' to allow boats to pass towards Chester along the River Dee and spanned 480 feet of the river which, at the time, exceeded the span of every other navigable river in Britain. Mr Gladstone was back in the area again on 21st October 1892, when he cut the first sod of the railway to Liverpool.

" Sir Edward Watkin, in opening the proceedings, said they were now beginning the very serious business of commencing the work of that new railway ; and he would at once ask Mr. Gladstone to do them the honour of cutting the first sod. (Cheers.)—Mr. Gladstone, who was presented with a silver-mounted spade, then cut the sod, and deposited it in a polished wood barrow mounted with silver."

THE CEREMONY OF CUTTING THE FIRST SOD OF THE WIRRAL RAILWAY, NEAR HAWARDEN BRIDGE, BY MR. GLADSTONE

Copy: The Graphic Illustrated Weekly Newspaper. 29 October 1892

The building of the bridge and railway line directly led to the arrival of John Summers and Sons Ironworks on the site as reported in the Cheshire Observer from 5th October 1895.

NEW INDUSTRY ON THE DEE.

Messrs. John Summers and Sons, of the Globe Ironworks, Stalybridge, have purchased upwards of 43 acres of land adjoining the Hawarden Bridge and the river Dee for the purpose of constructing extensive works for the manufacture of galvanised corrugated iron roofing sheets, &c. The works are to be proceeded with at once, and the firm expect that within six months they will be finished. They hope to find employment for between 300 and 500 people. The commencement of this important industry is due to the construction of the M.S. & L. Railway and the Dee and Birkenhead Railway from Hawarden Bridge, and there is no reason why before long the whole river frontage should not be taken up by similar works requiring large areas. It will be remembered that when the late River Dee Company attempted to construct an embankment between Connah's Quay and Burton, upwards of 20 years ago, it was then thought that a great part of the 2,300 acres of land enclosed would be used for extensive works requiring isolation and large areas, and 80 acres were actually sold for gunpowder works which were never constructed, owing to the embankment breaking 18 months after it was completed. The intended works of Messrs. Summers will be on the site of the Chester Golf Pavilion, and about seven of the most important holes in the links, and it will be necessary for the Golf Club to move, their pavilion and links to some other site either further away on the Marsh or elsewhere. As Messrs. Summers expect to employ so many hands, and consume about a thousand tons of coal per week at their Hawarden Bridge works, no doubt both Chester and Connah's Quay will reap some benefit, especially if other large manufacturers see the advantage of making use of the new railways and the River Dee, and constructing further works on its banks.

So it was that many people flocked to the area for work and the Davies family, originally hailing from the Ruabon area of North Wales, were no different. The Davies' family arrived in the area in 1916 and all became employed at the works. The works would become the biggest employer of people in the area.

Chapter Nine

'Bara Brith'

Lizzie had fallen back and had wanted to do nothing for the entire day after Gerald and Berty had left. Gerald's words had haunted her entire day's thoughts. <*'No one has bothered to check if she is all right or not AND she'll be lost and all alone in that asylum without a friendly face.'*>

She shook her head with disbelief and worry, fingering her lip nervously to the point where it bled. She didn't even stand up when Francis walked in from work. He knew straight away something was wrong.

"What's up love?"

"We need to speak with your dad about your mum."

"I thought we'd sorted this. We've just got things right and now you want... "

"Did you know he hasn't been to see her in that damn asylum since she's been there?"

"I suppose I did, yes."

"And that's okay is it?"

"No, it's not... but what can we do?"

"She's your mum, Francis. Your mum! AND he's now got another woman there."

"Edith is looking after the children."

"Is she? Are you that naïve? She's living there now."

"Looking after Gerald and Berty."

"I might look cabbage looking, but I'm not green. There's something going on and we need to talk with Frank. Today!"

"WE talked and got it sorted yesterday."

Lizzie rose from her chair and grabbed her coat. "Are you coming then?"

"Where?"

"To see Frank."

"To say what?"

"To ask nicely what we can do to help."

"Like what do you mean?"

"Like how do we go and visit your mother at the asylum. That's a start."

Within a minute the two were walking down the street towards Dee View. "Let me do the talking," Lizzie said as she linked arms with Francis.

*

"Oh, it's you!" a surprised Edith stammered as she pulled open the door.

"Is Frank in? Can we come in?"

"Ye... yes... Frank," she shouted. "It's Francis and Lizzie."

"Tell them I'm having five minutes."

It was too late, Lizzie walked through with Francis a yard behind. Lizzie saw the envelope on the side and saw the postmark of Denbigh. She missed nothing. Frank saw her eyeing up the envelope.

Gerald and Berty dashed down the stairs on hearing Lizzie and Francis come in.

"Aunt Lizzie has come around to see if you want to go there for tea." Frank said, seizing the initiative.

Lizzie seized it back. "You two head off to our house... the back's open. Go in and we'll be there in a few minutes."

The boys didn't need telling twice and dashed out of the house. Edith put the kettle on, but asked no one if they wanted a drink. She leant against the back room wall and listened.

"I know we talked just a day or so ago," began Lizzie with a watchful eye on Edith, "... and I'm grateful for that, er... and so is Francis. We love the boys and we want them to grow up with us in their lives."

"We do." Francis nodded.

"Yes, go on Lizzie dear... "

Lizzie took a deep breath. "Well, the boys haven't seen their mum in weeks and I was wondering if I might..."

"You might what?"

Lizzie swallowed. Her throat was dry. "Well. Yes… I'll come out with it. Can we. Can I go and see her at the asylum?"

Frank said nothing.

"I know that getting to Denbigh for us wouldn't be easy… a train to Rhyl and then Rhyl to Denbigh or a train to Chester and then to Denbigh. It's not an easy journey but we could do it. I've checked the timetables."

"You have? And what do you know about the asylum and if you can visit?"

"That's why we've come around Frank. To ask your permission and to make sure it's all all right with you. I… " Lizzie looked at Francis. "… we could go first and then take the boys the next time? It won't cost you a penny. We'll pay."

Frank looked at Edith. "Ede… Edith love, pass me that letter. I saw you looking at it Lizzie. Yes, it's from the asylum."

Edith passed the letter over. Frank opened it and stood up with his back to the fire. "Says here Lizzie and I quote, 'can have NO VISITS by order of the Medical Superintendent as it is injurious to her condition.' Is that good enough for you? We all want Elizabeth to be better, but visiting her seems will make her worse. I will let you know when they write to us to tell us any different, but for now that'd the end of the matter. All right?"

Lizzie looked at Francis. The two nodded at each other and then towards Frank. "But you will let us know when she's better and able to visit?"

"That's a promise."

"I thank you for that, Frank."

*

Frank had no intention of keeping to his word and later that night, with the boys safely at Lizzie's, a letter was written to Denbigh Asylum outlining the full facts as he and Edith saw them.

Edith was now a permanent fixture at Dee View, and it was more than apparent to wagging tongues in the area she was doing more than looking after Frank's motherless children. Lizzie knew even more and, despite Frank warning Gerald to never utter a word to Lizzie or Francis, he did. He told Lizzie everything. Lizzie knew some of the most intimate details, but couldn't say a word for fear of not being able to see Gerald again. These were tough times.

*

Lizzie did the next best thing she could and wrote a letter to Elizabeth at the asylum once a month, without fail. She even asked Gerald to do the same when he was around at theirs, and they would neatly tuck Gerald's letter in with hers before it went off in the post. Frank would never know about these secret letters, and Gerald understood why. Elizabeth never once responded from the asylum, but Lizzie was content at the thought she was doing her best to keep in touch. She never got a response once and was never sure whether any of her letters had even made it to Elizabeth, but it didn't stop her. She felt she owed it to Elizabeth and Gerald. Lizzie wished for a change of heart from Frank, so she may be allowed to make a visit to see Elizabeth, but he was always insistent Elizabeth was too unwell for any visits. He insisted he was in constant touch with the asylum about Elizabeth's welfare, but there wasn't a shred of truth in this. He made no contact at all.

Lizzie thought many times of making some sort of unannounced visit to the asylum, but its location in North Wales was remote, especially without a car. No one, except the rich, had a car in the late 1920s and potential visitors like Lizzie were excluded from visits by this fact alone. This impeded social interaction for patients, and an important element of mental health care, linked to making the place a good therapeutic centre, was squandered as a result. Neglect and cruelty were more appropriate words for the North Wales Counties Lunatic Asylum, but these were days of ignorance, when concern for locking people away usurped the need for cure and therapy.

*

The months passed and turned into years. Lizzie became pregnant in October 1928 and Cliff was born the following June, much to Francis and Gerald's delight. Berty still suffered from the occasional seizures, but luckily for him, Frank kept quiet and so he remained at home.

In the meantime, at Denbigh Asylum, Elizabeth's condition worsened with every passing month, no thanks to the concoction of drugs and treatments she was given to *'improve her condition.'* The only people improved by the treatment of patients though were the staff, as most treatments, although often given with the best of intentions, were intended to ensure patients were less troublesome. Anything to make the patients restful or sleep was believed to be beneficial. With little or no regulation over drugs doled out to who or why, some staff took advantage of the situation. Many staff self-medicated to alleviate the stress of working at the asylum and developed their own addictive recreational drugs habits, using opium and other powerful medicines from the unlocked cabinets. Worse still, it was common practise for others to overdose patients simply to pacify them; or when they got fed-up of troublesome behaviour. Either way, the long-term consequences of such uncontrolled drug use was detrimental to patient welfare. Therapeutics in the 1920s and before were of little concern to a mental health system which looked at its primary role as being custodial. The knock on effect of this was to lead to the stigmatisation of those incarcerated in asylums. No one and that included Lizzie and Francis talked about relatives in asylums, so Elizabeth was soon forgotten, even in her own community of Shotton.

At Denbigh Asylum, Elizabeth had more issues to contend with than drugs. About the same time as Lizzie became pregnant, she was told of a new form of treatment she would undergo for her increasing seizures. These were days when anything could and would be tried to cure epilepsy. Professional journals were replete with articles claiming cures for epilepsy. Besides all the usual and new drug therapy and brain surgeries, some claimed excision of an arthritic knee as a cure, whilst one stated that a hot iron should be applied to a patient's calves during an epileptic fit. Denbigh Asylum's new treatment for Elizabeth in 1928 was Cerebral Galvanism.

There was some logic to this treatment. Many leading physicians of the time understood the disorder of epilepsy to be because of a temporary change in the electrical impulses functioning in the brain. Neurotransmitters, the chemical messengers of the brain were guided by minuscule electrical impulses ordinarily sequenced in some orderly way. Epilepsy was when these signals became out of sync and imbalanced leading to seizures. Cerebral galvanism, a form of electro-shock therapy was commenced, as an experimental treatment of Elizabeth, to re-balance her normal brain functioning in attempts to control her worsening epileptic fits, which were brought on by the stress of Elizabeth being isolated from her family. This treatment was barbaric in its own right and was administered forcibly, without any form of anaesthetic, which caused untold stress to patients, many of whom broke bones or dislocated their limbs in involuntary movements or sometimes when they frantically tried to get away from what they knew was impending torture.

Elizabeth cried out daily for her family, but no one ever came. Medical notes now stated <'*she sleeps very little, and struggles to sleep. She is suicidal, and keeps saying she wants to die.'* >

A new Mental Health Act went through parliament in 1930 and the North Wales Counties Lunatic Asylum changed its name to the North Wales Counties Mental Hospital. There was less emphasis on the word lunatic and imbecile, but little would change in reality for the inmates of Denbigh. Visitors were few due to its poor isolated location with poor transport infrastructure. The people at Denbigh Asylum were the forgotten of their world and they knew it.

*

It was just before quarter past ten on the morning of Thursday 2nd October 1930, when Lizzie, Frank, Francis and Gerald boarded the train bound for Hawarden from Shotton. It was a one-stop, five-minute journey and no one spoke. All were in their Sunday best, with faces as sad as the trees lining the tracks, just shedding their leaves with the imminent approach of autumn. It was the first time Lizzie had been out without 16-month-old Cliff, who was now a demanding toddler, eagerly exploring the world around him. This was no ordinary day, and certainly not a day to have a young child with you. For a start, it was the first time since Elizabeth had been taken away from them, that Lizzie had been on any sort of journey with Frank. Yes, she'd sat a few places down the pew at Rivertown church on the odd Sunday since, but there was now a distinct coldness which existed between her and Frank. For Gerald's sake she did her best to make sure things had proceeded as smoothly as possible, but always felt guilty about Elizabeth and not being able to get to see her in what had now turned into over three and a half years. Worse than this she had even made excuses for Frank to Gerald who almost every time he had visited the house, had asked when they might get to see his mother. Gerald was now a tall twelve-year-old and this day, they would get to see Elizabeth.

It was a day when Lizzie had reluctantly agreed for Edith to mind Cliff for a couple of hours. Edith had said she didn't mind as she was already home and wanted to be there when Berty came back from his labouring job at the steelworks. Berty was now fifteen years old and brushed up around the canteen where Lizzie used to work. Berty was a world away from the academic prowess of Gerald and, in his latter days at school, had been employed to stoke the fires at the school or do any menial tasks as his reports deemed him *'incapable of academic work.'*

Lizzie still held a huge resentment inside for Edith, who she suspected to be the force behind Frank getting rid of Elizabeth to the asylum. It was unforgivable in her head, but for the sake of Gerald she put up with the situation. She felt her time would come.

It was a short walk from Hawarden railway station to the red sandstone of St. Deiniols in the centre of Hawarden village. Lizzie carried with her a small bunch of golden orange chrysanthemums, which she'd bought just before getting on the train. The church was almost opposite the Hawarden Castle estate of the Gladstone's. It was a church where the great Victorian Statesman and Prime Minister William Ewart Gladstone had once sat and prayed. Today it would the church was reserved for a small gathering of a steelworker's family. Gerald, Francis and Frank all sported dark trilby's, which they took off as they entered the church, greeted by the churchwarden, an elderly man who could hardly stand up straight such was his degenerative scoliosis.

"Ahead and right up the aisle," he quietly uttered, hardly heard by Lizzie who was at the back. "Mr Griffith Jones, your non-conformist preacher is here already in the vestry. He will be out shortly. Please take a seat either side of the aisle just before the rood screen."

They walked down the red carpeted aisle. Lizzie saw what she feared most. A modest wooden coffin. No flowers on it.

Nothing.

To the right of the coffin was the Gladstone Monument, a wonderful example of Victorian funeral art at its best. The plain coffin looked incongruous in its majestic surroundings, sat on its equally stark wooden trestles, which looked like they'd been borrowed from a builder's yard. Only five yards away, constructed from Sienna marble lay the great memorial to Gladstone and his wife lying regally side by side, an angel forming a canopy over the pair.

Whilst the inside of the pretty little church would have struck most people with awe, this was no such occasion for any admiration of surroundings. Lizzie put her hand to her mouth, fought back her tears, and gripped Gerald's arm as she walked up the aisle behind Frank and Francis. Gerald looked bewildered, after all he hadn't seen his mother in over three years and another woman was now at home filling her place. His head had been filled with many stories by Frank about why his mother had had to go away. Frank's narrative had carefully stitched into it many true elements which made the tales more believable for Gerald. Gerald just didn't know what to think other than he felt abandoned by his mother and Lizzie had been effectively gagged from revealing the truth by Frank AND it was only Frank truly knew the story behind Elizabeth's incarceration at the asylum.

Floods of tears filled Francis inside, but no one would have ever known. His face remained composed and funereal. Tears fell from Frank's eyes, but no one could tell whether these were tears of guilt, remorse, anguish, regret or whether they were tears of fakery and deception of the worst kind. Had Frank been seriously moved by his wife's death, no one would ever know.

The men sat down, Gerald pulled into place by Frank. Lizzie walked straight past where she had been told to sit and approached the casket with her chrysanthemums. She touched the wood and looked at the brass plaque adorning the upper centre of the lid. The inscription revealed what she had been told just three days before.

RIP
Elizabeth Mary Davies
57 years
Died 28 September 1930

Lizzie carefully placed the flowers onto the lid of the coffin. It seemed the most respectful thing to do. Inside, her emotions stirred. She felt angry and at once sad, but her eyes would cry no more tears. These had been used up in plentiful quantities in the days and years before.

Pettit Undertakers of Delamere Street in Chester had been employed by Frank to retrieve the body of Elizabeth from Denbigh Asylum. They had brought the body from the mortuary at Denbigh the night before in a converted Singer Super Six hearse with its beautiful new triplex glass windows, covering the coffin in a purple, gold braided, velvet cloth. In the darkness of the previous night, the churchwarden had opened the church to accommodate the coffin overnight.

On the stroke of eleven, Pastor Griffith Jones walked out of the vestry accompanied by four joyless faced men all dressed in black. The undertakers who'd come back for the committal.

Everyone knew Pastor Jones, he'd been the replacement for Pastor Herbert. The pastor made his way straight to Frank, shook his hand, offered his condolences and then shook hands with everyone else.

"Would you like to pay your last respects?" uttered the pastor grimly.

"It's not screwed down securely yet," coughed what looked like the lead undertaker, a man with a ruddy complexion and yellowed hands from the 80 Woodbines he got through every day.

Everyone looked to Frank.

"Thank you. Yes."

The lid was pulled back enough to see the head and shoulders of the corpse inside.

Everyone left their seats and congregated around the coffin.

This would be a sight no one would ever forget, least of all Gerald, who was shocked to the core to see his mother in the state she was. She resembled nothing like the person he'd last seen not long after his ninth birthday in 1927. The corpse WAS his mother, he recognised that, BUT barely. The frame in the coffin looked like that of someone who'd died in their nineties, not a person in their fifties. The sight was ghostly indeed, made worse by the physical appearance of the corpse, which, although only recently deceased, was barely recognisable as a human, never mind Elizabeth Davies. The sunken eyes, at the insistence of Frank, were covered over with Victorian pennies, one dated 1872, the year of Elizabeth's birth, and the other a brand new George V penny from 1930, to mark her year of death. The body was emaciated and lank grey needles of hair fell untidily to the plain off-white shroud, which covered every part of the body apart from the head.

Lizzie gasped at the sight. Francis stared on with disbelief, and Gerald couldn't look any longer. He turned his head away and walked back to his seat.

"That's enough!" Frank declared. "You can close it up."

"One last thing… " requested Lizzie quietly as she took hold of the golden chrysanthemums still on the coffin lid. "Can I place them inside with her?"

Frank nodded and walked back to his seat.

Lizzie carefully placed the flowers across Elizabeth's chest and with tearful eyes, bending over to Elizabeth's face she smiled and whispered, "Goodbye my friend. I'm so sorry I couldn't be there for you when you needed me most. Thank you for all you did for Gerald. I promise you I will be a good mother to him from now onwards. Promise. Goodbye."

*

The funeral was brief and quick. This wasn't their church and they were only here because this was the burial ground for Shotton. Within twenty minutes they were walking outside, following the coffin carried by the people from Pettit's, into the drizzle, which had had now descended onto the area.

They walked a good eighty yards around the back of the church and down the gradient into the cemetery fittingly overlooking the steelworks and the River Dee in the plains below. A few more words at the graveside and that was it. A life over and so cruelly over at the end. It seemed so final, as they all watched the men lower the coffin into the red clay of the ground. Lizzie picked up a piece of the sodden earth and threw it onto the top of the coffin. The brass plate shone no more, covered with clay and soil strewn across it. Gerald was the last to throw some dirt into the hole. For the first time, the emotions of the day got the better of him and his head fell into the arms of Lizzie, as tears erupted from his eyes. Tears which he had tried not to show and still hid from Frank's gaze.

*

The train back to Shotton was just pulling into Hawarden station as the funeral party arrived. Frank had unexpectedly invited everyone back to Dee View, declaring that Edith had prepared tea and bara brith for everyone.

"Today is a new start, " he said as the train pulled into Shotton, "... we shall never forget Elizabeth, despite burying her on this day. God rest her soul... " he quickly added, "she has been gone from our lives for some considerable time, so we must now move on." He directed his last words, looking squarely at Lizzie, eyebrows raised and added a "hmm?" with a few suggested nods.

Lizzie nodded in agreement. <'What else can I do!'>

True to Franks words, Edith had prepared food for the funeral party when they arrived back and they all sat in the parlour around the table, with no one knowing what to say for the best. Lizzie had been effectively gagged for some time, now she had agreed to it as well. She contented herself it was for Gerald's sake and vowed she would be the mother she had never had the chance of being from now onward. She was contemplating Gerald's future life when suddenly Frank stood up and clanked the side of Elizabeth's favourite teacup with a spoon, as if he was about to make a speech at some grand wedding.

"Stand up, Ede love. Stand up."

He beckoned Edith to come to her feet. On command, Edith stood up.

"Firstly, I'd like to thank you all today for being here, and I'd especially like to thank Edith for the lovely Bara brith and sandwiches. " He raised his Royal Albert tea cup to the air. "… and a good cup of tea, love."

Edith smiled appreciably. Lizzie was reminded of the day she was with Elizabeth and had drunk Horniman's tea from these very same tea cups, not two days after the death of Elizabeth's brother Herbert back in 1927. This was just a month before Frank had had his wife taken away. She could scarcely hide her reaction and turned away, pretending to cough for fear Frank would see her face.

"You okay Lizzie love?" Frank asked.

"Aha." Lizzie nodded as she looked back.

"Then good. There's no better time to say what I have to say AND… in the spirit of moving on… which I mentioned on the train, I do believe, I have an announcement to make."

Lizzie and Francis both looked at each other. The boys ate bare brith avidly. It was a real treat.

Edith moved closer to Frank. She knew in advance what he would be saying. "I know this may come as a surprise to you Lizzie and Francis… er … and you boys as well… er … it's me and Edith. Well, me and Ede are a couple."

The room was silent. Lizzie almost felt relieved. *<'Jesus and Joseph. Sorry God. I thought he was going to say they were getting married.>'*

Frank didn't end there. He turned to look at Edith "Edith and me will get married one day." Edith looked coyly at Frank and nodded.

The room was still and quiet.

"Well, aren't you going to say something Francis?"

"Yes, er, yes, we sort of knew anyway. I mean, Edith has been here for some time now… "

"Looking after the boys." Frank added curtly. "She's a good mum to you isn't she lads."

Both boys looked towards Lizzie for reassurance. Lizzie smiled.

The boys nodded.

"Then that's settled then. We all know where we are then don't we? We are henceforth moved on. End of conversation."

Lizzie felt gutted. It was like someone announcing their engagement on someone else's wedding day, only this day was THE funeral day of the wife of the person making the announcement!

Frank wasn't known for his tact but this was a real kick in the teeth for all concerned, apart from Edith and him.

Lizzie could have walked out there and then, but stayed for Gerald and Berty's sake. She was now even more resolved to ensure Gerald had a mother and that mother would be her.

*

It was gone four in the afternoon when Lizzie and Francis made for home. They'd stayed as long as possible for Gerald and Berty's sake but the lads had now gone upstairs to read so Lizzie had said it was time they were making tracks.

"One thing before you go… " Frank indicated for Francis and Lizzie to follow him to the sideboard.

He pulled out a formal looking piece of paper. "It's her death certificate. Your mum's… Want to see it?" He sniffed and grunted as he always did. The dust of the steelworks had done little for his chest over the years. "In case you don't believe she's really gone."

Lizzie looked at the certificate and read it several times. She openly wept for the first time in front of Frank, as did Francis.

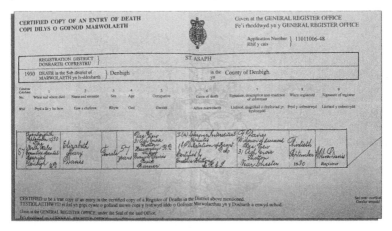

* * *

Death Certificate - Elizabeth Mary Davies (1930) [1]

Author's Note
[1]
The cause of death on the certificate is
a. Chronic Interstitial Nephritis
b. Dilation of Heart
Both of these conditions have doubtlessly been caused through ingesting toxins.

Chronic interstitial nephritis, which we now would call chronic kidney disease as an example, would be brought on through being prescribed (or injudiciously being prescribed) Potassium Bromide. Bromines mixed with other chemicals can cause damage to vital organs such as liver, kidneys, lungs and can cause stomach and gastrointestinal malfunctioning.

As regards Phenobarbitone, also prescribed to Elizabeth Davies, this is a Barbiturate, which is essentially a sedative-hypnotic drug, commonly used in the 1920s as an anti-epileptic. It is such a strong drug that many states in the US administer barbiturates for capital punishment by lethal injection. Respiratory depression is associated with the drug and prolonged use would exacerbate issues surrounding the amount of oxygen reaching the heart of the person, causing enlargement of the heart - respiratory drive is compromised with barbiturate toxicity.

Source: *US National Library of Medicine*
Essentially, Denbigh Asylum poisoned Elizabeth Mary Davies over a period of three years.

Dr Eustace Hutton who signed the death certificate for Elizabeth Davies was a medical doctor at Denbigh Asylum from 1915 through to 1947. In 1952 the Bishop of St. Asaph dedicated a memorial window to Dr. Hutton within the chapel at the asylum. Mrs Hutton, his wife, formally unveiled the window in the chapel, which is now derelict, with most of the windows being destroyed by vandals.

The hospital formally closed to patients in 1995.

By coincidence the author was a police officer for Nantglyn Police Station in Denbighshire from 1980 through to 1984 and the asylum, or the North Wales Hospital as it was then known, was on his patch. He did not know at this stage his great-grandmother had been a patient there as he attended the hospital many times to attend to incidents and sudden deaths, including the suicide of several patients and many other serious - and sometimes not so serious incidents. He played football on the pitch there for Denbigh Police against the staff football team and still has a scar on his back to prove the day he came a cropper during a match.

Chapter Ten

'Joining Up'

In the three plus years Elizabeth had been at the asylum, Edith Clarkson had been well ensconcing herself into the Davies' household at Dee View and her waist had increased in line with her enormous appetite and sweet tooth. For Berty, this was neither here nor there, but for the intelligent Gerald, this had been more of an issue. Well, it wouldn't have been an issue if everything had gone smoothly, but it hadn't. There was just something about Edith he couldn't get used to. Often, she scolded him severely for the most trivial of things, such as leaving his favourite reading book on the side or not folding his pyjamas in the right way when he left the house for school. Other times, she would wait for Frank to come home and complain the boys, particularly Gerald, had been causing her problems or plotting against her to make her life difficult. An actress extraordinaire she was at times, crying and bemoaning how badly they treated her and saying how much they disliked her.

"All I want is for them to like me," she complained regularly.

Frank had lost count of the number of times he'd heard Gerald say, "It doesn't matter what we do dad, she still complains about us - about me in particular. She just doesn't like me. I've tried to like her, but she makes it so difficult."

The months rolled by after Elizabeth's death, and things didn't improve for Gerald by having Edith around. He now had to do all his own washing and often that of Frank and Berty's. Edith refused to touch their washing and only did her own. Gerald had to make his own meals, sometimes in secret; very often Edith would cook for Frank and say the boys had eaten already, when, in reality, they'd had nothing to eat. She would send them to bed early with the threat that if they complained of feeling hungry, she would 'make things up' about them and tell Frank when he came home from work.

"I'll sort it!" Was the same answer Frank would give to both Edith and to Gerald. Truth was, he had no concept as to how he might resolve this situation. He had made his bed with Edith and now he was lying in it. The effect of all of this was to do exactly what Lizzie craved for, which was for Gerald and Berty to begin almost living at 6 Ashfield Road. Frank wasn't overkeen on at first, but he accepted this would be all right, as long as they slept in their own beds at night. Edith of course loved this, as it meant she had Frank all to herself and did her best to make sure the boys were away from Dee View as much as possible.

Lizzie loved stepping into the breach as parent to Gerald and felt she had got her own child back AND it was mostly Gerald who was there, morning, noon and evening. Berty's work was dirty, and his unsociable hours meant he couldn't always come. Gerald almost lived with Lizzie and Francis, apart from any time after dark.

*

The years rolled by and the happiest of times in Gerald's rapidly passing childhood were those he spent with Lizzie and Francis and their now growing family. Vince had been born in 1931 and on 15th March 1933, less than a week after his own fifteenth birthday, a baby girl arrived.

"Our own gemstone." Gerald had commented when he'd first seen her a couple of hours after she was born.

"Then we'll call her Ruby." Lizzie had smiled.

For Lizzie, the arrival of Ruby was tinged with a little sadness, though. She had planned at some stage to tell Gerald all about who he was and follow this up with an invitation for him to move in with them, instead of living with Frank and Edith. This had been put on hold when she found out she was pregnant, and Ruby signified the end to these plans. What little room there was in the tiny terraced house of two bedrooms was now to be taken up by the baby.

Gerald just adored his new niece. Of course, this was his sister but he was oblivious to any of this and he became a great help to Lizzie with his favourite niece, helping wherever and whenever he could.

This was in complete contrast to his treatment at Dee View, where Gerald and Edith's relationship now sunk to a new low. Edith had longed to become pregnant, but it just never happened. Gerald coming home and telling her how beautiful Ruby was didn't sit well at all, and she often flew into jealous rages. Edith fell into cycles of depression, binge eating and putting on lots of weight to the point where, by Christmas of 1933, she had gained over two-and-a-half stone during the year.

Christmas's for Gerald were the best of times when spent at Lizzie's house. The worst and most miserable times were when he was with his dad, Frank and Edith. There was singing and merriment at 6 Ashfield Road but only pessimism and moodiness at Dee View, so there really was no choice where Gerald wanted to be. Christmas 1933 was also Ruby's first Christmas and Gerald was determined it should be a good one despite the way he'd been treated at home.

New Year's Day of 1934 was when Gerald had his biggest surprise of the year. Unusually, he'd slept on the floor at Lizzie's welcoming in the New Year and hadn't gone home. He wandered back to Dee View with a smile on his face just before lunchtime. Frank and Edith were waiting for him.

"Where've you been 'til now, lad?" Frank demanded with some aggression.

"At Aunt Lizzie's dad."

"An' you thought it was okay to spend the night there?" Frank illustrated his point using his thumb to point toward Ashfield Road.

"I didn't think you'd mind dad."

"Mind? Ede 'ere made a meal for you last night, and you didn't have the decency to come back home and eat it. You could have even ran along the street and told us you wouldn't be home. Treat this place like a doss house you do. She's really upset. You've upset her yet again, lad."

In the background Edith looked on, bogus tears slowly filling her hostile eyes.

"Think you're just going swan in 'ere as you like, without as much as contributing a penny to the place, then you've got another thing coming, lad. I... er, WE, won't be used by you or anyone else, lad. You've had it too good for too long 'ere. Seems that damn education you're getting has made you too big for your own boots."

"I don't use the house. I don't. Honest!" pleaded Gerald.

"You'd better say sorry to Edith then, hadn't you lad."

Gerald looked over Frank's shoulder to Edith's cold and uncompromising face. He really didn't want to apologise to the smiling assassin at all. She had an insincerity and smugness about her lardy face which, in that moment, he thought about pushing into the bowl of cold custard which was on the table nearby. He didn't. He knew better and apologised. "Sorry."

"Sorry who?" shouted Frank.

"Sorry, Edith."

"You're not sorry to me then, lad?"

"Sorry dad."

"Tell him, Frank! You haven't finished telling him what we talked about," a snivelling Edith butted in. "Tell him!"

"Oh, yes, and we've decided. Thinking about that education of yours, lad. Er... these are hard times lad and education doesn't put food on the table or pay the rent. Gallivanting off to school is for people with money. It costs money you know to educate someone!" He ferociously shook a tin of pennies and loudly emptied it out onto the table. Two pennies rolled onto the floor. Gerald bent down to pick them up and put them back onto the table. "All we got this is. All we got between now and the end of the month!"

Gerald didn't quite believe his dad. Frank could afford his train journey's into Chester with Edith and the house always had a hearty meal, even if he didn't get a share.

"I can eat at Aunt Lizzie's," declared Gerald in desperation, knowing what Frank was about to say. The 1918 Education Act 1918, the brainchild of Herbert Fisher MP and afterwards known as The Fisher Act enforced compulsory education from 5 to 14 years in Britain and effectively stopped the employment of very young children in the factories of the land but it was now 1934 and Gerald was would be sixteen in March. No one tolerated people staying on in education in the working towns of the north in the 1930s, or even for decades after.

"... er... money doesn't grow on trees, it comes from hard slog at the steelworks. We need money in this house and schooling doesn't provide money does it!"

Frank pushed a small slip of paper before Gerald and hinted for him to look at it.

The form was headed *John Summer's & Sons - Basic Employment Form*. The job - *Steel Bar Counter*.

"The job is yours. Starting February. Just needs you to fill in your details take it over to the office."

"What about my exams coming up this summer, dad?"

It was Edith who spoke now. "You'll have to forget about these Gerald lad. I've decided... sorry, we've decided... " She looked to Frank for reassurance.

"Yes, we have," he agreed.

"... that you need to bring money into this house. Frank's kindly found you a job at the works and you should be grateful to your dad."

Gerald looked at the form with a slow shake of his head

"But I want to stay at school at least 'til summer. I promise that I'll look for work then. Promise!" He looked longingly at Frank, with tears coming to his eyes.

Edith shook her head. Frank looked at Edith and seemed heavy hearted. He shook his head.

"Please dad. Please!"

"No more please's and stuff. Go to your room! I don't want to see your face until tomorrow when you take that form over to the office."

Gerald's head sunk and he slowly left the room. As he closed the door to the stairs, he heard Frank saying, "It's not fair on the lad. Leave him until summer in school, Ede."

"He takes that job, or I'm out of here and there'll be no marriage later in the year and that's a promise."

*

January 1934 was Gerald's last month of full-time education. Friday 2nd February 1934 was his last day at Shotton Central. The day went quickly by, but as usual, Gerald worked quietly and studiously all day. He'd listened to the jingle of the hand-bell toured through the school by various bell-monitors during the day but there was one bell he was dreading more than any. The bell most pupils at the school loved, including Gerald before this day. The home-time bell.

The bell had rung and the class was dismissed. Whilst the others paraded out with shouts of 'see you Monday' or 'you goin' down the river after,' Gerald remained in his seat, slowly cleaning his nib with a piece of blotting paper, as Miss Winifred Jones prepared for home without noticing her solitary remaining pupil. It was only when Gerald tucked away his books and made a noise closing the lid of the desk, marked with years of ink and pupil etchings, that Miss Jones noticed him.

"Got no home to go to, Gerald?"

Gerald looked dejected. Miss Jones knew something was wrong and walked over to him.

"Can I help Gerald? You look awfully out of sorts. What is it?"

Gerald slowly shook his head. "No, Miss Jones. It's done."

"What's done?"

"School."

"School?"

He nodded again, fighting back the tears. "I won't be in Monday or ever again. Thank you for being nice to me since I've been in your class."

"You're welcome, but what is it?"

What Gerald said was no surprise to her; Miss Jones had heard the same story many times over. The children at the school never stood a chance of making it to sit their exams. Their families couldn't wait to get them to work to earn extra money for the house. Their wages wouldn't be their own and the young were expected to turn over most of their pay-packet as 'keep.' Miss Jones could do nothing. She had never been able to do. Home economics superseded any academic learning. That was for the privileged, and Gerald was far from that. All Miss Jones could do, was to give the same speech she had done to many others.

"Lift that chin up, Gerald. I know you've had a hard time, what with losing your mum and having to contend with a difficult home-life, but you are not on your own. These experiences make us strong people. What doesn't kill us strengthens us, hey?"

Gerald nodded and tried to smile.

"Do you know, when I was your age, I lost my dad in the Great War. We were destitute at one stage and we lived on a diet of eggs, eggs and more eggs from my uncle's farm but my mother always said to me, *'you're going to go on to great things Winifred provided you believe in yourself.'* Now Gerald, you listen to me. You have excelled here in school, and those silly exams you'll miss in the summer won't make a jot of difference to your life. Belief in yourself is worth a hundred pounds in the bank."

With that, Miss Jones gave Gerald a Victorian penny lying on the desk. "Think of this as your hundred pounds of belief in you." She folded his hand around the penny. "Now take this hundred pounds of belief and you go live the life you want!"

Gerald smiled one last time at Miss Jones and turned around and walked out, never to enter the school ever again. He went home via

Lizzie's and confided in her what Miss Jones had told him. He showed her the penny, which Lizzie said she would keep safe as his 'good-luck' charm. The fifth day of February 1934, penny safe at Lizzie's, he trudged over the Hawarden Bridge with Frank and thousands of others to what Frank believed would be Gerald's 'job for life.' Gerald had other ideas about how his life would pan out, but hadn't quite worked out what that would be yet.

*

Contributing to the household at Dee View made no difference to Gerald's relationship with Edith and it worsened in November 1934 when Frank and she married. Elizabeth had left £75 to Frank in her Last Will, which had gone to probate in April earlier in the year. The proceeds had been blown on a lavish 'wedding do' in Chester and a honeymoon in Brighton.

Berty and Gerald cared less and less for their home at Dee View and became more and more involved with Lizzie and Francis' household, helping with their growing family. Gerald in particular couldn't stand Edith's constant comments about how lazy he was and the relationship had grown almost intolerable. Life had to change and in 1936 it did. A poster on a wall outside the railway station in Shotton caught Gerald's eye.

HM Government 1930s RAF Recruitment Poster

Gerald saw opportunity written all over the poster. This would be his route out.

*

Gerald lived as close to an RAF base as you might want to be if this was an intended career path choice. Nearby was Sealand, not more than a twenty minutes walk down the railway where there was a huge airbase. In fact, more than one airbase. During the Great War there had been two airfields at Sealand, one at Shotwick to the north and one at Queensferry to the south. The railway ran in-between.

The airbase at Shotwick was a training station for RAF personnel in the war and had operated the latest aircraft - Sopwith Pups and

Camels, and later in 1917 Avro 504s. In 1924 the RAF station at Shotwick had been renamed RAF Sealand as there had been much confusion with supplies turning up at Sealand for RAF Scopwick in Lincolnshire, some 150 miles away on poor roads.

Initially, besides training personnel, RAF Sealand crated planes for transport overseas, but as the European situation worsened in the 1930s, the base took on the responsibility of training more and more pilots and flight crew. More hangars and barracks were constructed and by 1936 when a young Gerald Davies walked into the camp to join up, the base had become a massive logistic operation geared up for impending hostilities wherever and whenever they would be.

It was a hot July day when Gerald saw that fateful poster. It was as if the poster had been created for him and him alone. He was semi-skilled, and there was a promise the RAF would make him skilled. What more could he want and what an opportunity.

He acted there and then. He was on a day off and what else would he, or should he be doing. The poster said to 'apply to any RAF Unit or Depot,' so he walked the short distance along the railway to the camp.

The gates of the camp were guarded but the two guards were kindly and directed him to the main building of the site where they said he would be sorted. Polished floors and a picture of the king on the wall greeted Gerald. People in uniform milled about everywhere. This was a whole new world. A clean world. Not a piece of soot or metal dust in sight. This was where he knew he wanted to be. A rather stern but kind recruiting sergeant gave him the application forms to take home. "Your dad'll have to sign," he'd added, but Gerald knew this wasn't a problem. Edie and his dad would welcome him moving out. For Edith, this would be what she had wanted all along.

He'd completed and returned the forms that day and, as he'd predicted, Frank had signed them.

Gerald had opted to train as an 'aircrafthand' but had little knowledge of what that meant. It was what the RAF recruitment sergeant had suggested, so he'd gone along with it.

In the days and weeks after he'd submitted the forms he'd had to return to work at the steelworks, but in the meantime had had to attend RAF Sealand for a medical and to fill in other papers. Then the letter arrived. He signed up for six years and was in.

'Dear Gerald Davies,

Service No: 535005. Rank: Aircraftman - A.C.2

You are to report to RAF Sealand, Main Building at 10:00hrs. 'Training to begin on Tuesday 29th September 1936, where your initial training as Aircrafthand/Armourer will commence.

It was as short as that, but its brevity concealed the importance of this letter for Gerald. Now he could begin to believe in himself.

*

Gerald was nervous that first morning believing he might be on his own, but there seemed to be dozens of new recruits waiting to start their service in the RAF. The first job Gerald had, was to collect his uniform and kit. Then he was assigned to his barracks. It mattered not he was in a room with several others, what mattered was his freedom from Dee View. Lizzie and Francis and their children had bid him a fond farewell and given him little notes, wishing him good luck. They were very proud of him. Lizzie was particularly glad. She had worried for years about her own husband working in the dangers of the steelworks and had always wanted a cleaner job for him, but that was not to be. Gerald would be the lucky one to escape and have a proper career in the military. Yes, everyone was aware of Hitler but most people didn't see him as a danger to the peace in Europe in 1936, after all Time Magazine had been extolling his virtues and he had graced the cover of the magazine on 13th April that very year. The first of many pictures the magazine ran over the years - he would be named their *Man of the Year* in 1938.

For Lizzie, the RAF would be a safer job than the steelworks where people died horrible deaths regularly; crushed by heavy metal or burned to death when hawsers moving hundreds of tons of molten steel broke and molten metal spilled out.

The government in the 1930s prepared differently and the RAF increased the number of recruits going through the system. New accommodation blocks at Sealand meant they could train more 'flights' of men. So in September, Gerald began his twelve-week basic training course. This included drill or 'square bashing' as the recruits called it where they marched endlessly for hours and hours, looking more and more professional with every day which passed. Physical training formed a significant part of the initial training, and all recruits were expected to be in tip-top condition for whatever they would face in the future. Gerald found himself anti-gas training, fiddling around in the gubbins of the mechanics of aircraft and learning how to use weapons. He thoroughly enjoyed it all and wrote back to Lizzie telling her how wonderful it all was.

Gerald also studied as part of his training and finished what Miss Jones had started in school and getting paid for it, which was a bonus. After initial training he found himself moved several times, always training and getting better at his job working in and around aircraft. All this as a non-commissioned officer, but with a burning ambition to succeed inside.

*

By July 1937 Gerald was Class 1 Aircraftsman and within months a Leading Aircraftsman, now attached to 98 Squadron at RAF Hucknall near Nottingham where he had his first encounter with flying. It was a Sunday, and the camp was unusually quiet apart from a few crews and their Fairey Battle light-bomber aircraft.

Gerald had viewed with marvel the surrounding machines which flew off into the sky but he'd never been up in one. He'd just finished the final checks on one aircraft and watched as the crew came out.

"All checks correct, sir," he'd said to the Pilot Officer leading his crew out - a guy with an unusual surname which always stuck in his mind - Gordon-Finlayson.

'Good man Gerry," had been the response, but the second response he hadn't expected.

The Pilot Officer tapped his pipe out and began to fill it again. "Fancy coming up with us ol' man? Nice for you ground crew to get a feel for the way these things work, hey? We'll know it's safe then if you get on with us."

"Put that bloody pipe away, man! There's fuel everywhere!" came a shout from fifty yards away from someone who looked like a senior officer on the base. "Bloody idiot. You'll blow us all to bloody Kingdom come."

"Sir! Right away!" shouted the young Pilot Officer who winked at Gerald, putting his pipe into his tunic immediately whispering, "Jesus ol' chap, I'm in trouble now."

The other men laughed as the senior officer walked away without commenting further.

"Right, come on then lad, what are we waiting for. All aboard!" Gerald didn't need telling twice and within seconds was clambering aboard.

The flight lasted no longer than just over an hour. A quick training sortie with two other Fairey Battles, practising tight formations. Gerald was in his element and after that he knew what he wanted to do. Fly!

*

As 1938 wore on, war still looked far away to many, including Lizzie and Francis back home in Shotton. They heard from Gerald regularly about his progress in the RAF and wrote back regularly to wherever his latest posting was. Occasionally he would visit home in his smart uniform, but rarely did he visit Dee View unless Edith wasn't around. Lizzie still pondered whether to tell Gerald about his background and the truth behind his birth but she was reticent to do anything which might affect his career or cause him personal problems, so she once again she decided this conversation should wait until a more appropriate time but she couldn't quite get to grips with when and what that appropriate time might be. She was content in the knowledge Gerald looked at her as a motherly figure, so why might he need to know.

Author's Note

Aircraftsman Gerald Davies at RAF Sealand - 1937

Chapter Eleven

'Heinkel over Shotton'

It was 10.55am on the 3 September 1939, the first Sunday of that month, Gerald had been in the RAF for almost three years, working hard and had passed several promotion tests with flying colours. He was now at RAF Cottesmore in Rutland performing the role of Acting Sergeant and had been since the previous May. He proudly wore his Air Observers half-wing brevet with an O at the root, having earned these at Initial Training. He would remember this Sunday until the end of his days.

It was on this very day everyone had been told, Neville Chamberlain, the Prime Minister, would make a statement at 11.15 am, so all were gathered in good time in the 207 Squadron Crew-room, where the best wireless on the station was. The atmosphere was tense and serious, but at the same time upbeat. They'd all been preparing for months for a war they knew was imminent, but no one had any idea when this would be.

Gerald was at the end of months of training in and around the cumbersome Fairey Battle light-bomber aircraft. With its crew of three, it was almost obsolete before it even went into action, but Gerald was determined he would be the best air observer there was when the war started and start it would sooner than anyone on that day expected.

As he gathered around the radio with several of his RAF colleagues, the wireless crackled into life broadcasting live from London. Neville Chamberlain sounded broken to the core. All he had wanted was peace at any cost, now he would announce something chilling.

"I am speaking to you from the cabinet room at 10 Downing Street. This

morning the British ambassador in Berlin handed the German government a final note stating that unless we heard from them by 11 o'clock that they were prepared at once to withdraw their troops from Poland, a state of war would exist between us. I have to tell you now that no such undertaking has been received, and that consequently this country is at war with Germany."

The speech lasted for just over five minutes and was followed by a plethora of government announcements. The group of RAF personnel stood in silence throughout the entire broadcast. Their silence lasted for a minute after the wireless was turned off. Everyone looked at each other with disquiet at the unknown situation which now lay before them. No excited faces at the prospect of war. Some old lags remembered the carnage of the Great War; which ended the year Gerald was born - twenty-one years before. One or two showed their scars from their time on the Western Front and shook their heads with derision. Gerald looked on and listened.

"If you want to stay alive, keep your head down and volunteer for nowt," one man in the room said. "The war will come to you soon enough without you volunteering to get to it quicker!"

Around the land mothers, grandmothers, sisters and daughters wept. Many screamed *'not again, not again.'*

At Dee View, 31 Ash Grove, Shotton Gerald's father Frank and stepmother, Edie listened to their Philco radio with utter shock. No one wanted war. Not long afterwards they heard the wails in the street, as if a funeral of someone well-loved had passed by. There was no funeral that day in Shotton, but there would be soon enough right across the land. Those who remembered the Great War, and they were many, knew the hardships and losses of war. No one wanted this again, but here it was on their doorstep and loved ones were going to die before their time. Frank thought of Gerald and thought of Lizzie and Francis.

Lizzie and Francis had listened to the broadcast just along the street on their Cats Whisker Crystal Radio in its fine wooden box. The reception was rubbish, but good enough to hear provided someone was close at hand to keep the radio tuned in. Francis was a dab hand at this.

That first year of the war was a strange time for all. The blackout had begun right from the start, and as the dark nights rolled in for the winter of 1939, the street lights remained out. On cloudy moonless nights many a person walked into a wall or an iron gate gashing their shin open. Windows were tape covered and curtains drawn so no light could escape. Those who broke the rules found themselves before the magistrate, some with heavy fines, some with imprisonment. Rumours abounded, German spies were everywhere, so everyone had a national registration card. This meant the government knew who was who and where they lived. Spies and anyone not obeying the rules in any way could be more easily identified. It also meant men could be called-up with relative ease and from October 1939, all men aged between 20 and 21, had to register with the military authorities. This didn't affect Gerald at all; he'd been in the military since 1936 and his career was proceeding smoothly and so far, without a hitch.

May 1940 saw Germany invade France and the Low Countries and fears abounded: an invasion could take place at any moment. Francis was in a reserved occupation at the steelworks, but wanted to do his best for the war effort. On 31st May 1940 he joined the 19th Battalion (Shotton) of the Cheshire Regiment and began training in his new khaki uniform as one of the Home Guard for the area.

Lizzie's concern was for how Gerald was doing. Then on the morning of Wednesday 14th August the postman delivered a postcard to 6 Ash Grove, Shotton. It was a colour picture of a bridge at Henley-on-Thames with boats on the river and a church in the background. She turned the card over. It was from Gerald. She had posted a letter to him weeks before, but until now had received nothing back.

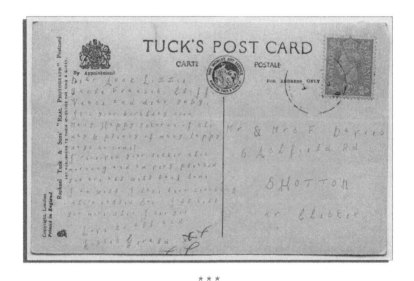

* * *

Dear Aunt Lizzie, Uncle Francis, Cliff, Vince and dear Ruby,
    It's your birthday soon. Many Happy Returns of the day & plenty of many happy days to come!
    I received your letter this morning and am very pleased you are all well back home. I am well. I have been courting - she's called Sue. I'll tell you more when I see you.
    Love to all and kisses.
    Gerald. xxxx

Lots of kisses were squeezed onto the bottom of the postcard.

It was a few minutes after seven in the evening when Francis came in from his shift at the works.

"Tradesman's entrance... It's that man again! I Don't mind if I do! Every penny makes the water warmer... " came the shout, mimicking Liverpudlian comedian Tommy Handley, as Francis walked in through the back door, throwing his flat cap at the hanger attached to the spench door. Francis loved the radio show ITMA (It's That Man Again), which had been broadcast late in 1939 and early into 1940. He just couldn't get the catchphrases out of his head, which he repeated endlessly. He could be heard walking around the house shouting, "Don't forget the diver." or the words of Mrs. Mopp, "Can I do you now, sir?"

Lizzie diverted him away from ITMA as much as she could. "You look worn out, love."

The humour of the ITMA catchphrases had long since worn off on the long-suffering Lizzie, but all the same, Francis loved to greet Lizzie with the same set of lines every time he walked in.

Francis wiped his forehead with a blackened handkerchief pulled from his trouser pocket.

"It's hot enough over in the works, without coming out into a second furnace at the end of the day."

"It's not that hot, love."

"You should try it after twelve hours over there!" Francis pushed the filthy handkerchief towards Lizzie's face in jest.

She ducked.

"You daft 'apeth, get those filthy things put away away. I got something to show you."

"Ooh, I like the sound of that," Francis grinned as he took Lizzie by the waist and slid his hand up along her stomach before being slapped across the hand.

"Nothing like that, you filthy beggar. Get washed and changed and I'll show you."

Francis was lathered from the heat and his red face showed it. He put his filthy overall on the back of the steelworks green spench door and grabbed himself a glass of water and swilled himself under the one cold tap, just inside the back door over the Belfast sink.

The wash and clean up didn't take long. The cold water ensured a quick swill.

Lizzie showed Francis the postcard.

"At least we know he is well and he's remembered your birthday's coming up. Got a girl by the looks of things too."

"A couple of weeks yet."

"A couple of weeks?"

"Until my birthday. Yes, he seems to be happy."

"What's the matter Lizzie?"

"He's been away a long time. The post card says nothing about what he's doing or what he's up to."

"Would you expect it too?"

"Probably not. Part of me understands. Part of me doesn't."

"And what else would you expect him to say?"

"That he loves me and I'm his mother?"

"We've been through all of this so many times. I thought we'd decided on that. He's not your son."

"He is my son. He's your son too."

"He is by birth, but Frank and Elizabeth took that responsibility on when he was born. You knew that... "

"I had no bloody choice."

"Language!"

"No choice at all. If I'd have gone home, they'd have thrown me out. So it all became a dark secret. Even Frank, after all what happened with Elizabeth still can't get his head around it. He was told the truth about Gerald's birth, but he just won't believe it. He won't."

"WE SHOULD BE CONTENT HE THINKS LIKE HE DOES!"

"Don't shout, Francis. Don't shout."

"If anyone heard you. Crimes! If anyone heard."

"So what, I think sometimes. He was my child. MY child." She filled up with tears. "He is my child and he always will be."

Francis put his finger to his lips and looked around. He closed the door which led to the stairs of the two up two down. "He knows nothing of that and he never can."

"When this bloody war is over, God willing, I will tell him who he really is."

"Oh yes, that'll be good. What will Frank say? What will Edie say?"

"He doesn't like Edie anyway. You know that. She's been a pig with him... and... and... she's vile to him. She's the reason he upped sticks and left in 1936. Poor lad, losing his mother in 1930."

"Oh, so my mother IS HIS MOTHER now, is she?"

"You know what I mean. When Elizabeth died in THAT hospital, Gerald's life changed for good. He was only 12 for God's sake... and just 9 when he put her in there."

"Don't take the Lord's name in vain."

"Who are you to tell me what to do?"

"Why are we rowing?"

"We're not. You're the one who's raised your voice and telling me to keep quiet."

"It's for everyone's good. Believe me."

"Everyone's good?"

"Who's everyone? When Elizabeth died, your parents' right to say they were Gerald's parents died with him. Look at this postcard... " She thrust it into Francis' face. "He calls us Aunt and Uncle and he thinks Cliff, Vince and Ruby are his nephews and niece."

"He doesn't say that."

"Well, he doesn't use the words nephew and niece, but he has used it. Look at the books he gave them for Christmas last year. He wrote in them all with black ink: Love and Best Wishes from Uncle Gerald. Says it all don't it?"

"I don't know. Where did all this start? Oh yes, that damn postcard. It's only a damn post card and it's Gerald's way of telling us he is fine."

"Who's swearing now."

"Damn is swearing?"

"You used it twice as well."

They both laughed.

"There's a serious point here, Francis. I don't want to fight, but I'm going to have my say on this. Gerald will know who he is. He has a right to know.

"It will destroy dad. He knows Gerald doesn't know. You know what he said, anyway."

"Your dad has no right to anything after the way he treated Elizabeth. He sent her to her death and WE were all expected to forget she ever existed. Well, I didn't for one. The truth hurts. Your mother died because of your father, and you know that. It's time we stopped living a lie"

Francis' face went serious again. "She was my mother. Yes. He's my father, yes… and I can't forget that either. And what's Edith in all of this?"

"She's the one who caused it all in the first place, for us, for Gerald, for everyone."

"What do you mean?"

"I can't explain this more simply. That floozy Edith was in your mum's bed as soon as she ended up in the asylum… three years before she died even."

"You have no evidence of that."

"No? Trips to Chester on the train on his own, dressed up like he was off to a wedding, when at home he sits in his vest and pants will his long-johns on display for all to see. He's reverted to type now, eh? I go there… God knows why…"

"Name in vain again… "

"… and there he is, pants unbuttoned and holes in his vest waiting to be waited on hand and foot either by me or fat Edie."

"Well, he is getting on now and Edie is younger than him by twenty years, so you'd expect him to be taking it easy now."

"Francis, Francis… you are missing the point. This is not about Frank, it's about us. It's about Gerald. Please, please understand, for my sake. I brought him into the world…"

"Shhh Lizzie. Someone will hear."

"There's no one in. The children are all out. They've gone for a long walk on the riverbank."

"The riverbank. I've told them not to go there."

"Stop fretting Francis. They're fine. It's a nice evening. They've got some jam-butties and have gone to watch a huge boat unloading at the steelworks jetty. It's just you and me. Look… Frank is with Edie now. I accept that. He wasn't nice to Elizabeth… I can't believe I'm even saying that… God, sorry God, he was awful to his wife, but now I have to accept that's a fact. That's what caused Gerald to join the RAF when he did, yet I don't regret that now either, he's doing well but the war worries me. Don't you remember him running here the day he found out HIS MOTHER had died?"

"Like yesterday. She was MY mother too. MY MOTHER."

"I know, I know, so you should understand more than anyone what was going on. Don't you remember the lies he was told by Frank about why she went into Denbigh?"

"Remind me. Go on…"

"He came here shouting *'it's not true. Mum is dead. It's not true, Aunty Lizzie. Tell me please.'* I can remember that now. I had to tell him Elizabeth was dead, and she'd died two days before. I so wanted to tell Gerald then that I was his mother anyway and that he still had a mother. Frank didn't even have the decency to tell YOU, his son, that your mother had died the day before in hospital."

"Dad had his reasons."

"Stop defending him. He was a bastard to Elizabeth."

"I'm not defending him and you don't know that for sure. AND stop swearing."

"Bastard, bastard, bastard… there, I've said it now."

Francis shook his head and sniffed. "You've changed."

"Well, don't go on about swearing then. I don't know what for sure? That he was a bas… "

"Yes, we've heard the word enough."

"She told me stuff, you know. I saw stuff. She hid stuff from you. Told me. We had a special bond from the time Gerald was born."

"You've hidden things from me."

"Your mum wanted to protect you. She told me not to say anything to you. She knew knowing these things about your dad would hurt you. I kept her confidence."

"You lied to me, Lizzie. We said we would never lie to each other."

"There were no lies. I just didn't tell you."

"You kept things from me then!"

"Stop being a tomato. This is not about you. Not about you! So Frank didn't tell you your mother had died for a day, then he didn't tell Gerald until a day later."

"Gerald was twelve, that's why?"

"You know that for sure?"

There was a pause. Francis shook his head and shrugged his shoulders. "Nope."

"Gerald hadn't seen his mother in … er … over three years. Not since Frank had her PUT AWAY in Denbigh. Don't you recall Gerald coming running to our place the day after Elizabeth was taken away?"

Francis nodded sadly and put his hand over his mouth, rubbing the days' growth of whiskers up and down. He looked up to the ceiling, hiding tears which wanted so much to fall from his eyes. He said nothing as he turned his head to secretly wipe his eyes.

Lizzie moved closer to Francis as he sat on the dining chair he always sat in, near to the wireless. She took hold of his arm. "You don't have to hide your tears from me. We are a couple; we've been through some rough times together. We gave away OUR child and now your mum has gone, it's only us who know this secret. No one else in the world knows."

"Except for old Mrs. Boswell, who delivered Gerald into this hell of a world."

"Mary Jane Boswell? No, she won't be saying anything. Unless she makes an appearance as a speaking ghost. She died in about '28, so she's long been pushing up daisies. She took her secrets to the grave... she must have had a head full of secret relationships and children given away in this area, hey?

"Suppose so."

"Our secret, makes us special. Our child who is now away at war and God knows if he'll ever come back. I pray every day he will, but I just don't know. I want to reclaim the child I have always known as my own and I will; God willing."

Now tears flowed from Lizzie's eyes. She turned Francis's head to face hers. "Look me in the eye Francis. Remember Gerald coming running to us after he got home from school on the day Elizabeth was taken to hospital. How callous was Frank? Don't you remember what Gerald said?"

"I do. He said, *'dad says mum is mental and they came in a yellow van to take her away. Please tell me it's not true.'* Something like that. I'll never forget his face."

Lizzie once again shook the post card in Francis's face. "That's why he deserves to know who he is. Your father hasn't cared for Gerald for years and we have failed him in his life. We can make up for that when the war is over and we'll have the chance to do what is right."

Francis nodded and clawed at his whiskers again, as tears flowed down his face.

It was then the war came to Shotton. Several very loud explosions disturbed the peace of the evening.

"What the hell was that!" shouted Francis as they both dashed to the back door to see plumes of smoke coming from nearby RAF Sealand.

"Jesus... sorry Lord... we're under attack Lizzie. Where the hell are the kids? Where was the air raid warning!"

There were more explosions from the direction of the airbase where

Gerald had joined up four years before. The base was just over a mile away from where Francis and Elizabeth lived. The Battle of Britain had been raging since the 9th July, mainly in the south of the country. The Channel Islands had been occupied by the Germans on the 30th June and there'd been air raids on places like Cardiff and Plymouth at the beginning of July, but nothing much up-north had happened. In fact, the battle had, so far, not disturbed North East Wales at all.

Then they saw it. The black cross on the fuselage was unmistakable. It was a German Heinkel *[1]* bomber with two engines on either side. The plane was no more than a hundred feet above the ground. The roar of the engines was deafening.

"They're after our steelworks, as well as the airbases here," shouted Francis, craning his neck upwards.

Shotton and the surrounding area would definitely be a target for Hitler. Unknown to anyone, least of all the Davies family in Shotton, the 14th August 1940 had been code-named *Adlertag*, or *Eagle-Day* by Hitler and his Nazi cohorts. It was the day Hermann Wilhelm Göring's Luftwaffe began their huge aerial offensive, which was supposed to be part of a grand plan to hamstring Britain's defences to pave the way for the invasion of Britain. In a daring attempt to confuse and split Britain's fighter defences, Göring sent out wave after wave of bombers to attack remote long-range targets in broad daylight - without the protection of fighters.

The reality of war was now over Shotton.

North East Wales and particularly Shotton was a prime target with its huge iron and steel works, working to capacity for the war effort, but there were also three airbases within the immediate vicinity. This is what the Germans had come for. The Luftwaffe was targeting RAF Sealand. The camps were a training base and fitted radar to Bristol Beaufighters.

The Heinkel seemed to hang over Shotton, as it circled slowly for some time with impunity. It was plain to see; the pilot was looking for targets in the area. Not a shot was fired from the ground, and there wasn't a sign of defence forces coming to tackle the aircraft.

Lizzie and Francis stood, bolted to the ground by the sight. It had been so low they could see the pilot and two others inside the glass front of the aircraft.

"Bastards!" shouted Francis, waving his fist.

"The Lord's not going to be happy with you today, Francis."

Francis took no notice and was still waving his fist. "Our Gerald is coming for you!"

"Never mind them, let's get the children."

For a short time, the plane disappeared over the rooftops of the many terraced back streets of Shotton, but Francis and Lizzie knew it wasn't far away as its thundering engines disturbed what had been a perfect summer's evening. Francis and Lizzie ran like two Olympic sprinters towards the bank of the River Dee, where the children were.

The Heinkel came into view again. It looked as if its pilot had decided to come in for a second run on a target.

"They could shoot our babies."

"They're not after children," shouted a puffed Francis, "but we need to get them back home."

The Heinkel flew low overhead, heading back towards the RAF base once again. Within less than a minute there were more explosions and smoke billowed up into the sky, just as Francis and Lizzie arrived at the riverbank, in the fastest time they'd ever made it. Ruby, Cliff and Vince were already running towards them.

The deafening noise of the first bombs being dropped had been heard by three spitfire pilots putting their aircraft away at RAF Hawarden, just 5 miles away and within seconds, the idling spitfires were off the ground and in search of the Heinkel.

The Heinkel had again circled around and was once again close to the Davies family, when the familiar thump of Rolls Royce Merlin engines could be heard. They'd heard the noise many times before as 'Spits' from RAF Hawarden, regularly roared over them. There were suddenly three Spits in the sky over Shotton. Francis breathed a sigh of relief at the sight and took time to catch his breath.

The three Spitfires thundered past to the cheers of the excited children. Francis whooped and cheered with delight too. Lizzie remained quiet, she'd expected the children to be scared and grabbed at them, pulling them closer, as she ran for more cover near to one of the brick pillars of the iron railway bridge which crossed the River Dee.

The children didn't want to be pulled and resisted. The sky was more interesting. Lizzie pulled away at them and shouted, "come on," constantly.

As she got against the brick pillar she whispered, "Thank God," to herself. Then she shouted at the three children. "Stay here, you hear!"

There were no houses to block their view now, and they watched the

Heinkel lose some height as it headed back towards them. Despite the Spitfires in the air, the plane circled around again and looked like it was going in for a second attack on the airbase at Sealand.

"Our lads'll have 'im," shouted Francis, as two of the spitfires opened fire. Loud *'rat-ta-tat-tats'* in short bursts filled the air. The cannon fire was so close, everyone spontaneously ducked their heads, but the urge to keep looking at the action overhead was irresistible, apart from little Ruby who covered her ears and screwed her face up, turning her head away. Lizzie hugged her close. "It's okay, it'll be gone soon."

Despite the attack on it, the Heinkel kept its path.

Two of the spitfires peeled away and the third spitfire fell in being the Heinkel. One long burst *'rat-ta-tat-tat.'* The planes were now almost all overhead and close. Very close. There was a solid noise of metal and a huge crunching sound. Some metal fragments from the Heinkel hit the water within feet of the family, now cowering against the brick pillar of the bridge.

"Crikey Moses, that was close!" shouted Lizzie. Everyone looked at each other and laughed nervously.

"He's gorrim though. Look at the smoke."

The Heinkel started spewing black smoke and sparks from both engines. It rapidly began to lose height. Two of the three Spits flew away as the stricken German plane headed down river towards Chester with one Spit pursuing, but not firing its weapons any more. The pilot knew the job was done.

"I'm glad he's not firing anymore," commented Lizzie.

"You are? He's a German and we hate them."

"That could be Gerald. That plane's coming down anyway without another bullet being fired. If that was Gerald and a Nazi plane kept on firing, would you want that?"

"Don't suppose so."

"Don't suppose so! You mean NO. They might be Germans, yes, but they're humans in that plane after all. Just ordinary people like you, me AND Gerald. All with worried families at home. Doing what they've been told to do, that's what they're doing Francis. War is damn stupid. STUPID."

The Heinkel was so low they watched it fly under electricity pylons and then it came down, landing wheels up, not 50 yards from a farmhouse.

As they sauntered back to the house, they heard explosions from the direction of the crash.

"I hope they're all okay."

"Soft, you are girl. Soft!" came the reply from Francis.

*

The next day Francis rushed in from work. It was just after seven again. He didn't even give his regular greeting or throw his cap at the spench door. He'd been to the newsagent's and held the local rag in his hand, shaking it about. "It's here in black and white. The headline - 'Heinkel Down in North-West.' This'll be the one. Didn't think they'd report it."

"Shhh, you three. Sit and listen." Seven-year-old Ruby sat on Lizzie's knee whilst Cliff, 11 and Vince 9, sat on the floor. Listening to someone reading was a treat. Francis often did this, even when there wasn't such exciting news to tell. Besides which, all three had been banned from going too far from the house after the air raid yesterday, so they had little to do.

"Well, what does it say then..." Lizzie asked in frustration as everyone listened carefully.

"It says here, *Two Heinkel 113s returning from a bombing raid on Wales provided inhabitants of a North West England town'* ... er, is Shotton in England now? I don't think so."

"They're probably not allowed to say exactly where it is are they?" Lizzie said, taking Francis's hat off belatedly. Francis sat down. A thing he never did in his overalls, but this was important news about the war.

"Come on, Francis, tell us more."

"Yes, come on dad. What does it say?" Cliff chirped up.

"I'm reading, yes okay... apparently children, we were provided with our *'first experience of an aerial battle last night.'* Kind of them to say so. *'The raiders'* Ooh, those nasty German raiders... *'were intercepted by British fighters as they approached the town...but...'* it says here, *'one managed to escape into the clouds.'* We didn't see two German planes did we children and there wasn't much cloud either!

They all shouted "no" together.

"It had clouded over quite a bit," Lizzie added.

"What does the paper say next... let me see. *'A fighter fastened on the tail of the other. Several bursts of fire were heard...'* Trrrrr....Trrrrr... Trrrr..." Francis threw his arms out in aircraft fashion and pretended to machine gun the children. The children cheered and clapped. Lizzie remained silent. Her thoughts were for Gerald and what he was up to.

"Yes...'and the bomber was forced down in a field on the outskirts of the town, where it afterwards caught fire.' ... "

"I hope the crew were all pulled from the wreckage safely."

"We'll see mother... Yes... it says here 'Four of the crew of the German plane were unhurt. One sustained a wound which is not serious, and he is in hospital. One of the crew had an Iron Cross.' ... "

"What's that dad?" Cliff enquired with interest.

"Something to do with being brave in battle... might've even been during the Great War. Who knows. Anyways, to go on, without interruption from anyone... ahem...'The raiders had previously attempted an attack on another objective in Wales, where they did some damage...' That'll be the camp in Sealand 'and there were some casualties.' Glad Gerald's not there now, love?"

Lizzie nodded, a picture of worry settled across her face.

" ... 'A few men were also admitted to hospital after the fight, with wounds, but none of them was serious.' Those are our lads, Lizzie. Thank goodness none of 'em are badly wounded.... 'Mr Llewellyn Jones, a farmer, was at his home with his brother-in-law, Corporal Anderton of the Home Guard,...' I know him Lizzie. Geoff. He's with the 19th Cheshires. He's with us... where was I, yes... 'when the bomber landed a short distance away.' ...It's got a funny bit here love. Says here... 'The five Germans got out of the machine, put up their hands and one remarked in English, ENDED.' Ha, ha, he said ended. Couldn't even speak proper English."

"I don't suppose they could. They're German. Poor things. Must have been a hell of a shock for them. One minute they're in the air and the next minute they're being fired at and have crash landed on foreign soil. Their families must be worried sick."

"They were still trying to kill us though, Lizzie. We are at war with Germany... Remember."

"How could I forget?"

"Finish the story, dad," chirped an irritated Cliff. Ruby paid not a jot of attention and no one noticed she had fallen asleep.

"Right, yes son, 'They were taken into the farmhouse and given tea and biscuits... ' See we do treat 'em with respect, not like I've heard they do to our lads."

He read on, "... 'They gave souvenirs to the children in the house. The bomber was badly damaged before it landed and one of the crew made certain *that the machine would be a total wreck by setting fire to it.'* Typical Gerry that, heh? Where are we now, yes… It says here *'continued in the next column' …"* He built up the suspense with a verbal drum roll. "… den den derrrn … yes, who… where is it, I can't see it."

Lizzie moved across to Francis. "It's there, you fool. Look there… it says continued from preceding column you nitwit."

"Oh, yes… *'Later the airmen were taken to the local police station, the first to arrive being the man with the Iron Cross and other decorations.'* He was like a Christmas Tree…covered in decorations. Ho. Ho. Ho."

Francis laughed as he rubbed his belly, mimicking Father Christmas. Vince and Cliff laughed. Ruby slept.

"Have you finished yet, I'll get this girl to bed."

"Nearly finished… *'Tracer bullets exploded while the bomber was burning, and scores of sightseers and souvenir hunters were soon attracted to the spot. While the air battle was in progress over Wales,'* Oh, they mention us now… *'Machine-gun bullets fell onto the streets of a town but there were no casualties.'* That would be us then, here in Shotton. We were lucky nothing landed on our bonces then hey kids. That's it. Here endeth today's news. Story all done dear."

"Thank goodness for that. Right… wooden hills time everyone. Francis… get a wash, hey!"

Over at RAF Sealand repairs were already underway to the Guardroom, the Sergeant's Mess and the Airmen's Block.

For the crew of the aircraft, their war was over and they became prisoners of war.

Author's Note:

[1] The German plane was a Heinkel He 111P-2 and the crew were:
Pilot: Oberleutnant (Pilot Officer) Artur Wiesemann
Navigator: Feldwebel (Flight Sergeant) Heinrich Rodder
Flt. Mech: Unteroffizier (Sergeant) Walter Schaum
Radio Operator: Unteroffizier (Sergeant) Heinz Kochy
Gunner: Unteroffizier (Sergeant) Gustav Ullmann
The Spitfire Pilot who downed the aircraft was: Pilot Officer Peter Ayerst who spent 8 years as an RAF fighter pilot, joining in 1938 and rising to the rank of Wing Commander. He died in 2014.

The other two Spitfires were piloted by Wing Commander John Robert Hallings-Pott CB, DSO, DSC, (RAF career 1926 - 1956. Rising to rank of Air Vice-Marshall) and Squadron Leader John S. McLean.

All three were based as training instructors at 7 OTU (Operational

Training Unit) in Hawarden.

In 1988 the five from the Heinkel 111 met with the Wing Commander Peter Ayerst for the first time and gave their version of events. They confirmed their target was RAF Sealand. They also revealed they did not see the Spitfire's from Hawarden coming and thought a shadow on the cloud was from their own aircraft, so made no attempts to take evasive action until it was too late.

More about this in: Spirit of the Blue: A Fighter Pilot's Story: Peter Ayerst - A Fighter Pilot's Story by Peter Ayerst and Hugh Thomas.

Image: Courtesy The Imperial War Museum.

Chapter Twelve

'The Girl at The Horns'

It was now early September 1940 and the Battle of Britain was in full swing. Britain fought for its very existence under wave after wave of German attacks. Mid-morning, Gerry was unusually sat alone in the Officers' Mess of RAF Northolt, [1] West of London. The boys were all out on various duties and he'd had to run an errand for the base leader Group Captain Stanley Vincent, so he was back early. As he looked out, sipping his hot cup of tea, he could see Hawker Hurricane fighters. He could hear them. He could smell them. The roar always sent a shiver down his spine.

Many of the pilots trained here had transferred to Biggin Hill to defend the south of England, and he knew of many who would now never come back. Losses were high amongst his friends. Making friends with someone was a frightening prospect, as those friendships were often short-lived and only reminded everyone just how fragile their lives were. He was twenty-two and had heard the scramble bell rung more times than he could remember, particularly for the men of 303 Polish Fighter Squadron, who were based there and who engaged enemy aircraft as part of the defence of London.

He reflected on the proud history of the place he was in. Northolt was the oldest RAF base in the country and predated the establishment of the Royal Air Force by almost three years, having opened in May 1915 as a base for the Royal Flying Corps.

The ghosts of airmen were everywhere. Every little object in the place was a reminder of someone who he'd never see again. Personal items left on the side which would never be collected again by their owners - collected by someone else and sent in envelopes. Reminders of lives that would never be lived.

Gerald had been training for most of the year and the year before.

'For longer even,' he thought to himself, thinking back to the end of 1938 when he'd completed his Elementary Air Navigation course. Things seemed to have moved on at a pace since then. By January 1939 he was an Air Observer under training and had some difficulty with the difficult maths every navigation officer had to succeed with. His tenacity and perseverance saw him through though, and he'd succeeded with some style in the end, proceeding first to Air Observer School at West Freugh in Scotland. By the end of May in 1939 he had achieved an 'A rating' on the Air Observers course and was posted to 207 Bomber Squadron at RAF Cottesmore, flying with the Squadron's twin engine Avro Ansons. He'd now flown more times than he could remember and just last April had been recommended for a Commission as an Officer, something which had come to fruition on 23rd July 1940 when he was made Pilot Officer Gerald Davies. The proudest moment of his life. Now it was all real as he stood in his RAF officers' uniform in an actual officers' mess. He couldn't quite believe it himself and constantly looked himself up and down several times.

'I'm the Shotton lad... destined to work with my dad Frank at the steelworks until I retire. Mum would never believe it if she could see me now. Oh mum. Oh mum, I wish you were still here dearest mum. Why'd you have to die so young?'

A tear came to Gerald's eye.

"Penny for them, Gerry Boy!"

He looked back to Michael, who'd quietly wandered in. Michael was his friend of a few weeks, completing the same training course as him.

"Was far away, Michael. Far away."

Michael came and stood by him and they both stared out of the window towards the aircraft and runway.

"You all right ol' man. Feeling sad, hey? We all feel sad from time to time. Be glad when it's a done deal and we're home."

"Bit of dust in the old eye, hey."

"If you say so." Michael winked and patted Gerald on the shoulder.

Gerald breathed out slowly to compose himself. "Thanks, Michael. It's a weird time, hey? I mean, look at the runway. A fake stream painted across it. No wonder so many of our boys miss it when they come in to land."

Michael took a slow drag from his beautifully polished pipe. Smoke filled the air. "The fake houses too ol' boy. Home from home, hey? Old Vincent has done a good job."

"I suppose he has."

"He has indeed. Hundreds of bombs the Huns have thrown at this place, but I think it's only a couple have hit the runway…and even then they've caused minor damage."

"Anyway, how would you like a couple of letters, old chap?"

"More than one letter for me? I am privileged today."

"Straight from the post room. Just in. Your name on both of them and one smells nice too."

Michael handed the letters over. Gerald looked at the envelopes. One was postmarked Henley and the other was Chester, this one was Lizzie's writing and he knew without a doubt who the first one was from.

"Is one from that Henley girl you're so fond of? Susan, is she called?"

"Yes… she is, Susan, well Sue, I call her." Gerald lifted the Henley envelope to his nose and smelled it. "Definitely her, Mike." He held the envelope out towards Michael. "This here envelope I shall treasure. I know it already, whatever it says inside."

"It might say you're dumped ol' man, or she's, you know, up the duff, or in the club." Michael laughed.

"Rather doubt any of those, but I'll never know unless I open it and if she's dumping me I'm taking you for a ride in the clouds and dropping you off at 10,000 feet without a parachute for your insensitive behaviour."

The two chuckled away.

"Well, open it then, ol' man. Let's hear what she has to say. Nothing private in here. I've got no letters, so read yours out. Any private bits you can omit." He winked and poked Gerald with the end of his pipe.

Gerald carefully used a knife on the table before him to slice open the first and what he considered the most important envelope, the one from Sue in Henley.

Inside was a brief note and a photograph. He looked at the photograph first. It was one taken of him and Sue on the river at Henley.

Michael surveyed the photograph from over Gerald's shoulder as he tried to light a pipe, which just didn't seem to want to get going. "Pretty girl!"

"She is." Gerald sighed. "Put some tobacco in that pipe of yours. Ashes aren't good for setting fire to."

"Does it say anything on the back?"

"Erm... " Gerald flipped the photograph over.

Our special time together.
  Never forget us.
  With my love.
  Sue x

"And what does the note with it say?"

"It says, keep this photograph as your lucky mascot. We had a day on the river to start a lifetime of memories into our future." That's what it says. It's just a short note.

"I can see a couple of kisses there as well."

"Just a couple."

"She has it bad for you Gerry ol' boy."

The full letter read:

> *Wargrave Road,*
> *Henley-on-Thames*

My Dearest Gerald

I wasn't sure whether we might have chance to meet up before you get posted away. When I see you, I'm never sure when I'll see you again. Our summer has been so full of fun and laughter, just as the photograph I've enclosed shows. I got the photograph developed so you can keep this as your lucky mascot when you're doing whatever you are doing in your plane. What a day we had, a day on the river to start a lifetime of memories into our future.

I miss you already. Do try to see me before you go anywhere.

With all my love always,

Sue

xxxx

Wargrave Road
Henley-on-Thames

My Dearest Gerald
I wasn't sure whether we might have
chance to meet up before you get posted
away. When I see you, I'm never sure
when I'll see you again. Our summer
has been so full of fun and laughter,
just as the photograph I've enclosed
shows. I got the photograph developed
so you can keep this, as your lucky
mascot when you're doing whatever you
are doing in your plane. What a day
we had, a day on the river to start
a lifetime of memories into our future.

I miss you already. Do try and see
me before you go anywhere.

With all my love always,

Sue
xxxx

As Gerald read and re-read Sue's letter, Michael searched for his tobacco pouch and was now refilling his pipe. "Well dear chap, what's the other letter say?"

"You'd think these letters were for you, Mike!" Gerald shook his head and smiled as he opened Lizzie's letter. Michael now had a pipe which he could light and was eager to listen. It seemed to be the accepted rule that people read out their letters from home. It made those who had received nothing from home feel so much better.

Gerald extracted the letter.

"Look! There's another photograph in the letter ol' chap."

The photograph in the letter was face down, so no one could see what was on it as yet.

"So there is, we'll see what that is in a minute. Right, here we go then... keep quiet, I know what you're like for butting in, so let me read...

6 Ashfield Road
   Shotton
   24th August 1940

"Full address and date. Nice Gerry boy."

Gerald looked up and then looked back at the letter again.

"Dear Gerald,

It was nice to receive your letter last week.

Thank you for your birthday wishes. You never forget your Aunty Lizzie.

Francis and me are pleased you have found yourself a lovely girlfriend. We must get to meet her someday. It sounds like you are very busy doing what you are doing. I bet life has altered so much since your commission. Officers' mess and all that now for you. We are very proud of you."

"I bet they are ol' boy... you're a determined blighter Gerry boy. You'll go far, mark my words. AND we all want to meet this Sue for sure..."

"Do you want me to read on Michael, my old man?" Gerald responded with a sardonic smile.

"Of course, of course... I'll keep my big mouth closed."

"Right...

I got the photograph developed of you which we took when you were home last time. Got two copies, so perhaps you want to give this one to Susan for her to keep of you."

Gerald turned the photograph over and held it aloft for Michael to see and waited for the comment.

Gerald Davies at home in Shotton 1940

"Smart, good-looking young man, you are Gerry. That your gaff there?"

"Thank you, Michael, my man. Yes it is… MY GAFF… right, where were we… yes…

What else do I say. Yes, little Ruby is fine and she misses you. Vince and Cliff are doing well in school. We are hoping Cliff will get a job in the office at your old works if he carries on like he is in his tests. He's almost as clever as you are.

There's nothing else to tell you. Oh yes, the same day as your letter came in the post, a German bomber was shot down by brave RAF lads like you. We saw it right in front of our eyes. The kids were on the banks opposite the works offices and we ran for them and it all happened above our heads. Some metal landed right in the river by us.

But we are all ok."

"Bloody damn Jerries. They get everywhere. Wouldn't surprise me if a full scale invasion doesn't come soon. At least our lads saw 'em off... good style by the sounds of it. Your family were lucky, hey?"

"Sounds like they were."

"When you write back, tell them we'll give Fritz one from us when we get the chance."

"I certainly will. Last bit of the letter to come now...

Reminds me of Mr Churchill's speech, which Uncle Francis is reading for me now from the Daily Post. It's called 'Tribute to Fighters.' - 'The gratitude of every home in our Island, in our Empire, and indeed throughout the world, except in the abodes of the guilty, goes out to the British airmen...' That's you Gerald... 'who, undaunted by odds, unwearied in their constant challenge and mortal danger, are turning the tide of world war by their prowess and by their devotion. Never in the field of human conflict was so much owed by so many to so few.' Uncle Francis says the paper says they all cheered at this. We all agree with Mr Churchill and YOU are in all our hearts here in Shotton.

We know how brave you are and you'll be getting your posting to somewhere soon I suppose. Let us know straight away where you are going. I know you can't say exactly but a hint will be enough.

Right, I must go now.

All the street send their love and lots of love from us here.

Keep well and safe.

Aunty Lizzie

xxxx

* * *

That's it... four kisses ends the letter."

"FOUR kisses again. She's a nice old girl, is your Aunt Lizzie."

"More or less brought me up, did Aunt Lizzie."

"What about your mother and father Gerry?"

"Frank, my father. That's another story. My mother's dead."

"Sorry to hear that, Gerry. What happened?"

"It's a long story. I'll tell you again, hey. Not now. Not now, Michael."

Gerald sat down and looked at the letter, reading it several times again whilst Michael headed to get himself a brew from what was left in the green enamel tea-pot on a side table. He knew he'd asked one question too many. Gerald scanned the photo of himself set onto a postcard, wishing his mother could see it.

"Nice-looking lad..." came the voice from behind. It was Ron, one of the chaps he'd been commissioned with.

"You been listening in as well."

"Just caught the end of it."

"You'd better get a letter back, old chap, before we get posted. Rumour has it some of us will be down south in Spits and others are off to North Africa."

Gerald looked at himself. "Yeh, I'm not bad for a lad from the back streets of Shotton, leaning against a ladder in his best bib and tucker."

"How's that girl of yours, Gerry?"

Gerald pulled out the photograph of him and Susan taken on the river in Henley. He touched Susan's face on the photo. "She's a real diamond is Susan. A real diamond."

"We all want to meet her."

"I've told him that already," shouted Michael from the side as he poured milk into his tea.

You seeing her before we head off on posting?"

"Tomorrow, I hope. Tomorrow."

Gerald placed both photographs and the letter into his tunic pocket, patting the pocket flat as he closed the button, just as the scramble bell rang frantically.

Someone grabbed the hand cranked siren and ran out with it shouting repeatedly. "Raid! Raid!" He stood it upright on the grass outside the mess and began winding frantically. The whirr started slowly and grew to a full ear-piercing siren. The base was now at full action stations.

Gerald was out of the door within seconds and had headed, as he'd done several times before, to meet with Czech Pilot Sergeant Josef František. [2] Gerald had been tasked to retrain Josef. Not a simple task. Josef was a rule breaker and not a rule taker.

*

Group Captain Stanley Vincent [3] the officer in charge of Northolt had taken Gerald to one side and pointed out a sergeant on a bench in the sunshine. "I have a little task for you Davies."

"Sir."

"Yes, you're just the man for the job. Northolt has a reputation to uphold, and we have a bit of a bandit here." He pointed to a sergeant sat on a bench smoking a cigarette. "There's the damn fool who landed his Hurricane last week with the gear up. Damn fool forgot. Thought he was in one of those out of dated monoplanes with a fixed under-carriage. Nearly wrecked the Hurricane, but it's salvageable. Just! We can't have that again. He's grounded until you tell me he's fit to fly again. Give him a day or so, then test him out again. Give me the nod and he can get his wings again. I'll introduce you and let him know who's the boss, hey Davies?"

"Sir."

Gerald was left alone with Josef and the two sat awkwardly together on a bench in the sunshine whilst Josef lit another foul smelling cigarette.

"Gerald Davies. Gerry." He held out his hand.

"Josef František, but you can call me Yo."

"As in Yo-Yo?"

Josef looked perplexed.

"Never mind. Bad for your health, those awful sticks of shit."

"So is flying in a war Gerry and getting shot at, hey?"

"I suppose. You been in many dog fights Yo?" Gerald commented, showing his naivety.

"More dan most here even I sink. Not many can claim my, how you say… experience. I have flown more combats than I can remember."

"You have?"

"Was in the Polish Airforce when de Huns came over de border into Polski. Den I was in de Battle of France. Now I'm in de battle for you country, Gerry! I very proud to be doing dis. Look you…" He pulled a square-cross medal embellished with two crossed swords, hanging from a green and red striped ribbon, out of his tunic pocket. He dangled it just above the three sergeant stripes on his arm and against the word POLAND on his shoulder. "It should say Moravia here, hey! One day I will go home. Yes, I like to…dis is my Crow do Gware boys…" Everyone knew he meant Croix de Guerre. "Yes, I have, yes I have bringded down nine of the hun planes and shot more up on de ground… so they gave me their biggest medal. Load of litter though, hey? What matters is staying alive, not a medal."

"Is it frightening being in a dog-fight?"

"You don't want to know, but I can tell you this. You sweat… you sweat fear. De fear runs down your face, past your nose and your fear, it enters your mouse. It tastes salty does fear. So salty! You will surely find out de way we are losing so many peoples. Your turn is soon to come for sure."

Gerald took a gulp of air and shook his head. "So it is terrifying."

"You don't have time to be terrified, Gerry. No time. It is a moment. For some it ends in death for others, well, they live to fear again."

"You can create your own fear too…erm… someone tells me you've been trying to kill yourself by landing without wheels, Yo!"

They both laughed.

Josef took a long drag on his cigarette and then threw it to the ground a few feet away. "I was doing the pancake making, but it is now your Shrove Tuesday, hey." He laughed again. "It's caused me much trouble. Now you are here, to tell me how to fly. One who has not flown with the enemy. Ha ha. Is funny but not funny."

"I'm only here to keep you out of trouble, Yo. You play ball with me and I will get you flying in a few days. Sooner! You can train me, hey!"

"Okay, we play de ball then. De first thing I will tell you is dis... 'Beware of de gun in de sun!' Repeat it now Flying Officer Gerry."

"Beware of the gun in the sun."

"Again."

"Beware of the gun in the sun."

Josef lit another cigarette.

"Again!... but tell me mores. Thinks abouts it? What must you be then to be a successful fighter, yes?"

"Beware of the gun in the sun.... and... er... " Gerald thought for a moment, then put his finger up, as if still talking to Miss Jones at Shotton Central School. "And be the gun in the sun yourself."

"Dat is so right. First lesson is done Gerry."

The two shook hands.

The start of a wonderful friendship had begun and within three days Josef was back flying at the say so of Gerald. In return Gerald learned many things from Josef, most of all how to stay alive in aerial combat.

*

Czech Pilot Sergeant Josef František was up and away in the Hawker Hurricane as the raid came in on Northolt. Gerald ran for his life to a sandbagged area as the Luftwaffe dropped bombs all around. All Gerald could do now was keep his head down and hope Josef, somewhere up in the blue, was doing his best for Britain. Josef would go on to shoot down the greatest number of enemy aircraft of any foreign pilot in the RAF in the war.

*

The memory of the raid on Northolt faded into memory as Gerald drove off to Henley the following day. Being bombed was just another occurrence of war. It happened and as long as it happened and you didn't get injured then it didn't matter. It was a good half hour's drive, but at least the threatening rain held off. It might have been faster but Gerald kept a steady pace in his 1932 British Racing Green MG J2 Midget. The 847cc car had a top speed of just over 80mph, but the car was Gerald's pride and joy so he avoided excessive speed. The car was as thrilling to drive as any aeroplane he'd piloted. He'd bought the car second hand, as a treat to himself on gaining his commission, which he knew was a surety several weeks before it happened.

Sat behind the wheel in his RAF officer's uniform, he felt like a film star. Years before, he'd seen Fred Astaire driving the same car in the film The Gay Divorcee and promised himself one day, would own the self same car. Just as soon as he could afford it that was. That day had come with his promotion to Pilot Officer.

Gerald drove down the leafy back lane of Henley-on-Thames with the river to his nearside. The very first signs of autumn pushed its way out from the leaves in faded greens. He'd been to Wargrave Road several times now to meet with Susan Hall, his girlfriend of that momentous summer of 1940.

The day after his commission, new officer's uniform on, with his 'new-to-him' car, he'd gone off to a grass airstrip in the middle of what he thought was nowhere, called RAF Henley-on-Thames. He'd been sent there for just a few days for what they called familiarisation training on Spitfires. "Get yourself to Crazies Hill Farm," he'd been told as he'd saluted the wing commander shaking his hand on commission.

He'd replied, "Yes, sir," as he was handed some papers, then had to ask 'where the hell is Crazies Hill Farm?' to more than one person on the base. RAF bosses were notorious for their practical jokes. It was a good way of alleviating stress and letting off some steam in dangerous times. Gerald made the initial assumption it might be a joke whilst someone high up decided where he was being posted, but the papers he had in his hand said differently. He was going on 'a course' at what had been the RAF's Technical Officers School of Instruction.

'Accommodation to be arranged,' the papers had said.

It was a pleasant drive in the Berkshire countryside to Crazies Hill Farm - RAF speak for the base at Henley-on-Thames. As he drove into the chocolate box hamlet of Crazies Hill, Gerald couldn't believe his luck. This was an idyllic place where the Luftwaffe wouldn't even imagine there might be an airbase.

It was 11.00hrs when he reported in for induction. The first day was definitely 'familiarisation' - looking at Spitfires, seeing how they worked and sitting in them, without as much as flying one. The remainder of his days there he found out would be helping to fit Spitfires, which the base tested and put together, receiving parts from the multitude of manufacturers around the Reading area. This was war, and there was no such thing as an easy course. The course was just another way of learning on the job.

The base was nothing to look at, just a few sheds at the edge of a long field which served as a runway.

On Gerald's mind, all the first day had been where he might stay. With the six others on the course, he soon found out this was in the local pub. Gerald arrived at The Horns Inn at Crazies Hill, after six in the evening with five others from RAF Henley whom he barely knew. They were on the same course as him but through the day, he just hadn't got the chance to get to know any of them any better. He felt he'd entered some great Anglo-Saxon hall, full of smoke, the atmosphere jovial as he headed towards the bar with the others in tow. There was wood panelling and yellowed plaster everywhere. The high beamed ceilings meant it should have been a less smokey place but, a bunch of men, who looked like they'd just wandered in from a hard days' toil in the surrounding fields, puffed away on pipes and cigarettes causing a constant haze.

A bald man in his sixties, wearing a dirty white apron, limped forward from behind the bar.

"Been expecting you lot. You're late. There we are. That's the way it is. Frank!"

Gerald held out his hand. "Flying Officer Gerald D…"

"No time for formalities, youngster. I'm Frank R Burrough, the keeper of this inn and chicken head chopper-off-era." He cackled gruesomely and made chicken noises, ending with a loud squawk, and beheaded a pretend chicken on the bar with a karate chop of his hand. "You can call me Mr. Burrough. Wife is Edith… she's the cook, bed sorter and all sorts else. I'm the boss, though. Don't forget it."

<'Uncanny. Dad is Frank and his wife is Edith. Edie!'> Gerald shivered. These two names sat uneasily in his head. <'There's too many Franks in my life right now!'> Gerald couldn't help but smile to himself.

"Thank you, sir."

"Don't thank me. The government is covering this for you lads and we are grateful you know. Very grateful." He didn't seem it. "You lads pass through here and we never sees you again. Being killed like flies I hear."

Gerald looked back at the others. "Well, we all have to do our bit."

"Done my bit. The Great War." He pushed his hand down his right leg. "Blown up. Metal still in there." He felt more down his leg, as if looking for a particular spot. "Somewhere! Yes, lucky to be here. Dead lucky! Was in a bunch like you lot, then BOOM... we were all on the floor, covered in shit and I never saw the others alive again. Surgeons told me they took part of John's bayonet out of my leg... explosion clean tore it off his Enfield and into my leg. They reckon it was him who saved me. Took the blast and here I am."

"Good for your sir. One of our heroes of yesteryear. Good for y... "

"Less of the yesteryear sonny... but more of the hero will do." He winked.

A door from the back opened. A thin legged 4' 6" tall witchy looking woman, with an out-of-place pot belly, walked in. Her face was bright red and matching her face was a crimson silk scarf keeping her grey hair off her sweaty looking face. She wouldn't have looked out of place in a rockery with a fishing rod in her hand.

"This is my good lady, Edith. Told you not to stand so close to the stove. You'll go on fire one of these days and that'll be the end of it."

His wife ignored the remark.

"Gooday all." Edith nodded.

"I've told them who you are, Mrs Beetroot."

She ignored the remark again.

"Ignore Frank. Thinks he's funny. You are all very welcome." She looked more stern than Frank and proceeded in the same vein. "No drunkenness! No noise! No girls in rooms! Lights off at ten-thirty. Hearty breakfast at seven and hearty evening meal at seven. All cooked by me from our little farm behind. No choice. You'll get what's done and enjoy....oh, yes and by the way... get up late and there'll be nothing on your plate."

< 'Nothing in the middle of the day to eat?' >

"I know what you're thinking, gentlemen? What about lunch? You'll be at the base but if you want, you can buy something here, but it's not included. Right. Rooms... three to a room. Lump it or like it."

They all headed up an old set of uneven wooden stairs which led to an uneven floored tunnel of a corridor. The place smelled decidedly old and damp in places but, all the same, it was a place to get your head down after a long day. That was all that mattered.

Edith pushed the door open for Gerald and his two RAF comrades, Simon and Colin.

"If you hurry up, there'll be a meal downstairs in twenty minutes." She left and took the three others to another room in the inn.

The bedroom overlooked the front of the pub where there was a red telephone box. A useless piece of technology for Gerald as he wasn't aware of a single soul with a telephone who lived in Shotton, apart from the doctor that was.

*

Everyone was starving, so they made haste and were soon back downstairs in their civvies. Jackets and ties.

All six sat at a table in a back room and afterwards headed to the bar area.

"Your round Gerry!" shouted Simon as the five laughed and went off to sit down. Gerald headed to the bar alone and leant against it, waiting for the girl who was pulling pints for someone else to serve him.

Whilst he waited he flicked through a beer-stained and thoroughly crumpled copy of the Berks and Oxon Advertiser, dated the previous Friday 19th July. He took a breath <'How much can change in a few days. That time last week I was Sergeant Gerald Davies. Now here I am… Commissioned.'>

The front page was full of ads and the only bit in the whole paper which attracted Gerald's eyes was the editorial on Mr. Churchill, which reminded Gerald of home and the sacrifices ordinary people were making. '… this is the war of the Unknown Warriors, the millions of humble folk whose deeds will never be recorded but whose labour and self-sacrifice are contributing to save our land from Hitler and to free the nations that he has enslaved.'

Gerald felt good he was doing his part for the war effort and was lost in his thoughts just staring through the paper.

"Yes sir, can I help you?"

Gerald looked up over the top of the paper.

"Erm… yes."

She was blonde, a little younger than him, he thought, and an absolute corker to look at.

The girl's eyes lit up. "Well sir, do you want to order anything?"

Gerald fumbled his words, "Yes, yes, er... yes... you can..." as he hastily made a hash of folding the newspaper which fell across the bar and onto the young lady's feet. Gerald stretched over the bar. <'Beautiful legs too.'>

"It's rude to stare, sir," she smiled coyly.

"Sorry, miss. Sorry. Just wanted the paper". If there was such a thing as love at first sight, this was it. Hearts were racing, faces flushed and lips dried out.

"I'll get it."

Gerald didn't know where to look, so he looked back towards his colleagues for support. He already knew the order but sought confirmation for no other reason than he felt awkward. "Pints all round, lads. Bitter?"

"Certainly ol' chum... and one for the lady, hey," shouted Simon who'd watched the ongoing episode at the bar.

Gerald felt even more awkward now.

"Ninepence a pint. Six pints it is."

The pints arrived on the bar one by one and Gerald moved them across to the table until he waited for his, the last pint to be poured. Gerald held a ten bob note in his hand.

The pint arrived, creamy froth pouring over the top. Gerald ran his finger up the glass and tasted the froth.

"Great. Nice beer."

"You must be a connoisseur to know that from swabbing the glass." She laughed. "Four and six, sir."

"It's Gerald. Gerald Davies."

He handed over the money. His hand touched hers.

"I'm Susan, but everyone calls me Sue. I prefer Sue. Yes."

"Hello Sue. Pleased to meet you."

Susan headed to the till, looking back as she went. "Pleased to meet you too, Gerald. That'll be five and six change."

Susan arrived back with two half crowns and a sixpence. She took Gerald's hand and wrapped his fingers around the coins.

"Sixpence in there for good luck. Keep hold of that coin."

"I will, I will. Do you work here? ... er... stupid question. I mean, are you here most nights."

"Some, but not all. It's my part-time job, but not tomorrow or the next day. Only when Frank needs me. You can't get blokes behind the bar nowadays. They're all doing what you're doing."

Gerald nodded. "Yes. I do rather like the beer here."

"You haven't tasted it yet."

"Do I detect you're trying to find any excuse to hang on at the bar?"

"I could be" said Gerald, now tasting his beer.

"So it's good then?"

"Rather good. Served rather well too."

She smiled warmly. "Thank you."

Gerald saw no rings on Susan's fingers.

"I see, erm…" He touched his ring finger. "So what are you doing tomorrow evening?"

"That's a bold and quick proposal, young airman. I have a date, I'm afraid."

"Oh, you do. Sorry. So Sorry."

Gerald flushed and made to head off from the bar.

"Wait, you fool. Come back." Susan went into her coat pocket, which was hung on a nearby door. She pulled something out of the pocket and dangled a khaki armlet at Gerald. It read U.T.P.

"What's that?"

"It's my date."

Gerald looked perplexed.

"Upper Thames Patrol."

"Still means nothing."

"It's Home Guard. Patrolling the river and all that."

* * *

Image: Tatler Magazine - 13 November 1940. The Upper Thames Patrol Home Guard Women

Mrs Wider, General Commander of Women's Section (third from left at front) and **Susan (Sue) Hall** *on left front sitting down.*

"What, you're armed?"

"Not the girls. We can drive the boats, though. Maybe I'll take you on a boat one day. Maybe it'll be this week."

"Maybe it could be tomorrow."

"It's UTP at 7."

"I'll walk you there."

"Pick me up, can you. At six? Let's see if I can't arrange a boat ride and a date at the same time."

"So that's a date then Sue."

"Perhaps it is. I'll leave a note with Frank and when you get back tomorrow from base, ask him for it."

Gerald headed back to the table with his RAF colleagues but kept his eye on Susan for the rest of the night.

Author's Note

[1] Northolt Airbase - used during Second World War by both Royal Air Force and Polish Air Force. First RAF station to operate the Hurricane.

[2] Josef František, DFM & Bar (7 October 1914 – 8 October 1940) was a Czechoslovak fighter pilot and Second World War fighter ace who flew for the air forces of Czechoslovakia, Poland, France, and the United Kingdom. He was the highest-scoring non-British Allied ace in the Battle of Britain, with 17 confirmed victories and one probable, all gained in a period of four weeks in September 1940.

[3] Group Captain Stanley Vincent.   Northolt Commander. He camouflaged the base, so it resembled civil housing. The result was so effective that pilots flying to Northolt from other airfields often struggled to find it.

Chapter Thirteen

'Goodbyes'

It was September 1940, and it was Friday the 13th, when King George VI narrowly escaped what the Daily's would describe as a *'thoroughly nasty bomb-shower'* which hit Buckingham Palace and 10 Downing Street in unprecedented daylight raids on London.

That very same day, the Italian Tenth Army advanced into Egypt, causing the small British force at Sollum to retreat in haste to a more defensive position near Mersa Matruh. The Italians advanced 59 miles in three days, stopping close to a Bedouin village called Sidi Barrani, which they began to fortify whilst waiting for reinforcements and supplies. Thus began Operation Compass for British forces, and the Western Desert Campaign swung into action with an immediate build-up of British forces. Despite the disaster at Dunkirk, the RAF were ordered to move bombers closer to the Egyptian frontier to support ground troops and so on 14th September 1940, Gerald had been posted to serve with 211 Squadron who were already fully engaged in actions against the enemy in the area.

It was the day after the palace bombing, and it all happened at an alarming pace. He was back at Northolt again for a few days. He'd been due an evening off and had arranged to see Susan later that evening, then at 11:00HRS sharp a briefing had been called by Group Captain Stanley Vincent. Vincent led from the front and wouldn't ask anyone to do something he wouldn't do himself. Frequently, when the base was under attack, he'd flown up alone on what he called 'station defence sorties' and had a considerable number of enemy bombers under his belt. He would later be wounded in the back flying one such sortie and would be awarded the DFC for his skill and bravery.

So, Vincent's reputation went before him and he was highly respected. Everyone stood up as he entered the room.

"I have called you gentlemen to this briefing as you are my finest airmen," he had begun. "Some of you have already seen action in the skies above this glorious land. Some of you haven't but you are all here because you are men I can trust to do a magnificent job."

Gerald had now flown several sorties from the Henley area in Fairey Battles and had gone over to France on propaganda leaflet drops. He'd had flak and some near misses from enemy fighters, but had always come back to base in one piece. Base had always been Britain, too. Where would they be going?

"The enemy are preparing themselves for an invasion, that is for sure. We have seen their preparations on the French and Dutch coast, but our bombers have done well and we have inflicted some considerable damage on their forces. Still, they are ready to come over and invade."

Vincent owned the room when he spoke and everyone listened enraptured, captivated by every last word. Everyone expected to be detailed to a local bomber or fighter squadron. They were all pilots and all were expected to fly whatever machine they were given, with the minimum of training.

Vincent pulled down a map. It was a map of the southern Mediterranean. North Africa and Egypt. The map was replete with black and red paper arrows showing on the ground troop movements.

"This is the Western Desert gentlemen. Make a mental note. This is where you'll be headed."

There was a quiet mumble of chatter across the room. No one had expected this.

"Quiet gentlemen!" an officer at the side shouted.

"The Western Desert is hotting up, if you'll excuse my pun."

The room laughed nervously as one. Quiet descended again without a word having to be spoken.

"Yesterday, the 13th, the Itis, in the form of the Italian 10th army, invaded Egypt from Libya. There's a whole bunch of 'em. Possibly up to 150,000 on the march towards Sidi Barrani here."

Vincent used a baton he picked up from the nearby desk to point to a nondescript town on the north coast of Egypt.

"Our boys, marked with red arrows, have headed to the area to stop them in their tracks. The Kingdom of Egypt and more importantly, the

Suez Canal are at risk if they are not stopped. We have over 35,000 troops already in the area with another 27,000 or so, we can call upon who are based in Palestine." He pointed Palestine out with some aplomb.

Palestine in Gerald's head was the place of Jesus and the Bible. Egypt was the place of the pyramids.

"Strategically the Suez Canal is our gateway to the Far East and our empire beyond…Australia, India, you name a pink place on the map and it'll be got to via the canal."

Everyone in these days knew pink was the colour of the British Empire. Schools taught geography by pink coloured nations.

There was more mumbling and quiet talking as Vincent took a sip of water.

"Right, settle down gentlemen. Complete silence and attention to the front."

Vincent moved nearer to the front of the gathered servicemen.

"So, I still hear you say, what the hell in damnation are we headed there for, when we have a country to defend from the huns? Well, I'll tell you this, the Itis have been buoyed-up by our little setback … and yes, it is a defeat of sorts at the hands of the krauts at Dunkirk between 26th May and 4th June last. Mr. Churchill himself has called this a colossal military disaster for the country. So the nasty little Itis are trying to take advantage of our misfortune at Dunkirk and are assuming an imminent German invasion of our shores… "

Vincent walked further forward amongst the men in the room who numbered no more than a dozen. He was nodding to himself in a self-satisfied way. "They presume wrong, don't they gentlemen?"

All nodded quietly and people looked at each other approvingly.

"I can't hear you. They presume we will not jump in to defend Egypt by deploying more of our forces there. But they are wrong, aren't they?"

Everyone nodded and shouts of "Yes!" They do!'" "Bastard Itis!" could be heard in the room.

Gerald nodded quietly.

Vincent went back to the map.

"They are no more than sixty miles into Egypt, and the French on the Tunisian side here have ensured the Itis can't throw their full weight at their offensive by opening up a second front on their western side. Major-General Richard O'Connor is commanding our forces there, and his brief is to prevent those Italians from reaching Suez. The eastern front of this offensive."

He slapped the map with his baton to reinforce this.

"Our job will be to help them from the air."

"When do we go, sir?" came a question from the floor.

"Impatient already, Jennings! You'll get your turn at them and soon enough. O'Connor has demanded reinforcements from the air as a matter of urgency, so we are making plans right now for urgent departures of much needed aircraft."

Vincent hadn't finished with the map yet.

"The Italians are under the command of someone called Marshal Rodolfo Graziani. Don't know him, but if he's like the other Iti leaders we know of, he won't be fit to run a boarding kennels for poodles."

Everyone laughed and there was the odd dog bark from the room, which gained disapproving looks from the officer at the side.

"Having said that, we must NEVER underestimate the enemy. As we speak, they pour along the North African coast and may be capable of overwhelming our lines. They get no further than the coastal town of Sidi Barrani." He slapped the map again.

"Tonight gentlemen, many of you will go into action for the first time. Even getting there will be a dangerous journey. We have suffered heavy losses just making our way over France to Malta, which is your first stopping point. Over three quarters make the journey, but that means a quarter doesn't. Your individual orders are on the side over there, and you will be given them one by one as soon as I vacate this room. Good luck and godspeed gentlemen."

With that Group Captain Vincent called Gerald across. "Follow me, young man." Vincent walked out , closely followed by Gerald, as everyone stood to attention at their departure.

Gerald followed Group Captain Vincent to his office. There was another man stood there in an RAF uniform - a corporal. He couldn't have been no more than 18 or 19 years old and was a good five or six inches over six foot.

"Pilot Officer Gerald Davies, this is Corporal... er... it's Frank Lee [1] isn't it corporal?"

The two shook hands as Gerald looked up at the enormous frame before him.

"You can call me Chris, sir," replied the man being over both. "Christopher is my first name. Frank's the middle handle."

Hello Chris!" Gerald replied confidently, still not knowing who the person was or why he had been introduced to the corporal.

"Fran… Christopher will be coming with you later, so you know. He is an important passenger. Intelligence Officer, that's all you need to know. You will need to look after him and the plane to make sure his precious cargo gets there."

"Yes sir, you can rely on me," replied Gerald. He looked at Chris. "You do know we… er… we only have a Blenheim at our disposal, not a huge Vickers Wellington, don't you Chris? Rather small inside… are you ready to be a sardine?"

Christopher smiled and the others laughed.

It all happened at a frightening pace, but luckily he had the afternoon to get a message to Sue. At least the pub had a phone and he knew she would be working at lunchtime.

*

It was just before two in the afternoon when Gerald managed to get to use the phone at Northolt. The phone rang to the point where he thought no one would answer and he was just about to put the phone down when Edith, the landlady at The Horns Inn answered.

"Horns Inn, Crazies Hill. How can I help you?"

"Gerald here, Mrs. Burrough."

"Who?"

"Pilot Officer Gerald Davies."

<'*Christ I'm there all the time. Don't you know who I am by now?*'>

"Ah, yes, Gerald." She was very formal and was using her best phone voice. "How can I help you?"

"Can I speak with Susan… er… Susan… Sue please."

"She's just serving at the bar at the moment."

"It's urgent."

"Can you wait one moment, please?"

Edith never waited for the reply, and Gerald heard the phone being placed down onto a solid surface. In the background he could hear people laughing and glasses being collected together. He heard shouts of "Sue! Sue! Telephone for you. Your gentleman, I believe."

It seemed minutes but wasn't when he heard glasses being placed down next to the telephone receiver.

"Hello."

"It's me, Sue. Me."

"Gerald. We're seeing each other after. Why are you calling now? I'm working." She went into a whisper. "You know Mrs. B hates me using the phone in work time."

"I had to call you. I can't come tonight."

"You can't come? But I haven't hardly seen you this week."

"I can't come, darling. I can't come. I'm… I'm…"

"You're going away. That's what you were going to say, wasn't it?"

"I'm afraid that's the truth. You know I love you and I want to stay but…"

"You don't have to say it. This is war. When are you going?"

"It's today. I have my orders. It's today."

"And it's away? I mean proper away?"

Gerald nodded and said nothing. Tears filled his eyes.

"Are you there still, Gerald?"

He nodded again.

"GERALD?"

"I'm here and yes. Don't know when I'll be back, darling."

I can't know where you are going?"

"You know not to ask."

"I'm sorry. I care for you dearly and want to know you are safe."

"I'll write to you when I can. I'll write to you."

Behind Gerald another RAF officer had arrived and although he said nothing, it was obvious he was next in line for the telephone.

"Yes, you must write. Please write. I love you, darling."

Susan was in tears. Gerald was in tears.

"I love you."

"Love you."

With that, Susan was gone. Gerald was left holding a phone and looking at the officer waiting to use the phone. He tried to hide the tears in his eyes but failed. The officer had seen it before. Now the officer had to give his wife the same bad news Gerald had just given Susan Hall.

*

Departure hour was midnight. He was heading to join 211 Squadron and he'd heard so much about them and their charismatic leader Squadron Leader James Richmond Gordon-Finlayson whom everyone either called 'G-F' or 'The Bish.' He'd been in charge of the squadron for a year bar a week - since 21 September 1939. The Bish was only four years Gerald's senior, but from all accounts he was a force to be reckoned with and his dad was a big-wig in the army. General Sir

Robert Gordon-Finlayson. *[2]*

Gerald and The Bish were from such different rungs on the social ladder, he wondered how he would get on with his new leader but there was one thing bugging Gerald. <*'Gordon-Finlayson? I know that bloody name. Where the hell do I know it from?'*>

Gerald contented himself that he'd probably heard of The Bish's rather infamous father and thought no more of it.

Gerald thanked his lucky stars he had managed to speak with Susan and he thanked God the weather was very unsettled for the time of year. It was raining in Northolt and there was a forecast of thunderstorms in all areas including over the English Channel and into France where heavy cloud might help make his journey safer and keep the hun fighters away. He had asked one of the lads on the base to take his beautiful 1932 British Racing Green MG J2 Midget to Susan in Henley for safekeeping and gently caressed the steering wheel one last time before he headed off.

A truck took an unusually quiet group of men out into the blackness of the airfield and they were dropped off by their respective 'kites' as the ground crew hailed them. The ground crew wound the engines vigorously and each of them sputtered into life with a huge roar. Three Blenheim Bombers would leave that night precisely on the stroke of midnight. All were full to the brim with fuel, just enough to make the journey to Malta and not much more. Gerald had planned the journey meticulously. There could be no room for error. Usually, they would be a three up crew but for this journey, with added cargo, they were just a crew of two.

Gerald thought of Susan going to her warm bed as he gave the thumbs-up to the barely visible ground crew at Northolt and taxied onto the runway in the Blenheim. Gerald was a pilot in his own right, but first and foremost he was a highly respected navigator and bomb-aimer. This was the start of his night flight to Malta. He'd only had a few hours to plan the journey, but after the call to Susan, he'd gathered his crew together and planned the journey in every detail. This included Corporal Chris Lee, whom Gerald had only just met and who Gerald had instructed would take on the role of Air Observer.

"If you've got such an important message to deliver - I assume that's what it is, then you'll need to be as sharp-eyed as anyone to make sure we all get there without a hitch."

The corporal had nodded as he'd squeezed his big legs into a space not fit for legs six inches shorter.

Gerald wanted to ensure nothing would be left to chance, and this new member of the crew would have to play his part. The ground crew pulled the chocks away and bid the flight crews 'good luck.' They had been responsible for the last minute inspection certificates being signed up, so the Blenheims could safely taxi away. The aircraft, plus their cargo was much needed on the battlefront. On board with Gerry was also Pilot Officer Arthur Geary, whom he would get to know more than most in his time away. Both had their regulation twenty pounds personal luggage with them - each individual's bag had the things they valued most. For some it was their favourite pipe. Most carried images of their loved ones, whom they thought they might never see again. Chris Lee's luggage contained a brown envelope which no one had seen.

Taking off at the same time were others he would get to know really well in the coming year. All headed to join 211 Squadron.

"Right chaps, let's get these kites up up and away. Safe flight all. Keep radio contact to a minimum," Gerald firmly implored on the radio as he waved to ground crew who gave thumbs up galore in return. Gerald was first down the runway, the lead aircraft of three making the journey that night. Gerald's Bristol Mercury engines roared away in the black of the wartime aerodrome. All you could see was the blue after-burn from the twin engines as the planes one by one roared into the night sky. Then they were gone.

It was a formidable journey to Malta and the aircraft flew out of sight of their comrades at 10,000 feet, down towards Le Havre and Honfleur where they saw some battle raging below. No one had thought to tell them there was a night raid by the British on the go. Bombs were being dropped and German searchlights harassed the sky, followed by colourful shell bursts well below.

Gerald crackled on the intercom, "We should be safe at this altitude gents. The flak is set to explode anywhere below 8,000 feet."

"Let's hope the calculations are correct then," someone crackled back.

There was always a concern some different settings may be used, and Gerald hoped none of his colleagues had bought it and felt nervous seeing the flak lighting the sky below. Luckily, too far below to be a worry to them. There was still the concern of enemy fighters though and all eyes were on the night sky which was lit up by an almost full moon looking like a lustrous white puff-ball in a sea of twinkling button mushrooms. Gerald couldn't help but marvel at the night sky and, despite the war raging on and the dangers this brought, he was thankful this was his lot. He thought of the Lizzie's kindness to him and felt comforted but she had her own life to live and the RAF was his family now. The service had taken him away from a home he hated to a place he loved. He pulled the collar of his jacket against the cold of the inside of the cockpit and thought of Susan.

<'I've found the right girl for sure. My beautiful Sue. She'll be my family, when this lot is over.'>

The turbulence was almost constant as Gerald's aircraft lurched and jumped its way through the darkness of the night, heading towards southern France and on over the Mediterranean towards the southern tip of Sicily. This was a good eight-hour flight and fuel would be an issue. The plane was flying to the limit of its fuel capacity. For sure, Gerald knew the fuel endurance of the plane he was flying, having checked and re-checked it again and again in missions up and down Britain. He flew on through the darkness and as the darkness became the light of a beautiful Mediterranean day, the roar of the engines created a calm and tranquillity of their own. The noise was the security they were working well. He knew engines inside out, having worked on them before his commission. The engines tonight sounded better than ever and he was comforted. In his comfort, his thoughts once again turned to Shotton, and he wondered what Lizzie and Francis and their young family might be doing. <'Sleeping you idiot.'>

He laughed out loud.

"What you laughing at my old mate?" Arthur Geary asked with a yawn on the crackling intercom.

"Nowt. Nowt. Just keeping myself awake."

"You'd better not fall asleep or I'll be chucking you out me'self and you'll wake up floating down over a hun's gunboat," laughed Arthur Geary.

The three planes were now completely out of sight of each other. All were full to permitted weight of urgent supplies and spares for Malta, which was in the process of being reinforced to threaten the Italian supply route to Libya. Luckily, the weather was kind once they were away from northern France and made the journey a lot easier. Soon, in the early morning sunshine of the day, Gerald eased back the throttle and they glided down into Malta alone, the engines now almost functioning solely on fumes, such were the tight fuel margins involved. Valetta aerodrome beckoned, and Gerald was happy to see the other Blenheims safely already on the ground there.

A night spent in Malta would have been just the ticket, but these weren't times for catching your breath. Ground crew unloaded the essential supplies and refuelled the empty tanks. Gerald and the others debriefed and caught up on some much needed shut-eye. Not enough though before dusk arrived and they were all back in the Blenheims again.

Destination Ismailia. Egypt.

Author's Note

[1]   Christopher Lee, famous for many things including being Dracula in films enlisted in the RAF in 1940 and worked as an intelligence officer. He was posted to North Africa, specialising in decoding German cyphers. He was based with the Long Range Desert Group. The LRDG eventually became the SAS.

After arriving at Ismailia in Egypt, he made his way across Tobruk to Benghazi and beyond. He was fluent in several European languages and could therefore move easily behind enemy lines. He made his way through Italian and (eventually) German bases, sabotaging planes and airfields along the way.

Little is known of his heroic deeds during the Second World War, as Lee rarely spoke about his exploits and his records remain classified to this day. He was decorated for his services in several countries following the war.

[2 General Sir Robert Gordon-Finlayson KCB CMG DSO (15 April 1881 – 23 May 1956) was Adjutant-General to the Forces. He became General Officer Commanding-in-Chief, Western Command in 1940 Knight Commander of the Order of the Bath, Companion of the Order of St Michael and St George, Distinguished Service Order.

He was responsible for the Army Council introducing a colour bar, whereby only those of pure European ancestry could be commissioned as officers.

Chapter Fourteen

'Meet The Bish'

As the Blenheims headed in the general direction of Alexandria in Egypt, a decision was made to follow the Libyan coastline for ease of navigation. The crews found themselves staring out across beautiful serene blue water to port and to starboard, desert interspersed with fertile spots where people and crops could be easily seen. It looked idyllic.

The surprise of the early morning was when Gerald inadvertently flew over Italian forces at Sidi Barrani, 80 or more miles east of Tobruk. The Italians were as much surprised by the arrival of the Blenheim as its crew were and sprung into action thinking a raid was imminent.

"Jesus! Itis!" shouted Gerald, as he pulled the nine boost lever for emergency speed and banked to port, gaining height to get out of the way of pop shots now coming up from the ground and exploding around the plane. The crew laughed with nervous excitement at the near misses and felt relief as they left the enemy without a kill. A lesson learned for both sides. Gerald was sure he wouldn't repeat that mistake again.

For the remainder of the flight they kept the coast at a reasonable distance, but always still in sight as the emerald sea shone below them like verdigris on some vast flat roof in the sunshine.

As they saw Alexandria in the distance, Gerald flew low to the coast and looked out below to a scene reminiscent of books he had read in his childhood about Ali Baba and the Forty Thieves. Men in long flowing robes with heads almost fully covered by patterned shemagh scarves flowed along poorly made up roads, or lolloped awkwardly behind ungainly looking camels loaded to the hilt with goods for market in Alexandria. Horrible little dust devils spiralled nastily on the road, as if looking for their next victim to throw sand at.

"Looks hot down there, Arthur," Gerald shouted.

"Hot enough for a cool beer, I think Gerry lad."

Chris Lee gave the conversation a quiet thumbs up. He hardly spoke all journey. Gerald put it down to one of two things. Speaking wasn't within the remit of Intelligence Officers, or he was just overawed as a young corporal with two officers on board.

They all licked their lips at the thought of cool beers and proceeded on, flying right over Alexandria, following the fertile plain of the Nile south towards Cairo. This was a different world and the British who flew over it for the first time in 1940 were at once besotted with its beauty and its mixture of medieval with modern. Great feluccas, with their huge white sails, looking like something more akin to the Mary Rose, moved serenely along the waters with their cargoes, whilst the city bustled with noise and traffic. There was much military activity below, and preparations for war could be seen everywhere.

The pyramids before them and the great sphinx were a marvel to behold and Gerald flew around the great stone objects more times than he could care to remember to take in this awesome, once in a lifetime sight, peeling off east after a few minutes to head toward the West Bank of the Suez Canal and the city of Ismailia, their eventual destination.

*

A pale blue RAF flag with a Union Jack at its corner welcomed them to the RAF base at Ismailia, which was enormous compared to Malta where they had left just a few hours previously, this was testament to the build-up of allied forces in the area. A nice smooth landing on a tarmac runway and Gerald taxied the plane as directed by ground crew to a stand alongside other 211 Blenheims and several dated Gloster Gladiators from 80 Squadron. These would be the planes, with their crews who would fight the Italians they had just been shot at by. He could see no new Hurricanes or Spitfires here, everyone knew they were the poor relations and the need to defending British shores from the Germans was paramount. Dunkirk was still fresh in the memory and Gerald recalled the day at the end of May when he'd been scrambled, as part of Operation Dynamo, to help defend the stranded troops on the beaches of Dunkirk. He felt helpless as he dropped supplies for the scurrying little ants huddled below, who waited patiently for Churchill's armada of small boats to arrive to take them back across the Channel to the safety of British shores. He knew the boats were on their way as he'd passed them, flying almost at the mast level of some boats, to keep under the radar. People on the boats had waved and they'd waved back. Everyone was glad to see an aircraft. It made them feel safer. Gerald didn't feel that way. He felt pretty vulnerable. The Blenheim wasn't a powerhouse of a plane and he'd had several run-ins with the Luftwaffe before. The Blenheim was no match for the speed and firepower of a Messerschmitt 109, so they had to be careful and keep low. This was a time of no respite as the Battle of Britain raged at home and invasion worries were of paramount concern to every soul in Britain. Now he was fighting the same war but had been called to stranger sandier shores for that purpose.

In grateful thanks for the plane getting them to Egypt with the minimum of fuss, Gerald patted the side of the dusty Blenheim. "Good old girl." He whispered, but loud enough for Arthur Geary and Chris Lee to hear.

Chris Lee expressed his thanks for getting him safely there as Arthur Geary shouted, "You're a big softie, Gerry lad."

Gerald was thinking of a reply when they were approached by one of the ground crew. "You're the last to arrive today, so you're all here, apparently. The Bish wants you three to go straight to the Officers' Mess. Debrief and brief, I believe. I'll show you chaps along."

The walk to the Officers' Mess was a few hundred yards through a plethora of hastily erected temporary buildings with tents flapping noisily in the ceaseless arid wind. There were other buildings which looked like they'd been there for decades, such was the build-up of sand on the side from those prevailing scorching desert winds. Gerald, Arthur and Chris were shown in to the Officers' Mess and both couldn't believe their eyes. The place had been decked out like some country bar at home. It even had wooden beams, or at least what resembled heavy wooden beams across the ceiling and walls, rather like The Horns at Crazies Hill. The only thing which gave away its location were patches of sand which had blown through cracks in the walls. The bar was surrounded by about twenty or more men in uniform, some in their long trousers, but about two-thirds of them were in their desert shorts AND they needed to be. It was sweltering hot. A portrait of the King overlooked the noise of jolly conversation on the go, which was interspersed with regular bouts of laughter. Beer and spirits flowed freely at the bar, behind which were shelves full to the ceiling with bottles of pale ale, brown ale, whisky and a variety of other beers and spirits. One or two noticed the newcomers walk in. Gerald noticed the others who had flown across with them. They were already in conversation with the most senior officer there, the man with three shoulder stripes, which gave away his rank. He was the newly promoted Squadron Leader and Commanding Officer of 211 Squadron, James Gordon-Finlayson, who'd been in Egypt just short of a year. His brown sun-seared leathery skin, with deep eyes giving him a distinctive young Churchillian look. He was incongruously stood next to a captured Italian flag and was dressed in shorts and a shirt, looking like a boy-scout touting for bob-a-job work. He immediately shouted across, in a rather eloquent upper class twang, "Gentlemen, come in. Come in!" He shouted loudly for all to hear, "The last of the sprogs are here gents!"

Most of the bar turned around. Glasses were spontaneously raised and several shouts of 'welcome chaps' resounded across the room. As people returned to their conversations, The Bish beckoned them across.

"Gerry ol' boy. Nice to see you again." The Bish said, shaking his hand warmly.

"Yes, sir." Gerald looked slightly puzzled. The Bish looked across to Arthur Geary and shook his hand "Ol' Gerry doesn't recognise me, hey? And he's brought me a new kite to play with."

Gerald was thinking quickly. Then it came back to him.

"Pilot Officer Finlayson from Sealand back in '36 or thereabouts. I knew I'd seen you before. You took me on my first flight."

"Gordon-Finlayson. G-F. The Bish as I'm called."

"They called you The Bish back then. I remember. So, so good to see you sir. You've done ever so well. Squadron Leader now, sir."

"Despite nearly getting fired for trying to light-up near a fuel dump!" The Bish laughed ferociously. "Yes, dear boy, I'm the best there is... er, but less of me. Thinking of doing well, you've come a long way too. I saw lots of potential in you then." The Bish looked across to Arthur Geary. "He started off as the lowest of the low and now look at him. Pilot Officer Gerry. He's a good man is Gerry. A hard worker." The Bish looked back at Gerald. "Hard worker you are. You'll go all the way to the top I can see it. Wing Commander Gerry Davies. Suits you ol' boy." He winked.

"Well, I never sir. It's great to be back with you."

The Bish looked back at Arthur Geary. "What this man doesn't know about planes isn't worth knowing. Stick close to him, I should."

"We're a team already, sir."

"Good show, boys. Right, who is this man here?" he asked, looking at Corporal Chris Lee.

"I have an envelope for you, sir," the corporal replied, patting his bag knowingly.

"In good time, young man. In good time." The Bish then looked back at Gerald. "Right, what can I get you boys to quench those sandy tongues of yours?"

Within a minute The Bish had cool beer ordered and both downed the drinks as if it was their first ever taste of beer. The three clinked their glasses together joyfully, and with that he grabbed the corporal and took him off to one side.

The two sat at an empty table and chatted over the contents of the brown envelope, the papers of which now were being closely examined by The Bish.

*

Chris Lee came over to Gerald and Arthur and shook their hands. "I'm off, gentlemen."

"So soon?" enquired Gerald.

"Have my orders. The Bish has his and he'll talk you through them soon. Good luck!"

That was the last Gerald ever saw of Chris Lee but not the last of what he came to know as Intelligence Officers with sealed orders from H.Q. The Bish called everyone to order and began to speak, welcoming the latest arrivals and once again singing the praises of Gerald who felt a little embarrassed at the attention. The de-brief, if that's what it could be called, turned into an easy-going briefing about the latest orders brought in directly from London by Gerald's flight.

"Italian bombers are massed along the Mediterranean coast as are their tanks and heavy equipment. We know some of this already… "

Someone shouted, "Bloody Itis… we've seen 'em. They're everywhere."

"150,000 and more coming our way. A major attack is imminent by air and land. We now know a little more about their strategies, their positions and strengths… of course knowing this we now know their weaknesses and tomorrow we employ our best men… i.e. you chaps, to bomb the hell out of the little buggers."

There was a loud cheer followed by immediate silence. The Bish was an expert at motivating the men in his command, but he was noted for his easy laid-back style. He was in his usual high polo-neck sweater, which stood out against his slate blue RAF officer's tunic. The monochrome blue shade for the RAF in 1940 wasn't quite the colour as chosen and designed by Major General Mark Kerr when the Royal Flying Corps ceased to be with the establishment of the RAF, as an independent service when it came into being on April Fool's Day in 1918. The colour of the very first RAF uniform came by chance. In 1917, a Russian war department had bought in large quantities of a wonderful pale-blue cloth for use by the Imperial Russian Cavalry. Then the October 'Bolshevik' Revolution occurred, rendering obsolete the need for this vast swathe of material. The entrepreneurial Mark Kerr bought it up and so the RAF uniform colour was born, but as an exact colour of blue for the RAF, it was to be short-lived as it was unpopular, making its wearers, especially with the gold-braiding, look like some attendant at the front of some posh hotel. By 1919 the pale-blue had been superseded by a more serviceable blue-grey colour which The Bish and his gathered team of officers now smartly sported, as they talked informally together, planning the missions ahead.

Gerald was more than ready for his bed, but there was more to do. The Bish wanted all of 211 Squadron gathered in the Ops Room to go over what the officers had discussed, so everyone knew what would happen, particularly tomorrow. Gerald headed over to the Ops Room with The Bish and Arthur Geary. Gerald expected the Ops Room to be some grand building, but it turned out to be only a crude and roughly built wooden cabin-like structure set in a depression in the ground on the air base. It rather looked like Dorothy's house from The Wizard of Oz, which Gerald had seen with Susan Hall at the Regal Cinema in Henley just a few weeks before.

<'One strong gust and it'll be away into the sky.'> He laughed to himself but immediately ducked down to the sound of shots fizzing and rattling out from a Lewis gun not far behind him on the base. Arthur Geary had ducked down too, as had a few others new to the camp.

"Save the nerves for another day chaps. We don't have the luxury of a bell at Ismailia to call everyone together for a briefing, so the order of the day is for everyone to show up at the sound of the Lewis."

Gerald breathed heavily and tried to look as if he hadn't been frightened by the gunfire. "Just testing us hey, Skipper?"

The Bish elbowed Gerald and winked. "Does us all good to know when to duck. You never know when it might be the real thing, hey, Gerry ol' boy?"

Gerald sighed. The Bish heard the sigh but said no more to Gerald, continuing his welcome speech to those gathered, some of whom had heard it before.

"So, here we are in Egypt, the land of the pharaoh. Been British since Napoleonic times and we want it to stay that way. The Suez is important to us and to our ships so, our mission is to stop the Iti in his tracks, turn him around, and stop him getting anywhere near Suez. Right, gentlemen!"

"Go Greyhounds!" *[1]* several shouted as Gerald watched on.

"And if we can we'll have time to have a look around at the antiquities... tell them about the place Willie. Incidentally, Pilot Officer Williams, for you newcomers is one of the SIOs *[2]* we have with us, he's our more permanent one, aren't you Willie.

Willie nodded.

"Willie is our resident Egyptologist. Yes, I kid you not, he used to lecture in Cairo University, didn't you dear chap? Clever man."

Pilot Officer Willie Williams, a man who looked like he should be at home retired and in his slippers with a pipe and a black Labrador, stood up. He'd done this speech twice before. And, yes, before the war, he'd been a lecturer at Cairo University.

"You are in a very special land, gentlemen. I know we are at war, but take time to appreciate your surroundings too. It is a privilege to be here in the land of antiquities. To follow in the footsteps of distinguished men like Flinders Petrie... "

<'Flinders Petrie?'>

"I see the puzzled looks on some faces. Sir Flinders Petrie was the founder of modern archaeology. He's the chap who first devised a system for dating archaeological finds through looking at the least important things, such as pottery fragments, which until then everyone ignored. You know what people were like then... they went for the artefacts that might sell. That's how he funded his work back at the University College of London, where he was Britain's first professor of Egyptology."

The officers nodded, lots of them disinterested, but others like Gerald were attentive and interested to hear more. This was education the likes of which Miss Winifred Jones at Shotton Central had never given.

"So, as a lecturer at Cairo in Egyptology, I've followed in the footsteps of Flinders Petrie. Did you know he was interested in eugenics chaps?"

Gerald quietly shook his head. <'Eugenics?'>

"You know, the science of improving a population by controlled breeding, rather like the Nazis with their Aryan 'Master Race' nonsense. He sent pictures, even skulls and things back to his friend Francis Galton in Britain. Galton was architect extraordinaire behind the world theory of Eugenics. They put people away, even in Britain, because of his theories on the subject. You know undesirables, the sick, weak… imbeciles and insane they called them."

Gerald drifted away into his own thoughts as Willie the Egyptologist carried on with his impromptu lecture on Egypt. All he could now think about was his mother, who'd been taken away from her home AND HIM, many years before.

<'Eugenics took my mother from me!'> kept repeating in his head.

*

As The Bish dismissed everyone, he could clearly see Gerald was consumed by a complete daydream. "Gerry ol' man. Wakey wakey."

"Sir!"

"Ah, with it are we?"

"Sir."

"Got a minute?"

"Sir. Yes, sir."

The room was now empty save for several irritating flies and the noise of the incessant ceiling fans rotating away, doing their best to keep the room cool but failing miserably.

Gerald looked worried. In his head he thought he'd done something wrong. Perhaps he'd flown too close to the Italians and risked losing the plane. Perhaps he should have avoided going over Le Havre. All these thoughts cascaded in his head. Either way, he thought he was in for a bollocking of sorts.

"Just wanted to say again a big welcome to the squadron, Gerry. You're not here by accident, you know. When I spoke to old Stanley Vincent at Northolt about the men coming to the squadron, he mentioned you were there. I couldn't believe my luck. I told him I just had to have you in The Greyhounds."

"Thank you, sir."

"Don't thank me, you're the man with the skills," he said, as he held out his hand for a firm handshake. "I've sort of watched your career develop and I've heard great reports about you Gerry ol' chap, since you got your commission. You're going places, lad. You need a bit of neatening around the edges to make you one of us, but you're a superb pilot and a navigator beyond reproach I hear. Look Gerry lad, you're a good all round RAF man and that's difficult to find nowadays. Everyone seems to have joined because of the war and has barely five minutes in the job. You're different. You've got RAF written through you like a bar of Blackpool rock. You're so like me, ol' boy. You joined up the same year, so you've been in the service since '36."

Gerald nodded and listened. He thought he wasn't like The Bish. The Bish was confident to the point of being arrogant at times and had an ego Gerald could only dream of. His rudeness and contemptuous manner was legendary, although Gerald had never experienced this. The Bish had been nothing but kind to him and the two had formed a bond even as far back as 1936 when they would all head out to Chester for the odd night out together.

"I was in the Cambridge University Squadron… did Law by the way ol' man… before joining up, and I always knew what I wanted to do. Like you, I'm RAF to the core."

"Sir."

Gerald couldn't match that education or intellect. He'd been to Shotton Central School, and even with great teachers like Miss Jones, it was a place for the production of factory fodder which, in the main, taught woodwork or, if you were a girl, cookery and home management. Gerald didn't have a proper exam to his name, save for the dozens of RAF tests he'd successfully passed of which he felt proud of. And of course he had his Sunday school and school reading awards. That had to count for something.

The Bish had a first in Law and lived in a big house on the coast. The coast he could match, as he lived alongside the tidal flow of the River Dee, but the house no. Lizzie's house was a terrace, as was the inaptly named Dee View, but it sounded good on his service record.

The Bish continued. "You joined because you wanted to make a career of the job. Four years' experience these days is, for me, like coming into possession of a gold bar. As you know, I joined as a Pilot Officer and look where I am now. Just over four years later and I'm Squadron Leader. As I told your friend Mr. Geary, you're heading the same way Pilot Officer Davies."

"Thank you, sir. Thank you, but I'm... "

"No condemning yourself, ol' man. Take the compliments as intended. It's all your hard work and commitment which has made you what you are. A good RAF officer and a credit to the service, and I know you're going to be a great asset to The Greyhounds."

Thank you, sir."

"We're going to get along just fine, you and me. I so know it. I suppose you want to know where I'm going with this conversation, dear chap?"

"I do, sir, yes."

"Look, not wanting to blow my own trumpet, but I'm here in command of this squadron because I'm the best pilot and leader there is... "

<'Not because your dad is General Sir Robert Gordon-Finlayson, General Officer Commanding-in-Chief, Western Command, including forces in Egypt and Adjutant General to the forces, appointed by King George.'>

"... I want a man I can trust right with me in the plane. Several little birdies tell me you are the number one at your job - flying, navigating, bomb-aiming. You name it, you can do it, so I want you with me from now onwards. Where I go, you go. Got it?"

"Thank you sir, yes, sir."

"Oh, and when I'm not here, you know, attending high-level meetings and the such like, within a year, you'll be the one running the show. You know, ensuring the ground crews are on their toes, giving us aircraft in tip-top condition and all that, hey. "

Gerald WAS taken aback! So much adulation coming his way from G-F. "Sir." He added with a solid conviction.

"And Mr Geary? Should he be our third man in the Blenheim?"

"Most definitely, sir. He's a good man, is Arthur Geary. A good and trustworthy man."

"Good, that's settled. It's me, you and Mr. Geary. Now go and get some rest or see the sights and sounds of the area. Tomorrow you might be in the thick of it - not much down time here for any bugger, I can guarantee you that."

Gerald saluted and left the room with the biggest smile possible on his face.

Egypt seemed a far cry from Britain and felt like going back to the dark ages. Fields were irrigated by hand with water being drawn from the Nile by a variety of archaic means, counterweighted pots called shadoofs, swung water from the river whilst others used a hand cranked Archimedes' screw to do the same to water their crops of cotton, maize and wheat. Flocks of colourful birds flew from the Nile reeds and a fangled tractor ploughed a field, but the main ploughing was done with oxen and a wooden plough; the sort we all learned about in school which farmers in the middle-ages used.

Thin cats sat in the sunshine everywhere, as people rode by on donkeys as if anticipating some second-coming. Camels were the dominant beast of burden though, and could be seen everywhere carrying weighty loads or just simply transporting humans around the place. It was reminiscent of biblical scenes Gerald had studied at Sunday school and it wouldn't have surprised him had Moses stopped him to say hello.

*

He found his bed in a tent strapped down with sturdy guy ropes on the outskirts of the aerodrome and at once set about writing letters home. One to Lizzie and one to Susan Hall.

In Britain, Autumn was well on the way and wet Atlantic westerlies had settled in across the country, when the letter fell on the mat at 6 Ashfield Road in Shotton. Francis had headed off to the steelworks and the children were all in school when Lizzie picked up the letter. The writing once again gave away the identity of the sender. Lizzie eagerly pulled the envelope open, careful not to rip it.

H.Q. RAF M.E.
Cairo
Egypt

Dear Aunt Lizzie, Uncle Francis & children,
I'm now thousands of miles away from you, living in a damn tent like some soldier in the American Civil War, but you shouldn't worry, it's very comfortable and it's never cold. The opposite is true, as it's just so hot here all the time. It took one heck of a long time to get here and we saw action on the ground below us as we came, but nothing which caused us a problem. I assume the RAF have notified Frank I am on posting, but I doubt he might have told you.
<'He hasn't, damn fool of a man.>'
I miss you all, but it's an exciting place to be is RAF xxxxxxx.

Would you believe it, I've seen the pyramids (I flew right past them and then did it again just for fun) and I've seen Cairo as well, what a busy city that is. Glad I don't live here permanently, although I could get used to the warmth. Then there's the sand. The sand is bigger than the ocean across to America out here and it has dunes as big as any wave on the ocean in a storm. You could get lost in a moment if you were unlucky to go down into it. No intention of doing that, so don't worry.

Oh yes… and the sun is so bright here, we've been issued with new-fangled tinted goggles so we can see better and they stop that damn sand getting into our eyes. I'm with a great crew here and am making new friends every day. The old hands here call us 'sprogs' as we are new to the place and it's a keen learning exercise as there are local customs we have to watch out for. I think the actual locals like us, we're a dammed site better than the alternative for them.

Some good news to end with. I'm now working as second to our squadron leader. Who said the boy from Shotton couldn't come good?

I'll sign off now and try to write in a few weeks. Goodness knows where I might be and what I might have done by then. Keep smiling and give all my love to the children.

Love to all and kisses.

Your Gerald xx

HQ RAF ME
Cairo
Egypt

Dear Aunt Lizzie, Uncle Francis & children,

I'm now thousands of miles away from you, living in a damn tent like some soldier in the American Civil War, but you shouldn't worry, it's very comfortable and it's never cold. The opposite is true, as it's just so hot here all the time. It took me heck of a long time to get here and we saw action on the ground below us as we came, but nothing which caused us a problem. I assume the RAF have notified Frank I am on posting, but I doubt he might have told you.

I miss you all, but it's an exciting place to be in RAF [redacted] Would you believe it, I've seen the pyramids (I flew right past them and then did it again just for fun) and I've seen Cairo as well, what a busy city that is. Glad I don't live here permanently, although I could get used to the warmth. Then there's the sand. The sand is bigger than the ocean across to America out here and it has dunes as big as any wave on the ocean in a storm. You could get lost in a moment if you were unlucky to go down into it. No intention of doing that, so don't worry.

Oh yes... and the sun is so bright here, we've been issued with new-fangled tinted goggles so we can see better and they stop that damn sand getting into our eyes. I'm with a great crew here and am making new friends every day. The old hands here call us 'sprogs' as we are new to the place and it's a keen learning exercise as there are local customs we have to watch out for. I think the actual locals like us, we're a damned site better than the alternative for them.

Some good news to end with. I'm now working as second to our squadron leader. Who said the boy from Skitton couldn't come good?

I'll sign off now and try to write in a few weeks. Goodness knows where I might be and what I might have done by then. Keep smiling and give all my love to the children.

Love to all and kisses

Your

Gerald
xx

Lizzie was thrilled to read the letter and couldn't stop holding it in her hand, looking at it constantly and repeating the phrase quietly, "working second to our squadron leader… clever lad."

*

Squadron Leader James Gordon-Finlayson 'The Bish,' Gerald Davies and Arthur Geary, flew their first operation as a crew together on 21 September 1940. This would be the first of many raids they flew together and they would become a formidable team. It was a night raid on Sidi Barrani and the ack-ack was as intense as Gerald had ever experienced, but they were there and back before Gerald had had time to worry about anything.

Gerald found himself at The Bish's side as air-observer, in Blenheim L8511, watching the rising Egyptian sun, as their plane, almost hidden by a huge vortex of sand, left the sandy runway. The Bish was lead aircraft of just two which took off early that morning. The plane headed out over the immense expanse of the Mediterranean, with the island of Crete visible dead ahead. About thirty miles from the North African coastline, they altered course and headed west over a warm Mediterranean Sea. Gerald was content to be with the experienced G-F and knew exactly what he had to do as air-observer and bomb-aimer. With Arthur Geary as air-gunner he contented himself he had found his niche in this awful war. This was the very first time this team of three had flown together, but it wouldn't be the last by a long way and thereafter the formidable team became known as 'The Bish Boys.'

Gerald sat over two cells, which made up the Bristol Blenheim bomb-bays. Today the aircraft was carrying four 250lb bombs winched into the bomb bays by ground crews at Ismailia.

It wasn't long before they were over the Italians at Sollum, on the North African coast, just west of Sidi Barrani where the Italians had fired at his aircraft just a day or so before. And they were firing again.

"AA coming out boys," shouted Gerald calmly though the fizzing intercom, as he saw the bursts from the ground followed swiftly by thuds and black shell bursts around them which rocked the aircraft.

"Damn Itis. Target dead ahead." The Bish crackled back.

The Bish and Gerald communicated constantly, even though the din in the cockpit was almost unbearable. Close co-operation was key and the intercom, despite its crackly nature, was vital.

"Good wind speed skip."

"Straight and level Gerry."

"Drift correct."

Gerald, as bomb-aimer, was in his fold-down seat, which he'd readied for the run-up to the target area. He folded himself over, almost prone over a sighting panel which was mounted on the starboard side panel enclosing the control and instrument panel at the very tip of the nose of the Blenheim.

Credit: Wings Over Olympus. T.H. Wisdom. Gerald to the right, in the fold down seat and The Bish piloting to the left. 'Height bar and scale' is the 'stick object' centre front. See [3] below.

"Almost over target skip," Gerald cooly replied, as he eyed up the ground, looking at Italian armament dumps and heavy equipment visible through poor camouflage along the coast below.

Then the primary targets came into view. What the briefing had described as the main core of troops and heavy equipment - tanks and lorries amongst little white buildings below. Now Gerald could do what they had come for. With his right hand he gripped 'the tit,' the bomb release button he'd used many times before when dropping propaganda over France in what now seemed like the distant past of the war but in reality wasn't that many months behind him.

"Bombs gone."

The plane jerked upwards with the loss of the weight and The Bish banked away tightly with some gusto, as the following Blenheim dropped its load. Ack-ack came fast and furious and the plane lurched with the explosions once again, sometimes flying directly through the smoke which, had they fired moments later, would have downed the aircraft. Beads of sweat had appeared on the faces of all three of the crew of L8511, not that anyone noticed. All had been too busy fighting the fight to notice how terrified they all were. The fear only kicked in once they had done 'the business.' To a man, they all wanted to get away as soon as possible. Of course, no one talked about being terrified, but everyone knew it. As they headed away, Gerald looked through the plexiglass which gave him a splendid view of the ground below as huge white smoke clouds from the exploding bombs appeared and fires raged in the aftermath. Gerald couldn't help but think, <'Jesus, that could be me down below.>

He thought of the futility of war and hoped he had caused damage to enemy equipment and not caused loss of life. He knew this wouldn't be the case though and tried to dismiss the negative thoughts from his head.

His machinations over the chaos on the ground were forgotten when the intercom once again fizzled into life. "Good job gentlemen" The Bish crackled out. "Rather, a good job, I think chaps. Gerry ol' man, do you play bowls?"

Gerald laughed with some hint of nerves in his voice. "No skip. Why?"

"Those bowls you dropped hit the jack spot on. You should take bowls up, hey?"

"Perhaps I should skip. Perhaps I should."

"Job done, boys, let's head for home. Drinks are on me tonight."

Not all the raids were simplistic and without their trouble, though. After an intensive raid on Tobruk on 25 September 1940, Gerald's aircraft developed a fire in the starboard engine. It had been touch and go whether they would ditch in the sea, with their plane constantly losing power, but they were able to nurse the aircraft over 90 miles to a forced landing at Ismailia.

*

Over the next weeks, planes and supplies arrived constantly at Ismailia, ferried in by RAF personnel from Britain from places across the globe. Bomb dumps were replenished and everyone on the base below the rank of Sergeant was issued with a rifle, such was the proximity of the enemy. New communications were installed across the base, so there wasn't the same need to fire the Lewis Gun to call everyone together.

The raids continued on Italian positions at Tobruk, Sidi Barrani, Buq Buq and Sollum almost daily, except for the odd day. The vulnerable Blenheims of 211 Squadron were protected on most occasions by the

Gloster Gladiators from 80 Squadron who regularly flew missions alongside them. All bomber crews were thankful for the protection, despite these planes looking like they would be better suited to flying over the trenches of the Somme in the Great War.

Night raids also began with regular drops of 25lb and 4lb incendiary bombs, which destroyed Italian fighters before they'd even taken off. With the air support, the British ground troops, who now were numbering in their tens of thousands, made significant advances against the Italian forces, driving them back into Libya.

Besides Ismailia, over the next weeks and months Gerald operated from several bases in North Africa, depending on the job in hand, some of which had the most unpronounceable names you could imagine - El Daba, Fouka, Ramleh, Abu Suweir, Semakh and Quotafia. He knew first hand why he was now part of The Greyhounds.

Author's Note

[1] The Greyhounds - nickname for 211 Squadron. Because they could move easily from one place to another and did so frequently during the Second World War.

[2] SIO - Senior Intelligence Officer

[3] The Air Observer's Equipment - Gerald's bread and butter!

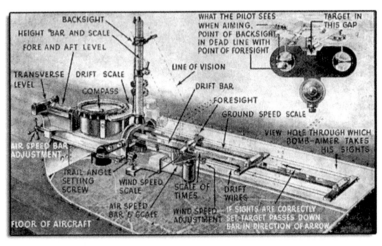

Illustration: Britain's Wonderful Air Force.

Chapter Fifteen

'Gloster Gladiator Giant'

On the morning of the 18th September 1940 The Bish had led a team of eight Blenheims with their escort of 80 Squadron's Gloster Gladiators on a daylight bombing raid of Italian air strips in Libya. The Blenheims had attacked in twos and Gerald, as bomb-aimer, honed his skills to perfection, scoring several direct hits on enemy planes before they'd had any chance of taking off. One had even been taxiing along the runway when he'd caught it with a direct hit. Momentarily, he'd thought about its poor unfortunate pilot then, shaking his head, had put the thought away somewhere deep into his mind.

Flying in the desert was unrelentingly hot and tantamount to flying around in the mouth of some huge dragon. The heat was often intense and only made bearable by the thought of a swift scoop or two back at the bar in Ismailia.

These were also strange times in more ways than one. It was obvious from the outset to Gerald that there could be long periods of inactivity and he had to make the most of these as those periods of inaction were, with much certainty, followed by moments of downright terror.

Gerald had been a new arrival on the 15th, but by the end of the 18th September he felt like an old hand at the base. New arrivals had arrived through the week and had bolstered the numbers at RAF Ismailia. All would get the customary 'gippy-tummy' which Gerald had succumbed to and was just getting over. So having a toilet was a great welcome relief. The other 'welcome relief' was the Officers' Mess where the constant dangers of flying bombing raids against the Italians could be shelved for a couple of hours. So it was, that evening, Gerald found himself with The Bish and Arthur in the Officers' Mess at Ismailia.

The Bish was recounting a tale from a few days before Gerald had arrived at Ismailia when a group of the lads from 211 Squadron had headed off to the horse races at Alexandria.

"Won £30 I did," he said swilling the last of his beer around the bottom of his glass in readiness to drink it. "That's why I'm buying the drinks at the moment" he chortled. "Won't last forever, so enjoy a free one on me whilst you can. Barman, same again!" he shouted as he emptied the glass. He came closer and whispered in Gerald's ear, "Was a bloody mistake too, ol' man. I backed the wrong horse, which turned out to be the right horse, by mistake!" He roared with laughter.

These were early days for Gerald and flashbacks of the heavy ack-ack fire constantly flew through his mind. He shivered and tried to forget these thoughts, concentrating on getting to know the people who now circulated in and around the bar. 'A-flight,' which The Bish led, were a tight bunch but Gerald was himself a newcomer to the place and he hadn't got to know people properly yet, even from his own squadron, so he excused himself and mingled with others in the bar. The men weren't just from 211 Squadron but were from at least two or three other squadrons. Some of these were fighter pilots from 80 Squadron and he'd seen there had been new arrivals again to bolster the fighting power of the RAF in Egypt. Gerald knew these people would be his protection and the more he got to know them, the more likely they would be to come to his aid.

He'd also seen the arrival of Hurricanes that very day and he felt even more secure now the bombers he flew in might be afforded the protection of this much heralded aircraft. He knew of Blenheims shot down in the past month by Italian bi-plane fighters, the last of which was a Squadron Leader Bax [1] who'd gone down after a lone Fiat CR.42 had strafed him from behind over Derna, a city to the west of Tobruk - this was only a week before he'd arrived in Ismailia. From all accounts he was now a prisoner of the Itis, but he no one knew for certain, such were the unfortunate circumstances of a war where communications were poor on all sides.

As Gerald observed the people in the bar, his eyes were drawn to one big smart chap in his best RAF shorts. He couldn't help but notice him, as the man was even taller than Chris Lee, who had travelled to Ismailia on the plane with them on the 15th. He even thought it was

Chris at first, but then he saw the Pilot Officer single bar insignia on his shoulders. Then he remembered watching him coming in to land at Abu Suweir on the Suez Canal, in a Gladiator fighter a day or so ago. He'd seen him struggle to get his six feet six frame out of the cockpit. How a man of his stature could fit into any flying machine was a wonder to behold. In fact several of 211 Squadron had stopped what they were doing to watch him several times get himself in and out of his plane and they'd all laughed and joked about him calling him the Gloster Gladiator giant. The *Triple-G* as they shortened it to.

The Triple-G was standing on his own, pensive and sipping slowly a cool beer.

He walked over. "Gerry Davies." He held his hand out and the two shook hands.

"Roald. Roald Dahl."

"Roald? Unique name."

He nodded. " Erm... yes... named after Roald Amundsen, the great Norwegian explorer."

"The one who beat Scott to the South Pole?"

"Well, I haven't heard of another one."

The two smiled.

"I, er, we, er... saw you and the Gladiator Roald. It's a small cockpit."

"Containing a big friendly giant, I know. Everyone has had their pen'th of laughter over it. Do you know all the fighter lads back home are in Hurricanes and Spitfires and they gave me this heap of camel dung when I got here the other day. The Gladiator would have been out of date for the Battle of Agincourt, never mind the Western Desert."

"That inspires me with confidence." Gerald laughed. "You fighter pilot lot are supposed to be the ones protecting us when we're on missions."

"Are we? Jolly well hadn't thought of it in that way. I haven't been here long enough to know yet, dear chap. Tomorrow one has told me to go off and find my squadron, which is now camped somewhere in the desert. The place name sounds like a Camel fart at the dead of night. Mersa Matruh or something similar to that it's called."

"Yes, that's where 80 Squadron are, I believe. Flown over the place this week but know little about it, other than the place is right on the coast. Beaches as white as snow there. It's right at THE FRONT, you know... next place along the coast is Sidi Barrani, where the Itis are holed up. 211 have bombed the place to buggery a few times, but they're still there, glued to the place like limpets. They're raiding us from there all the time.

"So I hear. We'll jolly well have to put a stop to that then won't we? You and your Blenheims... er... and me and my Gladiator!"

"You got much experience in that kite?"

"Experience. Erm... don't make me laugh. I enlisted in Nairobi... "

"Nairobi?"

"It's a long story. I'd been working for Shell in Tanzania when old Bwana Hitler - that's what the locals called him - came on the scene, so I jolly well thought it my bounden duty to join the war effort. Hell's teeth and bloody damnations, though! It was 600 miles from Dar-es-Salam in my old Ford Prefect to the nearest RAF recruiting place, which was Nairobi in Kenya."

Gerald listened on eagerly, fascinated by this imposing man.

"Nearly getting eaten by crocodiles on the damn way as I crossed a river, I was! Anyway, to cut that long story short ... er ... Gerry is it?"

"Yes, Gerry, it is." Gerald took a gulp. He knew the Nile contained huge crocodiles. Everyone had been told not to go swimming in there. "Crocodiles!"

"Yes dear man. Crocodiles... " Dahl came in closer to Gerald, snapping his teeth together and hissing heartily, like some great story teller in front of a big audience. "Lots of 'em there were. Snap, snap, snap, they went. Their long mouths... big enough to swallow my car had they wanted... were full of sharp bayonet-like teeth, which they could have easily chewed the metal to pieces with." He hissed again as his eyes widened, as if the fear of that day was still with him. "Surrounded my car they did and they bloodthirstily eyed me up as their next meal... " He sighed and went quieter. "But three shillings lighter in my pocket... and six sturdy chaps who charged me that exorbitant sum, pulled me out and I was back on my way."

"Lucky escape."

"A good ol' jolly more like in the African bush. Let me give you some advice dear man. Jolly well live your life and live it to the full. That's my motto! If one lives a mundane everyday existence, all one will jolly well have, at the end of the day, will be mundane tales to tell... er... or no tales at all. One has to live a life of adventure to have lived, but in all of that, don't try to get killed dear chap. That doesn't help ones future life."

"I think we're in one huge extraordinary adventure right now,

Roald!"

"Where was I, erm... yes. I enlisted at Nairobi. First things first, they sent me for a medical and the rather good humoured RAF doc told me *'big legs and planes don't mix'* but he passed me anyway, saying there was no height restriction on pilots as far as he could tell from the regs... and added, rather meaningfully, it was my funeral if I couldn't get out in an emergency. He wished me good luck all the same."

"You are pretty tall, Roald - we watched you getting in and out of the Gladiator. *Triple-G.*"

"Triple-G?"

"Gloster Gladiator Giant. Was our little joke you know, seeing you struggling folding those knees up to your chest. It was just like seeing someone stuffing a jack-in-a-box into a box two sizes too small... you got in part way, then you kept springing back out again."

Gerald laughed away.

"Hilarious for you all. Well, at least that's a new joke, I have heard no jokes about my height before... EVER. So it was you lot chuckling away at my expense. I see. Well, you won't be laughing when you need my expertise to shoot down the Itis coming for you." He elbowed Gerald's arm and smiled. "Good to get to know you, Gerry. Drink?"

The two ended up at the bar with their backs to The Bish and Arthur, who were propping it up.

"There were sixteen of us who trained to fly in Nairobi. Leading Aircraftsman rank they gave me at first."

"Ditto Roald. I came through the ranks."

"Learned to fly in a Tiger Moth. What a plane! Loved it. The workhorse of my flying training it was. One seat for the instructor and one for me. Great plane. Trouble for me was once again my height. Sitting on the damn brolly..."

"The parachute..."

"..., yes, the parachute turned me into something like a giraffe piloting the plane. My face was stuck eight or more inches higher than anyone else's, so the wind caused me havoc and I could hardly breathe once the plane was in the air."

"So how did you sort that then?"

"Well, the instructor asked me enough times whether I wanted to continue. *'Your tall build,'* he kept saying and then he would add *'hmm... not good!'* I think he wanted me to pack it all in. Parkinson was his name. I sorted it by wearing a cotton scarf. Simple as that.

Have you ever flown a Tiger Moth?"

"Worked on one, but nope, never flown one."

"You should try the Tiger. Thinking of flying... let me tell you a little story. When I got here in Ismailia, I spoke to some idiot of a Flight-Lieutenant who showed me to the Gladiator I'm flying. It was him who told me about joining the rest of the lads tomorrow. Well, I jolly well smiled at him with, you know, the sort of grin one has when one wants more information. Then I asked him who would train me to fly the plane and he laughed at me, calling me an ass. He said *'how can someone train you in it, there's only one cockpit, you idiot!'* He told me to just get in it and try it out for myself. That's when you must have seen me - going between here and Abu Suweir."

"So how did you get your commission Roald?"

"By chance, I think. As I said, there were sixteen of us training to be pilots. It jolly well seemed an arbitrary thing, they gave half of us commissions, so I became Pilot Officer with seven others and the other half became Sergeant Pilots. Then they split us again into either bomber of fighter pilots. So I'm a fighter pilot. You?"

"I started exactly like you as an Aircraftsman. 1936 I signed up. Long story. I had such problems at home and I just had to leave. I didn't even consider flying, but this bloody war started and here I am."

"Yes, us going to war with Germany and Italy has moved things on at a faster pace. I've come a long way since I joined up in Nairobi just after the start of the war as a Leading Aircraftsman, but all wanted to do was fly."

"So where you from?"

"I spent my first few years in a little place in South Wales. You wouldn't know it, it's called Llandaff... near Cardiff."

"Well, you might have a Norwegian name old chum, but it seems you're Welsh then like me... only you're the southerner and I'm the one from the better part of Wales. The North. Little place called Shotton."

"Never heard of it and, as I said, I'm not technically Welsh not with a surname like Dahl. I'd be Jones, or Roberts or whatever your surname is again?

"Davies."

"There we jolly well are then. Davies, a good old Welsh surname you've got there."

"So are your parents living back in Blighty then?"

"Only my mother alive now and yes she is. So where does the

Gerald come from?"

"I'm apparently named after some First World War army officer and it's my mother who's dead."

"Sorry to hear that old chum."

"Been dead since 1930 and... you wouldn't want to come to Shotton away. Filthy, smog ridden, industrial hole, on the banks of the Dee."

They both laughed.

"So, I thought you might get to fly one of those Hurricanes that've arrived?"

"I was hoping so, but right now it looks like I'm stuck with the out-of-date Gloster Gladiator. Last in and all that... er ... yes, the Gladiator... er ... couldn't chase a bag of dates with wings and it hasn't got a radio, would you believe it. No navigation stuff either."

"So I hear?"

"One has to find one's own way by map on the knee apparently, but, hey-ho, it's got great fire-power. I suppose I should thank my lucky stars for that. I still can't get my head around the fact the machine guns fire through the propellers. First time I did it, when we were on a training exercise, firing at a canvas drogue behind an aircraft, I thought I was going to shoot my own propeller off."

Gerald laughed.

'Do you fly the Blenheim Gerry?"

"I fly, but right now I'm a navigator with The Bish" he nodded back over to The Bish, who was only a couple of yards away.

"Ah yes, I've heard of G-F. Jolly good man."

"He certainly is. Great pilot, too. Just before coming here, I was flying at Woodley Aerodrome. Training Polish pilots. Great lot."

"No Gloster Gladiators for those fighter boys in England, so I hear. It's Hurricanes and Spitfires all the way now with Bwana Hitler ready to cross the channel... and rightly so. I just hope we get more Hurricanes here and I get to fly one. The Itis won't know what's hit them then."

"Tell me about it. Love the Blenheim, but the old girls are struggling nowadays against the speed and capabilities of the new bombers out there. We all could do with something better but as you say, it's Britain's defence which has to be a priority for Mr. Churchill."

"You should be proud to be one of the Blenheim Boys. You're pretty famous everywhere nowadays."

"Even in deepest darkest Africa?"

"Even in Dar-es-Salam. All I can say is hats off to you, lads. You're the bravest of the brave flying in those things. Right at the front of everything going on, but it's the Spit lads who are flying high with praise nowadays."

"Yes, and they surely deserve it, Roald."

"And you lads don't? Don't jolly well do yourself down, Gerry. You must have been in the thick of it so many times."

"Just once or twice."

"Where did you train to fly then Gerry?"

"Back home, lots of places. Going solo is by far the most frightening thing, wouldn't you say?"

"Funny you should jolly well say that dear man, the biggest problem one has encountered so far is flying solo. There's no training goes along with a Gladiator, after all there's only one cockpit. They put one in it, sometimes they show one the relevant controls, but they assume one has learned all that in the Tiger. They pats one on the back and then they says *'off you go!'* One taxis about gingerly getting used to the rudder control, throttle and all that... er ... and then comes the time one has to head down the damn runway. It's a steep learning curve and a killer one if one doesn't get it right."

"Tell me about it!"

"After a few circuits and one or two dodgy landings when you get away by the skin of your ass. Fly or die, we call it."

"What squadron are you with again?"

"80 dear chap. It's going to involve air-to-air combat and not a soul can teach you about that. It's the deep end and we've all been chucked in before we can swim properly. Flying is great. Being shot at, not so great, hey! Those who survive will be those who learn quickly, the lucky ones are those who get chucked in near the side, so they can cling on without getting out of their depth. "

"So bloody true. Tell me about it. We've had new close calls already. Luck is the right word. I have my lucky photo."

Gerald pulled the now tatty photo of himself and Susan from his shirt pocket.

"Pretty girl. A veritable Vera Lynn doppelgänger."

"Dopple... what?"

"Lookalike, dear chap."

"Yes, she is. Shall we sit down? Fancy another Gerry?" Dahl made a drinking gesture.

Gerald had hardly finished the drink he had. "What the hell. Just a small beer Roald, thanks."

Dahl headed to the bar and was soon back with two Whitbread beers.

"The locals don't like us having a drop of the old ale here, but for God's sake we're defending the place from the Itis and soon the Jerries, if you'll excuse me using that word Gerry."

"That's the joke I've heard a million times before, too."

The two clinked bottles and laughed, just as The Bish and Arthur Geary came across to sit down.

"Couldn't help but overhear ol' man, you came from Nairobi here?"

"Yes. Nairobi," answered Dahl.

"I'm Squadron Leader James Gordon-Finlayson... "

"Roald Dahl, 80 squadron, sir." He raised his glass as a quiet cheers.

The Bish continued. "Nairobi... January to September last year was there. Aide-de-camp to His Excellency, Air Chief Marshal Sir Robert Brooke-Popham."

"The Governor of Kenya."

"Then you know him?"

"He was well gone by the time I got to Nairobi. He'd resumed his active service with the outbreak of war."

"Yes, I knew he'd been put in Nairobi to prepare for a potential Iti invasion, after the damn Itis had invaded Ethiopia. Clever man, do you know, the first thing he did in Kenya at the outback of war was to intern all the Jerries... " G-F looked at Gerald and smiled. "Sorry, Gerry ol'man."

"Gerald looked at Roald and chortled. "Just as I said... "

"Yes, he did that and commandeered all the kites in the country. Shame I couldn't have helped him, but the very day war broke out I was on a plane to Cairo. By the 21st of that month I was with 211 and here I've remained ever since. Old Brooke'm is back in Blighty I believe."

"Well, from all accounts sir, you are the right man for the job here in Egypt and you and your lads are certainly keeping the Itis in their place."

"We like to think, so don't we lads?"

"Yes, we'll drink to that," added in Arthur Geary.

"Then I'll do my best to be as protective to your squadron as I can and I look forward to working with you boys."

"We'll all drink to that" Gerald said.

The ale had been flowing freely that night and G-F spontaneously burst into song, gathering all the men from the squadron around him they sung the squadron song all to the tune of *Everybody's Doin' It, Doin' It…[2]*

Early in the morning, ate the break of dawning,
  See all the Blenheims, lined in a row,
  See the flight mechanic, turning little handles,
  Chuff, chuff, chuff, and away we go.
  Two Eleven's shaking 'em, shaking 'em, shaking 'em,
  Two Eleven's shaking 'em, shaking 'em, shaking 'em,
  See that shower of sand over there,
  That's the Greyhounds doing their share,
  You'll get a salmon sandwich if you get there,
  Two Eleven's shaking 'em now!

*

The sun was just leaving the sky and a beautiful orange glow pervaded the cloudless Egyptian skies as Gerald looked out from the airbase at Ismailia the following evening. Darkness came at around 7.30pm and this was a welcome break for everyone, as it seemed the only time of the day when the flies ceased their endless attacks on the exposed skin of anyone who they came into contact with. No raids were planned for the night of the 19th September, so The Bish had invited all to the infamous Canal Club by way of welcoming them into the squadron. Gerald was on his fifth day away from Britain, but he felt like he'd been here forever gauged by the amount of things he'd done in such a short time.

When 211 weren't bombing the hell out of somewhere or someone, the socialising never stopped. Tonight would be no different, despite a few people having ghastly heads and husky throats from the raucous singing which went on until later than Gerald could care to remember.

So it was, gone half nine at night, Gerald headed off with The Bish, Arthur and what looked like almost everyone from 211 Squadron to what everyone described as the most special place in the area. This was Gerald's first visit to the tall colonial Canal Club building, sat on the edge of a welcome cool breeze from the Suez Canal. The streets of Ismailia bustled with locals going about their business now the temperature had dropped, but it was still what anyone in Britain might term the hottest day of the year at anyone's guess. Oxen pulled cart loads of every conceivable cargo you might think of and women dressed as if they'd just walked from a straight out of the Gospel According to Saint Luke, limping and gliding their way in noisy sandals along narrow streets, some with loads looking like they should be on the back of an oxen cart. Filthy, half-naked children and beggars, some with limbs missing, hung around street corners with doleful eyes cadging money and goods from passers-by, especially from the throng of western military people now in the town. All in apparent contrast to the ruler of Egypt, King Farouk I who lived a lavish lifestyle whilst his people often couldn't afford one square meal a week or even a month.

Gerald had had little time to see the sights and sounds of the area, other than from the skies, and this was his first glimpse at a life he could only think of as being something akin to what medieval Britain might have looked like.

The inside of the Canal Club was altogether different. The club exuded colonial charm and smart waiters in white moved graciously amongst lavish dining facilities which Gerald had never experienced in his whole life. It was a far cry from anything he'd ever seen. Certainly a far cry from his days at home in Shotton, Flintshire.

Gerald's eyes were wide as he walked through the main entrance.

"Nice place Gerry ol' man, hey?"

Gerald cast his eyes everywhere. "Superb Skip. Wow."

"You'll have to get used to places like this after the war you will."

"I will?"

"Certainly. No more two up two down lifestyle for you, my man. You and that girlfriend of yours will quaff champagne at Henley Regatta when this lot's over. You mark my words."

He patted his pocket with *that* photo in. "I certainly hope so. Certainly hope so."

"You can't go wrong with a name like she's got, anyway. Susan is my wife's name."

"I didn't know you were married, skip?"

"Got married as the war started. You never know, do you ol' boy." He looked sombre. "Haven't seen her much since. Pretty old girl she is."

"Susan too."

"Yes, I've seen."

A waiter showed the groups of men from 211 Squadron to their various tables. Gerald and Arthur Geary sat with G-F. Gerald still marvelled at the interior, awash with history and resplendent in its luxuriant and grandiose fitments which seemed to be everywhere.

Modernity wasn't amiss at the Canal Club either; electric light bulbs shone through the pretty crystals of chandeliers and electric fans spun their magic on the air in the place, creating a feeling of utter calm.

"First time I came here was with father, you know."

"General Sir Robert Gordon-Finlayson. "

"Yes, father is the very same man. Decorated soldier. Served in the second Boer War you know chaps and in the Great War he got his DSO fighting with Wellington's famous fighting third. Until recently he was Commander of British Troops in Egypt. I called him General Gordon, you know, him of Khartoum fame. Gordon saved the Sudan and father… "

<'Father! *The General in charge of British Forces!'*> Gerald smiled inside.

"… is now General Officer Commanding-in-Chief, Western Command. He's just the man to sort out the Western Desert campaign… ably helped by us from 211, of course. "

Both Gerald and Arthur nodded in agreement. They liked G-F immensely, but had heard the stories of his famous father a few times now. Usually after a few beers.

"Here's a fact for you chaps. Did you know, only last May, father was invited to dinner with the British Ambassador, Sir Miles Lampson, in Cairo. The two chaps dined with Marshall Italo Balbo, the black-shirted filthy fascist Italian Governor-in-Chief of Libya, General Walther von Brauchitsch, the Commander-in-Chief of the German Army and General Alberto Pariani, I think he was the Iti Minister for War, but of course we weren't at war then were we? This was all before the war started and these lot of Krauts and Itis were on a visit to the interior of Libya; no doubt eying up what they would attack later in the year."

"Load of bastards," added in Arthur Geary.

"They are dear chap. We got our own back on the bastard Balbo, though. You weren't here then, but on the 28th June 211 bombed the hell out of Tobruk airbase. We were also after that damn crane again in the harbour. Remind me to tell you about the sweepstake going on for that! Anyway, just after we'd finished our raid the idiot Balbo [3] was coming back from high-level meeting and was a passenger on one of his own planes when the stupid Itis thought it was us again coming for a second run at bombing them, so they shot the bugger down themselves killing everyone on board. They're a mad lot the Itis. Do you know, they have even created new villages in Libya and named them after their so-called famous pilots. Maddalena, Razza and some bugger called Baracca , so father told me."

Gerald shook his head. "I bet they've got a village called Balbo now!"

Everyone laughed.

"Shows how useless they are, hey?" Then G-F beckoned Gerald and Arthur in closer to him across the table. "It's Sir Miles who worries me, though..." He looked around cautiously and whispered even more quietly than he'd been talking before. "Ol' King Farouk and Sir Miles don't get on, you know." G-F touched his nose knowingly. "Did you know Farouky boy has kept all the bloody lights burning away at his palace in Alexandria, despite blackout? So when we can't see a bloody thing after dark, he gets to keep his lights on. That's like putting the illuminations back on in Blackpool for the Luftwaffe to see the place. Stupid bastard. I've informed father that Farouk is obstructive and non-co-operative. I've suggested getting rid of King Farouk would be a good thing. That'll get back to Churchill, believe you me. I mean, Farouk could do an Edward VIII and no one would be any the wiser he'd been forced to do it. Keeps the people on-side. But lads, there's one thing father told me about this... "

Gerald and Arthur naturally moved in even closer for the pending secret.

"... Farouk has got a palace full of Iti servants, to this day, as we speak, so he's a security risk without a doubt father says. That's why the Itis don't bomb the place. They'd be bombing their own, so he can keep his lights on. Worse thing is though, the damn lights are a guide down to us. Father says that's why we keep getting the raids on our bases. Mr. Churchill, I am told, has informed Sir Miles to be tougher on Farouk. I do believe, bottom line is, Mr. Churchill wants Farouk interned, ie, put out of harm's way, if he can't behave himself. Do you know what I think, chaps?"

He didn't wait for any reply.

"They should intern the lot of them, but the diplomats won't do it."

G-F checked again around him. "There's another thing too."

"Go on, what is it?" Arthur asked with much interest.

"It's Sir Miles himself, the Ambassador. Guess what his wife is called?"

Gerald and Arthur shook heads.

"Well lads, she was Jacqueline Aldine Castellani before she married him. What does that tell you, hey?"

Silence.

"She's a bloody Iti. Jesus lads! The ambassador... OUR AMBASSADOR is married to an Italian, no wonder he lets Farouk leave his lights on and doesn't intern his servants. My father told me that Farouk had said to Sir Miles, 'I'll get rid of my Italians, when you get rid of yours.' Cheeky bastard! Egypt remains neutral in this war, but I wouldn't trust any of them. Anyway, have you heard the news from today about our pal last night Gerry ol' man?"

"News? What pal? I've been nursing my head for most of the day, so I'm afraid I've been out of the loop skip."

"Ol' Pilot Officer Dahl is missing."

"What? Missing?"

"Just before leaving to come here tonight, I was asked to see if his Gladiator was parked up anywhere on the airfield or whether I'd seen him at all."

"And was it?"

"What did they teach you in Shotton, Gerry lad? They wouldn't have been asking had his plane been around. Seems that earlier today he crammed his massive crazy crane legs into the Gloster and set off to meet 80 at their base in Mersa Matruh. I've been on the line to our airbase at four and have spoken to the C.O. there. Seems he made it to his first refuel at the airbase at Amiriya west of Alexandria. Then an hour later he had his second refuel at Fouka. From there, the C.O. gave him details of how to find the rest of his 80 Squadron crew. We don't know what's happened to him since. He could have turned around the C.O. thought as there was a bit of a sand storm, but equally he could be lost somewhere out there in the desert. There's. A good chance he's been shot down too. The Itis are everywhere in that area. All we can do is hope he's all right."

"Well, I know why no one has heard from him for a start. He ain't got no radio in that jalopy."

"Yes, a radio would help ol' man."

"He was a nice chap, was the Gloster Gladiator Giant."

Author's Note

[1] Squadron Leader Alfonso Rudolf Gordon Bax - Blenheim L8376, shot down at Derna, Libya on Wednesday 4th September 1940. He broke a leg in the crash and became Italian Prisoner of War. Held at Benghazi in Libya and afterwards Italy. Following this he was held by the Germans, at Stalag Luft I, at Barth in Pomerania (Baltic Coast), where he remained until the end of the

war.

It wasn't until many months after that 211 Squadron found out he was even alive after he'd been shot down.

[2] Song courtesy of: Blenheim Over the Balkans - James Dunnet

[3] Such was the chivalry of war at this time, Arthur Longmore, Air Officer Commanding the Middle East, ordered 211 Squadron to fly over the site of Balbo's death (the Italian airfield at Tobruk) to drop a wreath. The wreath contained the following message signed by Longmore: **'The British Royal Air Force expresses its sympathy in the death of General Balbo – a great leader and gallant aviator, personally known to me, whom fate has placed on the other side.'**

Chapter Sixteen

'The Anglo-Swiss'

True to his word, the next day, The Bish showed Gerald the sweepstake board for *'scoring a hit'* on the floating crane in Tobruk Harbour. Everyone, with any chance of being involved in its destruction, had signed their name on the board and chucked in a few Egyptian piastres to add to the fund. Gerald duly signed up, feeling he was in with a good chance of toppling the massive floating crane in Tobruk harbour. He's heard people talk about the attempts to bomb it without success and knew its strategic importance to the Italians to bring ashore their valuable supplies for the Italian war effort. The crane should have been an easy target as it sat atop a massive floating barge, but remained afloat despite a tremendous effort to destroy it on more occasions than the lads of 211 Squadron could remember.

Gerald pulled out some coins from his trouser pocket, examining them before committing them to the jar next to the sweepstake board. The head of King Farouk in his Fez looked sternly out to the side, like some Pharaoh of the second millennium B.C. Gerald examined the Arabic script, but couldn't make head nor tail of it. Everyone, including Gerald, understood the value of the coins though, as their silver content was high. He threw some coins into the jar.

"There must be over 150 piastres in there now!" the gambling eyes of The Bish commented. "With you as bomb-aimer, we're on a cert!"

Gerald nodded. "We'll see Skip! We'll see."

"Some of the lads have claimed a hit on it, but the shufti-kite [1] always comes back with pictures of it still going about its business, moving along the harbour to replenish the Iti war effort. It's vital we get it. Tobruk is of huge strategic significance. It's the best deep-water harbour anywhere along that coast and the crane makes it even more of a strategic place... plus, if we do the business, we can earn a few free drinks along the way, dear chap."

"When do we go?"

"Shame we're not due to target the place today. Other plans in the pipeline. And so to the second sweepstake, my ol' chap."

"Another."

"Oh, yes, dear Pilot Officer Davies! The water storage tanks at Buq Buq!"

"I'm aware of the water tanks. Seen them when we raided the airfields near there the other day. Hitting them would be like trying to hit a pack of ten Players Navy Cut in the middle of a football pitch, from a 1000 feet above."

"So you can guess that the STEEL water tanks are intact then. Damn *Muddle* East H.Q., that's what I've renamed those desk parasites, who told us we could only use 4lb incendiaries to blow the STEEL buggers up! The raid before last we did was at 250 feet. Damn dangerous. Could easily have lost a few crews and all for what? The incendiaries couldn't crack a Bakelite pot in Susan's kitchen from two inches, never mind 250 feet! I told them outright, but they messaged me back, the smarmy buggers telling me to *'do as I'm told!'* Cheeky bastards! Last raid, same again happened. Incendiaries bounced off like ping pong balls, so no bugger has managed to damage any of them in a month of Sundays of bombing raids. Now you're here, the odds are in our favour. I've given Muddle H.Q. a good what-for, so game is now on to make the Itis a thirsty lot when we're up our game next raid. Get some pennies in the jar Gerry boy and sign the sheet for Buq Buq."

Gerry emptied the last couple of piastres from his pockets and he was signed up to the Buq Buq sweepstake.

Whoever hit the target at either Tobruk or Buq Buq would surely be in for a week's free ale at the bar.

"Do we know how Pilot Officer Dahl is skip?" enquired Gerald as they walked away from the sweepstake table and headed for the morning briefing.

"I thought you'd ask, so I've made some follow up enquiries with the C.O. at Fouka out of interest. Bad news, I'm afraid. There's still no word about Dahl. Though no news is heavenly good news, I keep telling myself."

Gerald nodded and thanked The Bish for updating him.

"Between you and me," went on The Bish, "the damn fool of a C.O. at Fouka, mentioning no names right now, sent the poor bugger to the wrong place."

"What?"

"6.15 last night, it seems Pilot Officer Dahl was directed to a place thirty miles south of Mersa Matruh where he was told his squadron was. Damn fool idiot sent the poor blighter to the middle of an empty desert. Dahl would have been losing the sun by the time he got there and worse still, he'd have no way of making it back without the fuel gremlins getting him. "

" ... and couldn't radio anyone for help because he didn't have a radio as we know."

"Correct Gerry ol' chap, so I'm afraid, if I was putting my piastres into a sweepstake as to whether he's alive or dead, think I might be opting for the dead option as he's sure to have gone down into the rugged terrain there without a chance of landing safely. Fried alive too if the fuel has caught fire. That's my fear, Gerry man. If the plane goes up and there's no hope of getting me out and you're still alive, I'd hope you'd use that revolver of yours and shoot me point blank dead. I'd do it to myself if I could or I'd do it to any bugger screaming out in pain."

"You're too good a pilot to succumb to the enemy, skip."

"Very kind Gerry ol' man. Mind you, thinking on, the unlucky Dahl could have come across bandits in that jalopy of a Gladiator he was in so he would have bought it, anyway."

"We can hope he's alive somewhere, hey?"

"If he is, he's in no-man's-land and he's a sitting duck for the Itis. Poor bugger. All we can hope is that he's got down safely and if the Itis have him, like it seems they might've got ol' Bax who went down at Derna on the 4th, then fingers crossed they look after him."

It brought home to Gerald just how vulnerable they now were. He hadn't felt it so much when bombing from some altitude, but the disappearance of Dahl made him think about the dangers now facing him. These dangers would become even more apparent with low-level bombing missions in the pipeline - orders brought in by Chris Lee, the contents of which had only been seen by The Bish.

•

It wasn't long before everyone was gathered with The Bish for the day's briefing in front of a map of the coast of Egypt along to Tobruk in Libya and beyond.

Everyone quickly became silent as The Bish walked before the maps. He pointed straight at Tobruk.

"As much as we'd love to get that smart-Alec captaining the crane in the harbour here, we have a different job today. Low-level attacks on enemy shipping chaps!" He pointed to an area of sea to the east of Tobruk.

"We know there's a convoy coming in to Tobruk tonight. It'll be under cover of darkness. Our objective is to get to it before it reaches the harbour. As you know, the Itis have a knack of using that damn crane to lift stuff off and away from sunken and sinking boats, so we need to get to the convoy before it gets anywhere near the harbour. There are one or two of you here who've done no low-level stuff, so today will be your first go at it."

Gerald knew this was him.

"We get in as fast as we can without being seen, flying low to the target and then just before the target, the bomb-aimer releases the bomb and the pilot pulls away sharply. For those who've no significant experience of this, I'll show you afterwards the two wires we've attached across the front of the inner cockpit. They're there to help the bomb-aimer and the pilot to correctly sight the target. The bombs won't explode straight away as they have an 11 second delay on them to give us a chance to get away. We'll be as low as the top of the ship's masts, and we'll head over the top and be away before the bombs go off. WE don't want to be taken down by our own bombs, do we, hey?"

Everyone nodded and gave a quiet, nervous laugh.

"You'll know from your training that the bombs drop short and bounce along the water until they hit the ship... or sink short, if you don't get it right. We won't get it right unless we all fly in at a fairly acute angle and LOW. Low is the key. Air-gunners..."

The Bish looked across the faces and one or two, including Arthur Geary, put their hands up to show who they were.

"Yes, air-gunners, you'll be at the ready to keep the heads of the Iti crew low, firing the single forward gun, so the buggers don't fire back at us."

"Questions?"

There were several questions about exact timings and bomb loading. The Bish had his hand well on the pulse and everyone felt confident once they left the briefing.

* * *

*

The bombing of the convoy in the darkness over the Mediterranean off Tobruk, went with no loss of the six Blenheims which took off in the darkness from Ismailia. Ships had been hit, but no one knew whether or not any had been sunk. The days ahead were one briefing after another and the targets intensified as part of the softening up of the enemy under Operation Compass which was being ramped up daily by H.Q. There seemed little time for relaxing in the weeks following, and sometimes Gerald found himself on more than three raids in one day. No sooner had the Blenheim dropped its load of bombs than they were back up again over a variety of targets along the North African coast.

Several times Gerald found himself over Tobruk with the bomb-aimer sights firmly set on the floating crane in the harbour, but it remained untouched according to the regular flights of the shufti-kite, as did the water tanks at Buq Buq. The sweepstake on the table in the Officers' Mess remained unclaimed. Gerald hated the Tobruk raids more than any of the raids. Tobruk was heavily defended and the flak always heavy and unforgiving. Several times Blenheims returned from raids looking like pieces of Emmental cheese, such was the amount of shrapnel holes in them from ack-ack fire. There was a lot to lose, and the Italians didn't intend to lose any of it. Munition dumps abounded, a power station gave life to the place and a vital radio station remained completely undamaged, billowing out propaganda to the region. In and out of the deep-water harbour, freely flowed convoy after convoy, keeping the Italians fully supplied. Ably supported of course, by that damn floating crane, its shadowy steel criss-cross frame boldly highlighted against the sky as richly blue as any Queen Trigger Fish living in and around its barge support. The crane stood, like Christ the Redeemer, untouched by the bombing of 211, or any other squadron for that matter, symbolising Italian power over the port. Everyone wanted to bring it crashing down but no one could.

Then there were the raids on the camp at Ismailia, which the Italians invariably conducted at night. The Italians were aware of the arrival of Hurricanes in the area and dared not venture out in daylight, fearing big losses to their planes. Everyone hated the disturbed night's sleep, but knew it would be short-lived, as the Italian advance of late had been stopped in its tracks at Sidi Barrani. These raids were rarely troublesome. Gerald knew to don his tin hat and head for trenches dug outside in the sand. After the raids were over, there was a new and ongoing danger to watch out for. Alongside high-explosives, the Italians also dropped what the people on the ground at Ismailia called Thermos bombs, for the simple reason they looked like a Thermos flask and could easily be mistaken for one. One or two people had in the months gone by and had paid the price for picking them up as vibration triggered their deadly cargo of explosives. Anyone who now saw one would know to shout for Fat Willie. Gerald never learned his full name, but knew to call him when he spotted his first Thermos.

"Over there Will" he shouted, pointing to the dangerous looking object lying in the sand, as Willie arrived, whistling merrily and singing made up lines from Gracie Fields' ditty 'Wish Me Luck.'

'Wish me luck as you wave the bomb goodbye
Cheerio, here it goes, on its way... '

He looked at Gerald as he nonchalantly took the rifle from over his shoulder. "Keep your head down, sir."

Gerald ducked into a small trench nearby. Willie stood against a parked lorry and took aim, singing again.

Wish me luck as you wave me goodbye
Not a tear, but a cheer, when it's gone... '

He took careful aim and fired. He'd done it more times than he could remember and the bomb exploded with a deafening thud, sand, bits of rock and metal raining slowly down as he sang again.

'Gives me a smile I keep all the while
In my heart bombs gone away
So till we meet once again, the bomb and I
Wish me luck, da de da de da da... '

"Right sir, you can come out now."

Gerald extricated himself from the dusty hole, bashing his uniform down as he stood up.

"Good job, Will. Good job."

"No, my thanks are to you sir for letting us all know it was there. Take your leg off would that if you'd a happened to kick it, or worse still, you'd 'ave no eyes or head if you picked the beggar up by mistake."

*

Gerald had arrived at Ismailia when the desert campaign was just heating up. Now 211 Squadron was making as many sorties in September as they had in the three months previous. Gerald was out on sortie after sortie with hardly any chance to take a breather in-between. Night raids intensified and often the Italians would follow the Blenheim raiders back to Ismailia, trying to blow up the airfield, so the Blenheims had no chance of landing. The Blenheims then made for alternative airfields until the heat was off.

As September 1940 changed to October, the scale of operations 211 Squadron were involved in hadn't diminished one iota and, if anything there was a huge intensification of effort to ensure the Italians could advance no closer to Egypt. 211 Squadron's task was to hinder and delay the Italians to give allied troops some chance of success, even in retreat, on the ground. Within all of this, Gerald did his best to win the sweepstake, but still the crane at Tobruk stood tall.

Gerald was feeling positive he could get that crane, as on the morning of Wednesday 2nd October he'd done what no one else had done and that was to hit one of the water tanks at Buq Buq, for which the crew of Blenheim L8511 were rewarded the sweepstake totalling 62 piastres.

"We're going to get that bloody floating crane tonight and we shall be quids in at the bar for the foreseeable future," Gerald declared late on the night of Saturday 12th October 1940 as The Bish briefed his crews for a low-level attack on Tobruk. Everyone knew this was a dangerous mission, as the ack-ack from Tobruk was always thick and heavy.

"Absolutely, we're going to nail it tonight!" The Bish had replied, "especially, because the damn Luftwaffe have bombed the hell out of Wimbledon yesterday and father informs direct from HQ, via a note from our SIO Willie, er...   Pilot Officer Williams... er, yes...   they've destroyed the   Centre Court Stand. [2] I'm not having that. I've sat there many times having my afternoon strawberries and cream. We're going to let the Itis have tonight chaps good and proper and it'll be one in the eye for them and their damn kraut friends."

The crew cheered, but all soon concentrated on the tasks in hand.

Six Blenheims took off for the raid on Tobruk, loaded with 250lb bombs.

It would be Gerald's last raid for two weeks.

*

* * *

A sensation of floating consumed Gerald as he drifted in and out of a dreamlike state. Ethereal visions drifted through the blinding white light which consumed his eyes. He saw his mother Elizabeth and his Aunt Lizzie. They spoke to him and he reached out to touch them.

<'Are you all right Gerald? Are you all right?' Speak to me?>' repeated endlessly in his head. Then Susan arrived, stepping off a boat on the Thames. She was trying to get near him, but people seemed to pull her away.

<'Susan! Sue! Sue> A silent scream, heard by no one.

Gerald tried to run after Susan trying to be heard, but a paralysis gripped him. No words came forth. He wanted to hug the visions before him, but the nearer he tried to get the more he seemed to drift away.

<'I'm dead. I'm no more. This is heaven. I'm in heaven.'>

Everything became nothing until Gerald was awoken by the incessant roar of, what seemed like, an entire fleet of Blenheim engines in his ears. He sat bolt upright in panic. He could see the rotating propellers of the Blenheim and could do nothing to save himself from falling into the blades.

"Ah, God, I'm falling into the engine. Christ! The engine. The engine… " He screamed and tried to open his eyes to save himself, but there was just nothing except awful stinging white light and engine noise.

"You're orrite Gerry," a young woman's voice softly declared with a janner accent. [3] "You're okay, you knows. You're safe now here with us."

Gerald felt the woman grip him kindly by the shoulders. She rubbed up and down his upper arms gently.

"Sue, thank God you're here," he shouted.

"Sue? Dear boy, I'm Mary… Mary Welland, a nurse here at the Anglo-Swiss… er, the Hospital in Alexandria. You're safe now, Gerald. You is safe."

Gerald tried to open his eyes but couldn't. The panic in his voice was obvious. "Nurse… nurse! I can't see! I can't see! I'm blind!"

"You've got bandages over your eyes and you've had a nasty bang on the head, Gerald."

His panic continued. "I'm blind! I'm blind!"

Once again, the soft tones of Mary Welland spoke. "You've had fuel in your eyes and it's only temporary. Only temporary Gerald! You'll see when the bandages come off. You will see. Promise you."

Gerald's eyes were stinging intensely. Despite not being able to see, he could now feel the comfort of the hospital bed. He felt he was on a bed of feathers compared to where he was billeted in Ismailia. Gerald was oblivious to what had happened to him and couldn't remember one single detail about how he ended up in hospital. The last thing he could remember was the thick ack-ack over Tobruk, then little else.

"You need to rest now Gerald. Plenty of rest. The doctor thinks you have severe concussion and rest will dos you good. Your C.O. did a good job getting you here. He landed the plane not too far away, especially for you dear boy. He's probably saved your sight."

Gerald listened but was still groggy. His head thumping away like some great Victorian mill machine in Lancashire. Then he thought about the Blenheim... and Arthur and The Bish.

"So they're all right then. The others... The Bish .... Arthur.. they're all right are they?"

"Apparently so. Squadron Leader Finlayson tells me a shell exploded near the port side of the plane and the plexiglass on your side was pieced with a lump of metal. Knocked you clean out he said and a broken fuel line gave your face a good wash... but not with soap and water."

Gerald heard the nurse gently laugh. "There was all sorts of gunk in those eyes of yours when you arrived, my dear, but, as I said before, the doc says you're probably going to be fine. Now rest, Gerald, rest."

Gerald fell asleep again and hadn't a clue how long he'd slept, when he was awoken by the sound of air-raid sirens wailing away. Gerald heard the noise above; it was a familiar noise he'd heard before and always at night. Italian bombers, with their distinctive engine hum, always attacked after dark, that was their M.O.   Then constant ack-ack fire began all around and the explosions of nearby falling bombs began. The explosions were loud and came near.   TOO NEAR. The building shook and Gerald clung on to his bed, arms outstretched, finger gripping crisp clean sheets he hadn't felt in some weeks.

Even in hospital he couldn't escape being a target.

<'If I get through this war in one piece, it'll be a miracle.>

*

What day it was, was anyone's guess, never mind the actual time of day; unless it was meal time or time for the medical rounds, when the noise on the ward increased exponentially giving some sign as to what time it was.

It was during one of these times when Gerald heard a voice he thought he recognised in the bed right next to him.

"That feels so jolly well soothing Nurse Welland," were the words he heard as Nurse Welland tended to a nearby patient who's face had been completely covered with bandages like something from a scene in The Invisible Man.

"Yes, much better," Nurse Welland declared as she delicately wiped around vicious injuries on the man's face. "Still very swollen are those peepers? Won't be doing any peeping for a while, but you will, you will."

Nurse Welland was ever optimistic.

Gerald would have recognised that 'jolly-well' voice anywhere. "Dahl? Dahl, is that you?"

"Who jolly well calls me?" The voice shouted back.

"You two know each other?"

"Well, I know this man. He's a fellow Welshman, the Gloster Gladiator Giant. Well, he's sort of Norwegian Welsh aren't you, dear chap."

Roald Dahl sat up more. Nurse Welland ticked him off. "Be careful Mr Dahl, I'm in the middle of sorting those eyes out. We want no more damage do we."

"I knew it was you, Roald. We thought you were dead old chap. The Bish told me you'd probably bought it in the desert."

"Then the reports of my death were premature ol' man. I was rescued... " It then dawned on Roald Dahl who he was having a conversation with. "Gerry. I know who you are now. The North Walian from the bar! How are you my man and what brings you here? Christ, it hurts to talk!"

"Well, keep that mouth closed then," smiled Nurse Welland, unseen by either Gerald or Roald.

"She's a jolly lovely nurse is Mary Welland. She's a naval officer, Gerry. I'm mad about her. She's one hell of a nurse. Beautiful eyes she has... "

Nurse Welland nudged him hard and smiled. "Says the man who can't see a finger in front of him."

"Steady on, Nurse Welland, you jolly well hurt then. Yow. It hurts to smile, Gerry man. What was one saying then... "

"You were asking Gerry how he got here," Nurse Welland

interjected as she carried on working on Dahl's face. "Keep still, Mr Dahl. Keep still."

"A bump on the head and fuel in the eyes." Gerald said as he tried to figure out just exactly where Roald Dahl and Nurse Welland were.

"Your comrade Gerry can't see at the moment either" declared Nurse Welland. "Blind leading the blind, eh?"

"All one need is one more and we can jolly-well sing *Three Blind Mice*" laughed Roald Dahl.

Nurse Welland finished off her session tending to Pilot Officer Dahl and he was soon bandaged up again with no more than his nose and mouth free.

"Don't tire yourselves out too much. I'll leave you two to catch up then shall I?" Nurse Welland chortled as she walked away to tend to someone else.

"So how come you're alive then, Roald?"

"No thanks to the C.O. at Fouka who jolly-well had no idea where my squadron was."

"We heard you'd been given duff coordinates."

"I think the damn gremlins had been at work on the C.O's brain, never mind the plane I was in. He sent me on a mission to die in the desert without firing a bullet. Well, I jolly well did get fired at. Yes... by my own bullets, they were exploding in the fire like something from the Glorious Twelfth and I was the red grouse jolly-well ducking the bullets."

Dahl sighed again and took a few deep breaths through what looked like minuscule holes in his head bandage.

"Yes, jumped ahead of oneself there... so, I ended up over the desert with light fading and not an airfield in sight. One had to decide... erm, yes... try to land the old kite or crash the bugger trying to head back to where I'd come from. The latter wasn't an option. Not enough fuel."

"Go on."

"I went down to the darkening desert twice to look at what the situation was. There just wasn't a flat landing spec. Place below me was jolly-well full of boulders. Trouble was brewing, dear chap. Trouble. The gremlins were sucking the fuel out of the Gladiator quicker than a thirsty camel sucks at a trough. Focusses the mind, dear chap. Focusses the mind. I came in as at slow a speed as one dares. Just over seventy or so miles an hour I would hazard at a guess. The wheels touched down and I throttled back. Too late, though. I hit a boulder and the nose ploughed into the ground. It's not the speed you're doing dear Gerry, it's what you hit which causes the problem and did I hit ithard."

"You remember it all?"

"As clear as a goldfish sees out of its bowl. Within a flash, the whole kite was ablaze. The machine guns were firing on their own and the bullets exploding all around me. One thought one was a goner dear chap."

"At least I was out of it when I was injured. I'd have had no idea if I was a goner or not."

"Best way, best way. I was like Joan of Arc. The flames lashed up all around me. I know what a turkey feels like now on Christmas Day. The damn oven was hot and getting hotter. I had to get out, but one was well strapped in."

"How did you manage to get out?"

"Magic fingers worked on the seat and parachute straps, as the bullets from my own plane whizz-popped by. Damn sure those gremlins had turned my own guns on me but... er... yes... one was determined to survive and not get turned into a Sunday roast. I rolled out like some Olympic gymnast going over the horse, doing a somersault in the process. One landed on the sand and clawed one's way from the burning wreckage like some dirty beast escaping from hell."

"Good God, Roald, you are one heck of a lucky blighter have come out of that in one piece."

"Hardly one piece yet ol' chap. Hardly one piece. Gremlins would have had me back in there, if they could have done, but I wasn't having that. My crawl might have been as slow as a tortoise, but they ran out of bullets and the kite burned them all up, thank God." Dahl signed. "I just went out of it completely. I suppose dear chap I was jolly well relieved to be out of the fire."

"Proper old phoenix, you are Dahl."

"Apparently, the boys from the Suffolk had seen one of 'their boys' go down in the no-mans-bit between them and the Itis, so luckily their C.O. ... one with a bit of sense this time... told a few of his lads to check it out. Was easy to find me. The burning bush, which was the Gladiator marked X on the map for them."

"Proper good fortune they were there."

"Yes, I rather think they thought they might find that Sunday roast I mentioned, but they found a bloodied and burnt me in the sand... and here I am. Whether it was good fortune or not, one is not sure yet. Do you know Gerry ol' chap, if I ever get away from this war alive, I'm going to write about those gremlins. Pesky creatures!"

They both laughed.

"I have to say Roald old chap, I'm quite surprised no one thought on to tell The Bish you were alive."

"That's war. Everyone's too busy saving their own bacon to think about passing messages on. If you're missing or dead in these times, it seems to be the same but there are exceptions... those lads from the Suffolk and the nurses and doctors here at the Anglo-Swiss of course."

"What injuries do you have them Roald, have they told you?"

"Nose has become a wandering figure on my face. They think my eyes are well burned, but the lovely Mary Welland thinks I'll see again. How's your sight ol' chap?"

"They itch and hurt like mad, but apart from the headache I don't think I should be here too long. I just hope we both get our 20/20 eyes back."

"We'll drink to that one day, dear chap, we'll drink to that."

*

The next day Gerald awoke to find Roald Dahl gone from the bed.

"What's happened to Dahl" he enquired of Nurse Welland when she came to take off his eye dressings.

"He's got a few more issues than you and is having some pretty major surgery on the next few days, so we've moved him to a room on his own. He's fine and will be fine though, but he'll be in for a few more weeks or even months I should think."

Nurse Welland removed Gerald's dressings and he slowly opened his eyes as the nurse bathed them in a warm saline solution. The light was almost unbearable and everything was blurred.

"It's blurred, I know, you don't have to tell me. Your eyes might take a couple of days or even longer to get back to normal, but the doc say they will."

"So when can I get back to the squadron?"

"You will, soon enough, you will. Be patient. All you lot are the same. You can't wait to get back to the front line. I can't for the life of me understand why."

"You know nurse, I don't think most of us know why either, but what we know is we have a sense of duty towards each other and for our country, or the countries we are protecting. We are fighting for freedom. Pure and simple. Freedom, to preserve our much cherished way of life which generations before have built up on a steady rock we call Great Britain."

Nurse Welland smiled. "You should be a politician Pilot Officer Gerald Davies."

"Perhaps after the war I will, who knows."

Author's Note

[1] Shufti-Kite - Shufti is an Arabic meaning 'look.' Kite is the word used for a plane, so the two words were commonly put together by the RAF to describe reconnaissance planes which often flew over targets after bombing raids to ascertain the damage caused by the raid and from this future raids could be planned.

[2] Friday 11th October 1940 - Several bombs landed on Wimbledon, the All-England Lawn Tennis Club. The roof of the Centre Court stand was extensively damaged and 1,200 seats were obliterated. The stand wasn't fully repaired for another nine years.

[3] Janner Accent - from Plymouth and associated with the navy. The Anglo-Swiss Hospital in Alexandria was a naval hospital at the outbreak of war and all the staff were naval personnel. As the war progressed, the hospital began accepting casualties from all the services.

Chapter Seventeen

'Hotel Grande Bretagne'

Just before dawn on the Thursday 28th October 1940 Mussolini ordered 140,000 of his troops into Albania and Greece; so began the Greco-Italian war which would see the involvement of British forces and seal the fate of many involved, including that of Pilot Officer Gerald Davies. Greek Prime Minister General Ioannis Metaxas vowed to resist the invasion to the last man. The Greeks were ill-prepared for war, but brave Greek soldiers resisted with all their might and fought tenaciously in the mountain passes of Albania and Greece to bring the invasion to somewhat of a halt ensuring the Italian advance remained on the Greek/Albanian border.

*

Air Vice-Commodore John Henry D'Albiac, the Greek Prime Minister, General Ioannis Metaxas and many sombre faced Greek and British Officers stood in the sunshine of Greater Piraeus in a small civil cemetery in a suburb of Athens called Kokkinia. It was afternoon as the coffin of 20-year-old Royal Air Force Volunteer Sergeant John Merifield from County Durham was lowered to his resting place in the town cemetery. Full military honours were accorded to John Merifield [1] who was a wireless operator and air gunner operating with 30 Squadron. Merifield had been killed in action on 6th November. He hadn't even fired a bullet when the Italians strafed the plane he was in as he sat at his air gunner's seat in his Blenheim bomber. His C.O. had commented he would have known little about it and the other people in the plane thanked their lucky stars the attack had not been sufficient to bring down the plane in its entirety, otherwise all three crew would have perished. So, bad news as it was, when the Blenheim touched down that fateful day at Tatoi aerodrome in Greece, it DID manage to land and carried with it the body of John Merifield, the first RAF casualty of the British arrival in Greece. He wouldn't be the last and it was a reminder to all just how dangerous a place this might be.

As the funeral ended, General Metaxas offered many condolences to the British and spoke with John D'Albiac agreeing to meet later over dinner.

It was gone eight that night when John D'Albiac sipped his wine at a table at the Hotel Grande Bretagne in Athens, where he had hastily set up an RAF nucleus H.Q. for the RAF in Greece. He contemplated his thoughts and what he might discuss with the Greek Prime Minister, who was just ten minutes away.

He'd flown over to Athens from Egypt on 6 November 1940 aboard a Bombay transport plane closely protected by Gloster Gladiators from 80 Squadron and followed by other aircraft, including a Sunderland Flying Boat accompanied by several of D'Albiac's staff plus one other notable person; Squadron Leader Tommy Wisdom, a revered journalist who worked alongside 211 Squadron. Wisdom was a qualified pilot, but his job was W.C. (War Correspondent) in the Middle East for the Daily Herald and other newspapers back home. Now it seemed his duties would involve reporting on a developing war in Greece. Squadron Leader Wisdom was someone who already knew Gerald, and soon they would be brought together again.

Just days before, he'd been Air Officer Commanding, RAF Palestine and Transjordan, now he was ready to embark upon another mission. The survival of Greece as a nation!

General Metaxas arrived at 8.15pm on the dot, as he'd promised, this time with an entourage of aides and armed guards who sat or stood around the edges of the dining room, making everyone nervous in the process. There were a variety of RAF personnel around but sat with D'Albiac at the table was his second in command, Wing Commander Alfred Henry Willetts.

The General sat down and there was an initial conversation about the sad loss of Sergeant Merifield, as meals were ordered and drinks arrived. Then the Greek Prime Minister turned to more pressing matters.

Greek forces were struggling on the border with Albania, their airforce was well under strength, something General Metaxas was well aware of.

"Your support in this campaign is much welcome, Mr. D'Albiac. We are a strong-willed nation and we have the heart of a pride of lions, but even a pride of lions can be no match for too many guns and too many soldiers... or even too many aeroplanes."

"Dear Prime Minister, I can assure you, I would not be here if Mr. Churchill was not fully behind you and your country. We must at all costs keep the Iti from his menacing colonial ways in Greece."

"You know, I thought at one stage, you British had colonial ambitions here, but my thinking has altered since '36, when Berlin and Rome became best of friends. I have to say I was wrong about you British, but I've never been wrong about the Italian."

"Mr. Churchill will surely be glad to know that Prime Minister."

"Yes, the Italian is AND has been our enemy for some time. Mr Mussolini is not to be trusted. It is seventeen years this last August since the fascist attacked our island of Corfu, killing and maiming dozens of people."

"I am aware, yes."

"Mr Mussolini invaded Corfu with many thousands of his ill-guided troops, and it was only by the grace of God the League of Nations forced him out. We have never forgiven him here in Greece, you know, especially as we were forced to pay to get him out from OUR lands."

"I understand Prime Minister." John D'Albiac responded with an air of calm. "The RAF... "

"Needs to be helping us to support our ground troops in northern Epirus, where the fighting is at its heaviest. Our small air force is struggling to cope against overwhelming Italian air superiority. We need help and we need it now."

"As I was saying, the RAF, wants to help, indeed an advance element of our air support has already arrived. More will be coming. The force already here... erm... what are they Willetts... "

"Gloster Gladiators and medium range Blenheim bombers, sir."

"Yes, thank you, Willetts. This force now awaits my instructions... "

"And those instructions are?"

"Willetts and I have much experience in the art of air combat and use of planes in zones of conflict. Willetts will explain." D'Albiac took a further sip of his wine and lit a cigar.

"Thank you, sir," responded Willetts, sitting up and pushing his glass of wine to the side.

"Dear Prime Minister, sir, I thank you for inviting us to meet with you this evening but I have to say, from the outset that supporting your ground offensive would be a bad idea."

Metaxas shook his head with a little disbelief.

"Give me time to explain, sir. I think you'll like our plans. Supporting ground forces in this case is NOT a good use of our resources. We have a limited amount of RAF planes. You will understand that the Battle of Britain has raged and most planes have been directed to the defence of Britain."

"Yes, I can understand and I appreciate, in these troublesome times you have been able to offer support to Greece, but our ground troops in northern Epirus face a threat which could destabilise the region and they need help."

"Yes, and we will give them that help. The small force we have we will concentrate on disrupting the Italian lines of communication and their disembarkation ports in Albania."

Wing Commander Willetts unrolled a map of the coast of Albania and Greece, placing wine glasses on the corners to hold it down. He pointed to places on the map. "Our intelligence tells us Durazzo, Valona and Tepelenë will be amongst our prime targets. Here the Italians are busy going about their war business by the hour. We bomb these places and they can't get supplies to their troops in the mountains fighting your troops. Why do we need to bomb troops in trenches in mountains and perhaps just hold them down and undercover for a few minutes when we can stop their ammunition and relief getting to them at source?"

"And where do you intend to base your planes in Greece?"

John D'Albiac leant over the map. "That was our next question, Prime Minister. We hoped you might have some suggestions for us?"

"Well, we have airbases, as you know here in Athens. You landed at Eleusis this morning before we met at the funeral of your poor unfortunate RAF sergeant."

"Prime Minister. Yes."

"Athens, is the most beautiful of places, especially Phaleron. It has a lovely beach, you should try it some day. Good for bathing!" He smiled, then became serious again. He pointed to the map and at Athens. "The airfield at Eleusis is about 18 km northwest of the city but, for you, looking at deploying your forces against the Italians in Epirus, it shall be unsatisfactory in the extreme."

The Prime Minister looked more closely at the map.

"You have a difficulty sir, Greece doesn't lend itself to creating aerodromes of any size. Especially for bombers to land and take off from."

One of the Prime Minister's aides bent forward. "If General Metaxas might excuse me sir. I might suggest the Larissa plain here."

He pointed to the Thessaly region of Greece.

"I've heard of Larissa," D'Albiac puffed on his cigar. "It's mentioned in Homer's Iliad. That's as much as I know, though. Are there any all weather aerodromes in this country of yours?"

Metaxas looked at his entourage. People shook their heads. "That's possibly a no then, Mr. D'Albiac."

"Might we do some reconnaissance of the countryside in the north to see what's on offer Prime Minister."

Metaxas gathered his aides closer. Greek whispers and shakes of heads followed. "We will do our best to help, but we can't have planes of yours flying all over the place. It might cause issues with our countrymen."

Metaxas could see D'Albiac shaking his head in frustration. "We will do out best. We will do our best to find you places to fly from. It won't be sorted today, but we will do it."

The group settled to finish their meals and talked amongst themselves. At about 10pm Metaxas approached D'Albiac to bid him farewell.

D'Albiac wasn't finished. "One more thing Prime Minister."

"What is that Air-Commodore?"

"Your Greek airforce WILL come under my command, this is straight from Mr. Churchill. No bargaining on this."

Metaxas had few options and all shook hands and departed, agreeing a timetable of meetings in the coming days and weeks. There was even a suggestion John D'Albiac might be able to make an accompanied tour of possible aerodrome sites further north in Greece. *[2]*

*

The meeting at the Hotel Grande Bretagne would seal the fate of the immediate future of 211 Squadron, who had now moved base to Fouka on the north coast of Egypt.

* * *

*

Gerald could never understand why he'd had to spend almost two weeks at the Anglo-Swiss in Alexandria. Once his dressings were removed, he felt ready to head back to Ismailia at the double, but the hospital had strict rules around how and when they let their patients go back on active duty. Mostly the rules surrounded giving the service personnel a break from the front line, even when they didn't want that break. Everyone's sense of duty was so intense at this time, and Gerald was no different. The RAF had given him a home, a family he could call his own and a financial security he knew would set him up for life. He'd met the girl of his dreams and even though she was now far away, he hoped, to the depths of his heart, he would see her again and soon.

Over the two weeks Gerald was at the hospital, he did his best to visit Pilot Officer Dahl in his sick bed as much as possible and the two became firm friends. Gerald doubted Pilot Officer Dahl might ever fly again such were his injuries, but Dahl was a determined personality.

It was the day Gerald was discharged and he waited for his lift from H.Q. to arrive.

"Taxi for a chap called Gerry!" came the shout around a medical screen.

"G-F! It's you. How are you Skip?"

"More's to the point, how are you ol' chap? You were looking at death's door the day we dropped you off here. Now look at you, a bit of a war scar on the head but you look 100 per cent."

"And I feel it too," a glad-hearted Gerald replied. "So pleased to see you. Never thought I'd see the day."

"You need that uniform sorting out Gerry lad, there's blood all over it still."

"They said they tried to clean it, but yep, you can still see the tide mark."

"Battle scars Gerry lad. Welcome to the club. Let's hope this is the voodoo to keep you from harm in the future."

With that, Gerald frantically searched his pockets. "My photo!"

He felt the familiar shape in his pocket and extracted the photo of himself and Susan from Henley.

"Stop panicking ol' chap. It's there."

Gerald pulled it out. The corner now had a slight wash of blood on it. "It's the only photo of Susan I have. Will marry this girl one day."

He kissed the photograph.

"Soppy bugger!" retorted The Bish. "Right we need to go. If you're fit, then I'm fit. We need you back. I need you back. I thought I'd lost my right-hand man and I'll be honest with you Gerry, it's not been the same at all. There's no one in the squadron like you. No one."

"That's very kind, skip. Right come on let's head off. Can't wait to get back."

Gerald said his goodbyes and thanked the staff, giving Nurse Welland a particular hug for being so kind to him. Then he remembered. Dahl! [3]

"There's someone I want to say a particular goodbye to skip."

The Bish followed Gerald to the room where a poorly looking Pilot Officer Dahl lay, arm strapped to a board with tubes feeding into his body. Nurse Welland followed the two into the room.

"Just a couple of minutes chaps. A couple of minutes, He had an op on his nose yesterday and he's feeling rather rubbish today."

"Rather rubbish?" came the voice from under the bandages. "How dare you gorgeous Nurse Mary Welland. You wait 'til I can get out of this bed I'll give you a jolly good what for."

"Well, blow me down with a flamingo feather, if it's not the damn tall lanky chap from the Gladiator."

"How jolly-well dare you sir, I object to the word damn."

"No bugger told me they'd found you, well I'm heartily glad Pilot Officer Dahl. Very glad."

"Gerry knows the full story, I'll let him tell you, but I can say with some certainty I'm glad someone found me." A hint of a painful laugh came from under the bandages.

"You'll be soon back and at em, like Gerry here. Rest assured. You're 80 Squadron, aren't you?"

"I was, sir. Do you think they'll have me back after I obliterated one of their prize Gladiators?"

"Have you back? They need you back, Dahl man. They need you. What's more, I can tell you now, they've had more Hurricanes in. Seems you might have done them a favour by crashing your plane as it's prompted H.Q. into action.

"Well, I'll keep my toes crossed sir." Dahl tried to raise his arm. "Crossing my fingers is still painful." He gave a feeble, tired attempt at laughing.

"Think you chaps need to leave Mr Dahl to rest, eh?" Nurse Welland directed more sternly now.

Pilot Officer Dahl spoke again. "Just before you chaps go, just a word of thanks to Gerry for keeping me company for a couple of weeks. Would have gone mad without him."

"Been my pleasure, dear chap."

"Yes... and... I'll see you when I'm out of here, dear chap. Will make sure I'm there to protect you Blenheim boys in that new Hurricane kite I'm so looking forward to get... "

With that, Dahl fell asleep.

Gerald whispered, "Then you'd better get on the mend quickly Pilot Officer Roald Dahl. We need chaps like you. The world needs chaps like you."

*

Gerald was so glad to be out! The bed at the hospital might have been more comfy than his sleeping bag and camp bed back at the air base, but the place was stuffy and he couldn't wait to get out. He took a deep breath of the fresh morning air.

It felt good! It felt good to be alive too.

The Bish led Gerald to an Austin 10/4 Cambridge staff car in desert garb parked just outside the main entrance to the Anglo-Swiss. Gerald sat in the passenger seat and they headed off. Gerald said very little. His mind was awash with a myriad of thoughts.

It was now striking home to the 22-year-old Gerald just how close to death he had come.

<'I might never have seen Susan or any of my family again and I'd have known nothing about it.'>.

He shook his head to clear it of the cascading thoughts, but he could still see Pilot Officer Dahl laid up in a hospital bed, his face heavily bandaged and his long body motionless on the bed, a tired and buckled frame. The thought of going to war had frightened and both excited the 22-year-old Gerald at the same time but now he realised, for the very first time, this was no game he was in. No one was playing. This was a grim reality of bandages and blood.

As he daydreamed with the warm wind of the Egyptian day blowing through the wound down window of the Austin 10, he was conflicted. He had felt sorry and somewhat guilty in the past for the little ants he had bombed. He'd watched the ants running, or driving, or trying to get a plane off the ground as his bombs touched ground. He'd watched ants die before his eyes many times and always,

ALWAYS... he felt they were someone with a family... someone's son or father. Now, because of him, they were no more. There would be empty places at dinner tables across the globe and some of this empty places would be down to him, but the guilt was wearing off fast.

Gerald daydreamed his way along the route back to base, accompanied by the soothing ticking noise of the tappets of the Austin 10 which lullaby'd him in and out of sleep. The Bish, as ever, looking relaxed, had his left arm hung out of the open window and looked across towards his passenger every now and then to check he was well. He was content to let him doze. <*'He must have had a fistful of drugs in that place. Poor bugger. We'll all be back in action soon enough so sleeping is a good thing!'*>

After a period of deep relaxing sleep and a dream of being on a punt on the Thames with Susan, Gerald woke up.

"Are we back at The Horns yet Sue?"

The Bish elbowed Gerald. He could see he was still help asleep. "Gerry ol' boy. Wake up!" Another elbow. "Wake up! The bloody Horns, what's that ol' chap. That bang on the head has sent you doo-lally-tap lad."

Gerald sat up straight, coming to with an enormous yawn. "Yes, with it now G-F."

Gerald wiped his eyes and took a few deep breaths. "I'm fine now."

"I bloody well hope so. I need you back fully compos mentis Gerry."

"Just dreaming. Just dreaming. Was back at The Horns in Henley."

"With that Susan of yours?"

"Good days, they were good days."

"You'll have plenty to come. Plenty to come, when this war is through."

It was then Gerald noticed the sea. He stared out through his window across empty white sand beaches lapped by the turquoise Mediterranean Sea which, had they been in Britain, would have had more than their fair share of people crowding them, even in wartime. What was even stranger was that the sea was to the car's nearside. The car... THEY were heading west. He looked back through the rear split screen window. He wasn't wrong.

Gerald suddenly became more awake and alert. "Are we taking a new route back to the Suez skip?"

The Bish looked back and with his usual laconic manner said, "We've abandoned all our planes and we're going ground only. We've struggled to get that damn crane at Tobruk, so we're going incognito and attacking it with hand-grenades later today. Hence I'm heading west for the Iti lines."

"Say again, G-F."

"That bang on the head has done you no good." The Bish winked.

"I'm 100 per cent and counting, tickety-boo I am."

"Just testing you're still all there ol' chap."

The Bish was famous for his mischievous ways, but Gerald was well used to this.

"Where are we going? Base moved, has it?"

"You guessed first go. Fouka, here we come. Your Blenheim awaits, sir."

*

It was now two days since his discharge from the Anglo-Swiss. Gerald stood on the ground at Fouka inspecting Blenheim L8511. It was late evening and once again the sun was saying its quiet goodbye to the day. There wasn't a sign of any damage having ever occurred to it whatsoever. Gerald watched Arthur Geary clambering in to his air-gunner position. He'd already seen The Bish haul himself on board and head towards the pilot's seat. Gerald nodded his head with incredulity. "Not a trace, hey!" He looked back at the ground crew preparing the aircraft for take-off. "Great job, boys. Great job."

One shouted back with a thick cockney accent, "Glad to 'av you back guv."

Gerald gave him the thumbs up. Glad to be here!"

"You lot take care out there. We wants you backs in one piece you 'ere!"

With a "gotcha thanks" Gerald climbed aboard and the doors and hatches of the bomber were sealed closed. It was as if he'd never been away.

Tobruk once again lay ahead and the six planes heading there were loaded with their cargo of bombs.

The damn floating crane was still the talk of the briefing and this perhaps was the last chance to do anything about it from the private conversation he'd had with The Bish on the way back from the hospital in Alexandria.

"Between you and me," the conversation had begun, "we won't be in North Africa much longer. It's hush hush, but I can trust you. Seems we might be heading for somewhere across the Med. Intelligence tells us an invasion is on the cards, and soon. It may be the Itis or it may be the Itis and Krauts together. There's also talk of India or Singapore as potential places we might head, so be prepared for upheaval at short notice. Our motto of being the Greyhounds will come into play again for sure, as we'll be heading to pastures new and soon. I'm expecting a call to H.Q. any day to discuss things further."

It wasn't long before they were over Tobruk. Gerald was determined the crane would have it that night, especially now he was aware they may have precious little more time to get at the sweepstake in the bar.

Squadron Leader James Gordon-Finlayson flew the Blenheim at as low a level as possible as they flew over the mess of ack-ack heading their way. The plane shook and was thrown around by the upcoming flak, but The Bish maintained a steady course. The crane was dead ahead between the home-made aiming wires on the front plexiglass of the cockpit.

"Close as we dare," the brassy spitting intercom message from The Bish hissed out. "Target dead ahead."

"Keep it steady, skip. Coming in line. Top wire... barge into view. Almost there... crane lifting to wire... top wire. Yes... between... and on target... " Gerald pressed The Tit hard. "Bombs gone."

"Bombs gone!" he repeated with some gusto as the plane pulled sharply away with a thunder of its twin engines. Gerald stretched to see down below as bombs skipped onto the blackness of the enclosed . The flashes from the ack-ack gave the target intermittent light as the Blenheim almost scraped the brontosaurus like neck of the 20 ton floating crane. Gerald strained back to see as the bombs exploded against the barge.

"Strike skip. Strike!" cracked Gerald.

"We got it, Gerry?"

"The barge for sure. The barge. The blasted crane looks to be still standing."

"It was built in Britain then for sure," laughed The Bish, as they headed away from the rumble of the ack-ack.

*

The de-brief was short. Gerald and the crew of L8511 felt sure they'd hit the crane. No one else claimed even a near miss.

"The shufti-kite will let is know - we'll convene again after we've had word back," were The Bish's last words on the matter.

The next day the answer was in. The observer on the reconnaissance plane reported *'some damage'* to the barge but added *'the crane I fear is intact and with some repairs, it'll probably be serviceable again within a few days.'*

The Bish didn't a care jot. The pertinent word on the sweepstake was 'hit,' so as far as he was concerned they had indeed won, but he announced nothing straight away, despite several of the squadron asking for an update on the crane. Over the next few days 211 Squadron bombed Italian troop movements along the coast of Libya, from Sollum to Sidi Barrani, bombing Italian forts, paying particular attention to Fort Maddalena which was part of a new frontier of barbed wired created by the Italians to defend their new territorial acquisitions. These were the latest instructions from H.Q., to keep the Italian onslaught at bay, to support allied ground troops who were doing an excellent job and the crane at Tobruk would remain a target 211 Squadron would never attack again, but the sweep stake announcement remained for The Bish to decide on.

That announcement came in the second week of November.

The officers were called to a briefing. The Bish looked solemn.

"I have three announcements to make gentlemen… "

Someone at the back, eager to know about the Tobruk crane, shouted across "It's the sweepstake boss. The sweepstake!"

"In good time, gentlemen. In good time. Now, less interruption please. Firstly, I can tell you I shall be away for a week or more. Big things in the offing, but you shall know of that in due course."

There were mumbles and nodding but no one enquired why The Bish was going away. It was expected for the C.O. to take instructions and go off strategic planning from time to time, and no one wanted to be in possession of 'need to know stuff' anyway.

<'It's to do with us moving on for sure. The Itis are in Greece now.'>

"Second piece of news is, a break for us of sorts. Whilst I'm away, barring disasters, you can have some leave chaps."

Tremendous cheers.

"What's third!" someone shouted.

"Third is an awful piece of news, gentlemen."

You could hear a lace fall undone. Faces went serious.

"It's that damn crane in the harbour. We might not have destroyed it but we sure crippled the bugger, so the sweepstake is won by…"

"Gerry!" Another voice shouted.

"Gerry? Well, but for my fantastic flying skills, Arthur's gunnery skills and you other buggers keeping us from getting shot down, so yes, Gerry got the nearest bomb on target but we all did the job, so the sweepstake is... "

He hesitated to create tension.

"WON BY ALL!"

Great cheers abounded, accompanied by many hard pats on Gerald's back.

"Now I won't be here to share in your great fortune, but I can tell you gentlemen, when the jar was emptied there were 172 piastres counted. AND it's behind the bar, so you all get a free bit of what does the soul good!"

*

Gerald found out the break from duties wasn't for everyone, him included, and although he was on leave of a kind he was expected to remain on base supervising ground crew and making sure the Blenheims were operationally ready. The parting words from The Bish had been, "We'll be out of here within a day or so of me getting back, mark my words. I'm now certain it's not the far East or even Turkey. It'll be Greece. Greece! Mum's the word." He tapped his nose twice.

*

In those days of the second and third week of November 1940, Gerald travelled between Ismailia and Fouka (and one or two other places) more times than he could remember. This certainly wasn't a period of leave but was more relaxed as no bombing raids or enemy action took place for the whole of 211 Squadron. The other squadrons took on the responsibility of keeping up the daily and nightly onslaught on the Italians along the coast and to Tobruk. Gerald and a few of the men ferried supplies up and down the length of the Suez and along the coast as far as Mersa Matruh where Pilot Officer Dahl might have been had he not still been in hospital.

On quiet evenings Gerald walked the five-minute walk to the most beautiful beach he'd ever been on and imagined himself walking down the sand, hand in hand with Susan before walking through the gently rippling shoreline to immerse himself in the cooling and soothing waters of the Med for a refreshing skinny-dip. This was his treat to himself and he would lie back and float with squinting eyes on the sun as it altered its shade from pure white to gold to blood orange.

<'I'll be bringing you here one day, my sweet. You wait and see.'>

Author's Note

[1] John Merifield was re-interred at Phaleron War Cemetery, Athens on 6th February 1945. King George II of Greece sent his personal representative and Prime Minister Metaxas attended. A Greek newspaper reported: 'The coffin was covered with two crossed flags - the flags of Britain and Greece. The dead, a young English airman, the first to be killed on Greek soil, came down out of the blue sky wounded while chasing the assassin of Greek women and children - the Italian aviators. He was the first British Eagle, his wings broken, to fall on the sacred soil of Attica, the first hero of the new generation of the Philhellenes of 1940.'

[2] In his report to the Air Ministry dated 9 Jan 1947 John D'Albiac states he pressed the Prime Minister of Greece to undertake the immediate construction of all-weather runways at Araxos and Agrinion and if this was not provided, this would limit the support the RAF could give to the Greeks. Metaxas agreed and stated runways would be ready by Jan 31st 1941. Severe weather and construction issues meant this would not be the case.

[3] Pilot Officer Roald was in hospital for approximately six months recovering from face, back and other injuries following his crash in the desert on 19th September 1940. Pilot Officer Gerald Davies was in hospital from 12th to 23rd October 1940.

Chapter Eighteen

'The King Comes to Henley'

It was Tuesday 19th November 1940 and The Bish had returned from his time at H.Q. He wasted no time in bringing together his team of officers in 211 squadron to brief them on the outcome of the discussions and orders given in his time away. The news given at the briefing was as suspected by all. They would move on but where they had never been certain, although there had been lots of speculation. The betting was that it would have something to do with the Italians in Epirus.

The Bish left the team in no doubt. They would be headed for Greece within 48 hours.

Gerald had a good idea what the outcome of The Bish's visit to H.Q. would be, he just wasn't aware of the precise details. It wasn't only the Bish's H.Q. visit, or even the conversations he had with The Bish, which had made him fully aware of where he might be heading. There had been another clue. Gerald had made good friends with the war correspondent who'd been with 211 Squadron since before he'd arrived in mid-September. Squadron Leader Wisdom had been with 211 since the last week of July, but at dawn on the on the 6th November he had flown off on a 'hush-hush meeting' to Greece, in a Sunderland flying boat from Alexandria. Gerald had sat with Flight Lieutenant Luke "The Duke' Delaney the previous day and, over beer, they had talked about The Duke's trip to Palestine in the past few days with Tommy Wisdom, who had a big background with racing cars before the war. The two had hired a big old American car and had headed for Jerusalem across the Sinai Desert, breaking down one or two times in the process in a car they'd nicknamed *Wisdom's and Delaney's Folly*, such were the problems they'd had with it. The two had stayed at the King David Hotel in Jerusalem and for the first time had managed to bathe and drink without a hint of sand interfering with the fluids.

"I'll tell you this… " had added The Duke, pulling Gerald closer to whisper. "It was on the way back, we'd called to see friends at Beersheba and we found out about the Itis invading Albania and declaring war on Greece. Tommy called it the lighting of the Balkan Bomb!"

Gerald nodded and listened intently.

The Duke came in closer. "On the way back to Cairo, we were stopped by a guard. He told Tommy that his C.O, a Charles Bray wanted to see him… cut a long story short, I ended up taking him there, and we went for a jar with old Wing Commander Bray." The Duke became even quieter in his speech. "Tommy's off to Athens… staying at the King George Hotel in Constitution Square. Place full of 'German tourists' Gerry ol' chap. German bloody tourists, my arse."

They giggled together at the phrase.

"Seems that Air Commodore D'Albiac will be there, hence the reason for sending Tommy Wisdom our personal correspondent. Important matters must be afoot, hey? Some high-level meeting with the old dodderer Metaxas as well ol' chap."

"Metaxas?"

"The Greek Dictator… you know, The Prime Minister as he's called."

Gerald shrugged his shoulders. The name was a new one on him.

*

During the early evening of that Tuesday of the third week of November, the officers from 211 Squadron were called together for a group photograph. It would be their last photograph together before the squadron left Egypt for Europe. Everyone knew it was Greece, but the precise location was being kept a secret, or as most men suspected, Muddle East H.Q., still didn't know the exact location where anyone was going.

In Britain it would be the day over 900 people would be killed in a Luftwaffe raid on Birmingham.

The officers laughed and joked with Harry Hensser, the Air Ministry's official photographer, who'd been given the rather insalubrious title 'Photo Joe.' Harry... Photo Joe, wore an RAF uniform, but held no rank although he'd been on more missions than many of the crew and had flown in France earlier in the war. He was the official photographer on site and directed proceedings as to who was sitting or standing where in the photograph. There was only one person who wasn't given any direction. He knew where he was going from the outset. The Bish was centre image seated at the front, with his faithful band of brothers around him.

Image: Officers of 211 Squadron: November 1940

Front Row (left to right): Flying Officer Luke Sylvestre Delaney, (The Duke) Flight Officer Allan Leonard Farrington (Dinkum), Flight Lieutenant Graham Danson Jones ('Potato'), Squadron Leader James Gordon-Finlayson ('The Bish'), Flight Lieutenant George Brunton Browne Doudney, Flight Lieutenant Kelly, Flight Lieutenant Henry Fremlin Squire ('Doc').

   Middle Row (left to right): Pilot Officer 'Willie' Williams, Pilot Officer Ralph Barnes (Buckshot), Pilot Officer Wingate-Grey, Flying Officer George Ritchie, Flying Officer Dennis Charles Barrett (Keeper), Pilot Officer Guy Inglis Jerdein (the Airedale), Flight Lieutenant Lindsay Basil Buchanan ('Buck'), Flight Lieutenant Robert (Bobby) Douglas Campbell, Pilot Officer Chapman, Pilot Officer Ronald William Pearson.

   Back Row (left to right): Squadron Leader Kenelm (Ken) Crispin Vivian Dundas, Pilot Officer Eric Bevington-Smith (Smithy), Pilot Officer Gerald Davies ('Gerry'), Pilot Officer Arthur Geary.

   See [1] below for more information.

* * *

"Hurry up, gents" he dictated. "It's damn well hot out there and our night out at the Club beckons."

Photo Joe, Kodak Folding Autographic Brownie camera held steady in his hand, framed up the motley crew before him, with one eye on the sometimes capricious G-F, who from time to time was shouting, "Hurry up Harry man, we've not got all day… " followed by guffaws of laughter.

With a shout of "looking this way, gentlemen… AND… " the shutter clicked. The camera film was wound on and two more shots were taken for 'good-luck' and that was it. Session over and the image recorded for posterity. Everyone could now head off for the farewell dinner which beckoned at the Canal Club.

The sun had long departed the evening sky when The Bish, Gerald, Arthur Geary and the other officers of 211 Squadron headed for the Canal Club in Ismailia in an enormous group.

The waterfront club was the regular haunt for members of the RAF stationed nearby. It was a place to relax, where everyone felt secure in this strange arid land.

Gerald looked around the place with a hint of nostalgia filling his head.

<'I might never come here again.> He looked around taking everything in. <'How could I ever describe this place to Sue or to Lizzie and the others back home? They'd never believe what I've seen. I've flown over the great pyramids more times than I can remember, I've seen The Sphinx and swam in the Mediterranean like some rich playboy in Monte Carlo. What a privilege and all at the expense of the RAF.'>.

He smiled to himself. Then he thought about the amount of times he'd been shot at and how close he'd come to death on so many occasions already.

<'I just want to get this done and get home to see Sue.'>

The Bish interrupted his thoughts. "If I give you any more pennies for those thoughts, you'll soon have ten-bob, ol' chap."

"Sorry, boss. In a world of my own."

"Again! You can get put in the loony-bin for that, you know ol' chap."

Gerald looked seriously at The Bish. He really could have said something there and then. His mother Elizabeth had been put in the 'loony-bin' and the comment touched a raw nerve. He'd never told a soul in the RAF about any of this and bit his tongue to stop himself coming out with something he might regret.

"Come on ol' chap, I know you're going to miss this place." The Bish gripped Gerald with one arm around his shoulders in a fatherly way. "You deserve this tonight. You're my guiding light when we're up in the blue yonder. We'd not be here now, if it wasn't for you and Mr. Geary there…" Arthur Geary nodded as he collected drinks for the group, and handed them out. "… we're a great team and we'll be that same elite team over in Greece."

"Here's to a glorious future and a great partnership for The Bish Boys."

The group clinked glasses together and cheered.

Others arrived, and the noise of the place was raucous and happy. All had booked in advance and the hand-written menu was a soup starter, followed by a good old roast chicken dinner with traditional roast vegetables.

The whole evening was accompanied by music from the RAF Middle East Command Dance Orchestra, who'd come down from Cairo specially for the occasion of The Greyhounds leaving.

"Great band, hey!" Arthur Geary commented. "I believe one of their guys is from your neck of the woods."

"He is?" Gerald said, looking across to the band.

"The young lad there… " he said, pointing to a talented trumpet player who looked no more than sixteen.

Gerald looked across. He'd never seen the lad before in his life. "Don't know him." Gerald added with a hint of disinterest.

"Said something to me about being from a place called Shotton."

"Shotton!" Gerald's ears picked up. "That's where I'm from."

"Go over and speak to him then, when this number's finished. You might know him."

Within ten minutes Gerald had made his way across to the young lad. The two shook hands.

"Gerald Davies. You're a dab hand with that there trumpet."

"Syd Lawrence.[2] Well it's Sidney George Lawrence actually, but I go by Syd with a Y! Sounds better"

"Arthur tells me you're from Shotton?"

"He'd never heard of the place when I said I was from Shotton. No one has, although occasionally people mention the nearby Sealand and Hawarden airfields."

"Well, I've heard of it! Shotton born, bred and educated!

"Ditto, sir! Salisbury Street me."

"No kidding! I know Salisbury Street. Just up the road from me."

"Where you from in Shotton then?"

"Ash Grove."

"Down by the line."

"Small world, hey! ARTHUR!" he shouted. "Over here."

Arthur Geary made his way across. "This is my new mate, Syd. He's from Shotton, like me."

Arthur Geary shook his hand. "Yes, we have met.   I was complementing Syd on what a great exponent of his art he is. So you're from the same place as this reprobate?"

"Certainly am, sir.   No better place to be from.   My mum was a Phillips? She was from Sealand originally. Know them?"

"There's Phillips' working over in the Steelworks."

"You worked there?"

"I started work there before the RAF."

"Dad was from Wrexham, he worked at the works as a draughtsman. Sam Philips he is. He married my mum Lily in 1919 at Hawarden Church."

"My mum's buried there." Gerald sighed heavily. "Er… yes… Sam, your dad.   Name rings a bell.   There's many people in the works, though. A LOT!" Gerald sighed again, still thinking about his mother Elizabeth. "Anyway, Syd, do you still live in Shotton?"

"Well I did, but music and the war dragged me away and I find myself here in sunny Egypt… with a fellow Shottonite! Amazing. Bloody amazing. So you chaps are fighting the Nazis for us?"

"Well, the Iti at the moment, but who knows when that might alter."

"Hun or Itis, they're all the same.   Trying to kill us off when all we want to do is live a peaceful life. I couldn't even escape them in Shotton, you know chaps."

"No?" Gerald listened with interest.

"Just this last summer, before I came away, a bloody Heinkel I was told it was, flew over my house.   Nearly took the damn chimney off. When was it now?… It was… "

"Don't tell me," interrupted Gerald. "It was August… "

"About the middle of the month. The 14th I think."

"That's it.   I got a letter from my Aunt Lizzie telling me about it. The krauts bombed Sealand and were shot down by Spitfires from Hawarden."

"I saw it with my own eyes. The Hun bomber went over and bombed the hell out of Sealand.   Then our boys… I mean, er, you lot arrived and chased it. All in broad daylight. Three Spitfires."

"Good old Spits."

"Rat-a-tat-tat fires one, then another rat-a-tat-tat and another." Syd Lawrence used his trumpet to make the point. "They had a good go at it. Then BOOM! The engine goes on the hun plane. Last I saw, it was going down, smoke billowing from it."

"Well, blow me down with a feather, Syd. You're from Shotton and saw what I read in a letter from Aunt Lizzie. Now you're here. Small world. Get you a drink?"

"I don't mind if I do. Was wondering when you'd ask," answered Arthur Geary. "He doesn't need asking, get the lad from Shotton a drink."

In-between playing with the orchestra, on and off throughout the evening Syd came to sit with the lads from 211 Squadron and told Gerald more about his time in Shotton from playing at the famous Vaughan Hall in Shotton itself to playing in venues around Chester city centre.

Gerald and Syd agreed to meet up when they could, the uncertainty of the future permitting. Gerald couldn't say where they were off to tomorrow, but did his best to let Syd know he wouldn't see him anytime soon. "It might be when this bloody war is over," Gerald added, shaking his head pessimistically, "… whenever that might be."

"Give my regards to Shotton!" Syd retorted.

"You too, if you get back there before I do."

The two parted with a handshake.

Everyone ate and partied until just before midnight, singing songs from the First World War, but no one had wanted to stay too late, nor become so intoxicated that it might spoil the following day. For the first time they had all, to a man, remained sensible as tomorrow at noon, they had a trip across the Mediterranean and a new task. The Greco-Italian War.

Several times during the night Gerald had retrieved the precious photograph of Susan and him, which he took everywhere, and looked at it to savour the time they'd had the day the photograph was taken. He'd even showed the photograph to Syd as he was desperate for someone different to share his story with. In-between Syd heading back to play a piece with the orchestra, Gerald told him the story of his girlfriend, the person he'd fallen madly in love with, who was now thousands of miles away. Each time he looked at her, he wondered if he might ever see her again.

Part way through the night, Syd announced on the microphone, "This is for Sue in Henley, from my Shotton buddy Gerry. So for all you lads in Ismailia missing your loved ones at home, here's Our Love Affair by Glenn Miller."

Gerald listened and drifted off into his thoughts. He didn't want it to be a brief encounter or even just a stolen moment. He'd found the girl of his dreams and he intended to go back for her. These were times of snatched moments and brief flings for many. He could cope with the snatched moments, but not a brief fling. Susan was so much more than a brief fling.

"Pretty girl Gerry lad." The Bish said surprising Gerald from behind late in the evening, as he put his arm over his shoulder, looking down onto the photograph now lying on the table of the Canal Club. "Got the look of Vera Lynn." The Bish gently picked up the precious photograph.

"Careful boss. Only one I've got of her."

The Bish took no notice, but handled the photograph with care anyway. "Even got her eyes Gerry. Thing is... can she sing like Vera Lynn."

"She has a warm voice. She certainly sings to my heart."

They both smiled. Both were missing their loved ones at home.

The Bish held the photograph away tantalisingly, inspecting it even closer. "Blonde. Nice cheeks,   Have you , you know..." He winked suggestively.

Gerald grabbed the image back. "Filthy mind G-F, hey?   That's for me to know and... "

"You haven't then."

"You'll never know Skip." Gerald winked, as The Bish handed the photograph back.

"Look after it, ol' chap. Look after her, if she's THE ONE."

Gerald looked longingly at the close up black-and-white image of him and Susan on the boat. "She is. We've danced the Blackout Stroll together..." he reminisced. "Yes... I remember changing partners mid-dance when they put the lights out."   He laughed. "Neither of us wanted to swap."

The Bish had his own memories of good times dancing with his wife and walked away, leaving Gerald with his memories of a warm July day when they'd sat in a relaxing chauffeur driven launch from Hobbs of Henley, meandering their way on the Thames, heading gently along the famous Regatta course. It had been Susan's idea.   Their second date. It wasn't a boat for hire. Just a favour.

"Why don't we take a trip on the water. It would be such an agreeable thing to do on such a lovely day. I've got my camera and we can take some pictures of the ducks and any wildlife we see. Besides, what else would we do. We are walking out together, I mean… courting aren't we? AND I get a perfect discount," she had joked.

This had been the first time Gerald had heard Susan use the word courting and he supposed now they were officially a couple, well at least the beginning of being a couple.

Susan had volunteered for duties on the river weeks earlier as an unofficial auxiliary on the Upper Thames Patrol who were part of the Home Guard in the area.

"If the Nazi's invade, I want to be here to safeguard this beautiful river from being a conduit inland for their forces," she had declared with some vigour, deeming this to be her important contribution to the war effort. If she couldn't fight or fly an aircraft, then this was the least she could do. Susan Hall had recently moved to the area from Hove on the south coast and now lived with her parents in a Riverside bungalow just off Wargrave Road in Henley. Coming from the area originally, her parents had moved nearer their roots and she had naturally come along with them. She loved the riverside and as the war progressed she became more and more involved with security activities on the river.

"What can I do ya for today Sue my love?" Harry from Hobbs had shouted.

"Private trip for two?"

"Gotcha girl!" Harry winked. "I'll get our quietest boatman to sort you out. Leave you lovebirds in peace then, eh?" Harry had winked again at Susan, who's cheeks flushed red.

"Let me pay. Let me pay." Gerald insisted, fumbling in his pockets for change.

"Er… that'll be the huge price of… nothing. Me and Sue know each other, don't we Sue. Hush-hush, like." He touched his index finger to his nose as if to suggest a secret. "So, as you're her friend today, then it'll be no charge."

"What he means is… isn't it, Harry. This is UTP stuff, so we are going out on patrol. Well, as good as." Gerald and Susan sat aside each other on the beautiful old wooden launch, the motor purring away as the boat made its way upstream.

True to Harry's word, the boatman, a guy in his late fifties, who took them, never uttered a thing and tried his best to avoid eye contact with the couple he had in his care.

Anyone looking on would have known the couple in the boat were recent acquaintances as they sat somewhat apart as the boat chugged along a short distance in the Oxford direction.

Neither knew how to begin the conversation they both longed for, then both said the word "So… "

"Go on, ladies first," Gerald smiled.

"Thank you. I was going to ask where you're from."

"You wouldn't know it, it's a little town on the banks of the River Dee called Shotton.   Nothing like as posh as here in Henley.   The river's nothing like this one here either…well in Shotton it isn't anyway but at Chester, now there's a difference. The river at Chester by the weir is just like here. You can hire a boat, have ice-cream and walk into the city quite easily."

"Sounds a nice place. I've never been."

"One day, er… I shall take you, if you'd come?"

"I might," she smiled teasingly.

"So what do you do when you're not on the river then Miss Susan Hall dear?" Gerald gazed into her blue eyes, awaiting a response.

"Careless talk and all that, hey. I might have to kill you if I say. You could be a spy?"

"What? In this uniform?"

"My day job or my other job, well you know I'm in the Home Guard, patrolling the river…keeping communications going on the river and the roads around the river. You know that."

"You have a proper job?"

"Cheeky boy! The Upper Thames Patrol is a proper job in a way. I do a few hours at The Horns but I'm a shipping clerk in my main paid job. I file things away. It's boring, so there's nothing more to say about it."

"So could you shoot a gun if you had to then?"

"What do you think?"

Gerald laughed.

"Don't laugh. I might be a wizard with a gun."

"Are you?"

"I could be, if there was a German coming up the river." Susan made her hands into a machine gun and strafed the river with a burst of her vibrating lips. "There, you see. All the Germans are dead."

"Wow, you can use a gun, but you use your eyes better. Oh, those beautiful eyes."

The two stared at each others' eyes, becoming lost in the blue gaze. They fell slowly towards each other and Gerald remembered what his dad had told him about putting his arm around a girl.

'You don't go at it like a bull at a gate, lad. Gently lift your arm and watch the girl's eyes. If she doesn't move away, then put your hand on her opposite shoulder and lay your arm behind her neck. All gentle mind. Then pull her gently in closer to you. That's when you get to k...'

Gerald followed the instructions in his head. Susan didn't move away. Her neatly pencilled eyebrows arched slightly and the light rouge on her cheeks seems to brighten even more. He'd not kissed a girl before and didn't even know if this was the right place to be doing it. With an audience of one!

He looked at her eyes. She had a light eye-shadow on, with a hint of gold to match the sparkle in her eyes. Susan's black mascara flashed wickedly a few times as their eyes collided and an involuntary urge kicked in, which neither Gerald nor Susan could do anything about. Their heads gently fell towards each other and Susan lifted her hand to caress Gerald's face. Lips met, a gentle collision of skin with Red Velvet lipstick being the only barrier between them. The touch of lips lingered as both closed their eyes. No one wanted to be the first to pull away.

The boatman turned his head further away. He'd seen it all before, especially now in wartime. Romances were different in these times, people got together quicker. No one knew for certain how long their romance might survive. This world was a fleeting glimpse for many soldiers, airmen and sailors, so they would make the most of it.

The need to breathe in had kicked in at the same time for the couple and their lips gently peeled apart, momentarily sticking together as if their bodies were telling them not to move away from each other. Hearts were beating fast and breaths were drawn in quicker.

Susan looked at Gerald and laughed. He looked surprised.

"You look lovely in my Helena Rubenstein."

"Helena... "

"My lipstick. On You."

She took a clean white handkerchief from her leather handbag and wiped Gerald's lips, showing Gerald the results, before she put the handkerchief away. They both giggled like teenagers.

"Sorry!" Shouted Gerald to Henry, their chauffeur.

"No worries, my old mucker. Seen it all before. Just jealous I'm not thirty years younger."

They giggled again.

Susan squeezed Gerald's hand and they kissed again, both taking a quick look to ensure their chauffeur still had his gaze averted.

The old boatman lit a cigarette and kept the launch at a steady, slow speed. He had no intention of rocking the boat either for himself or for the young couple now lost in each other's eyes three yards down the launch.

The couple laid back in each other's arms contented in their brief escape from the war which pervaded everything in their lives as swallows darted down to the river and played without a care in the blue sky above.

As they turned mid-river it was Susan who remembered the box brownie which she'd forgotten about.

"The camera, Gerry. Shall we take some photos?"

"Well, we've seen plenty of ducks, coots and swans... and a couple of squirrels on the banks a mile back and we ain't got a pic of one of them." They laughed.

"How's about, I take one or two of you two enjoying yourselves on this fine day hey?" Henry suggested. "Dab hand with a camera, eh. Give it 'ere."

"Splendid idea" said Gerry as Susan handed the camera over.

The couple sat arm-in-arm, with Susan sightly in front and Gerald holding her close in from behind and THAT photograph was taken, just next to Henley's Sailing Club's Headquarters at Wargrave.

The launch chugged its way back towards its moorings downstream, and Gerry kissed Susan again. "I believe I am falling for..."

The sentence didn't get finished, Gerald and Susan had been too engrossed in each other as Henry Hobbs brought the couple back to the mooring at Henley that first day they took a boat ride on the river.

"Hey, you two, we're back."

"That was over far too quickly."

"Watch the camera as you get out, you two. Don't want those precious photos going into the Thames, do we young lovebirds?"

"Henry!" Blushed Susan.

"Yes... Henry," winked Gerald.

"Are we lovebirds Sue?"

"We might be."

Henry tied the boat securely to its mooring, and the two held hands as they got off the boat.

"You can tell your grandchildren about this boat trip one day!" Shouted Henry Hobbs as the couple walked away.

"That's a bit forward, isn't it?" Susan said, looking at Gerald with a warmth in her eyes. "I mean, talking about children already with a stranger."

Gerald could see himself and Susan holding the hands of two young children, a girl and a boy.

The next thing Gerald knew, he was being tapped on the shoulder by Arthur Geary.

"You in there Gerry lad. Day dreaming about that girl of yours again."

Gerald shook his head and quickly placed the photograph into his tunic pocket and buttoned it securely. He tapped the breast pocket and thanked his lucky stars he'd had the fortune to meet Susan.

"Do you know Arthur... "

"Not another story about that girl of yours, Gerry lad. You're crazy in love."

"You've not heard this one. It's about the day the King came to Henley."

"George VI came to Henley?"

"Yep, an' I was there to see it."

"When was that dear chap?"

"I remember the day so well. It was July 28th this year. I'd been invited by Sue down to the Thames for the King's visit. I wasn't with her if you get my drift Arthur... "

"You weren't with your lady friend? Why on earth not?"

"No, she was part of the day's proceedings."

"Proceedings?"

"Yes, she's part of The Upper Thames Patrol - it's a Home Guard Unit. It's to stop the Nazis in their tracks if they ever get across the channel and intend using the Thames as a through-route."

Arthur Geary nodded.

"She was part of the flotilla behind the King's barge... she was in what they called the Guard of Honour for their stretch of the Thames. She told me she never even got to see any of them, except the back of their boat, but I stood on the side waving to the King, Queen and to Princesses Elizabeth and Margaret Rose as they passed by. It was a great day."

"You actually saw THE King."

"Yep, and THE Queen, so I know what I'm fighting for King... er... and er... Queen... and Country!"

They both laughed.

"And did you get to see your Sue afterwards?"

"Her boat dropped her off right next to me when she'd finished and we walked out together watching the rest of the day from the side of the river. We saw the King's barge waiting to go through Boulter's lock on its way to Windsor, so we got a real close-up view of the Royal lot. We all sang the National Anthem as they waited. Never been at such an occasion before."

"Do they look like royalty close up then?"

"I suppose they did... minus crowns on their heads."

"They reserve them for when they pose for the coins."

They both roared.

"Me and Sue went for a ride in the country in my MG after, ended up in a pub somewhere deep in the heart of England. What a day. What a day! It frightens me I'll never get back or even get to see her again." He sighed.

"Be optimistic young Gerry lad. You two will create a wonderful life together one day when this is all over. You'll see."

Gerald thought on. " I miss home so much."

"We all do! We all do!"

THE KING'S REVIEW OF THE UPPER THAMES PATROL
— THE RIVER SECTION OF THE HOME GUARD:
CRAFT PASSING THE SALUTING BASE ON JULY 28. THE
QUEEN, PRINCESS ELIZABETH AND PRINCESS MARGARET
ROSE ACCOMPANIED HIS MAJESTY. (*Wide World*)

Illustrated London News - 3 August 1940

Gerald took the photograph from his pocket and placed it on the table. He looked at it longingly and watched as the Canal Club emptied of RAF personnel. It had been a successful night and everyone seemed in a more positive mood. Gerald stood up as several officers approached and bade him farewell, shaking his hand warmly. There were wishes galore from people staying in North Africa, but other squadrons were leaving too. 80 Squadron and their Glosters were heading for Greece. Gerald was thankful for their continued presence and shook hands with several of them, telling them he'd see them over the other side of the water.

Tomorrow they would be in another theatre of war. Greece.

* * *

Author's Note:

[1] Officers of 211 Squadron (further information)
There are 22 men in the photograph. Nine were killed before the end of the war:

Flying Officer Dennis Charles Barrett (Keeper) - Killed (25 yrs) 2nd January 1941 - Athens
Flying Officer Luke Sylvestre Delaney, ('The Duke') - Killed in Action (21 yrs) - 6th January 1941 - Greece
Flight Lieutenant Lindsay Basil Buchanan ('Buck') - Killed in Action (24 yrs) 13th April 1941 - Greece
Pilot Officer Gerald Davies (Gerry) - Killed in Action (23yrs) 13th April 1941 - Greece
Pilot Officer Arthur Geary - Killed in Action (31yrs) 13th April 1941 - Greece
Squadron Leader Kenelm Crispin Vivian Dundas (Ken) - Killed in Action (26yrs) - 10th February 1942 - Malaya
Flying Officer George Ritchie - Killed in Action (30 years) 2nd October 1942 - Singapore
Pilot Officer Ronald William Pearson (Twinkle) - Killed on Active Service (30 yrs) 7th August 1943 -Kemble, Gloucestershire
Flight Lieutenant Allan Leonard Farrington (Dinkum) - Killed in Action (29yrs) - 29th August 1944 - Denmark

By coincidence , almost that very week, Susan Hall took part in a group photograph for Tatler Magazine of the Upper Thames Patrol Home Guard Women's Section - see Chapter 'The Girl At The Horns.'

[2] Syd Lawrence - was born Sidney (Sydney) George Lawrence on 26th June 1923 at Shotton in Flintshire. He dies on 5th May 1998 in Manchester. He was a famous Big Band Leader in Britain, in the style of Glenn Miller, appearing on many British Television Shows including working with Morecambe & Wise. The Syd Lawrence Orchestra, formed by him still lives on and plays to this day.

Chapter Nineteen

'Poisoned'

Gerald was with Arthur Geary in their encampment just outside Ismailia and had heard Arthur rush outside to be sick. There was hardly a man from 211 Squadron who hadn't woken up at some stage during the night with a severe bout of diarrhoea and vomiting. Gerry got up to check on Arthur but wasn't feeling too good himself. He put it down to the ale on offer at the Canal Club.

"Jeez, Arthur, too much of the old ale I see!"

Arthur retched again. "Like you, I hardly drunk a drop."

Then it hit Gerald. He was suddenly violently sick and dashed off to the khazi; a dirt hole in the ground thirty yards away. There, in the darkness of the desert, he met The Bish and four others from the squadron.

"Not you as well, Gerry lad."

Gerry said nothing. He couldn't.

"Some bugger has poisoned us last night!" The Bish commented as he wiped the water and spittle pouring from his eyes and nose. There were many rumours about Germans and Italians infiltrating the locals. Added to this, the locals weren't always happy about what some termed the 'occupation' of their land by a colonial power, so everyone thought it highly likely that dirty tricks were to blame for the illness now affecting everyone.

Gerry came out of the darkness. "At least we're not dead, Skip!"

The retching shout came back, "Not yet ol' chap. Not yet!" The Bish scurried for a private place to throw up as Gerald once again disappeared into the darkness without saying another word.

The most horrible gurgling, barfing and eructation noises could be heard everywhere. For hours!

Several hours later the whole squadron was laid up in their camp beds, all green as the markings on their aircraft. The Blenheims stood silent and no one moved from their beds for a day, apart from to-ing and fro-ing to the khazi. There were definitely no Italian spies anywhere near the camp this day, as this would have been the perfect time to mount an offensive. As it was, the enemy was quiet. Not even a raid had taken place the previous night.

Over the Mediterranean Tommy Wisdom waited for more reinforcements plus the people he knew and loved from 211 Squadron. Needless to say, the trip across the Mediterranean was cancelled and Tommy Wisdom saw nothing of the men for three more days.

*

Gerald flew out of Ismailia for the last time before dawn on the 23rd November 1940. The Bish headed the flight of all the Blenheims from Ismailia over to El Daba, the airbase at Fouka, where they refuelled for the first leg of the journey. Afterwards Gerald set foot for his one and only time on Crete to collect supplies and take on board more fuel. The Blenheim flight then headed across a clear blue sea to Eleusis, just north-west of Athens, The Bish completing a low pass of the Acropolis with the Parthenon siting on top, before landing to drop off some supplies and collecting, what the ground crew called *'mission important materials'* for their onward destination. This comprised food, drink and fuel supplies in the main. The flight of Blenheims was quickly loaded up and off to Menidi, a short flight to the north-east of Athens. This was the eventual destination of the day and would be their new home in what looked like a very mountainous part of Greece.

As The Bish descended the Blenheim towards Menidi, from a blue sky scattered with the wispiest of cirrus clouds high above, he pointed out something.

"Look, ol' man. The King's palace."

Gerald looked down at the rusty brown tiled roofs of what looked like a sprawling most un-palatial complex amongst trees. Then he looked the few yards across to a grass runway set in the trees.

As The Bish looked down, it was his time to reflect on the missions ahead now. *<'John D'Albiac has done a good job preparing Greece in* *advance for our arrival, but bloody hell there are still no hard runways for us. It doesn't augur well for when there's crap weather - and winter is just around the corner.'>*

"The King's place is right next to the runway, skip."

"Yes Gerry, my man." Crackled the intercom back. "Welcome to Menidi... er... as was previously called Tatoi. The King altered the name to stop the Itis bombing him." He laughed loudly. "It's the summer residence of George the Second of Greece."

"Lucky bugger. It's a right posh place skip. Look how green it all is as well. Jeez, skip. Greenery at last."

The Bish gave a thumbs up

As they landed it was 'Buckshot,' Flight Lieutenant Lindsay Buchanan, who reported that with minutes of his leaving Ismailia aerodrome, the Italians had dropped a stick of bombs across the runway, taking it out of action. Luckily all of 211's Blenheims had got away unscathed.

"If I'd have left a couple of minutes later, all three of us would've been fried meat by now!" had been Buckshot's way of laughing off the dangerous incident.

"One success too late!" The Bish commented at the briefing of the men later that day to much laughter.

One of the first people to get to The Bish's Blenheim was Tommy Wisdom, who greeted the crew with a huge welcome, the relief written across his face now that proper reinforcements to the Greece campaign had arrived. "The King will be impressed!" he'd said as he showed the men to the Officers' Quarters, near to some newly constructed hangars on the site. The place they were staying in was almost home from home, it was the old summer hotel of the palace at Tatoi and a veritable plush residence compared with what they'd been used to.

*

Menidi was base to other squadrons of the RAF and was now a powerful hub for the RAF in Greece, a place from which they could, if not easily, due the distances involved, attack the Italians in Epirus. As Gerald walked around Menidi on that first afternoon in Greece he saw men from other squadrons including the fighter squadron 30 and 80 who'd been over in North Africa. As he walked down a line of Gloster Gladiators from 80 Squadron, he immediately thought of Pilot Officer Dahl and wondered how he was recovering.

<'He could even be here?'>

He asked, when he saw the Flight Commander of 80 Squadron heading in his direction. Gerald had met the South African Squadron Leader Pat Pattle [1] in Egypt on a couple of occasions before but didn't know him very well. Either way, formalities between people of differing ranks had relaxed a great deal. Most young men had experienced near-death experiences so many times they all had a healthy respect for one another as people, not as a rank. The only snooty ranks they met were those who had no combat experience. Pilots and crew were here one day and gone the next. No one could afford the luxury of elitism in this cruel war.

Gerald stopped in front of Pat Pattle hold out his hand to remind him of who he was. "Pilot Officer Gerald Davies. Got a minute."

Pattle's weather worn features looked full of flu or something similar.

"Gerry, isn't it? I recognise you from… "

"Fouka or Ismailia it'll be."

"That's it. Blenheims. 211?"

"On the nail. Anyway, just a quick enquiry sir, I know you are busy."

"Happy to answer if it's something I can answer," Pat said, blowing his nose.

"It's a question about Pilot Officer Dahl's welfare. Last time I saw him, he was at the Anglo-Swiss. Is he all fixed-up now?"

"Visited a couple of days ago, Gerry. Still laid up I'm afraid, might never fly again so I'm told. Bad do in the desert with that idiot from Fouka."

<'Would love to know who the Fouka idiot is!'> Gerald smiled inside at almost sounding as if he'd sworn.

"Sorry to hear that, sir. If you see him again, tell him I'm asking for him."

"I sure will."

"Thank you. I'm grateful."

With that, one of the ground crew approached Gerald. "Briefing, Sir. The Bish is looking for you."

*

The outcome of the briefing was no surprise.

The Bish began with a detailed explanation why they were all there.

"You think we're here to save Greece's bacon, if you'll excuse the pun. Well, we are... BUT we are also the first forces to be back on mainland Europe since our troops were evacuated from Dunkirk. What do you think of that then gentlemen?"

No one had thought of the what they were up to in this way. Everyone cheered at the thought of making such a first.

"Winston Churchill, our great Prime Minister... " went on The Bish, "... expects us to do our duty and give the Itis a pasting and remove them from where they ought not to be. To that end we are assisting the Greeks, but we are doing more than that. Yes, we are. This is a moment of decisive action against Benito Mussolini following the invasion of October 28. The Greeks lads in the snowy mountains of the north are doing their best with inadequate resources, but from now on they will have The Greyhounds behind them. Are we ready for this gentlemen?"

"Ready!" Came the shout of a couple of dozen officers.

Right at that moment, Gerald knew the Blenheims were being loaded up with fuel and bombs to prepare for a raid. The Bish now told them where.

"Tomorrow morning at ten-fifteen we depart for Durazzo, a port on the Albanian coast in Epirus. The Itis unload their ships of men and supplies to fight the Greeks on the ground there. Tomorrow, The Greyhounds will give them the shock of their insignificant little Italian lives. They won't know what the hell has hit them."

More cheers.

"There's a BUT! The Itis may be a different kettle of fish here. We don't know for sure what they're about and we won't until we raid them tomorrow so my last words are some words of caution for us all. Be on your guard tomorrow and have your wits about you. Good luck, gentlemen. Good luck!"

There was a somber mood about the place which The Bish immediately recognised.

"One more thing before you go!" He added, stopping the men in their tracks as they made to leave the room. "There's still some money left from the sweepstake we won, so I shall expect everyone at the bar for a swift one!" The Bish announced as he ended the briefing.

Following the briefing and a quick drink at the bar, everyone readied themselves for the morning raid. No one knew what to expect. This was no longer North Africa, this was Europe and things were very different. The bar had been a quiet affair. The uncertainty of tomorrow's raid on Durazzo weighed heavily on the minds of everyone. The first raid on a new place was always filled with trepidation and anxiety. They knew the flak of Tobruk, Sidi Barrani and Buq Buq, but they had no idea what the defences were like around Durazzo.

The last thing Gerald did that night was to double tap his tunic pocket.

<'You're my good luck mascot, Susan. Where I go, you go. Night sweetheart.'>

Author's Note

[1] Marmaduke Thomas St John Pattle, 'Pat' - DFC & Bar was killed in action on 20 April 1941, during the Battle of Athens.

Chapter Twenty

'Spiro Amerikanos'

The morning was soon upon them and the Blenheims left in groups of three. Gerald, The Bish and Arthur Geary would, as usual, be the lead plane. The raid on Durazzo was a success, but the aftermath was a different matter. The aftermath had led to L8511 crash landing in shallow waters just off the narrowest of beaches at Lefkimmi in Corfu.

Gerald walked a few hundred yards further along the narrow strip of beach towards a small group of people ahead of him who had come out to see what the fuss was all about. They were a mixture of men and women, with several small children who were running around and playing, seemingly oblivious to the smoking Blenheim in the background.

<'Harmless locals for sure!'>

He momentarily stopped, then convinced himself it was safe to proceed forward, all the time thinking how he might need to draw his revolver from its holster should the need arise, which he touched constantly to reassure himself. He could see people from the group looking in his direction.

"Ahoy! Over here! Help!" he shouted and proceeded towards them at more of a pace, although still with some apprehension and trepidation. This was wartime and people carried guns, whether or not they were military.

There were shouts and screams of panic ahead of him. Parents gathered their children who needed to be carried, and the group of people melted away in haste with fright.

There was a shout from behind. It was The Bish, now stood on the wing of the stricken Blenheim. "You've jolly well frightened the natives Gerry, come on lad you can do better than that." Arthur Geary was sat astride the fuselage using a fire-extinguisher which was barely working. A trickle of some fizzing fluid emitted from the canister as he shook it with all his might.

Both laughed. Gerald still fumbled about looking for *that photograph.*

The Bish could see what Gerald was doing and shouted again, trying to lighten the mood. "You'll wear that uniform out Gerry ol' chap. It's not there! Just occurred to me, the last time I saw it was at the Canal Club."

The Bish was right. It was coming back to him now. <*'Shit! I left it on the table!'*>

Gerald smiled nervously and gave a thumbs up in derision as he proceeded forward, shaking his head at his stupidity for losing the photograph of him and Susan.

The crowd of people began running away even faster as they saw him coming, but one man stood his ground as the people passed him. Then he walked forward towards Gerald. He could have been no older than Gerald but his face was serious and Gerald stopped in his tracks when he saw the man was armed with a rifle, albeit a rifle which looked like it could have been used during the Crimean War. The rifleman before him went down on one knee, his finger to the trigger, and took aim.

"HALT!... Man from plane, I say HALT. I shoot!"

He motioned to Gerald to put his hands up.

<*'The people of Corfu are on our side, aren't they?'*>

Gerald complied instantly. He stopped and held his hands out to either side to show he had no weapon in them. If he had to die, he had no intention of dying through non-compliance.

"Inglese, Inglese!" Gerald shouted loudly, trying his best to look as friendly as possible.

The two were now about fifty yards apart. Gerald contemplated drawing his pistol but thought twice about it. The man before him had the advantage of having his weapon fully trained on him, and Gerald's .38 Enfield revolver wouldn't even make it out of the top of his pyjamas before the bullet hit him. The man motioned again with the barrel of the rifle for Gerald to put his hands up even higher, but this time it was accompanied by a shout. "Hands up, airman!"

The best course of action he could think of was to do what the man said and put his hands up. High!

He'd seen it many times in the western films he loved watching back home at the Alhambra Cinema on Chester Road in Shotton. He loved John Wayne and had seen him in quite a few films, the most recent being Stagecoach, which he'd seen just a few weeks before when he'd been at the cinema with Susan back in Henley.   Yet he still wondered, where was that photograph now of him and Susan taken on the River Thames during the summer.

<'*Some waiter has probably thrown it away.*'>

It had been his lucky charm and now he'd lost it, his luck had gone and here he was shot down and at the end of a gun. He felt like he was in a movie himself, hands held high like some outlaw in Arizona caught by the sheriff.

The man remained on his knee pointing the gun and Gerald remained hands above his head.   Both had never experienced this before. Luckily for Gerald, the man was not trigger-happy.

"English!" Gerald once again called out to the man who seemed not to have heard. Gerald walked forward gingerly, and then it seemed there was recognition of his uniform. The man stood up and lowered his gun.

"Say, you're English. You're sure welcome to our island brother."

The man had shouted back in plain English with what Gerry thought was a Canadian accent. Gerald had trained with Canadian airmen and recognised the accent straight away. This was no ordinary Corfiot.

Gerald walked up to the man and they shook hands.

"Gerry. Gerald Davies."

"Fokion. Nai *(yes)*… Fokion Halikiopoulos." *[1]*

"That's some name sir, I'll never get my head around that." Gerald said as he gently pushed the muzzle of the rifle, plus its lethal looking bayonet, away from his direction.

"Nai… Just call me Fokion! Welcome to Lefkimmi. Say, you seem to have a problem with your aircraft. Are you all okay? No one is hurt?"

"Just a teeny-weeny minor problem and yep, we're all fine, if a little shaken up. That damn rifle didn't help either. Just keep it pointed down. You'll have someone's eye out with that bayonet!"

"Nai. Sorry about that. Can't be too careful. We have the Italikos bastardos… they bomb us and we shoot at them, so they is crashing here sometimes. I wasn't sure you might be them… Now I know you not. Nai!

"Just one quick question, nai," said a bemused Fokion examining Gerald's uniform. "Why you wear pyjamas, my man."

Gerald looked down at the brown and red stripes of his nightwear peaking out of his uniform. He'd completely forgotten about them. He chuckled heartily. "It's a long story. A long story!"

They both looked back at the smoking plane down from which The Bish and Arthur Geary were now wading through the shallow sea.

Image: James Gordon-Finlayson Collection.

"There are Nazis around I hear too?"

"Nai, nai. Yes. They bomb... Italikos... Germanoi... they are all the same. Nai. Talk is they'll be here soon. They are getting ready to invade us for sure. Nai... We are very worrieds. I thought at first you were one of them, then I saw dis uniform."

"Well, we've just slowed them down a bit, so hopefully they won't be here for a while."

"Nai. You are good men."

"I knew someone from Canada once. Are you Canadian by any chance?"

"Corfiot born and bred but nai, I spent time in my younger years with family in Chicago. America. It's full of Greeks like me. I come home to look after my family, so did my brother Spiros. We shall call him here. He will be sure to help. He likes to help. He knew an English family once, they have gone back now. Mrs. Durrell and her children... nai... well, they were quite grown up. He liked them. He misses them, nai. I'm sure he will tell you the story when he meets you. He has a car. Nai… he can help."

Gerald felt a complete sense of relief filling his body. "You are a sight for sore eyes then, dear Fokion."

"Sore eyes?"

"It's a saying in English."

"Nai, yes I remember. I have heard of it. Means you are happy."

Gerald nodded and shouted back to The Bish and Arthur Geary, who were wading ashore as they spoke, but still some distance away.

"Okay lads, come on over," shouted Gerald. "It's all right chaps."

At the same time the throng of Corfiots, who'd been taking cover for fear the downed airmen were the enemy, started emerging from everywhere and soon the group were surrounded by hundreds, if not up to a thousand people. All cheering, patting them on the back and shaking their hands. One or two spoke English and now they were inundated with the words "Thank you!" and "Brothers Welcome!" spoken over and over again.

Fokion shook hands with The Bish and Arthur Geary.

The Bish was concerned about the aircraft and looked back from the shore thinking how it might be recovered, if indeed it was recoverable. He had collected the important logs and papers from the plane. These were placed in his canvas shoulder bag.

"I see you are worried for your plane." Fokion observed.

"Yes dear chap, I'm not sure if it will ever fly again, but I don't want the Itis getting their mucky paws on it."

"Nai, nai, I agree. I will arrange for us to rope it up and we shall pull it ashore. Then your people can decide about its future. How would that be for you?"

"That would be top dollar. Top dollar."

"Then we are set to go. We look after you whilst you arrange whatever you need to. You are safe here on Corfu though. Very safe, nai. We love the English. We love you."

No one had time to talk much more as the crowd took complete charge of the situation, which became carnival like. Gerald and the others were picked aloft and carried at shoulder height to the singing voices of the Corfiot throng. They headed through bamboo and olive groves towards Lefkimmi village, leaving the stricken aircraft half submerged in the shallows of Lefkimmi Bay.

This would be the last The Bish, Arthur Geary and Gerald Davies, saw of their beloved Blenheim L8511. The three had only been at Menidi for a day, this was their first raid of the Italians at Durazzo, and they had come off for the worst. Now they were stuck on Corfu until they could sort a means of transport for getting home.

<'And no bugger knows we are here,> contemplated Arthur Geary, who had failed to send out a radio message, because shrapnel had completely ruined the radio transmitter on the Blenheim.

Within twenty minutes the three airmen had arrived in the beautiful old village of Lefkimmi. Its orange roofed white buildings in narrow streets looking beautiful under the warm November sun.

"Come," shouted Fokion, "you are our honoured guests and I will take not a no for an answer. You eat, drink and be merry with us now. You are saved and by God's grace, nai, this is something to celebrate. So, nai, yes, we first go to the taverna. There is much room there."

The three had no option and were taken into what looked like the front of a small shop, but inside it was a little room with tables set out as if ready for people to eat. Everyone who had accompanied them to the village, including children, seemed to pile in and sat staring in wonderment at the airmen.

"Someone has sent a message to Spiro my brother and he will be here soon, but first you see and experience Greek, ochi (no), Corfiot hospitality, nai. "

The three nodded and replied as one, with their newly gained Greek language skills - "Nai!"

It wasn't long before wine, olives and sardines arrived at the table, followed quickly by bread, cheese, hard-boiled eggs and more alcohol in the form of beer and cognac. The treat was welcome, as was the black coffee which helped to maintain sobriety as the hour went on in the smoky taverna where everyone, including teenage children smoked away merrily, without as much as a word from any of the adults around them. Then there came a big honk of a car horn outside the taverna, as a dusty looking huge American Dodge Buick squealed to a halt, creating a plume of dust as high as the taverna itself. Out of the dust emerged a larger-than-life character. Fokion's brother had arrived.

"Told you, he'd be here. He can't resist. Spiro, come in, come in... " Fokion turned to Gerald and the others. "They call him Spiro 'Amerikanos' [2] here. Nai, he... Ochi! No... we, our brothers, we lived in America for many years and my brother Spiro, nai, he brought that big American piece of machinery shit back with him to use as a taxi here on the island."

Spiro was walking in any way, humming away merrily and greeting people in Greek as he entered the taverna, as he preened his big hairy moustache. Everyone cheered at his arrival. Some children even ran up to him and hugged his colossal frame.

"Fokion my brother, I heard that. Yes, I am the only ones with a car in this place... well, a working car anyways." A booming laugh followed. Everyone listened to Spiro Amerikanos. "Everybody's needs me." He burst into Greek.

«Όλοι με χρειάζεσαι!» (You all need me!).

The place cheered. Gerald hadn't a clue what was said, but this was the happiest he'd been in such a long time. He'd even forgotten about the lost photograph such was his star of merriment... aided by the cognac of course.

"Now Fokion, what have yous brought for me's... some British airmens I see."

Gerald and the others stood up from the table to greet Spiro who held out a hand which seemed bigger than all their three hands put together. He was a man mountain with a voice to accompany his size.

«Καθίστε! Καθίστε!»

"Sit! Sit!" Insisted Spiro. "No ceremonies here for me's. Yous gentlemen are our honoured guests here on Kérkyra... er... Corfu's. I am ordered to take yous to the British consulate in Corfu Town, but... what's the rush. We stays with Fokion and his family tonight."

Fokion nodded. "There is plenty of space in my house for you brave people, nai."

"Then it is settled for yous. I think we haves time for more cognac and, God, ams I hungry. I haven't eaten all these days. We shoulds toast our friends from England, I think first.. heh!"

With that Spiro nudged Gerald hard and indicated for him to pick up an empty cognac glass, which he filled there and then to the brim, filling the others' glasses and a rather large one for himself at the same time. He raised his glass to the room.

«Ψήνουμε τους Βρετανούς ήρωές μας.»

He repeated in English. "We toasts our British heroes."

«καλή υγεία!»

"Good healths, gentlemen!"

Everyone in the place responded, clinking their glasses together, some stretching across to clink glasses with the bewildered Blenheim three who were still wet from their impromptu dip in the sea. Something soon noticed by the effervescent Spiro Amerikanos. There followed a conversation in Greek between Spiro and Fokion, at the end of which both men stood up, as did several others, as if ready to part at an instant.

"My apologies!" Fokion doffed his beret as Spiro spoke.

"Fokion, my brother, has left yous poor mens in yous wet cloth, so we have to go now and finishes our celebrations at his house. We will dries yous clothes and we can let yous get some sleeps. I tells you before, he has plenty of room there."

"Nai, nai" Fokion responded. "You will be my honoured guests and MUST stay with me at my home until we makes you dry again."

With that the group of three airmen were driven away to cheers and even flowers thrown into the old Dodge Buick as they headed to Fokion's cottage, less than a mile away, surrounded by chickens, geese and a lone duck which made more noise than any other bird there. Gerald couldn't help but think it might have recently lost its mate who they could be eating soon. There was a fire burning bright in the grate as Gerald and the others entered the cottage where Fokion's wife, three daughters, two sons, his parents and two grandparents were all crowded in. Cigarettes were handed out as Gerald removed this wet clothing, exchanged for a modest woollen blanket which had temporarily been removed from someone's bed.

«Καθίστε, καθίστε! Φάε φάε! Πιείτε, πιείτε!»

"Sit, sit! Eat, eat! Drink, drink!"

Three repeated words Gerald could now recall with ease in Greek. There was now more food on the go than the three could almost cope with. Gerald felt it was a good thing there were plenty of dogs and cats about the place as he could give the odd tit-bit to the animals which constantly pestered for a bite to eat. There was black bread which Gerald had never seen before, warm goat's milk which Gerald tasted but wasn't overkeen on, but the chicken pie and marinaded veal was something to die for and the three felt like three kings come home. More than anything Gerald was glad not to have found duck on the menu, feeling relieved that the duck outside was just a noisy lone duck and not one pining for a mate in the pot.

With warm clothing, a belly fully of drink and food, the three airmen slept soundly that night, grateful for the kindness and hospitality of the Corfiot people who had comforted them and provided them with shelter. Even the loud snoring of Spiro Amerikanos disturbed no one's sleep.

*

* * *

They all rose late the following morning, apart from Fokion and his family who, as usual, were out at first light, unheard by their sleeping guests, tending to their daily chores around the animals in their care. Fokion had arranged for someone else to be on duty at the Church of St. Mary on the shoreline, so he could stay at home and tend to his guests.

The anaesthetic properties of a mixture of cognac, wine and beer had put them all soundly to sleep, including Spiro Amerikanos who needed no excuse to enjoy a good knees-up. By the time the airmen woke, sore heads to a man, it was almost midday. Oodles of coffee with bread, cheese and leftover meat were on the menu for brunch. Once again the three were treated like royalty and headaches diminished with gallons of water consumed by all provided regularly by Fokion's wife or children who were obviously under strict orders to be at the command of the airmen.

The day wore on and it was soon time to bid fond farewells to the Corfiots of Lefkimmi, but the three would never forget the way these kind and thoughtful people had treated them, never having met them before. As the three headed out to Spiro Amerikanos' ample Dodge car, with its engine rumbling away, there were tears in everyone's eyes and hugs galore abounded. No one wanted to see the three airmen go, and the three airmen felt the same too.

The afternoon passed quickly and Spiro wanted to get the three away before darkness fell, so drove at a racing pace along what seemed like a treacherous steep and windy dirt road following the coast, with the sea to the right. They were headed for Corfu Town and a meeting with the British consulate. No one spoke, and it was as if Spiro hated the silence as he hummed tunelessly (and constantly) as he drove.

"You don't have to drive so fast, Spiro... " a worried Bish uttered from the front passenger seat, with his hands gripping the leather seats. "We can... er... and would like to get to where we are going in one piece, please!"

"Don't worries Mr. Finlayson sir," replied Spiro with his deep rich voice from the driving seat. "I haves to drives fasts because we don'ts wants to be caught in the opens by the Italikos. They will be sure to shoots at us. They do's it all the time. Keep yous eyes opens gentlemens... not just the Italikos but the Nazis. They toos bomb us days and nights. I'm surprised we hasn't hads a raid already this day.

274

They musts be having a holidays from bombings" He roared out loud. "No's bombings holiday, hey airmens!" Spiro laughed at his own words and nudged The Bish next to him.

"So, how come you speak such good English Spiro?" Gerald said trying to change the worrying subject from his windy position in the back seat of the open-top car, where he was sat with a quiet Arthur Geary, still doing his best to shake off his muzzy head. The answer to the question had already been spoken about last night, but it didn't matter, it stopped thoughts of some Macchi 200 settling in behind them and strafing them on the road as they headed to their destination. He'd had enough of that over Durazzo. That'd been the final straw to break the back of the Blenheim now resting in the Ionian Sea at Lefkimmi.

"Listens my friends... we is the poor peoples here on Kérkyra. We haves to makes a livings in any ways we cans. My ways of makings a living was goings to Chicago. Eight years I was in the Americas, with my's brothers and we travelled fars and wides. Say, I even gots to Alaska and works in Bostons as well. Yannis... he stays in Boston to be police. He big mans in police now there I am tolds. Did I ever tells you I met the playwright Henry Miller [3] in America? It is a very strange story."

"That'll be a no" Bish sarcastically with a wry smile. He knew he was going to get the story anyway.

"Then I tells yous. Yes... Mr. Millers he works for the Chicago Tribune and... yes... it was very long time ago I knows, but I takes him places in this very car. He says to me that he hads heard of Corfu and would love to come, so I says to him to come then I leaves America. I think no more of it but I mention this to Lawrence Durrells who writes letter and invites Mr. Miller here. Yes... he invites the very famous playwright here and would yous believes it, Henry Miller he comes last year. Right here to Corfu! He stays with Lawrence and Nancy and I gets to meet him again. Mr. Henry Miller tells me I am always welcome to stay with him in America. We good friends yous see. When I am rich I intend to go back, but for now I have families to look after here in Corfu yous see." Spiro Amerikanos sighed heavily. "Anyways, nai, I dids makes moneys but the biggest of depressions came... yous knows of it?"

"The Great Depression. Yes."

"So yes, the Great Depressions came and moneys started to comes scarces, so's I ships out, but I's takes this great Dodge Buick with me.

It is way of making moneys for me's and my families. You likes?"

"Like it! It's like a much bigger version of my MG back in Britain." Gerald replied thinking of his green MG now parked up with Susan a thousand miles away.

"Ah! MG. Mr, Geralds. Good cars. Good cars. No goods for taxis though!"

"You're right. Fokion told us you were friendly with an English family who lived here in Corfu?"

"Nai - Yes, my's friends. The Durrells family. Nice peoples, especially Louisa... " He was nodding vigorously. Melancholy filled his leathery, sun-worn face, "... yes, she was the mother. No husbands, yous knows. They comes here in '35 I thinks it was. Yes, 1935. Lawrence and his wife Nancy they comes first, followed by the mother, nai, yes... and family not that long after. They lives on the other side of Corfu Town. When they first comes here, it was me who finds them the villa where to lives. This is the directions in which we is now headeds... nice people. Nice people."

"You knew them well?"

"Well! Mr. Geralds, I knew them likes my own family. They became my family here. By strange chance, the little boy they had, lovely boy... he had very strange habits though... always collecting insects and little animals he was. His name was same as yours Mr. Geralds. Little Gerry I calls him. Gerry he was like yous. Ten years old when he cames here with his brothers and sister."

With that The Bish let out an unusual belly laugh. The words 'Little Gerry' had amused him greatly. "Little Gerry, now there's a good name for you ol' chap," he said turning his head to look back at Gerald sitting forward in the back seat.

"I think just Gerry will do fine, thanks Skip," Gerald responded, pushing the back of The Bish's seat with some force.

"Nai, yes, I was the first persons to have a car on Corfu Island yous knows. This is how I comes to meets the Durrells family... taxi driving lets me meet many interesting peoples like yous." He boomed with laughter. "Yes, drivings is my life. Talking and meeting new peoples is part of this life."

The Bish asked the next question... "So Spiro, was Louisa attractive? I mean, did you fancy your chances ol' man?"

"Fancies my chances?"

"Yes, you know... did you like her. I mean, you said she was single."

"But of course, she was pretty womans and on her owns too. For sure, nai, I would have devoted my's whole life to her. Who wouldn't? I means, she was a few years older than me's. Not fifty years but nears that she was when she comes here to Corfu. Then for me, yous knows, virile man in my early forties… so she was attractive to me. A few years between us, but nai, what is age gentlemens when yous has a good woman!" Once again laughter as loud as the wind whistling over the bonnet of the speeding car followed as Spiro nudged The Bish, giving him a big grin.

Then Spiro's demeanour altered and he came over all sad again. "The war it comes and spoils all things. Spoils everything it did for me's. The Durrells, well all but Lawrence and his wife… they are still here. He is writer, I thinks… yes, but the others, nai, they go's back to England and I am yet to see them again. For sure, the Italikos or the Nazis will come. Big invasions taking place all the time. The Durrells they knows this and it is too dangerous for thems. I was heartbrokens by losings Louisa. Heartbrokens!"

The three airmen remained silent and listened to Spiro's sad lament, as Gerald kept an ever watchful eye on the sky at all times.

"The low life war mongering rats, they ruins my life." Spiro pretended to spit.

"Ftou, ftou, ftou!" He shook his head. "In Greek tradition it is common to spit when we talk of bad things. Anyways… Let me tells yous this my friends; there is only one worse things than Italikos or slime of the swamp Germanoi Nazis and thats is the Turks. Sons of bitches they are! Never trust one. NEVER!"

"We'll take your word on that ol' chap." The Bish spoke up. "Never encountered a Turk in my life."

"And yous never wants to!"

It was The Bish's turn to change the subject now. "So how did you get your first name, Spiro ol' chap? I noticed back in Lefkimmi there were more Spiros in the taverna than any other. Rather confusing…"

The car was still heading at speed and The Bish still clung to his seat, as if he was still being chased by a Macchi out of Durazzo.

"Firstly Mr. Finlaysons," said Spiro, nodding with an air of superiority. "I am THE ONE and THE ONLY Spiro Amerikanos on the island. Everyone knows Spiro Amerikanos. I helps them when they needs me. Dependable Spiro is me. The other Spiro's… fuff… " He shook his head dramatically with disappointment. "… there's Spiro the

Butcher, Spiro the Candle Maker, Spiro the Baker, Spiro the Saddler, Spiro the Priest, Spiro the whatevers... everyones on Corfu is called Spiro yous knows. No one knows who these Spiros are, but every other man here is called Spiro after our revered Saint of this island, Saint Spyridion. His mummified body is in the church in Corfu Town. A very special place. I will takes yous one day, to meet him!"

*

Incessant humming or conversations about the other unknown Spiros of Corfu carried on non-stop all the way to Corfu Town and the journey passed in the blink of an eye AND with no enemy planes being spotted much to the relief of all. They were soon outside the British Consul and it was Spiro who jumped from the car almost before it had come to a halt in the dust and banged loudly on the door of a bomb damaged building but which, in the main, was still standing because of the thickness of its stone walls.

"I have some of your mens for coffee," he shouted loudly as footsteps inside arrived at the door. He sounded as if he knew the people inside, and when the door was opened, it was obvious he did. The young chap who answered the door, spoke in Greek and directed him in without question, to which Spiro shouted back to the car. "Come on airmens, we needs to be inside."

There were four men and a woman at the consul and all knew Spiro very well, that was obvious from the outset and the way they welcomed him with open arms. After a quick coffee Spiro declared, "I knows the tasks in hand. I needs to go to sorts these matters out. Goods!"

Spiro took time shaking hands with 'Lefkimmi Blenheim friends' - Gerald, The Bish and Arthur Geary. "Bless yous my friend" he declared to each one. "I sees yous when I returns tomorrow. I makes arrangements with my friends to help yous back to Athens."

Unknown to Gerald and the others, someone had written in the log at Menidi:

'Missing, feared killed.' *[4]*

Author's Note

[1] Fokion Halikiopoulos. The author visited Corfu during October 2020. Fokion was identified as the male who came from the Church of St. Mary (pictured below) on the shore at Lefkimmi. He was purposely posted there by

the Corfiot Authorities to guard against/ warn of any invasion Corfu.

Images: Nigel Davies-Williams. Pictured above and below is the church with Papa Spiro Monasterios who showed the author the location of the crash landing.

Note: Only this side of the church was built at the time of the crash landing. The other side was constructed at a later stage.

* * *

[2] Spiro 'Amerikanos' Hakiopoulous 1892 - 1943

Corfu was bombed day and night by both the Italians and Germans during the war. Corfu was occupied by the Italians in April 1941, and the German occupation of Corfu began on 14th September 1943. It is reported that Spiro Amerikanos died of natural causes through stress brought on following the German invasion of late 1943. He had been trying to escape the island, but ways out were closed. He was 52 years old.

[3] In 1939, the playwright Henry Miller stayed with Lawrence and Nancy Durrell in Corfu, at 'The White House' at Kalami

Henry Miller refers to the death of Spiro in his book The Colossus of Maroussi :

<There was one other person whose presence I missed and that was Spiro of Corfu. I didn't realise it then, but Spiro was getting ready to die. Only the other day I received a letter from his son telling me that Spiro's last words were: "New York! New York! I want to find Henry Miller's house!" Here is how Lillis, his son, put it in his letter: "My poor father died with your name in his mouth which closed forever. The last day he lost his logic and pronounced a lot of words in English...He died as poor as he always was. He did not realise his dream to be rich.'>

[4] Documents sent from Greece in 2020 by Kostas Kavvadias shed more light on this.

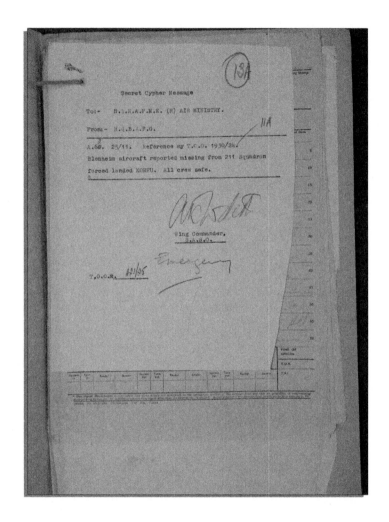

Secret Cypher Message

To:- H.I.R.A.F.M.E. (R) AIR MINISTRY.

From:- H.Q.B.A.F.G.

A.68. 25/11. Reference my T.C.O. 1930/24.
Blenheim aircraft reported missing from 211 Squadron
forced landed KORFU. All crew safe.

Wing Commander,
S.A.S.O.

T.O.O.R. 131/25   Emergency

Chapter Twenty-one

'Dodge Destroyed'

British forces in Greece were growing by the day. Besides the Blenheim Bombers 211 and 84 Squadrons had at Menidi, there was a smaller contingent of Blenheims *[1]* from 30 and 84 Squadrons at Eleusis on the other side of Athens. 70 Squadron was based in Athens too, with a few Wellingtons. Roald Dahl's 80 Squadron with its Gloster Gladiator fighters were based at Eleusis and were often at Menidi with 211 Squadron but minus Pilot Officer Dahl, who was still laid up in hospital over in Egypt. As yet, no Hurricane fighters had arrived in this new theatre of war.

*

The aerodrome at Menidi was now minus a plane and its crew and the newly arrived 211 Squadron was minus its C.O., the irrepressible James Gordon-Finlayson; this after less than 24 hours of being based there. Tommy Wisdom recorded in his notes on that first night, *'we spent an unhappy evening.'*   Of course, he wasn't to know the missing three were all fine, apart from the odd scratch here and there. He wasn't to know either that the three had partied that first night they were missing.

Across a few hundred yards of olive trees, on that very night Tommy Wisdom was writing his log book, unknown to anyone within 211 Squadron, Prime Minister Metaxas had come for a meeting with King George II at the 'Tatoi' Palace, to tell him they were *'proud of their success, the first allies to carry the offensive to enemy territory.'* Of course, it hadn't been reported back to Metaxas that the C.O. of 211 Squadron was missing with his crew following the bombing raid on Durazzo in Albania. There might have been a little more concern expressed then.

*

On the second day 211 Squadron was at Menidi, the landing ground was quiet. The lack of leadership had caught them on the hop, and no one knew what to do in the short term. The officers had met in the newly established mess and had agreed, as a mark of respect, to wait for at least 48 hours before deciding what to do next, although H.Q. had been informed as they were duty bound to do. Besides this, three other aircraft had suffered damage in the fateful raid on Durazzo, so urgent repairs were ongoing to make the Blenheims serviceable. One was severely damaged, Flying Officer Ken Dundas doing his best to save the plane had made a belly landing on the grass runway in the valley at Menidi.

Then there was the continued talk about where The Bish and his crew might be.

"I saw them. Smoke coming off the port engine pretty badly... and they had a Macchi on their tail. They'll be in the drink for sure." Flight Lieutenant Doudney had suggested. "We couldn't help at all. We were full of holes ourselves. Lucky to get back."

"The Bish, Gerry and Arthur are a tough crew. We need to wait. They might just turn up," had suggested 'the Airdale,' Pilot Officer Guy Jerdein, so called because his thick curly mop of hair looked like the dog.

Everyone agreed. Waiting was the preferred option right now.

*

The Bish, Gerald and Arthur now sat with the people from the consulate in what the lady had described as *'the least damaged room in the building.'* The lady turned out to be Winifred, the wife of Harold Allan Dilke Hoyland M.B.E, [2] an old-school Consul General who had been in the diplomatic service around many countries of the Mediterranean for almost forty years. Hoyland spoke little, but when he did, he carried an air of confidence which even surpassed that of The Bish.

283

In the space of twenty-four hours Gerald felt he'd seen the kindness of the poorest of people on Corfu and now he was experiencing the same with the richest of people. The crash landing had been worth it just to experience how the other half-life he thought.

<'Wow, if Lizzie or my mum could see me now - hobnobbing it with the great and good of society.'>

Hoyland was a distinguished consular official known far and wide across the region. His deputy at the Corfu Consul was Guy Hamilton Clarke, quite a fit looking young man, who'd only recently been appointed to the post having come from the Levant where he had been Vice-Consul.

All the consular officials wanted to do their best to help the airmen and the process of doing this had already begun but Guy Clarke became even more helpful when The Bish and him realised they had both been at Cambridge University, although at slightly different times. The place went from a warm atmosphere to an extremely genial one and the 'missing three' sat with him whilst a couple of staff made coffee for their impromptu guests.

"I see, from the look of this place, the war has come to you?" The Bish began as he sipped at his weak and tasteless coffee, whilst cigarettes were offered all round.

"Last packet in the consul. Enjoy." Guy Hamilton Clarke said with a smile.

"It's nice to have some different company. We're repeatedly under threat here from the Italians. They've already made a formal request to the Greek government for the island to be ceded to them. Of course this has been rejected but, the Italians don't take no for an answer and... er... well, look at this recent paper. Shows what's been happening."

Guy Clarke picked up a three week old newspaper flown in from Britain and showed it to The Bish. The headline read 'British Consulate Bombed,' It was the first British newspaper The Bish had seen in a while. He read the small piece out loud to the others.

"London Monday. During an attack on Corfu, the British Consulate was repeatedly singled out for bombing. It is believed that some British civilians were killed."

The Bish looked up towards Clarke and Hoyland. "Gentlemen, I'm so sorry to hear this.

Hoyland answered with a grim certitude about his voice, like some old general who'd just lost men at the Battle of Waterloo. "Bad news,

I'm afraid, Squadron Leader. They're after us good and proper here in this building. The worst raid took place on 1st of the month. That raid killed five people and injured 26 others. I lost two of my staff in that raid. There's just five of us left here now, and we're still under the Iti cosh at times. The dashed bombing! It's indiscriminate - we've lost women and children in the town to these scoundrels."

"And we thought we had it bad. At least we have the means to fight back... or at least we did."

Hoyland continued. "Do you know Squadron leader, the Iti even used the Greek ensign on their planes, to make it look like we were being attacked by our own country."

"Damn Italians. Can't trust them."

"Thinking of your plane, can we assume it will never fly again?"

"I rather think so. One of the engines is somewhere at the bottom of the Ionian."

Guy Clarke now took up the conversation. "I have taken the liberty to tell Spiro... er, yes... amiable rogue but an honest chappie at heart. We have met before a few times. He had a lot to do with a rather nice English family living on the island."

"The Durrells. Yes, he told us."

"Yes, Spiro is very trustworthy. He gets things done around here. Anyway, Spiro had more or less told me what you told me about your poor plane, so I've... I've taken precautions already to have the locals drag the plane out of the shallows and onto a flat area... er... where they drain the water away for salt production. It's safe there for now. With your permission, when I get chance I shall arrange for any parts which can be reused and any personal items belonging to you chaps to be returned to you at your base or to the RAF... whichever is easier."

"Yes, that's just the ticket, Guy. We have most of the personal kit we need, we ensured we rescued that yesterday. Any salvageable parts... yes, agree... anyway you chaps know the score. Anything we can reuse, or the Greek airforce can reuse, then we need it recovering."

"Don't worry, I shall do the right thing. The key thing for you gentlemen to do right now is to relax."

"I'll drink to that" Arthur Geary said, raising his cup as if it was a cognac. Gerald raised his coffee cup. He didn't want it to be a cognac. He'd had enough in the past day or so to last a lifetime.

"So gentlemen," continued Hoyland, "there is nothing we can do until tomorrow pending the return of our friend Spiro Amerikanos. Hopefully, he will have in hand the necessary plans and information to get you three back to your base on the mainland."

"Are you able to make contact with our base for us to let them know we are safe?" Gerald wisely added.

"I'm afraid that's out of the question, Pilot Officer. A recent Italian raid has destroyed our telephone lines and communications are completely down."

"Then, if you don't mind, we should enjoy your hospitality and I thank you for that."

The Bish spoke too soon. Sirens had belatedly sounded, and then there was the familiar sound of the whine of a bomb as it plummeted to earth. Explosions everywhere! The ground shook, but the building they were in remained unscathed.

Guy Clarke bolted up to his feet and eyes full open with concern.

"Another damn air raid!" He held his hands forward and suggested people remain seated and calm. "Discretion, gentlemen, would seem to me to be the better part of valour here. Those bombs are awfully close, but I don't think that close, so we have no reason to fear a ... "

Then the whine of a second bomb. A great explosion followed. The bombs were getting closer. This time Hoyland stood up. "Tis not the time to be brave gentlemen. We shall have to retire to... "

Then a third bomb exploded and the entire building shook violently, dust cascaded down and cups shook with coffee tidal waving over the edges. It was as if some earthquake had begun. Guy Clarke's eyes now told a different story. Gerald could hardly hear such was the deafening noise of the explosion.

All waited for Hoyland's instructions whilst everyone cowered, but strangely no one moved. The three airmen had no idea where to go anyway and, to a man, calmly waited for Hoyland to say something.

Then the whine of a fourth dropping bomb. Everyone knew this one would be too close.

Gerald held his breath. <'Jesus, we've had it!'>

The blast hit. It couldn't have been more than a few yards away. Glass shattered and the shock-wave ripped the small crystal chandelier from the ceiling at the centre of the room and most of the plaster from the ceiling with it. The falling fitting narrowly missed Gerald, crashing in a hail of plaster dust on the floor. His beautiful china coffee cup, which he'd been sipping at just a second ago and which reminded him of his mother's special tea-service at home, was no more. The blast had torn the cup from his hand and had smashed it to a thousand pieces against the wall. The pretence and the stiff upper lip attitude that nothing was happening ended there and then.

"The cellar! The cellar!" finally commanded a dust covered Hoyland, as he grabbed his wife Winifred "Winnie! Winnie, dear!" and pushed others toward the stairs.

Everyone ran for their lives.

*

There were more raids during the night. The cellar wasn't that comfortable and little sleep was had by anyone, but all were grateful the small room was a way below street level and so afforded excellent shelter.

Spiro arrived early, just as day broke.   He looked around the consulate and surveyed the damage.

"Is bloody crazy out theres but seems yous has had a crazy time here. Italikos having a good go all over the island. No one is hurts no?"

Everyone nodded to say they were fine and coffee was the first order of the day.

"I was worried they might get my car so I watches very carefully before I drives to you to tell yous what is planned. It is too dangerous to go in the car by day, so we's wait until just before dark. I arrange for fishing boats at harbour. Yous has to go to sea by night as the Italikos will machine guns yous if they sees yous in the day."

No one disagreed with that, and the eight bombing raids during that day confirmed they were doing the right thing.

*

It was dusk when Spiro took the airmen down to the harbour at Corfu, followed by several locals he had employed to carry bags and help with the clandestine operation.

It took less than two minutes for the little army of people to get things on board the fishing vessel and everyone waited on the shore to wave a great goodbye to the airmen, but any goodbyes were delayed, as the fishing vessel just wouldn't start no matter what its crew of three did. They made several attempts to get the boat going. Spiro was at all times in command of the operation and his Greek shouts could be heard everywhere and people could be seen running to his commands to fetch the various spares needed. Eventually, after two hours, the engine of the fishing vessel started, and the vessel began to pull away from the shore.

Gerald and the others had one last chance to express their gratitude to Spiro and the others there for all their support and assistance. They were more than grateful and wondered how they could ever repay this kindness. As Gerald stood on the fishing vessel, slowly moving from shore, he promised Spiro he would return one day with his beloved Susan. "I'll have a photograph to show you then" Gerald bragged.

"Be sures to Mr Geralds! Be sures to."

As the boat shifted more and more away from the harbour, Gerald shouted the few words he'd learned in Greek. Repeating them several times to make sure Spiro could hear.

"Efcharistó. Efcharistó. Sas agapáme Spýros. Mas échete sósei.

"Thank you! Thank you! We love you Spiro. You have saved us."

Spiro, the man with the big-heart and the big car next to him on at the harbour just down from Corfu Town was shouting back. He could just about hear the words... "Then, Mr. Geralds, I shall see you soon. You be sure to return. Goodbye! Good lucks!"

Gerald and the other airmen watched on, as the shore got further away and the people there became minute figures, just visible in the dark under the moonlight.

Then the airmen heard it. The sirens on Corfu wailed away again. Then they heard the drone of engines. Italian bombers! They knew what was coming next. The whining of dropping bombs began. Gerald could see the little figures on the shore running for cover.

One thing didn't move. Spiro's Dodge Buick.

Bombs landed all around and then one hit the car, smashing it to pieces and a fireball raged.

Gerald wanted the fishing vessel he was on to turn around but he knew he couldn't, it was hopeless. All he could do was hope Spiro hadn't been in the car. As quickly as the raid had started, it was over. The airmen were glad they hadn't been spotted on the open water, otherwise it would have been like a turkey shoot.

Then Gerald spotted something with relief. A man on his knees on the quayside. The burning wreckage of the Dodge Buick lit him up for all to see. It was Spiro.

Gerald could hear the crying from where he was and the shouts in Greek.

«Γιατί! Γιατί! Χάθηκα! Χαμένος!»

"Why! Why! I am lost! Lost!"

* * *

*

The fishing vessel wasn't built for comfort or speed. The airmen had joked it must have been built for the Trojan Wars, not the war they were in. It was ancient, and it leaked. The airmen, stuck on an open deck, with no shelter in a brewing storm, became cold and wet with every wave which broke over the bow of the boat. It chugged relentlessly through the blackness of the Ionian Sea, a sea which looked very warm and inviting in the day, but now, with a storm at full strength, it looked like they were sailing across hell's kettle, about to boil over.

The missing three did not know to which area of the Greek mainland they were headed, but hoped and prayed every minute they would make it. Gerald mulled over the disaster which had befallen Spiro Amerikanos' car.

<'*Thanks to us, he's lost his livelihood. How can we ever repay him? Bloody war. What the hell is it about people we have to fight and destroy each other.*'>

The night wore on and the unrelenting storm threw the fishing smack around like a raffle ticket in a tombola drum. Spiro had provided beer and rations for the journey. No one felt like either. The bread had become soaked through and Arthur had already thrown up several times, so drinking a beer was out of the question. The four-man crew understood no English and all conversation between the airmen and the crew was through some newly invented sign language which sort of did the trick, especially when it came to telling the hardened fishermen the beer was not wanted.

Before they knew it, the first shards of light from an approaching dawn appeared across the sea. The boat skipper showed his concern "Italikos. Rat-at-tat-tat!" he noised and motioned a plane coming in the strafe them and at once headed the boat towards the shore where the steep mountains cascaded down into the sea.

*

It was six in the morning when, damp and cold, Gerald and the others went ashore. Never had he been so glad to be on dry land, despite feeling like he could sleep for a week. The shore was pretty golden sand and a fishing village was a few hundred yards along the shore.

This was the island of Lefkada, they had sailed over sixty miles along the western coast of Greece. At any other time, any of the three airmen would have thought this was the most beautiful place to be on holiday in but a brewing war kept everyone on their toes.

One of the crew who'd obviously been tasked to take the airmen to safety shouted in broken English, "Lefkada! Come! Walk! Follow! Boat again later."

After a few minutes walk, Gerald and the others were in the village of Lefkada, after which the island was named. They all walked down the Main Street and into a grocer's shop which the fisherman guiding them seemed to know.

"English! Friends! Welcome airmen!" shouted the grocer and he at once cracked open a bottle of cognac. Everyone welcomed the drink which felt like pouring liquid fire into a cold oven and at once they all felt a sense of warmth they hadn't felt since leaving the harbour at Corfu. This was followed by squid fried over the open fire in the back of the shop, where the three remained drying their clothes and resting for more than two hours.

They were all asleep when the fisherman woke them.

"We go now!"

"Good lucks. They takes you to nearer Athens. The boat will hugs the shore to make you safe. Less trouble from Italikos!" were the last words of the grocer who gave them a full bottle of cognac to take with them. They headed back towards the shoreline where the fishing smack was moored and boarded the boat.

The weather was now sunny and a warmth filled the air, even though it was late November. The boat headed south down a small channel between the island of Lefkada and what looked like the mainland.

"I think they're now saying it's safe to travel by daylight here," The Bish had commented, seeing the boat sailing in what looked like an enclosed area of the Ionian Sea. Everyone hoped his words would not be spoken too soon, but it wasn't the Italians who stopped them going on, it was the wind. As the day wore on, the wind became so strong the fishing smack couldn't cope with it and they were at a standstill, or even being blown backwards occasionally. The crew and the airmen consumed cognac and laughed it off as much as possible.

"We could spend the war out at sea if we have enough rations to keep us going Skip," Gerald commented. All the three airmen could hear was the constant comment of the word "Astakos! Astakos!"

They soon found out that the crew had abandoned any hope of sailing on towards Athens and had settled on making some headway for a place called Astakos, where they hit land late in the afternoon. They had travelled another 30 to 40 miles south, so they were now a respectful distance south of Corfu, but the good news which the fishermen told them in their creed sign language and broken English was that they were now on the mainland at last.

Astakos would be another unforgettable day in Gerald's life. There they were heralded as heroes and mobbed by a crowd, some of whom were waving the Union Jack with their own Greek flag.

"Where the heck did all this lot come from?" Gerald commented as people of every age filled the narrow streets. He was kissed many times by young girls shouting in English *'beautiful man'* and his arms were filled with chrysanthemum flowers of all pretty shades which the girls gave to him. As he looked across to The Bish and Arthur they too had their arms full. Within minutes they were being carried aloft and headed up towards the town hall of Astakos where, still watched by crowds of people they drank more cognac, smoked cigarettes, which Gerald hated, but he tried one for the sake of not offending the locals who were so pleased to see them.

A meal was laid on and wine washed down the local delicacies a treat.

Everyone was feeling thoroughly good about themselves at Astakos, despite losing a plane, nearly being killed in that loss and afterwards nearly being killed by bomb and the sea. "This is what life is all about!" had joked Arthur Geary only to be reminded by The Bish "we're weren't home yet chaps by a long way!"

Gerald, as ever with his finger on the navigation pulse added, "By my calculations chaps we're still only about half way to our base at Menidi."

The others looked a little disconsolate at this news, despite the party atmosphere around them.

Gerald had at this time spoken with several locals with a view to getting a car out of the place now they were on the mainland. He had no intention of getting back in a boat when there were roads around, despite their awful state in most places.

Author's Note
[1] The Blenheim.
In 1934, the owner of the Daily Mail, Lord Rothermere, wanted a 'fast and

spacious' aircraft for his own use. He knew Bristol designer Frank Barwell who told him he could build such a craft. From design to manufacture took a year and in April 1935 a plane called 'Britain First' made its inaugural flight some. The plane was 30 mph faster than the RAF's fastest plane at that time.

The RAF took note of the speed and requested a military version of the plane which is how the Blenheim came to be produced.

Technical (**Wikipedia**): The Bristol Blenheim was a twin-engine high performance, all-metal medium bomber aircraft, powered by a pair of Bristol Mercury VIII air-cooled radial engines, each capable of 860 hp (640 kW). Each engine drove a three-bladed controllable-pitch propeller, and were equipped with both hand-based and electric engine starters. To ease maintenance, the engine mountings were designed with a split-segment to facilitate rapid engine removal without disturbing the carburettors. A pair of fuel tanks, each containing up to 140 gallons, were housed within the centre-section of the fuselage.

The pilot's quarters on the left side of the nose were so cramped that the control yoke obscured all flight instruments while engine instruments eliminated the forward view on landings. Most secondary instruments were arranged along the left side of the cockpit, essential items such as the propeller pitch control were actually placed behind the pilot where they had to be operated by feel alone. The navigator/bomb aimer/air-observer was seated alongside the pilot, and made use of a sliding/folding seat whilst performing the bomb aiming role. Dual flight controls could be installed. The wireless operator/air gunner was housed aft of the wing alongside the aircraft's dorsal gun turret.

Armament comprised a single forward-firing .303 in (7.7 mm) Browning machine gun outboard of the port engine and a .303 in (7.7 mm) Lewis Gun in a semi-retracting Bristol Type B Mk I dorsal turret firing to the rear. From 1939 onwards, the Lewis gun was replaced by the more modern .303 in (7.7 mm) Vickers VGO machine gun of the same calibre. A 1,000 lb (450 kg) bomb load could be carried in the internal bomb bay set into the centre section of the fuselage. Like most contemporary British aircraft, the bomb bay doors were kept closed with bungee cords and opened under the weight of the released bombs. Because there was no way to predict how long it would take for the bombs to force the doors open, bombing accuracy was consequently poor.

Rapid advances in technology which had taken place in the late 1930s had rendered the Blenheim mostly obsolete by the outbreak of the war. In particular, it had become heavier as extra service equipment was installed; much of this was found to be necessary through operational experience. This, coupled with the rapid performance increases of the fighters that would oppose *it, had eclipsed the Blenheim's speed advantage. In January 1941, the Air Staff classified the Blenheim as inadequate in terms of performance and armament for current operations.*

[2] *The British Foreign Office appointed Harold Allan Dilke Hoyland C.B.E. (1885(Constantinople) - 1959) as Consul General*

to Corfu on 30th August 1940.

Harold married Winifred Helen Wood (1891 - 1970) in 1918.

The British Foreign Office appointed Guy Hamilton Clarke (1910 - 2004) as Consul to Corfu on 17th September 1940.

Chapter Twenty-two

'Missing Feared Killed'

"We have a car for you, gentlemen." the Mayor shouted with some joy and within minutes a roomy rust red Ford 'Model A' roadster, with rust red leather seats, driven by an old Greek man in what looked like an outfit made from the same covers as the seats of the car, pulled up at the scene.

"Kalispéra Kýrioi Good afternoon, sirs!" The driver shouted. "Erasmo, your driver at your service. "

The missing three piled their belongings, flowers, food and drink given by the locals of Astakos and waved a sad farewell to the crowd of people still gathered around them. As the dust settled on the road behind, the three, tired from their exertions on the road, fell asleep and missed much of the journey ahead, as the car passed along treacherous mountain passes and through wild streams fording the roads.

They were soon at the next main village - Aitolikón.

It was as if someone was phoning ahead or telegraphing their arrival somehow, as once again the entire village was out to greet the car as it arrived. By this time Gerald and the others were well satiated, but more food and drink was to come, plus flowers and kisses galore from people of every age. Never were such humble men treated like heroes anywhere in the world.

"No wonder they call this the cradle of civilisation!" The Bish shouted to Gerald as once again they were carried through narrow streets. "How civilised is this!"

"It's great Skip," Gerald retorted as he held out his cheek to be kissed by a young woman whilst at the same time thinking about

Susan back home and wishing it was her.

All the time the people of the Aitolikón were shouting "Zíto i Anglia!" 'Long Live England.'

Yet again more cognac rolled forth and once again they ended up in the mayor's office being pickled, alive with more alcohol again. Gerald knew his limits and was raising his glass many times to all and sundry but not drinking a drop. Arthur Geary was the same, especially after his skinful at Lefkimmi. The Bish was a different proposition. Someone had found some pipe tobacco and for the first time since leaving Menidi he had filled his pipe and was as happy as he'd ever been. The others marvelled at his constitution as he never seemed to get affected too much, no matter how much cognac he was pouring down his throat.

The mayor of the town insisted on a speech and luckily for Gerald, who was unaccustomed to making public speeches, The Bish, as the highest rank was called up to speak to the people of Aitolikón from the balcony of the town hall. In front of him the crowd still chanted, "Zíto i Anglia!"

The Bish raised his hands in the universal language to get the crowd to listen.

The speech he made was all in English of course, a language not understood by most of the people in the village, but The Bish had speeches down to a fine art.

"Ladies, gentlemen, children, Mr. Mayor and everyone of Aitolikón."

The Bish gestured to men, women and children and particularly used his open arms to express gratitude which the people cheered at constantly.

"I thank you. We thank you for your generosity. For the cognac *(he lifted his glasses to cheers)*, for the wine *(he grabbed a bottle of wine to more cheers)*, for the food *(he grabbed a piece of bread and tapped his stomach gratefully)* we are most humbly grateful and appreciative. We thank you, the people of Greece *(more cheers)* for saving our lives and helping us to get back to our base. Lord knows where that is from here!" It was The Bish's turn to smile and laugh out loud now. People in the crowd laughed with him, but many didn't understand his words. It was the international language of laughter and humour which made them feel at one with the airmen.

"We applaud the bravery of your troops and their tremendous fighting skills in the mountains of Albania. *(He clapped and the crowd clapped back)* We airmen of the RAF *(The Bish made like an aeroplane, with accompanying engine noises)* are PROUD to be fighting for Greece and I can assure you all here today, we will defend YOU and the Greek people with our lives *(cheers)* AND we will not stop until we have routed this land of the Italikos! *(Tremendous cheers)* And as for Benito Mussolini... " The Bish then drew his hand across his throat with a grim face. The crowd hissed and cheered at the same time. "The fascist will have his wings clipped and never take over your precious country of Greece, not if I and my friends have any say in it."

The Bish ended his brief speech by shouting in Greek the few words he'd learned by being around the people at Lefkimmi.

"Sas efcharistó ólous. Zíto i Elláda!"

He repeated it in English. "Thank you all. Long live Greece."

The crowd erupted with patriotism, jingoism and general excitement as The Bish waved out across them from the balcony, beckoning Gerald and Arthur to do the same. The three airmen stood on the balcony, looking out across the throng of Greeks, all looking slightly bewildered and waving like George VI and his family stood on the balcony at Buckingham Palace for some royal occasion.

As they left the balcony, presentations were made to the three including pairs of tsarouchi shoes, the strange fronted shoes traditionally worn by the Evzones. *[1]*

The three sat at an official dinner once again, despite only wanting their beds, which they'd been told had been arranged at the main hotel in the village. At dinner, Gerald sat with a rather large lady who spoke English to perfection. He was glad of this as trying to communicate all day with hands and the odd word of Greek or English was wearing.

"I am related to Byron, you know. He is my long time relative. You know him? English poet?" the woman had begun the conversation as Gerald cut a piece of goat's cheese onto some black bread, which he now loved, having first had it at Lefkimmi. There was also some caviare which he tasted with the cheese.

"Ooh, caviare, that's an acquired taste." He tried to avoid screwing his face up, but the fishy taste got the better of him. "Mmm... Byron. Yes, we did him at school."

"Did him?"

"Yes, we read his poetry in class. I liked it but I can't remember it now."

"Well, you know he lived at Missolonghi?"

"No? Where's that?"

"You are truly near to where he came in January 1824. He write poetry about this place."

"He did?"

The woman's woman became even softer, eyes flashing as if splashed by wine. *"On this day, I complete my thirty-sixth year...* You know?"

"Doesn't ring a bell."

"'Tis time this heart should be unmoved,
  Since others it hath ceased to move:
Yet though I cannot be beloved,
            Still let me love!
Now you must know of this? It is famous."

"Not heard that one."

"Tis from the poem January 22nd, Missolonghi. He was a beautiful-looking man. Beautiful words. Beautiful lover. All the girls they fell for him. I have to say, including my great-grandmother. They had, how you say, a bit of a thing..."

Gerald felt uncomfortable as the woman ran her finger over the back of his hand as he spread more cheese on the bread. The woman, who could have been old enough to be Gerald's mother, leaned in closer to Gerald and whispered in his ear.

"Beautiful man... Erotic man... " Gerald pulled away and out seems the woman took the hint. "Beautiful man and very erotic was Byron, but unfortunately he was unwell and he died a few weeks later. He was all but 36-years old... but, not before their intimate time together brought forth my line of his family."

"You're related to Byron?"

"But of course, dear boy. Lord Byron was not only famous for his written work, but he is a great hero here in Greece. He was responsible for saving us at the sieges of Missolonghi. Besides this too, he was a famous womaniser and he and my great-great grandmother were linked forever by one night of heavy breathing and lust. She could not resist his erotic charms, dear boy."

She ran her finger along Gerald's leg. He moved it away as quickly as he could.

The Bish, who'd been listening in, elbowed Gerald and whispered, "Runs in the family then... womanising or whatever the opposite is called, dear chap."

Gerald did his best to involve The Bish in the conversation after that and thanked the woman for her history lesson as he moved to talk elsewhere, leaving The Bish in conversation with the woman whose name he never got to know.

This truly had turned into the most memorable day ever for the three, for more reasons than Gerald could imagine. Meanwhile, back at Menidi, the atmosphere was gloomy and dull, with the loss of The Bish and his crew.

The merry RAF team of three, formerly the crew of L8511 were showed to their quarters and Gerald was grateful he hadn't been followed by Lord Byron's great, great granddaughter, if indeed she was telling the truth.

*

Next day, Gerald rose early from his comfortable bed in a local hotel the people of Aitolikón had put the three airmen into. He hadn't felt this relaxed in a good while. As he put his uniform shirt on, he felt at the pocket where 'that photograph' should be, in the hope it might be there.

He ruminated on his thoughts of Susan and home.

<'*Definitely why we crashed. My lucky charm is gone.*'>

Today a taxi awaited the three, courtesy of the townsfolk, and once again they were off. This time the destination was known before they left. "I want you to see and feel Greece. To see and feel our country and know what democracy you fight for," the mayor of Aitolikón said as he shook the airmen's hands just before they left. "I have a treat for you at the end of the road at Missolonghi." This was just a few miles away and another stepping stone towards Athens. Gerald wondered what was there, then realised this was the place the woman had said Byron had been at way back in 1824.

At Missolonghi the taxi dropped the three off near a small square, at the centre of which stood what looked like a stone monolith in memory of someone. Nearby waited what looked like a well-healed man in his forties, dressed as if he was headed to some formal dinner somewhere. The taxi driver told the three their guide waited.

"Giorgios Seferis [2] at your service, gentlemen. I am at your disposal today," he began. "I know we are at war and you have you orders, but you can't come to this beautiful country without knowing more about our historic links, especially here in Missolonghi. Britain and Greece linked through time."

It was soon established the Greek authorities venerated the three airmen in their care. The man sent along to meet them in Missolonghi was none other than a Minister of State of the Greek Government. He spoke impeccable English and was an expert on Byron.

Gerald perked up. "I have some awareness of this. Lord Byron? He's the link."

"The lad from Shotton has some breeding!" winked The Bish, as Arthur Geary marvelled at the historic monuments all around in the warmth of the late Autumn sunshine.

"Maria, whom you met yesterday… "

The Bish nudged Gerald and whispered, "… your femme fatale dear chap."

"Er… yes… Maria," <'That was her name.'> "… she is very knowledgeable. She is reputed to be related to Lord Byron. Maria and I go back a long way *(another nudge came from The Bish directed at Gerald with raised eyebrows)* and she had made a request that I tell you the story of Byron and his presence here in Hiera Polis… our sacred city of Missolonghi."

"That's very kind. We are all ears." The Bish commented thoughtfully as he lit his pipe with his fresh supply of tobacco.

"Well, behind you is the monument to Lord Byron, your famous poet. Not only is he a famous poet, but he is the hero of Greece. Here in Missolonghi he supported the Greek struggle for independence and died here a hero! This monument contains his heart. You might have his body back in England, but we have his heart. Lord Byron is a war hero like you gentlemen. He planned attacks on the Turks *(he spat heavily at the mention of the word)* all the time and, despite his lack of formal military training, he commanded forces to great success. Then on 15 February 1824, he became very ill and never properly recovered, dying here in Missolonghi on 19 April. Noble man. Magnificent man!"

"Yes, he certainly was!" The Bish piped up, as smoke billowed from his pipe.

"Yes, I am sure had he lived and he would surely have defeated the Ottomans *(he spat heavily again)*, he would have been made the King of Greece."

Then began a tour of various places in the town, including many mentions of battles and sieges which took place in the town with lots of reference to the Turks and Ottomans. Any mention of these two names was always followed by three vicious spits from Georgios.

The complete tour of Missolonghi took up the remainder of the day, with meals and drinks provided along the way. The three were then led to a luxurious hotel and slept soundly as they dreamed of their adventurous trip around Greece in the past few days. Gone were the horrible memories of a plane hurling towards a crash landing in the sea to be replaced with beautiful memories of a beautiful people in a beautiful land.

*

The door knocked at Dee View in Shotton and Edith answered the door. It was a telegram being delivered by a young lad on a bike. Everyone called these lads the *Angels of Death*, such was the message they often carried to doors across the land. Edith at once read it. Hand over mouth, she walked into the back of the house where Frank had just come home from his shift at the steelworks. He looked at the small piece of beige coloured card and at once, he stood up, looking at the message on the telegram repeatedly. He read it out loud to Edith, with a hint of disbelief.

"MR AND MRS FRANK DAVIES - DEE VIEW ASH GROVE SHOTTON DEEPLY REGRET TO INFORM YOU YOUR SON - - 44072 P/O GERALD DAVIES - - HAS BEEN REPORTED MISSING - - FEARED KILLED ON WAR SERVICE
LETTER FOLLOWS"

Frank fell back to his chair and threw his face into his hands, squashing the telegram to his face. Edith looked on helplessly.

"Oh, my God. My God. My God Edie." Frank exclaimed. "Poor Gerald... he's gone. Just like that. A piece of paper and that's his life. Gone!"

It was the first time Edith had seen Frank so upset. Even the normally cold Edith had tears in her eyes. She did her best to console Frank and put her arm around him, taking the telegram from his hand. She read it again.

"It says feared killed, not actually, you know... killed. He could still be alive. We have to have some hope."

Frank looked up through tearful eyes. "Don't you think they'd have thought that through. I mean, they don't just write things like this for nothing. He's not returned to base for sure and when a plane doesn't come back that can only mean one thing... "

"He could be a prisoner of war somewhere, that's a thought, isn't it

Frank?"

"There are people around here who've had similar telegrams. If they're a prisoner, the Red Cross or someone says they are. When it says missing or uses the word killed, it means they think he's dead." Frank stood up with a purpose.

"Right Edie, we'd better get round to Lizzie and Francis' place. They need to know. We don't want anyone else telling them the news."

Within minutes the door knocked at 6 Ashfield Road, just a few yards down the road from Dee View. Lizzie opened the door. It was Frank AND Edith. She immediately knew something was wrong. The two walked in without an invitation, past the pastel shaded photograph on the wall in the parlour of Gerald in his officer's uniform. Francis was in the back eating a sandwich. He'd not long walked back with his dad from their shift at the steelworks and hadn't expected to see Frank so soon after leaving him and hadn't seen Edith at their door in some considerable time.

"The children?" Frank asked.

"Still at school."

"Berty is at work, so it's only us."

Lizzie trembled and didn't want to ask, but she knew she must. "Is it... bad news, Frank?"

He handed the crumpled telegram to Lizzie. She looked at it with Francis.

Nothing more was said. Tears fell from eyes in buckets and four people sat numb in the back room of a terraced house in Shotton, as many others probably did that day across the land.

*

In Greece, several days had passed and the missing three boarded a train for Antirrio where they would catch a ferry across the Gulf of Corinth to the east pier at Rio. From there they caught another train and headed into Patras, Greece's third largest city. As they sat on the train looking out across the Peloponnese and the huge mountains surrounding them they talked about their adventures over the past few days.

Gerald mentioned Spiro Amerikanos several times and hoped he would salvage something of his old Dodge Buick but deep inside he knew this wouldn't be the case as the image of the exploding car was indelibly imprinted on his mind, as was the picture of Spiro crying out on his knees before the car at Corfu harbour.

The Bish and Arthur tried to lighten the mood by teasing Gerald about his near miss with Byron's great-great granddaughter Maria.

"She'd have well cracked your nuts," Arthur quipped as suddenly things altered for the worse again. The train shook and juddered along the track, as an Italian bomber narrowly missed the passenger carriages with a stick of bombs which exploded all around the train. The pilot had spotted the train heading along the track and had done his best to destroy it there and then.

"We're sitting ducks on this damn bloody train!" The Bish said, calmly shaking his head and filling his pipe. "If it's my time to go, I may as well have a last smoke, hey chaps," he declared as other bombs could be heard dropping around and onto the city of Patras whose suburbs they were now in.

The air raid was over by the time the train pulled into Patras. Waiting for them, as had been arranged, was fifty-year-old Hellenic Naval Commander Gregory Mezeviris. [3] All the 'top-brass' had been employed to get the three missing men back to base.

Mezeviris had no intention of rushing off to Athens saying, "As you can see, the war comes to us, so we shouldn't be in any rush to get to the war. Today we eat, drink and be merry for tomorrow, who knows where we shall be." Wise words from a man who had already seen action in the First Balkan War of 1910, the Hellenic-Bulgarian War of 1913 and who was the first ever commander of a Greek submarine during the First World War. Gerald, The Bish and Arthur took his advice and thereafter were treated to a grand time in and around Patras, despite the place still burning from the constant bombing raids. It seemed too that the Greek people heeded the same advice, as most people carried on about their business as if nothing had happened.

*

It took a week for the missing three to arrive back at base in Menidi, granted their last few days were an impromptu holiday on the Greek mainland being shown the sights and sounds of the land by a variety of top Greek officials.

The Bish summed up these few days in his diary with a simplistic remark which downplayed the whole matter:

'The Naval Commander arranged lunch for us and a taxi brought us to Athens in four hours, after a series of hair-raising incidents with chickens, dogs, children, skids and precipices.'

The Bish and Arthur Geary atop a Blenheim at Menidi after their Corfu adventure with Gerald taking the photograph. The base 'staff-car' is in the background (see Chapter: 'A Bad Start').

Credit: Papa Spiro Monasterios who retains original image at Church of Saint Prokopios, Kavos, Corfu.

Author's Note

[1] The Evzones. Part of the Greek Presidential Guard.

[2] Georgios Seferiades (born: Giorgios Seferis) (1900 - 1971) - Greek poet (Nobel laureate) and Greek Foreign Office diplomat. He became Greek Ambassador to the UK from 1957 to 1962. Regarded as one of the most important Greek poets of the 20th century.

[3] Gregory Mezeviris (1891 - 1978) In 1906 he joined the Royal Hellenic Navy as a Cadet and served with the navy until his retirement in 1949.

During the Second World War he was Superior Commander of 10 Greek destroyers, serving himself aboard the King George, which the Germans seriously damaged on Easter Sunday, 13th April 1941. By coincidence, the same day Gerald Davies lost his life in Greece to the overwhelming German force entering the country.

Chapter Twenty-three

'Tommy Wisdom's Plan'

No one had expected to see The Bish, Gerald or Arthur Geary ever again when a taxi brought them   back from the dead, one rainy morning in the first week of December 1940.   One of the first people they met was interpreter and liaison officer for the Greeks, a chap called Constantine John Manussis. [1] Constantine had the nickname 'Embros,' (εμπρός) Greek for 'hello' or 'forwards' or 'come-in,' seems it was something to do with what he shouted in Greek when approached for advice or information.   It was the way he seemed to always begin a conversation, so the nickname stuck.

"Could have done with you back in Lefkimmi," commented The Bish as he shook his hand for the first time. "Need to get some Greek under my belt... "

"As opposed to Greek wine in your belly skip," Arthur Geary chirped in.

"Pot, kettle, black!" The Bish riposted. "Anyway, I hope no one else has assumed command of my squadron in my absence,"   The Bish said, as he entered the Officers' Mess with Gerald and Arthur in tow, to the surprise (and cheers) of all there. He followed it up with, "And how did we do in that raid on Durazzo?" Hoots of laughter flowed through the room. The Bish was back and he was none the worse for his experience, neither was Gerald or Arthur. The Greyhounds were complete again.

"Seems you damaged the jetty, sunk one ship and set another bugger on fire," commented Squadron Leader Tommy Wisdom, who was sat with the others from 211 Squadron. "So, where've you reprobates been until now then?"

"Been on holiday, touring this beautiful countryside, haven't we gentlemen?"

Gerald and Arthur nodded behind both looking tired.

"Without a good night's sleep for days," added Arthur Geary.

"And me... think of me, without my photograph of Susan!" Gerald said, still patting the pocket of his shirt where the photograph should be.

"He's be on about that damn photo gents, since we pancaked in Corfu." The Bish smiled across to Gerald. "Er... yet more importantly, I was stranded without my pipe tobacco, but no one moaned about that."

"Yes, because a kind local gave you a few fills to go on with Skip."

"All right Gerry, no need to gloat on my tobacco finding exploits in deepest darkest Corfu," The Bish gurgled, as he hovered his lighter over the bowl of his pipe.

The Officers' Mess listened on. The two were like Flanagan and Allen, a veritable double act in the making.

"Everyone needs a lucky charm, don't they? That photo was... "

"Was missing days ago... it's in Egypt, still enjoying the Canal Club."

He laughed and blew smoke towards Gerald, who ducked to avoid it.

"... was my lucky charm gents, hence the reason we were out of luck on that day over Durazzo!"

The Bish puffed away and was now covered in a halo of his own smoke. "It's bad luck to be superstitious ol' boy! Anyway, I doubt luck had anything to do with it on the day. Is that your way of explaining my success at landing the plane so skilfully so we're all here to tell the tale?"

"Fair point Skip! Yes, I think we were damn lucky to get away with it on the day, so perhaps not having the photograph was a thing, hey! Would still like to get that photograph back though."

"I think you've seen the last of it ol' boy."

"I know Skip," he replied "I'd like to just get... er... a message to her, to say I'm doing all right out here."

"You HAVE got it serious, dear boy. Here we are in historic Greece, surrounded by a culture second to none in the world, and all you can do is think of that girl of yours back home."

"I'm going to marry that girl one day for sure?"

"You are?"

"I am."

"Have you asked her?"

"Erm... no?"

"Don't you think she might want to have a say in the matter dear boy?" The Bish then posed the question to the whole of the Officers' Mess. "What do you think, gentlemen? I think our Gerry should write to this girl... er.. Susan... yes... to propose to her, hey?"

The whole place cheered away and there were shouts of *'marry me!'* and *'here comes the bride!'*

"All right gents, thank you," an embarrassed Gerald said. "I'm worn out with thinking."

"What he means... " The Bish interrupted, "is... erm... could it be that we've been plied with cognac for days and we're cognac'd out!"

A serious tone came across the face of Tommy Wisdom. "We did get a message through yesterday that you were all safe, but I'm afraid it was days too late to stop a message going out from H.Q., to your families to state you were missing feared killed."

"Well, that's easily resolved," a jocular James Gordon-Finlayson pointed out, "we can jolly-well un-inform them of the same. It'll be a pleasant surprise for the folks back home that we are ghosts become people again. Get a message to H.Q. right now to get the telegrams... or letter... or whatever the blighters send out."

"Yes, we'll sort that out, but Gerry I have an idea for you," Continued Squadron Leader Tommy Wisdom.

"That being?"

"Do you want to get a message to your Susan?"

"Sure. That would be a first class thing to do. As you know, we were banned from writing home for a while whilst we moved from Egypt and got settled here."

"What might you want to say to her?"

"Well, to tell her I'm safe and well, oh, yes, and to say I'd like another copy of the damn photograph I lost. It was my mascot and I'm sure that without it things were worse and we got bad luck."

"Poppycock!" shouted James Gordon-Finlayson from behind as he was walking away. "No such things as good luck mascots, and stuff like that. Getting that plane down was down to pure skill. Makes a wonderful story though, hey!"

"Ignore The Bish" winked Tommy Wisdom. "He's only jealous you've got a gorgeous girl at home. Yes, we can do that and I can see about trying to get a copy of the photograph. "

"Thank you, Tommy, appreciated."

"But if you really had to say something to your Susan right now… er… I mean face to face, what would you want to say?"

"I would ask her to marry me?"

Tommy Wisdom's face lit up. "Straight up you would?"

"I would indeed. I would propose to her on one knee."

"Then I can use my influence as a war correspondent to get something done for you."

"You can?"

"There's a few things here, Gerry. You Blenheim Boys are the invisible heroes of the skies. Mortal danger is part of your job, but you get on with it without an ounce of fuss. This is a chance for the British public to get to know a little about you. You represent every bomber crew and their loved ones out there, and it's high-time you lads got some recognition for it. The British public need a feel-good story, don't they in these dark days. I mean, how many awful stories get a happy ending nowadays. Answer is… well, I can't remember one like this. Pilot Officer goes missing with his crew. His family thinks he's dead…"

"They do?"

"Protocol. We had to inform them you were all missing. That's being rectified with a letter now… anyway, the good news is that the Pilot Officer and his crew then turn up a week later all safe and well. What does that do for the morale of everyone out there who has a family member missing in war?"

"It gives them hope."

"It gives them so much hope, dear Gerry and you'll be the face of that hope. I can't promise you anything but I've been chatting with Richard McMillan, the B.U.P. [2] War Correspondent in Athens and Richard Dimbleby, another journalist there. They know a few key people, so watch this space dear boy! Watch this space!"

"Well, thank you indeed, Squadron Leader. Thank you."

"I could do with a picture of you in those Tsarouchi shoes to go alongside the article."

"I think that would be a step too far, Tommy. A step too far!"

They both laughed.

Squadron Leader Tommy Wisdom took down every detail possible from Gerald and the wheels were set in motion to get a story into the press.

* * *
*

It all happened at quite a pace.

November had ticked over into December, and Susan Hall hadn't seen Gerald since he'd had to rush off on his posting way back in September. Like everyone else in Britain, whilst loved ones were away, the people at home got on with their lives. Yes, they thought every day about their loved ones, but life still carried on. Susan Hall was no different and her life was equally divided between her duties with the Upper Thames Patrol and her time at The Horns in Crazies Hill where she still pulled a pint and served meals.

Despite the war, The Horns was gearing up for Christmas and Susan was fully at the beck and call of the landlords Frank and Edith Burrough when she was on duty. It was early evening and Susan went to open up when she encountered two men as if they'd been waiting for the place to open.

Susan was used to the odd customer waiting for the pub doors to open, so this was nothing unusual. She hadn't seen the two ever before though, so was a little suspicious of who they might be. Nevertheless, she ushered them in, seeing that the younger of the two had a camera, with a large circular flash hung over his shoulder, she assumed they were something to do with an event on the river, after all the Thames in the area always had something or other on the go which the press were covering - AND these two looked as if they had been born in Fleet Street, so they had to be press.

"Come in gentlemen, what can I get you?"

"Two pints of your best please," the older one of the two, with the Errol Flynn pencil moustache, politely asked.

"Coming up. Take a seat."

The two, neatly attired in long taupe macks, trilbies and dour brown ties followed her to the bar and watched as she pulled the pints.

Susan looked over at them, as the pair stared hard back at her. "You're press aren't you?"

"No flies on her," the older man said, nudging the one with the camera.

"You wouldn't happen to be Susan Hall, would you?"

"No flies on you," replied Susan.

The two men lit cigarettes.

Susan was cautious and careful about what she might say, after all these were the days when everyone was warned careless talk cost lives. She poured the bitter into two glasses, saying no more.

"We really need to speak with Susan," the man repeated as he watched the two full pints being placed onto the beautifully polished wooden bar. Susan carefully wiped a small spill from the bar and carried the two drinks to the men.

"And who is asking?"

The man from the press intuitively knew he was talking with Susan Hall. He gave her some coins.

"Five-bob, cover the cost of the ale?"

"More than enough."

"Keep the change. So, I bet you are wondering what we might be about then? We are from the press."

"You said." Susan looked at the two half crowns in her hand. "Thank you."

"I have a message from someone special in your life."

"Who might that be?"

"Pilot Officer Gerald Davies."

Susan perked up at the sound of Gerald's name, but at the same time worry filled her face. "Is he all right? He's not... you know... is he?"

"You'll be glad to know he's fine... er... now."

"NOW?"

"We're doing a story about him. Seems his plane came a cropper and crashed somewhere on a Greek island. Him and the others got out safely... "

"Was he hurt at all?"

"We've been told no, so I have to assume that's the truth. Long and short of it is... he has mentioned you. He's struck on you, you know, and we think it'll make a delightful story."

"Story?"

The journalist retrieved a notepad from his pocket.

"Seems he had a photograph of you and him, taken on the river in the summer..."

"Yes, yes, he would have had it. It was the last thing I gave him before he left."

"Er... but... he's lost it. It was his lucky mascot, he says. We said we'd try to get a copy done for him. Do you have... "

"A copy? Yes, I do and the negatives... here in the pub, as it happens."

"Well, that's the first one ticked off the list, then Ronny." The two press men smiled. "We can get the photograph to him. There's transport for supplies going out there regularly, so I'm sure they wouldn't mind adding a little envelope marked 'urgent' on it, with a note in it."

"I can do that?"

"Do it right now, but we need to know more."

Frank Burrough the landlord had walked through. Susan looked at him. "Can I chat with these gentlemen for a few minutes?"

"Take a long as you like. There's no one in yet." Susan began to put a quick note for Gerald together and wrote a few words on the back of the photograph.

"A few more questions while you write away... so how did you meet?"

"Right here in the pub." Susan Hall explained the full circumstances and told the two pressmen about the precious time the two had had together in the summer after they had met when he was a flying instructor in the area.

"He says he wants to marry you after this is all over?"

"He does?"

"Yes, he's asked us to make a marriage proposal by proxy to you."

"Goodness, that's something of a surprise. A nice one, though. What a wonderful thrill."

"And your answer is?"

Susan laughed heavily and teasingly. "Hmm... that's for me to know and you to find out. My answer might be in the letter, and it might not be. I can't give YOU an answer to this question, can I?"

"You do play your cards close to your chest, young lady. Right Ronny, all we need is a nice photograph of the young lady and that letter when it's finished and we're away from here."

*

"We couldn't have you down or thinking you might get bad luck because you didn't have that photograph now, could we Gerry ol' boy" Tommy Wisdom had commented as he presented the newspaper before Gerald. The Daily Herald had been flown out from Britain as part of the deal to sort Gerald out and keep morale high amongst the men. It did the trick.

Tommy Wisdom's Plan had gone like clockwork.

Gerald stared at the front of the newspaper and there was the actual image in the press of him and Susan taken on the river at Henley that summer. A summer which now seemed so far away in time.

"It can't be Tommy. Is it?"

"Take a look."

Gerald looked at the front page of the Daily Herald and there it was. The photograph of him and Susan for all the world to see.

PRESS "POPPED QUESTION"

This is Susan Hall, the girl who received a proposal of marriage via the newspapers. The young man is now Pilot-Officer Gerald Davies, on service in Greece, the sender of the proposal. He was explaining to a reporter that the reason he got lost on a bombing trip was that he had left his mascot—a picture of Miss Hall—behind. No, it wasn't his wife, but . . . "you can tell her I am going to marry her after this job is over. She doesn't know it yet, but this goes as a proposal."

Original Copy of newspaper cutting kept by Lizzie and Francis Davies, then passed on to the author via Ruby Davies

"Oh, my goodness, it is. It is!" Gerald became silent and his eyes filled with tears.

Gerald could quite believe what he was seeing. "You mean this is it, the original photograph I had taken with Susan at Henley… "

"Yes, of course it's the photograph Gerry lad, just in a daily paper for everyone in the country to see."

"It's only been a day or so since we talked about it."

"We press can work our magic on anything. One phone call and hey presto, the ball was set in motion."

"How did you get it then?"

"I got a message to the lads on The Herald via our team in Athens, and they did the rest. Went to see your Susan they did in Crazies Hill… "

"They actually spoke to her."

"And had a pint to boot."

"Lucky blighters!"

"They told her you're fine and she gave them a copy of the photograph, which is now before your very eyes."

"How is she?"

"Apparently fine."

"The paper is yours to keep."

"Tommy, how can I ever repay you?"

"You lads have done enough for us already. The paper is yours to keep."

"I have one more surprise for you Gerry dear chap."

"More surprises. What a rather great day this turning out to be."

"Go on then, close your eyes."

Gerald squeezed his eyes tightly as he heard Tommy Wisdom extricate some papers from his canvas bag. Something slid across the table in front of him.

"You can open them now."

Gerald opened his eyes. On the table before him was an envelope addressed to Pilot Officer Gerald Davies and another envelope marked 'URGENT,' with almost the same address on it, but this time he recognised the handwriting. The handwriting was that of Susan Hall.

It was a letter.

"Open the one you don't recognise the writing from first." Tommy Wisdom suggested.

Gerald slowly opened the envelope and there inside was a copy of the photograph he had lost.

"My photograph!" Gerald almost squealed with delight.

"Well, a copy of it anyway. Look on the back."

Gerald turned the photograph over.

* * *

My dearest Gerry
  Glad you have our photograph back.
  Keep safe.
  All my love.
  Susan x

"Now you won't have to go on those raids without the photograph Gerry ol' chap."

"Thank you. Thank you so much… and here was I going to cut the paper to shreds to put the cutting in my pocket."

"You know who the other letter is from then?"

"Certainly do."

"Well, you'd better open it then.

Gerald carefully opened the sealed envelope.

Wargrave Road
  Henley

My Dear Gerry,
  The men came from the paper today. They were very nice. One took a photograph of me outside in the rain, so I had my hood up. The other one other spoke to me about you. I told him everything about how we met and how we hadn't really known each other long. It only takes one day to know each other though, doesn't it?
  They told me you had been missing on a bombing trip. I didn't know because, of course, no one tells me and I don't have any contact with your family in North Wales but I hope to when you are next back on leave, whenever that is? Perhaps you will then take me there, to where you live? I would like that very much, darling.
  The man from the paper told me about the photograph you had lost or mislaid. You're hopeless, Gerry. He told me that you didn't feel happy to fly again unless you had the photograph with you. So what else could I do but find the negatives so they could make another one for you.
  What you were thinking of, losing the photograph, you naughty man.
  What's more, what is this the man from the press tells me? You want to marry me? He said you had requested the press make a

proposal of marriage from you far away. How sweet and lovely a man you are.

I didn't want to say yes and I didn't want to say no to a man I didn't know, but you can be assured I will tell you when I see you and you will like what you hear.

Much much love and more.

Susan

xx

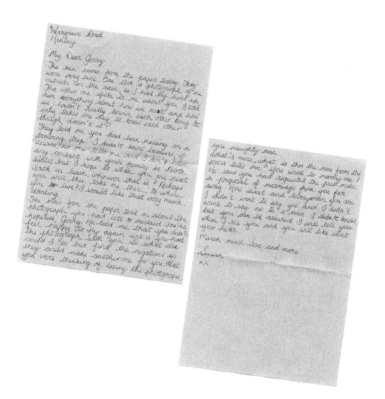

It was just after six in the morning, not long after Frank had called for Francis and the two had headed across the Hawarden Bridge on their cycles to the steelworks, when Mrs. Sprake hammered on the door of 6 Ashfield Road in Shotton.

Inside Lizzie Davies was busy preparing to light the fire in the grate

<'Who the heck can that be now. Francis forgotten his snapping, no doubt. Useless he is.'>

"Coming, coming, wait your sweat, wait your sweat!" She shouted, as she hurriedly tried to wipe the black soot marks from her hands.

"Lizzie, Lizzie" came the shout from the other side of the door. "Open up! Open up!"

Lizzie at once heard it was her friend Audrey and rushed to the front door with some concern, past Gerald's photograph on the parlour wall, over which a wilted and drying chrysanthemum hung. The telegram informing Frank of Gerald being 'Missing Feared Killed' still lay on the sideboard next to the Coronation jug of King George V. Frank had left it there. "Best left with you this, for the reasons we only know," he had commented before he and Edith had left the house on the day the telegram had arrived from the angel of death.

<'Something is wrong, something is wrong. Audrey never comes here at this time.'>

Lizzie opened with door. "What's wrong Audrey, has something happened to Jim?"

"Happened to Jim? What are you on about Lizzie. Let me in! Let's go through the back!" In her hand was The Daily Herald. "Have you seen the paper?"

Audrey was already walking in as Lizzie closed the door and followed her through to where the unlit fire was still in a mess, half laid with papers and coal.

"The war's over?" Came Lizzie's speculative comment.

"No such thing. I wish. You haven't seen the paper, have you?"

Audrey slapped the paper into Lizzie's hands. "Look! There! It's your Gerald. He's alive."

Lizzie looked at the aper with disbelief. She fell back in to the chair. "It can't be. The telegram. The telegram."

"It says there, in black and white. He's alive! It's not just in this newspaper either. It's in ALL the papers!"

Courtesy British Newspaper Archive - a selection of several newspapers from December 1940

"Oh, my God. Sorry, God. Oh, my God. Can it be true? Gerald is alive. I've had no letter or anything Audrey."

"Says so there. Let me finish sorting the fire and get a pot of tea on for us. It's a shock Lizzie, I know, but a good shock. You wait 'til your Francis and his dad knows."

"I have to tell him, I have to tell him Audrey. Mind if I take the paper. Can you mind the fire for me? Oh, and mind the children, they're still upstairs. Surprised they haven't come down with all the noise… anyway, I won't be long. Won't be long!"

With that, Lizzie ran out of the door and headed across the footbridge which ran alongside the railway line. Dozens of cyclists were either going to or coming from the steelworks, and she did her best to weave in and out of the throng of workmen in their flat caps and clogs.

Then she saw him. It was Francis heading in her direction. He was waving a paper. The Daily Herald.

Lizzie stood still and waved her paper back at him.

Francis pulled to a halt and let his bicycle fall against the side of the bridge just as a goods train noisily clattered by, steam filling the bridge and the clank of the wheels on the track blotted out any sound anyone made.

Lizzie and Francis never heard what either person said, but it didn't matter, both cried with delight and hugged each other as tight as they ever had.

Author's Note

[1] Constantine John Manussis (1917 - 1964) known as Embros - Greek Liaison Officer and interpreter attached to 211 Squadron. After the war he settled in Britain.

Source: Wings Over Olympus and 211 Squadron website. More information at www.levantineheritage.com - the Blacklers Resident in Greece.

[2] B.U.P. - British United Press. Several War Correspondents were based in Athens at the time.

Image: Courtesy Wings Over Olympus. War Correspondents in Athens 1940

(Left to right with Acropolis in background): Lee Stowe, Jan Yindrich, J. Aldridge, Martin Agrinsky, Richard Dimbleby, Arthur Merton, 'Happy' Woodward, Ed Sevens.

Chapter Twenty-four

'DFC'

"You can dump those pyjamas under your uniforms now, lads!" was one of the first announcements made by Squadron Leader James Gordon-Finlayson upon his return with the others from the dead. Laid across the table in the Officers' Mess were warm looking Irvin suits for each of the crew of 211 Squadron.

"Now we can fly to the stars and not freeze our bollocks off, gents," had been the follow on comment, as everyone collected their garments with great joy and appreciation.

No one had expected Greece to be so wet and cold, but it was December after all. Wet and cold it was! Bombing operations had been hindered by the weather but had not stopped. The crews were constantly reminded that they were the lucky ones, as the Greek troops on the ground in the Albanian mountains were often poorly supplied, without food and freezing.

"At least most days we come home to our beds. Those Greek boys haven't even got warm boots on and are stuck week-in and week-out in freezing conditions. It's our duty to help them and help them we will. If we die in the process, so be it!" This was how The Bish had finished his briefing before they ventured out again in L6670 a replacement Blenheim Mk I from 84 Squadron. In that first flight back, The Bish, Gerald and Arthur might have lost L8511, but they considered themselves lucky to have the opportunity to fly once again.

They could be at the bottom of the Ionian Sea, so all were grateful

211 Squadron were now fully engaged in Wing Commander Willetts' plan, as outlined to John D'Albiac and General Metaxas' team

at the Hotel Grande Bretagne to on 7th November, to engage the Italians at three main strategic locations: Durazzo, Valona and Tepelenë.

So it was, in their newly gained Irvin suits, The Bish Boys once again flew out to bomb the Italians at Valona harbour. As usual, everyone was terrified but on task nevertheless.

"Bombs gone," was the familiar cry as once again they came under heavy fire and Italian fighters chased them in the skies. Arthur Geary sweated as he loaded and reloaded to keep them safe, firing at anything resembling an Italian fighter.

Photo: Courtesy Wings Over Olympus - 211 Squadron Bombs dropping on Valona Harbour

Then it happened. Several strafes from an Italian fighter peppered the Blenheim before it peeled off.

Smoke poured from the Blenheim and flying it was a task in its own right with some of the tail section shot away.

"Bloody déjà vu, this is chaps!" shouted The Bish across an intercom crackling worse than ever. "Are we all fine?"

Gerald gave a thumbs up and tapped the photograph in his top pocket.

"Roger that skip" came the response from Arthur Geary "Bandit has gone now. Seems he had no more ammo."

L6670 limped back towards Menidi.

This time they made it back.

As they landed on the rain sodden runway at Menidi, Gerald once again tapped the top pocket of his new Irvin suit "told you G-F, our luck was in. It's down to the photograph."

"Photograph! You may be right ol' boy, you may be right! It's also thanks to this old bird. Seems to fly when there's bugger all left of it."

They all laughed nervously as the ground crew arrived and immediately set about repairs to the plane.

As Gerald walked away, looking back at the damaged Blenheim, he breathed a sigh of relief. He grabbed the photograph out of his pocket, looked at the writing on the back and kissed it. "Thank you, Sue. Thank you!"

The Bish slapped him hard on the back. "Soppy bugge,r Gerry!"

It mattered not to Gerald what The Bish thought; he was now down safely back on terra-firms and to his mind, carrying the photograph with him brought him luck. He intended to take it wherever he went from now onwards, without fail.

*

During November the Blenheims had carried out 235 sorties, of which 56 were aborted for a variety of reasons. December continued on at a pace and the weather further north seemed to deteriorate with a pace no one had expected. The Blenheims were restricted to two airbases in the south of Greece, Menidi and Eleusis, all because the Greek government were still intent on not provoking any Nazi hostility by allowing the RAF bases closer to the north of the country where they might be seen as a threat to the Germans. This meant all raids on Albania took place at the limit of the fuel capacity of the Blenheims.

Deteriorating conditions in the mountains, where the peaks rose above the clouds meant that bomb loaded Blenheims struggled to safely make it through and it was only the skill of the pilots and their navigators which prevented disasters happening on a grand scale. A timely reminder for the men of 211 Squadron was when 'The Airedale,' Pilot Officer Jerdein [2] and his air gunner, Sergeant John Munro nicknamed 'Pickers,' were returning from a raid on Valona on 7th December. Their craft struck the peak of the mountains in atrocious weather near Lamia. At 23,000 feet, the air temperature had been minus 50. Everyone considered themselves lucky not to have kissed any mountains themselves that day.

The Bish announced it in a matter-of-fact manner, but as respectfully as he could. "Bad news gents, Pickers and The Airedale won't be in their beds tonight. Iced up kite in the mountains." They said a prayer and everyone carried on. They had to.

The weather also exacerbated the problems and low cloud over the targets in Albania meant the brave crews often had to fly at a level where they could get to see the target but which put them at extreme risk of being shot down by the Italians.

Despite the dangers, throughout December the Blenheims with their brave RAF crews flew north over the mountainous and freezing Greek terrain to bomb Italian targets along the Albanian coast and further inland. Sometimes they were accompanied by Gloster Gladiators from 80 Squadron and other times with planes from other squadrons. On more occasions than they liked, the crews flew on missions with no fighter protection at all. Their mission was succeeding though and the Italian invasion of Greece had been stopped in its tracks, thanks to the tenacious fighting of the Greeks in Epirus, ably assisted by the British Royal Air Force but the Italians held on inland at Tepelenë, which made the place a regular target for 211 Squadron.

The sodden grass runways were a problem and not conducive to heavy bomber wheels rumbling along them, let alone landing on them with some force. D'Albiac's wish for hard core runways hadn't materialised and few doubted it was something which could be now be achieved, nevertheless everyone just got on with the job and the occasional moans were few and far between. One thing on the sodden runways which had increased were the amount of dummy aircraft lining the sides. Before The Bish had gone missing, he had spoken with Willie, the Intelligence Officer, about his concerns as regards the amount of Nazis in Greece.

"The Nazi shufti-kites are always up and about the place. If they see how many planes we don't have in this place, they'll be sure to invade, so we need dummy planes everywhere."

"Leave it with me," Willie replied and got on with setting in place arrangements to get dummy aircraft strategically placed all around.

*

* * *

With Athens not too far away, Gerald regularly travelled into the city. The rain of the night, soaking the runway, seemed to melt away here and each time he found himself in Athens there was nothing but sunshine.

He marvelled at the architecture and had even been up to visit the Parthenon sat atop the Acropolis overlooking the city. He'd thought the sights and sounds of Egypt were a marvel to behold, but the flies ruined his perception of the country. No such thing here in Athens. The city was a clean and modern European city. Its people looked clean and modern as they walked along wide tree-lined avenues with tall marble buildings either side. Gerald had been to Liverpool a few times on the train and the two cities looked so similar, except every time he'd been in Liverpool it had rained and here, the sunshine fed the warmth of his heart.

The city centre was a strange place to be though. He would regularly be greeted with "Guten Morgan" or "Guten Tag" as he walked about Athens. The place seemed to be full of Germans, but there was nothing anyone could say as, after all, right now Greece was not at war with Germany. This was a real odd situation AND a worry.

At nighttime, the officers of 211 Squadron frequented one of two nightclubs, either the Argentina or Maxim's. During the day their regular haunt was Zonars café in a street with an almost unpronounceable name - Voukourestiou, which was Greek for Bucharest Street. The place had only been opened the previous year by the enterprising chocolatier, Karolos Zonaras. Like Spiro Americanos from Corfu, Karolos had worked and lived in America and wanted to bring back to Greece what he had learned there. He wanted Zonars to be the best restaurant in Athens, and it was. The best chefs in Europe filled the place and in 1940 it had become the premiere place of café culture in Athens.

Zonars was the place to meet for artists, intellectuals and the like. Remarkable people with remarkable talents met here and created their poetry, music or artwork over a coffee. Now amongst these people was the RAF.

On his first visit to the café Gerald and the others met with Yannis Tsarouchis [1] a noted Greek artist who was talking with a young lad, Manos Hatzidakis, [1]* who looked no more than fifteen years old but these were times when people had to grow up quickly and the young lad had a solid and fearsome look about him.

The two saw the uniforms of the RAF and approached the table where The Bish, Gerald, Arthur, Tommy and Willie were sitting.

Yannis spoke first.

"Can we joins you gentlemens?"

"Take a seat," a confident James Gordon-Finlayson announced. "As long as you're not Nazis."

Three spits immediately came from the two men, who looked around the place furtively.

"I am Yannis and this is my friends Manos. We are Greeks, yes, through and through, you knows," Yannis said as the two men sat down.

"Good to hear. Good to hear." The Bish replied.

"I sees, you have not ordered yet. Then it is for us to get you your coffees in appreciation for alls you do's." Yannis burst into Greek and set the order in motion.

"That's very kind, thank you." Gerald added. All the airmen remained cautious of their new guests, knowing the amount of Germans around in the city.

"It is the least I can do," Yannis whispered quietly. "I am now ons leave from the war in the mountains of Epirus. Is a cold and bloody war against our foes, the Italians, but we are driving them back slowly but surely."

As Intelligence Officer, Willie listened with interest. Any news he could pick up was useful to pass back to H.Q., and this was first hand information coming from someone at the front near Tepelenë.

"That's good to hear." The Bish responded.

"I wanted to personally say my thanks to you gentlemen for being in the skies above us and dropping us supplies." He looked around and whispered even more quietly than he had been. "We are short on so many things. Food, warm clothing, ammunition… you names it, thens we is shorts of it."

The airmen all said nothing. Tommy Wisdom noted everything too.

"So whilst here in Athens we all lives a Bohemian life, a few hundreds of miles away, life is so different but mades better by the efforts of you men, so is why I buys you coffee."

The coffees arrived as if on cue, as did another man, The Bish, Gerald and Arthur knew well. It was Giorgios Seferis, the Greek Foreign Office diplomat and expert on Byron, who'd shown them around Missolonghi.

The Bish, Arthur and Gerald stood up immediately and shook hands.

"You know each other?" Tommy Wisdom asked.

"It's a long story. All I can say is Byron." The Bish commented, putting his finger knowingly to his nose.

"Yes, gotcha," Tommy Wisdom responded. He now recalled his conversation with Gerald when he'd interviewed him to get the story into the Daily Herald. "Small world G-F!"

Everyone sat down.

"I was coming to meets with my friends Manos and Yannis when I saw they had company. I thoughts to myself, I knows these peoples. Now we are all friends together and I am so pleased to see you again. These men..." he whispered to Yannis and Manos "... are formidable warriors and I have lots of respect for them. They are heroes of this nation and follow in the footsteps of Byron to be saviours of our great nation."

"I'll sip a coffee to that," Gerald said, raising his cup to all the people around the table who reciprocated.

Giorgios altered the mood again.

"Gather in gentlemen...." Giorgios beckoned the group to all come closer, whispering to a point he could hardly be heard. "We haves to be particularly on our guards here, as much as Zonars is the most beautiful of places in Athens... " He looked around. "Yes, but it is, we must not forget a place of dangers. My government work tells me many things. Yes, we are not at war with the Germans, but I wants to warn you, their spies are everywhere. You knows the Nazi swastika hangs proudly from the German Embassy just around the corner?"

Willie knew for certain, but Gerald certainly wasn't aware of this, yet nodded as if he knew.

"It is just my warnings to be careful, gentlemens, when you are sats in here. Ears is everywhere. You see that table over there?" He nodded without looking and his eyes directed the others towards a table where a smart man, of about twenty-five years old, dressed in a natty suit was sat with a pretty blonde who looked like she was five years his junior at least. The pair could have been a young couple from Henley on holiday as far as Gerald was concerned. The girl reminded him of Susan.

"Tourists gentlemens, you thinks?" he whispered. "Ochi! No... they are the G.S.P."

"G.S.P.?" Gerald whispered to Willie.

"Geheime Staatspolizei. Gestapo for short. Hermann Göring's creation, but now led by Heinrich Himmler and his henchmen. You wouldn't want to be interviewed by any of them, believe you me. I believe the Geneva Convention is null and void when it comes to these guys."

Gerald nodded with a look of concern.

Giorgios looked at Gerald. "Your friend is not wrong. These are bad, bad peoples!" he said shaking his head with derision. "Anyways, lets not talk of those filthy Nazis. He spat three times quietly. "Yes... my friend Yannis here, who fights courageously in the mountains to the north, wants your continued support without the interference of Hitler's jackboots. Did I mention those Nazis again?" He spat once more.

"We are always at your service, Giorgios," The Bish replied honestly. "We owe you much for what the kind and beautiful folks of Lefkimmi did for us and for everyone who helped us get back to base, we are eternally grateful."

"One more things, James, if I can ask a favour then?"

"Try me out then and I'll see if we can help," The Bish smiled.

"It's not what you can do for us, I think it is what we can do for you." Giorgios once again reduced any volume to his voice. "The King, he wishes to come and inspect you at Menidi. Can yous arrange this for him as soon as possible. Perhaps January?"

Gerald had never seen The Bish taken by surprise. The Bish, not sure what to say, even stuttered his words a couple of times. "The... the ... King!"

"Shhh! Mr Bish!"

"Ye... ye... yes... yes. We can arrange for that."

Willie spoke up. "We will confirm it with our team and let you know the arrangements made."

With that Giorgios gave The Bish a card with his details on and the three Greeks got up and left. The three airmen looked at each other and raised their coffee cups.

"The King!"

*

The mundane days were few and far between, as 211 Squadron headed towards Christmas. On Christmas Eve, Gerald once again diced with death at Valona and it wasn't just the weather causing a problem this time. The Bish Boys, led by The Bish headed for the aerodrome at Valona through the cloud shrouded snow-topped peaks of the Pindus

Mountains. Sheer determination and exceptional navigation skills got all planes to their target and as they dropped out of the low cloud over the airbase they surprised the Italians, attacking without any retaliation, but more was to come. As they sped away, they headed over Valona harbour and straight into the loaded guns of an Italian Cruiser. The nine Blenheims strafed the ship and were lucky to escape the huge barrage it put up as they passed.

"Well, we're still airborne Skipper," a sweating Gerald calmly commented.

The intercom crackled. "It might be Christmas Eve, but it's just another day at the office. Just another day at the office, chaps.

All nine aircraft headed back to Menidi, taking with them some Italian shrapnel as usual. Italian fighters interrupted their journey further south and increased their shrapnel load more but all made it back safely and without injury to one person. Planes could be replaced and crews could be replaced when lost, but on the front line, lives were valued by everyone and any mission where no one was lost was regarded as a success.

*

On arrival back at base that Christmas Eve, everyone had headed for a quick beer.

"Where's the Skip gone?" Gerald observed to Tommy Wisdom as he looked around for his boss.

"Called to a meeting. The A.O.C. John D'Albiac and his wife are here and they've asked to see him."

"Christmas drink, no doubt."

"Yes, and they won't be inviting you, Gerry ol' man. You've had all the publicity for everyone in this place, what with you and that damn photo. You still got it?"

"Still got it? I pat it every five minutes, dear Tommy." He pulled the photograph out, and they both looked at it. "Saved my bacon again over Valona today, I reckon. I can't thank you enough for getting it for me. Makes me feel secure and safe, like a bullet deflector it is."

A good hour later The Bish walked in to the Officers' Mess, accompanied by the A.O.C. John D'Albiac and his young looking wife Sybil, who instantly and warmly shook hands with all, to everyone's delight. Those who weren't already standing, stood up instantly at the unannounced visitors.

The room went silent.

"Thank you. Sit down, gentlemen." John D'Albiac urged.

"I want to thank everyone for their loyalty to the RAF, their loyalty to me and their loyalty to the Crown. These are testing times for us all but we have, in YOU, the team who are 211 Squadron, a group of people with metal and determination built into their very core. Just this morning I understand you gave the WOP a Christmas Eve whopping at Valona…"

All cheered.

"Well done gentlemen, you are doing a splendid job with the minimum of materials. You fly dangerous missions each and every day, and I am grateful for that. The mountains are a hazard in their own right, causing us regretful losses. Pilot Officer Jerdein and Sergeant Munro, we have lost of late and they shall never be forgotten. Indeed, ALL lost in this epic struggle, we will remember for all time."

"Hear, hear" came the shout from The Bish, followed by the others.

John D'Albiac continued.

"I understand fully what you boys are up against. Even landing your kites back at base on these damn awful runways can be fraught with danger. We have done our best to get access to better airfields and I sincerely hope we can achieve this in the new year. We are looking at bases further north which will give us better access to the Albanian coast and other strategic areas without flying a marathon before we get there."

Everyone nodded in agreement. Everyone knew they were flying to the fuel limits of the Blenheim, and this was a concern every time they went out on a sortie.

"Valona is, as you know, the biggest sea-port on the Albanian coast and it is the key point of access for the wop into Greece. Operations to destroy their logistics operations will continue until they are totally defeated. We have them on the about turn, we know that. It is now just a matter of time before we defeat old Musso's men and return them to where they belong. Either a watery grave or back to Rome."

Once again everyone cheered.

"Many of you will wonder why I am here with my good lady."

Sybil D'Albiac smiled at everyone.

"I have a special announcement to make. Squadron Leader James Gordon-Finlayson is a phenomenal leader and he is a pilot of extraordinary skill. In recent times, as you know, we thought he'd abandoned us all to our own devices," he chortled heartily. "The bugger went missing with his crew... where are you gentlemen..."

Gerald and Arthur Geary tentatively stretched their hands out.

"He took you two on holiday to Corfu, landing on the narrowest strips of beach and then having a tour of the island, free bed and board and caviare galore." He looked at The Bish. "I jest James... er ... yes... Squadron Leader Gordon-Finlayson has flown umpteen raids against the Iti, both day and night with his trusty team..."

He looked directly at Gerald and Arthur, who nodded and smiled. Then he looked back at G-F.

"Your skill and determination Squadron Leader, in bringing to fruition, then leading and completing those raids and many shufti flights over enemy territory not only here in Greece but back across the Med in the Western Desert has been outstanding. You're a damn brave man Squadron Leader and so are your team. You know Squadron Leader, I began my service with the Navy in 1914 and then joined the air service, which is where gentlemen, I was awarded my D.S.O. in 1916 [3] as, what you chaps call a shufti-kite pilot. The flak I received over many months and attacks against me by enemy fighters bears no resemblance to what you gentlemen have had to go through, and through all of this you have a VERY determined leadership. I mean, what can be more determined than bringing down safely his aircraft onto a strip of beach in Corfu no wider than several yards. To this end I can tell you all that Squadron Leader James Gordon-Finlayson, colloquially known to you boys as The Bish or G-F or perhaps other things sometimes hey... "

Everyone laughed.

"... has been awarded the Distinguished Flying Cross, [4] so huge congratulations to The Bish. Merry Christmas one and all!"

The room burst into spontaneous applause and shouts of "The Bish" and "DFC."

"I am so pleased to accept this award, Sir," began The Bish, "But I must let you know, this is FOR ALL OF US. Well done lads!"

Once again, applause and smiles filled the room.

"One last thing I want to mention sir, particularly from myself, Gerry and Arthur are the gallant people of Corfu. Their kindness and generosity is second to none. Right now the citizens of that beautiful island are as good as defenceless and all suffering at the hands of the Iti. We have witnessed this first hand... (he laughed), ... the Iti even tried to kill us at the consulate but failed miserably like they always do. (all cheered) This is why tomorrow, on Christmas Day, I have arranged for 84 Squadron, whose pilots will dress as Father Christmas's by the way, to return our thanks for their generosity. Tomorrow they will fly from here, their holds not loaded with bombs but loaded with hundreds and hundreds of gifts for the children of Corfu." Everyone cheered again.

"So, fill your glasses, gentlemen."

All grabbed their drinks.

"To our esteemed guests, Air Vice-Commodore D'Albiac and Mrs D'Albiac, to the people of Corfu and to defeating the enemy. Gentlemen... The Greyhounds!"

All repeated it loudly. "The Greyhounds!"

Author's Note

[1] Yannis Tsarouchis (1910 - 1989) - Famous Greek painter who exhibited internationally after the war.

[1]* Manos Hatzidakis (1925 – 1994) - Greek composer and songwriter.

[2] Pilot Officer 42312 Guy Inglis Jerdein, 211 Squadron. Killed in action 7th December 1941, aged 22 years. Phaleron War Cemetery.

Sergeant 638862 John Munro, 211 Squadron. Killed in action 7th December 1941, aged 21 years. Phaleron War Cemetery.

[3] Distinguished Service Order John D'Albiac 22nd June 1916

long-distance reconnaissances.

Lieutenant John Henry Dalbiac, R.M.A.

In recognition of his services as an aeroplane observer at Dunkirk since February, 1915. During the past year Lieutenant Dalbiac has been continually employed in coastal reconnaissances and fighting patrols. The Vice-Admiral Commanding the Dover Patrol, in reporting on the work of the R.N.A.S. at Dunkirk, lays particular emphasis on the good work done by the observers.

[4]

James Richmond Gordon-Finlayson DFC.

7th January 1941 - Awarded the Distinguished Flying Cross.

The KING has been graciously pleased to approve the following awards in recognition of gallantry displayed in flying operations against the enemy:

This officer has completed more than 40 day and night raids and reconnaissances over enemy territory in Greece and the Western Desert. Undaunted by continual severe antiaircraft fire and attacks by fighters he has shown superb courage, determination and devotion to duty. The accuracy of his bombing has resulted in great damage to enemy positions and transport concentration, and his determined leadership of his squadron has enabled most effective results to be secured.

THE LONDON GAZETTE, 7 JANUARY, 1941   151

Acting Squadron Leader Douglas Robert Stewart BADER, D.S.O. (26151), No. 242 Squadron.

Squadron Leader Bader has continued to lead his squadron and wing with the utmost gallantry on all occasions. He has now destroyed a total of ten hostile aircraft and damaged several more.

Acting Squadron Leader James Richmond GORDON - FINLAYSON (36078), No. 211 Squadron.

This officer has completed more than 40 day and night raids and reconnaissances over enemy territory in Greece and the Western Desert. Undaunted by continual severe anti-aircraft fire and attacks by fighters he has shown superb courage, determination and devotion to duty. The accuracy of his bombing has resulted in great damage to enemy positions and transport concentration, and his determined leadership of his squadron has enabled most effective results to be secured.

In November, 1940, when his squadron commander was engaged by eight enemy fighters, Captain Boyle alone succeeded in taking off from a waterlogged aerodrome, and attacked in an attempt to extricate his comrade. Though wounded and covered with oil he continued to fight, after his squadron commander had been shot down, until his engine was so damaged that he was compelled to land, being rescued from his wrecked aircraft by the front line troops. Captain Boyle has repeatedly led his flight into action over enemy territory and against superior enemy forces with skill, courage and determination.

Flying Officer Hugh Norman TAMBLYN (40862), No. 242 Squadron.

Flying Officer Tamblyn has shown the greatest keenness to engage the enemy and has destroyed at least five of their aircraft. He has set a splendid example to the other members of his section.

Pilot Officer Eric Simcox MARRS (33572), No.

London Gazette No 35037

Squadron Leader James Gordon Finlayson DFC publicity.

Liverpool Evening Express - 28 December 1940

Chapter Twenty-five

'Liberate the Swastika'

The 'scroungers' had been at work that Christmas Day and, as usual, when special events were planned, had 'come up with the goods.' The goods on this occasion made by 211's Maintenance Team Section was to create a pub called The Greyhound. Miraculously and with limited materials, they had turned a tent into what looked like a home-from-home pub, complete with a mock log fire which they'd lit red from behind with some electric bulbs and a car battery. Above the bar was a large sign which read BEER IS GOOD FOR YOU.

Outside 84 Squadron had left with their loads for the people of Corfu and to coincide with this Air Vice Marshall D'Albiac sent a message to the Prefect of Corfu, Evangelos Averoff-Tositsas *[1]* saying: *'These gifts are a token of our admiration and of your courage in the face of heavy and constant enemy attack, and an appreciation of your kindness to our airmen who had to land in Corfu.'*

For the people of Corfu, receipt of the gifts was a great boost to morale which was soon dampened as whilst everyone sat down to eat Christmas lunch at Menidi, the Italians, unbeknown to he Christmas revellers, had bombed Corfu mercilessly.

Preparations for Christmas Dinner at Menidi were all about making the day as normal a Christmas Day as possible, to lift the mood of everyone and to put the war away for a few hours at least. Invitations had been sent out to attend 'The Greyhound' and, as was customary, the Officers and NCOs of 211 Squadron would serve everyone else before they themselves sat down to lunch.

Image: James Dunnet. Blenheim Over The Balkans (Ron Thompson)

Talk between Gerald and the others near him on that Christmas Day surrounded the men they had lost and the visit to Zonars in Athens.

The conversation quickly moved on to the amount of Nazis in the city and then on to the German Embassy where the swastika hung proudly, by chance, next to the stars and stripes of the U.S.A, whose Embassy was next door. Of course, neither of these countries were at war in 1940, although surreptitiously the yanks were helping the British in more ways than anyone knew.

The Bish, with his penchant for gambling, had set the tone of the conversation and everyone laughed when he said, "Ten bob of my own money to anyone who fetches the Nazi flag back gents."

The laughs were followed by several people shouting "I'm in" and "You're on boss."

Air Vice Marshall D'Albiac and his wife Sybil stayed for Christmas dinner and John D'Albiac proposed the toast, "To health, happiness and thoughts to those empty seats at the table."

The war just could not be compartmentalised that easily, even just for a day.

*

With full stomachs, you would have imagined Gerald and his cohorts would have remained on camp at Menidi, but these were the days of short-lives and everyone wanted to make the most of the time they had. No one knew when life might be cut short, so several of the squadron headed into Athens for more fun. The Bish had stayed at Menidi with the D'Albiac's, but lots of the others traipsed around several bars and wandered several times with a thoughtful eye under the German flag, which now had a hostage value of ten shillings.

*

Gerald sobered up quickly late that Christmas Day when he learned the Italians couldn't leave Corfu alone for even one day. Everyone felt the same when they heard the news. The Bish had already turned in for the night knowing what had happened but he spoke with Gerald and Arthur on Boxing Day over a coffee and breakfast.

"The Itis have to have it back hard and good gents for what they've done... on Christmas Day of all days," he began. "Valona tomorrow! It's our prime target but we're going in full strength gents. FULL STRENGTH!"

"The only way 211 can deal with this." Gerald concurred as The

Bish's right-hand man. Arthur Geary nodded.

So it was, twelve aircraft, 211's full compliment took off from Menidi on 27th December 1940, all loaded with 250lb bombs, heading for both the harbour and the aerodrome at Valona. The last words of The Bish before everyone parted for their aircraft were, "Give them hell gentlemen and we'll see you all back here afterwards."

The aircraft travelled in very close formation with The Bish Boys at the front as usual. Close in to them were James Dunnet and his crew, Sergeant Pilot Jimmy James with Andy Bryce and Pongo, almost touching the tail of The Bish such was their proximity. Everyone knew the dangers and stuck close.

Valona was no easy target. As The Bish Boys approached, leading the twelve aircraft, the tracers from the ships in the harbour hurled their way skyward like some lethal firework display, immediately followed by intense ack-ack. The Blenheims shook time and time again as deadly black clouds exploded around them. Gerald was almost too busy to notice. He had become so used to focussing on bomb-aiming and the compass. He quietly stared towards the ground, shouting his instructions in a matter-of-fact way as usual.

"Coming up… 30 points to port. Turn now!

Bomb doors open.

Left. Left.

Too much, right a little.

Hold it. Hold it.

Steady… steady.

Bombs gone! Bombs gone!

Bomb doors closed."

Italian fighters did their best to chase away the attackers but had arrived on the scene a few minutes too late, except for the unlucky crew of Blenheim, L2533 who caught a machine gun blast from a Fiat CR 42, which luckily for the crew injured no-one but irreparably damaged the underside of the aircraft. Luckily the crew managed to limp back to Menidi, where they discovered the true impact of the damage as their undercarriage had gone.

The crew fired off a flare to inform the ground a belly landing was in the offing. Gerald, who was already safely on the ground and out of his plane, held the photograph of him and Susan in his hand as he prayed the crew would make it down safely. The hapless Blenheim made its final approach to the grassy runway, smoke streaming from underneath it. Within seconds it had crunched into the ground, its propellers buckling to a stop as they hit the ground. Debris flew everywhere, and the crash and crunch of metal was appalling to hear. No fire! Not yet, at any rate. That was a bonus. It was James Dunnet's plane and he and his crew, Bill 'Jock' Young, the air-gunner and Willy Arscott extricated themselves from the plane at break-neck speed.

The crew stood a few yards away from their stricken aircraft and thanked their lucky stars they were down, but not out. Death had escaped many that day by luck in the main. Italian bullets and shrapnel had once again damaged things but these could be repaired.

There was no let up to the attacks on Valona following the Italians' decision to bomb the defenceless people of Corfu on Christmas Day. New Year's Eve came around quickly and another low by the Italians was uncovered. As Gerald bombed Valona, the radio crackled to life and they heard the voice of Flight Lieutenant Bobby Campbell.

"Skip. Just taking a photo of a hospital ship steaming towards the harbour. It's white and clearly marked with nothing less than a huge red cross on its side. Bloody thing has just set full guns blazing at us. We've headed for cloud cover, but permission sought to bomb the bastard."

There wasn't even a moment's thought involved from The Bish.

"Granted!"

The next thing Gerald heard on the radio was Campbell's crew.

'Low in the water, God, it's loaded with munitions. Must be surely…
Steady skipper…
Bombs gone…'

The Bish had turned to take a shift at Campbell's observation. Gerald was now in a position to see the ship. It was white with an enormous cross. A split seconds later the bombs hit. Tremendous explosions followed. Then nothing except debris. If it had been a hospital ship or even masquerading as such, whoever was on board was no more. It had exploded like he'd never seen before. Every soul on board would be gone.

<'Those people on the boat had families and photographs of them in their pockets just like me.>

The Bish crackled in, "Good job gentlemen, good job. It's New Year's Eve, let's head home. We all deserve a good drink tonight."

But it wasn't over at all. The Bish had spoken too soon.

Arthur Geary, as usual, had his eyes peeled for bandits and it wasn't long before the Fiat CR 42s and G.50 Freccias arrived in frightening numbers. The Bish and Gerald knew the exact moment Arthur spotted them, as his machine-gun burst into action and the intercom crackled red hot with the news of the location of the bandits.

The three were a formidable team and The Bish trusted his crew implicitly to do the right thing when the occasion arose. All twelve aircraft were now engaged in life and death struggles with the Italian fighters, but all crews, despite their mortal fears knew their roles and each of the planes fought with passion to ensure they would not end up in the Ionian Sea where they saw at least two of the Italians hurtle towards in a smokey death throw. The Blenheims headed east for the cloud cover of the Albanian mountains, chased by their foe.

Then Gerald saw it, at a time when the majority of the attacking Italians were either short of ammunition or running low on fuel, a solitary Fiat G.50 had lined up behind Blenheim L1540 [2] of B Flight, for one last attack. The air gunner Les France, fired away repeatedly as the pilot Syd Bennett did his best to manoeuvre the sluggish Blenheim out of harm's way but the plane was in a bad position and a burst of machine gun fire saw the Blenheim heading down in flames towards the ground.

"Bennett's bought it!" shouted Gerry as they headed into the clouds and safety.

"All we can hope is that he can level out and pancake it down. Doesn't look good though." The Bish added as the plane buffeted about in the clouds above the mountains.

Gerald was quiet all the way back and kept his hand on the pocket with the photograph in. Death was all in a day's work. He'd now lost so many friends he'd almost lost count, but these were people he never forgot and their names lived on in his head. He thanked his lucky stars his luck seemed to be in for yet another day.

All but Syd Bennett's plane got back to Menidi, although a few were shot up good style.

This was a New Year's Eve no one would forget and matters were only going to get worse as 1941 beckoned and the war had nothing to do with it.

*

The Bish hardly said a word after they'd arrived back, and he drove off to H.Q in Athens to see if there was any word on Syd Bennett and his crew. There wasn't a shred of hope in the camp he would come back with good news, especially with those who'd seen the plane heading down in flames.

Two hours later, The Bish was back "Gentlemen! Bad news, I'm afraid. It's *'Missing Feared Killed'* I've agreed which is to go out. There's nothing been heard since of Syd and his crew, so we have to assume the worst. H.Q. have sent on the dreaded news to their families back home. Another three households at least turned upside-down. God, I hate this job sometimes."

"We turned up after a week away, so there is the faintest of hope I suppose," a dejected-looking Gerald added.

"There's only one thing for it chaps, we have to carry on with the plans we had for tonight."

"Plans?" Arthur crewed up his face.

"You forgot already?" The Bish shook his head. "You've been with young Gerry too long. It's Potato's birthday today. We have a surprise party arranged for him at Maxim's."

"Yep, cook has done a cake specially for him and that's already gone ahead to the place." Gerald smiled.

"So we can't NOT have a do, can we now?" The Bish asserted. "Besides with, we all deserve a good blow out on the town tonight. Get a few down our necks for Syd, Les and Will."

*

There were now three reasons for celebrating; it was Potato Jones' birthday; The Bish had heard about his D.F.C and it was New Year's Eve. Gerald didn't head straight for Maxim's in the centre of Athens. He headed for Tommy Wisdom's place, known to all the airmen as The Pension Wisdom; this was Tommy Wisdom's B&B for want of a better description. It was his place of abode in the centre of Athens, where men enjoying a night in Athens could bed down to save them the journey back to their base at Menidi. Tommy spent a fair amount of time in Athens with the other journalists putting together a daily news sheet for the forces' stationed locally called the B.A.F.G. Bulletin, which is where he first published the story of Gerald and 'that photograph.' A weekly radio show called The Bafflers, a half-hour show of tom-foolery, on Athens radio for the forces locally, had become a much loved programme with the Greeks who lapped it up. The Athens based journalists mucked in, acting to a script, whilst Richard Dimbleby's contribution and party trick was banging two beer tankards to make it sound like they were in an authentic pub in

England. John D'Albiac had listened in and likened the show to listening to a 'taproom brawl.' The broadcast always ended with 84 Squadron's Flight Lieutenant Hubert 'Jonah' Jones, shouting the phrase *'time, please, gentlemen, please'* which confirmed John D'Albiac's sentiments.

Photo Courtesy Wings Over Olympus
The Bafflers performing their first broadcast. Third from left is Richard Dimbleby and next to him, second from left is Tommy Wisdom.

Gerald dropped his night things off at The Pension Wisdom and headed out with Tommy to meet the others at Maxim's nightclub where the party for Potato Jones' birthday was now warming up. It seemed the whole of 211 Squadron was there for the 'private party' but it seemed the 'private' bit was just a corner of the restaurant. Maxim's was known for its great floor shows, music and excellent cuisine, and was a favourite place for 211 Squadron, besides other squadrons, Athenians… and Nazis too, as Gerald would find out this night.

Amongst the people Gerald spotted the two Gestapo which Giorgios Seferis had pointed out just a short time before. The two were trying to blend in but were doing a poor job. Everyone knew who they were. Flight Lieutenant Luke Delaney - The Duke was already sat down with Keeper, The Bish, Twinkle, Buck and Potato. Keeper had brought them along in the staff car. Gerald and Tommy sat down with the group.

"Did you know, those two there are Nazis?" Gerald nudged The Duke almost immediately he sat down

"Know?" responded The Duke. "Yep, I do. The Provost Marshal pointed them out to me before. Bastards! Shouldn't be in here. Did you know Gerry ol' man, the Nazis are sending the Greek troops propaganda on the front in Albania, saying we are dancing away and fraternising with their girls when they are fighting for their lives against the Italians."

"Is that right?"

"What's more, the Greek Chief of Police here has issued an order telling the Greek girls they cannot fraternise with us RAF chaps because of these rumours. The cheek of it."

"Well, I've got my Susan back in Henley, so I'm just here to enjoy Potato's birthday."

"Good on you 'ol man. Keeping celibate. You'll change your mind one day. Love's young dream and all that." He laughed. "You couldn't do anything else 'ol man what with all the publicity surrounding you and that girl. Still got that photo by the way?"

Gerald patted his pocket. Where he went, the photo went nowadays.

"Anyway..." went on The Duke, "bloody Nazis, that's why they should't be in here. They're nothing but trouble. They need throwing out! It's Potato's night not a Nazi rally! I'm gonna throw the bastards out."

"Whoah! Hold on." Gerald said, trying to deflect his anger. "Leave it with me. We don't want to get into any argy-bargy that might get us kicked out on Potato's birthday, do we? Mac from 84 is your man. He speaks German, I've heard him taking the mick out of Hitler. I'll go and have a word."

Gerald headed off to where he could see Mac [3] sitting with some of the lads from 84 Squadron. No one knew what Gerald said but Mac was up like a shot and within seconds was stood at the table where the Gestapo man was sitting with his 'girlfriend.'

The Gestapo man was shouted in German "Was glaubst du wer du bist? Du kannst uns nicht zum Gehen bringen!" *(Who do you think you are? You can't make us go!)*

To which Mac looked back at the lads of 84 Squadron and bade them "Stand up lads."

Numerous men in uniform stood up, many not even in 84 Squadron.

Mac looked back at the Gestapo man and quietly said, "Denken Sie und Ihre hübsche Dame nicht, es wäre klug, ruhig zu gehen, hey? Wir mögen keine Probleme, aber wir rennen auch nicht davon!" (*"Don't you and your pretty lady think it would be a wise thing to leave quietly, hey? We don't like trouble, but we don't run from it either!"*)

The Germans got up and left to enormous cheers and people banging the tables in delight.

The staff at Maxim's had thought a fight was going to happen, but it all came to nothing thanks to Mac and his character, which almost got him into trouble the following day for fraternising with the enemy, until the powers that be heard the full story and he was congratulated for his efforts.

Getting the Germans removed from Potato's party wasn't enough and Bobby Campbell brought up The Bish's ten-bob wager which was still on the go for anyone who could get the swastika hanging outside the German Embassy.

"You up for it if we slip out?" Bobby suggested to Buck.

"I'm in. Let's liberate the swastika!" he slurred back.

"Gerry, you gotta come with a name like that. We need a look-out."

Gerald was a little hesitant, but his inhibitions had been lowered by the flowing retsina, and so the three slipped out of Maxim's with no one noticing.

They headed around the corner, towards the King George Hotel and then around the next corner where the German Embassy stood next to the American Embassy. The flag of the Third Reich, as much as it was a symbol of hate and oppression across world, looked resplendent against the white marble building. To Gerald, the vibrant red depicted the bleeding heart of Europe and the dreaded black swastika in the white circle, was a symbol of a blitz-krieg, yet to come to Greece, but everyone knew it was a case of the inevitable. Either way, the flag hung there, on a windless Athens' New Year's Eve, like a trouble maker waiting to gate-crash a party.

These thoughts gave the airmen the courage to do what they needed to do.

"You keep watch," whispered Buck in some sort of alcohol induced hysteria, trying not to laugh. "We're going in! Come on, Bobby."

The two headed down the street with their arms outstretched, noisily mimicking their Blenheim Bombers.

"Shhh! They'll hear you!" shouted Gerald.

Bobby and Buck looked at each other and giggled quietly. Fingers to their lips and repeating the words of Gerald.

No one was about as Gerald surveyed the scene.

He watched as Buck gave Bobby a bunk-up a woody old vine growing up the Embassy frontage. The first few efforts he fell back laughing, followed by 'shush' noises from the pair. Bobby got into a climbing rhythm, like a scene from Jack and the Beanstalk and he was soon level with the halyard holding the flag to the building. Gerald could see him fumbling in his pocket and soon he was sawing away at the cord with a pen-knife he'd produced. Inside, noise could be heard. The Nazis were partying away and hadn't a clue their territory was under invasion.

The flag fell away from the building and Bobby grasped it before it fell to the ground, stuffing it unceremoniously into the front of his tunic jacket. Clambering down the vine took a shorter time and the last two yards Bobby fell back into the arms of Buck, the pair laughing like two teenagers on their first ever trip out to a pub.

"Come on" shouted Gerald as he saw some Greek guards coming down the road at a pace. "Come on! Someone's coming!"

They all ran at top speed to the nearby Constitution Square in Athens, where crowds were gathered for New Year's Eve celebrations and the three melted into the crowd. From there they headed back to Maxim's where everyone had broken out into singing happy birthday to Potato, who teetered infused with alcohol in front of his cake with its 26 candles blazing away. Potato was an old man compared with some there who were barely out of school.

The candles blown out, everyone settled to eat a piece of cake and imbibe of the freely flowing wine. Midnight struck and Auld Lang Syne was sung with much gusto but all felt the sadness of the occasion missing their families and loved ones a thousand or more miles away across a war torn Europe. Gerald thought of Lizzie and what the family might be doing in Shotton, then he raised a glass when the toast came to absent friends, thinking of Susan in Henley. He looked at the photograph and quickly put it away again. He didn't want a repetition of what had happened at the Canal Club in Ismailia.

Melancholy was a fact of life away from home, but most kept their sad thoughts to themselves. Gerald looked around the table at the end of the night and contented himself he was with the best group of lads one could wish to be with. He looked at Bobby Campbell and smiled to himself at what he had secreted under his best dress tunic. He laughed even more when The Bish accused Bobby of getting fat in his old age. This group of men were his family and what they had been through together held them together like some unseen magnetic force.

Not long after midnight, the decision was made to head back. Gerald already had his plans to stay with Tommy Wisdom, as did one or two others who were staying at The Pension Wisdom.

Gerald shook hands with all the others as they parted for the night.

As Luke 'The Duke' Delaney and the squadron's equipment officer Dennis 'Keeper' Barrett headed away from him, Gerald looked puzzled. "Thought you two were staying with us at Tommy's place?"

"Afraid not," Keeper replied. "Better get the C.O. back to base, there may be something on tomorrow he tells me. You can head back with us if you want, the car's pretty roomy."

"Er… I don't think so, Keeper ol' chap. I've got a bed waiting not more than two minutes' walk away and when I'm sound asleep, you lot will still be on your way back to base."

"Good point, Gerry. But at least tomorrow I'll be back at base and sipping coffee whilst you are heading back with a headache."

They both laughed

"All right then chaps, see you tomorrow" Gerald shouted to Keeper as he headed for the staff car, keys in hand, to ferry The Bish, The Duke, Ron 'Twinkle' Pearson, an army officer they'd met that night and birthday boy George 'Potato' Jones back to base at Menidi.

But Gerald wouldn't see Keeper in one piece, tomorrow or ever again.

Author's Note

[1] Evangelos Averoff-Tositsas (1910 – 1990) Appointed Prefect (Regional Governor) of Kerkyra. After the Italians invaded Corfu in March 1941, he was taken hostage and imprisoned in Italy. He escaped in 1942 creating the 'Freedom or Death' (Ελευθερία ή Θάνατος) resistance group, whose aim was to liberate Greek and Allied war hostages.

Freedom or Death (Eleftheria i thanatos) is the motto of Greece.

[2] Blenheim L1540 Crew:

Pilot Sergeant Sydney Lewis Bennett (742975) Royal Air Force Volunteer Reserve (21 years)

Sergeant Leslie Ronald FRANCE (580854) (Wireless Operator/Air Gunner) RAF (22 years)

Sergeant William Henry TUNSTALL (749318) (Air Observer) Royal Air Force Volunteer Reserve (20 years)

All three were from 211 Squadron. Killed in Action 31st December 1940 (21 years) Commemorated at Alamein Memorial. Bodies recovered and all buried at Mavrovo, North Macedonia.

[3] Squadron Leader Hugh MacPhail, DFC.

Chapter Twenty-six

'A Bad Start'

It was a bright sunny day three days after New Year when Gerald, The Duke, Potato and Buck carried Keeper's coffin down the centre of the Church of the Resurrection on the royal estate at Tatoi, just a few hundred yards from the airfield. The coffin bedecked with Keeper's *[1]* well worn cap, signs of its use in the deserts of North Africa engrained into its surface.

The service was a simple one and afterwards the party of pall bearers headed to a piece of ground just outside Athens where the burial was to take place in a section given over by the Greeks to the British.

Tears filled Gerald's eyes. Losing people so far in this war had been almost surreal. The others they'd lost from the squadron no one had seen, they had just 'gone missing.' This was death brought home good and proper. A friend in a box who was no more. Gerald was taken back to the day when as a twelve-year-old, he'd travelled on the train with Frank, Francis and Lizzie to attend the funeral of his mother Elizabeth. The images were embossed into his brain.

Carrying the coffin of Keeper, he felt numb and shocked to the core.

<'It could have been me. I said no to the car journey back to base. That saved me.'> He looked up with thanks. <'Someone up there is looking after me.>

Then Gerald thought of the photograph in his tunic pocket.

<'Lucky photo, I guess!'>

The coffin was lowered into the ground with full military honours and a guard of riflemen from 211 Squadron fired three volleys in salute to fallen warrior Flying Officer Dennis Barrett. The firing of three volleys was an old tradition used to halt fighting on a battlefield so dead could be taken away. After the dead had been removed, three-musket volleys were fired and the battle recommenced. As if in cognisance of the old tradition a flight of Blenheims from the Greek squadrons passed over on their way to bomb Elbasan, a large Albanian city to the south of Tirana.

The group gathered at the graveside one by one threw soil in on top of the coffin and Keeper's hat. Gerald walked away talking with The Duke.

"Do you know, Gerry ol' chap, I heard of a funeral of some poor RAF chap taking place over in France when a damned Luftwaffe plane came over and spotted the lot of them stood around the grave. Do you know what he did, ol' chap?"

"I don't."

"The bugger came in for a second run and began to strafe the whole lot of them. The priest and everyone dived into the grave before the coffin went in. Was the only safe place.'

"Well at least we have been saved that today Luke."

"Damn huns; they riddled the coffin with bullets. The only RAF man killed twice so far in the war. Huns have no thought for anyone, least of all corpses."

They both smiled as they carried on walking.

*

New Year's Day had started in bizarre fashion with banging on the door of The Pension Wisdom. This heralded the news of the accident which had taken Keeper's life.

"There's been a dreadful accident," the messenger from 211 Squadron shouted as he gave the bad news to Tommy Wisdom, half dressed men groggy with alcohol standing in the background listening on.

Within minutes Gerald was out of the house with Tommy and the others, on their way to hospital to find out just what had happened.

Keeper lay badly injured, unconscious, and was at death's door. On the outskirts of Athens, just around 1am on New Year's Day, as the car headed towards Menidi in blacked-out wartime Greek streets, Keeper had lost control of the staff car trying to avoid an unlit sand-bagged air raid shelter which seemed to jut out into the road. Keeper had done a good job of avoiding the shelter, but the car veered out of control and left the road to the offside and the car had impacted with a gnarly old olive tree. The driver's side had taken the main impact and all of this side of the car had crushed Keeper in his seat.

The Bish had been the front passenger in the Ford staff car, WD 16070, and was now sat in hospital with a broken leg. Potato Jones had suffered relatively minor injuries, but all the same was detained in hospital with The Bish.

The Duke and the army officer hadn't been injured at all and luckily for the others, The Duke had sprung into action to get Keeper and The Bish to Kephissia General Hospital with some haste, but the haste hadn't saved Keeper who died from his injuries 24 hours later.

In the absence of The Bish, who was laid up in hospital until the 11th January, it fell to Tommy Wisdom to ensure Keeper's parents, Richard and Eileen Barrett, who lived in Croydon were sent a telegram from H.Q, to inform them of the tragic death of their 25-year-old son.

*

As the first fortnight of 1941 wore on at Menidi, the RAF personnel there tried to be as positive as they could, after all there was a war on and no one could afford to sit moping about the loss of a friend no matter how close they were. Other distractions helped and on the 5th January several from the squadron, including Gerald, had been selected to play a charity football match, with the proceeds going towards Greek wounded. The match was against the semi-professional team representing Athens. Gerald played in goal. He'd played in goal back in school and no one else had volunteered for this position. He'd learned from experience no one ever wanted to play in goal but was disappointed to be on the receiving end of a good four goals from the Athens side. The British forces team managed a respectable two goals back, so no one complained at a couple of goalkeeping howlers made by him.

In that same week the German's had unusually gone through diplomatic channels to accuse the British of stealing their flag, which the British of course denied, despite there being two Greek guards who reported they had witnessed the theft. In the meantime, back at Menidi, Bobby Campbell had come clean and had pinned the flag up in the bar, next to an Italian flag, taken by British forces from Fort Capuzzo on the Libyan-Egyptian border. Someone had commented the bar now resembled the trophy room of the Duke of Wellington.

When everyone saw the newly acquired flag, they sang joyfully and dedicated its presence in memory of Keeper.

John D'Albiac had been informed of the missing flag and it had got back to him that it might now be in the possession of 211 Squadron. It was a Saturday when The Bish was released back to the fray, leg in plaster, so his driving and piloting were put on hold for a short time. John D'Albiac brought The Bish back from hospital and at the insistence of The Bish, who to quote was *'gagging with thirst,'* their first port of call was the mess. As The Bish hobbled in with John D'Albiac in tow, there was no 'might' about where the German Embassy Swastika was.

"I see we have a new arrival in camp" John D'Albiac said with a wry smile.

"So it seems, sir, so it seems."

They both stood looking at the swastika as they ordered a beer and a glass of wine.

"Hmm, colour scheme has altered in here G-F"

"It has, sir, its has."

"I hate the new colour scheme intensely."

"Yes, sir."

"But I like the... er... how would you say, the panache of the decorators in their inventiveness. Very droll sense of humour, very droll."

"Very droll sir, yes. My men have a sense of humour."

"Make sure the decorators are told off, will you G-F."

"I will, sir, yes."

After John D'Albiac had gone, The Bish hobbled to speak with Bobby Campbell and one or two others, including Gerald. He stood them in a line, looking very serious.

"Today, I have seen the German flag on base, as has A.O.C. John D'Albiac."

Everyone looked worried.

"Step forward Flying Officer Delaney and Pilot Officer Gerald Davies."

The two stepped forward, much worry fell across their faces. Bobby Campbell smiled, "It was me sir, not these two."

"Oh, it was, was it? Step forward Flying Officer Campbell."

Bobby Campbell stepped forward with the others.

"You are a very naughty boy, Flying Officer Campbell! Ten-bob goes straight to you!"

The place exploded with laughter and the whole Mess clapped with jubilation.

*

The Bish was out of action as regards flying and commanding the squadron. Flight Lieutenant George Doudney had taken temporary control. He was a very experienced Blenheim pilot and highly regarded by everyone.

Gerald took control of the Blenheim on the raids or supply drops which took place over Albania which followed that first week. On the ground in Epirus, the winter had ground fighting to a virtual standstill. Then more tragedy followed. This time it was The Duke. He'd escaped injury in the car accident of the New Year's Day, but by the night of the 7th January his bed at Menidi lay empty.

It had all happened on the 6th, five days before The Bish was back at base, when The Duke's Blenheim had been in formation with Gerald attacking Valona. Fiat CR 42s had attacked the squadron after they had bombed Valona and several planes, including Gerald's had sustained damage, but The Duke's Blenheim was fatally damaged in the Italian onslaught and lost an engine.

"Still have some control, but no power to keep going. Am afraid I'm going down chaps. See you back at the Mess hey!" were the last words cracked out over the radio by The Duke as his plane circled down to the ground. Gerald felt helpless as he watched as The Duke struggled with the plane as it headed ever down to the ground in the province of Argyrokastro, near to Gjirokastra in Southern Albania. The Duke did his best to straighten out for a belly landing, but as the Blenheim struck the uneven ground it flipped and wreckage was strewn everywhere. Gerald knew the three crew wouldn't have had a chance. [2]

The 6th January saw two planes lost to enemy action and one near fatal hit. Temporary squadron leader, George Doudney, had a close call with a bullet from an Italian fighter and the bullet had cut a neat line in his flying helmet.

Another casualty of the raid was Blenheim L1487, [3] piloted by Bobby Campbell, the swastika thief. His plane ended up in the Aegean Sea and the crew were reported as missing.

*

* * *

Never had there been such a terrible start to a year in anyone's memory. These were times to forget and times no one would talk about for many a long year, even if they were fortunate enough to survive. Even those who survived took their memories to the grave with them in old age, such was the trauma of these times.

The worst was yet to come.

*

The Bish had been told in hospital about the losses and had hobbled about agitatedly, although he'd joked about George Doudney's near death experience, but one thing was certain, The Bish was more furious than ever at the losses mounting up and wanted to exact revenge on the Italians. Even from his hospital bed!

Gerald missed the company of The Bish, although he visited him in hospital and relayed any news from the base. Gerald, for the first time in ages, felt homesick but at the same time, he firmly didn't want to let anyone down and wanted to do his duty, to the best of his ability, for the squadron. The photograph in his top pocket was the only thing that kept him going, and the one thing he felt had kept him safe through that first week of January.

As for The Bish, on the 14 January he was occupied at Menidi all day with the Court of Enquiry, into the accident on New Year's Day which was led by 49-year-old Squadron Leader Henry Frederick Levell, who'd joined up during the First World War as a storeman and rose to the rank of Sergeant by the end of the war, then to go on and gain a commission in-between wars. Henry was known to be a strict, yet kindly man who took a pragmatic view of situations like this. The Bish's broken leg would have been enough to ensure the enquiry was viewed with some leniency, but the loss of one of the team in the accident was punishment enough for everyone. The enquiry put the blame squarely with the Greek authorities, who, with no consideration of life and limb had placed a black obstacle on a pitch dark road, which anyone would have crashed into. As it was, the driver, Flying Officer Barrett - 'Keeper;' the only fatality of the accident had miraculously avoided the obstacle, therefore saving lives in the car at the expense of his own.

On the same day as the enquiry, just a few miles away in Athens, General Archibald Wavell, the commander in charge of British forces in the Middle East had convened a high level meeting with Greek Prime Minister Ioannis Metaxas and his top General, Alexander Papagos. A request was made to the British for nine divisions plus more air support. General Wavell offered less than a third of what was requested and the Greek General declined such a derisory offer, thus once again settling the eventual fate of the future of Greece and 211 Squadron in Greece.

Replacement crews arrived within the month and The Bish was back but not fully up to speed with his leg in plaster, although the raids against the Italians in Albania continued without abatement and with a vengeance through the month; a month which ended with the injured Graham 'Potato' Jones getting his DFC, a great belated birthday present for the whole of the squadron.

London Gazette: 11th February 1941

By coincidence, the same day Potato was awarded his DFC, Gerald and The Bish had been listening to the radio, when the death of the Greek dictator Ioannis Metaxas was announced to the nation. The base flew the RAF ensign at half mast as a sign of respect and The Bish announced, "tTat'll be the bloody end of it chaps, what with Wavell denying us more support, the Nazis will seize on this, you can be sure. Going to have to watch it now, chaps."

"So I believe… " added in Gerald. "Seems their spy planes have been seen over Athens of late."

"I know. You mark my words. They'll be rolling over the border before you know it from the north. We have to be on our guard and ready."

"With the out-of-date planes we have and even those we don't have in numbers. Three gone in one day this week."

"I'm on the case, despite what Wavell has told the Greeks. I have my irons in the fire through father so, let me let you into a little secret Gerry ol' chap, we might even have Hurricanes here and soon. Watch this space, Gerry boy. Watch this space."

Author's Note

[1] Flying Officer Dennis Charles Barrett ('Keeper') 211 Squadron RAF Volunteer Reserve (75922) - Seriously injured in a car crash on 1 January 1941. Died aged 25 yrs, on 2 January - Athens. Phaleron War Cemetery, Athens. Re-buried in military cemetery, January 1945 from original resting place.

[2] All of 211 Squadron. Killed in Action - 6th Jan 1941.
Flying Officer Luke Sylvestre 'The Duke' Delaney, Pilot RAF (21 years).
Sergeant Vynor 'Vic' Pollard, Observer. RAF Volunteer Reserve (22 years)
Sergeant.Thomas Alexander "Jock" McCord. Wireless Operator and Air Gunner. RAF (19 years)
The crew of Bristol Blenheim L8537 were all killed outright and buried near the village of Këlcyrë by locals.

[3] Blenheim L1487 - shot down 6th January 1941
Flight Lieutenant Robert (Bobby) Douglas Campbell - Pilot
Sergeant Raymond ('Ray' or 'Apple') Appleyard - Wireless Operator and Air Gunner
Sergeant John Beharrel - Observer
All three survived their plane ditching in the sea south of Valona port. Initially, the three remained on the wing of the Blenheim for some time. Beharrel was eventually rescued by an Italian destroyer, but Campbell (with a broken leg) and Appleyard swam away and made the shore. All three were eventually captured and made PoWs. The exploits of Bobby Campbell in 'The Elephant on My Wing' describes his PoW experiences thereafter and escape attempts.

Chapter Twenty-seven

'Parymathia'

On the very first day of February 1941, The Bish Boys were back as a full team in the air. Nothing could hold The Bish down, not even a plaster on a broken leg and he led a raid of six Blenheims on Valona.

As the first week of February rolled forward, the weather began to improve. Early spring was in the air and the birds were singing away all around Menidi. 211 Squadron had now become used to flying north along the line of the Pindus mountains to Larissa where they refuelled. Since November 1940 they had headed north towards Mount Olympus, the 10,000 feet tall legendary home of the Greek gods, and from there north-west, crossing the treacherous cloud covered peaks of the Pindus Mountains in Epirus. Out of the clouds the Blenheims came like the Gods of Olympus themselves; with surprise and awe they dropped their deadly cargo on ships, aerodromes and troop movements below concentrating on Tepelenë inland. Mercy missions of food and supplies for beleaguered Greek troops on the ground interspersed the bombing raids. Sometimes, the Blenheims were accompanied by the archaic Gloster fighters which Pilot Officer Roald Dahl had crashed in the desert but more often than not the Blenheims were on their own. Surprise attacks didn't remain a surprise for long and the Italians hastily swung their ack-ack or fighters into action, chasing Blenheims away as speedily as they had arrived, but most of the time too late to prevent the attack.

Getting away from the scene of an attack was an art in its own right and almost every man for himself. The Blenheims usually headed south down the Aegean coast towards Corfu, then out towards

Missolonghi and home to Menidi, but often would head for cloud cover if chased by Italian fighters. Cloud cover meant heading for the mountains where other hidden dangers lurked - ice and unseen peeks, and several Blenheims had come to grief as a result.

Nothing lasts forever and the days at Menidi were numbered. Giorgios Seferis the poet and diplomat's arrival at Menidi would change everyone's lives for good. Spring warmth was in the air on the day he arrived. He asked straight away to see his *'Byron friends.'* Everyone knew what he meant and soon he was sat having a coffee and a chat with The Bish, Gerald and Arthur. No one thought anything unusual about this, after all important visitors were in and out of the place by the minute, except one, the King. The Bish still had the visit on his mind when Giorgios arrived, so after the niceties were over he asked the question.

"Giorgios, my dear friend. There's one thing you promised more than a month ago now and that was a visit from the King."

"Ah, yes, James... The King."

"I've been keeping this place shipshape and Bristol fashion for weeks now, yet no visit. What's going on old man?"

Giorgios nodded and nodded again. "Yes. News is... erm. Yes, I do not thinks he might be coming now. He is a busy man. I mades a promise to Eleusis too, and you knows he went there to visit with Prince Paul?"

Credit: Wings Over Olympus. T.H. Wisdom. King George II of Greece and

his brother, Crown Prince Paul inspect the RAF base at Eleusis, near Athens 1940.

"I had heard, but he hasn't been here."

"He cannot be everywhere and I have to say this, you know of Metaxas?"

"Yes."

"Things have alerted substantially since the death of our Prime Minister."

The Bish turned to Gerald and Arthur. "What did I say?"

The remark was ignored by Giorgios.

"So, I have news to brings you. In the past day or so I have spoken with your commanding officer John D'Albiac about how we progress the war with you, our British friends and allies. You know there was resistance to offering the RAF anything further north as we did not want to upset our German friends."

"I wouldn't call them friends," The Bish said with a firm element to his voice. "The huns are no one's friend and not to be trusted."

"We are not at war with Germany right now, so we have to tread carefully, I suppose I should have said."

"Perhaps. I'll forgive you."

Giorgios smiled, looking more nervous than he ever had. "Anyway, yes, so what I was saying, was now Metaxas is not influencing any more, if that's how I can say it, we have more flexibility where you can be based, so you will be pleased to know we have a new place for you to be, much nearer to the frontier with the Italians but far enough away not to be in the zone of war."

"Don't keep me in suspense any longer, ol' man. Where is it?"

"It is a beautiful place called Paramythia." He broke into Greek. "Tópos ton paramythión - it means a place of the fairy tales in old Greek. Yes... yes... now, to the west... inland from the southern tip of Kerkyra, yet only 20 miles from the border with Albania. When the Itis invaded last October they briefly occupied Paramythia and did much damage to the village there. Of course our brave army routed them from the area in just three hours, so therefore it is important to have you British there now. It is a symbol the to people that we are on the ascendancy and we will win this war."

Everyone nodded in agreement.

"Embros, our liaison officer has been on the case and has been sorting things for you in the background as we speak."

"Sounds pretty good. So much nearer for us all," Gerald smiled. "When do we get going?"

"Sunday!" replied Giorgios "The ninth."

"That's the day after tomorrow!" The Bish ruminated for a minute after he'd commented. Giorgios and the others waited to see what he might say next.

"Splendid. Splendid. That's enough time to prep six of the planes and their crews. Yes, that's fine," The Bish was nodding vigorously and lighting his pipe. "So how do we... "

"Carry out the logistics of this?" Giorgios intervened.

"Yes sir, how do we get all our stuff from A to B ol' chap?"

"We will loan you an Iron Annie... a Junkers 52 transport aircraft... "

"A Gerry plane! Sorry, Gerry! Taking your name in vain ol' chap." The Bish exclaimed.

"Looks on the bright side James, a German plane will be very safe from being shot down, so all your supplies will get to Paramythia in one pieces."

"Hmm."

"It is Greek Air Force plane, so we will be piloting it. What is more, Paramythia will be a first for 211 Squadron and others who comes there. It has been used by our planes for some time now... "

"So it is a hard runway? Concrete or tarmac?" Gerald said hopefully."

"I am afraids not. Look on the bright side gentlemens, grass is easier to hides from the enemy so is not easily seen. Your Blenheims will be safe there, hey?"

"From our experience," The Bish began, "air raids come whether or not it is tarmac. Damn Itis have their spies and the Huns... well... they have their tourists everywhere. We have had air raid warnings this week here, as you know."

"But no attacks. It is not easily spotted from the air, even when they know about it and neither is Paramythia.

"What about ack-ack defence at Paramythia, Giorgios?"

"All part of the service from us to you. The Greek army will defend your airfield at Paramythia. All of your tents there will be camouflaged and trenches will be dug to make you safe in case of any attacks. We have our local volunteers in action to helps you."

*

* * *

Giorgios hadn't been wrong and as Gerald approached the runway at Paramythia on the Sunday afternoon, he could hardly make it out in the landscape. The runway was a little bumpy, but what more could they expect. This was so much nearer than Menidi and a change for the better as far as Gerald was concerned. Menidi now held too many bad memories. Too many friends had been lost there. He needed to put these dark memories behind him. Paramythia, with its illustrious name as Valley of the Fairy Tales, was a fresh new start and as long as he had his photograph with him it would be a safe new start.

Gerald, Arthur and The Bish stepped from the Blenheim and took in the air.

"We shall be happy here," The Bish said blowing smoke into the air which, even in February smelled like some lush meadow on a warm spring day back in Britain.

"No more Zonars or Maxim's for us Skip," Arthur said, almost with a hint of disappointment in his voice. The airmen had loved being close to Athens and the social life it provided. Now they were in a part of Greece which looked like the poor neighbourhoods of Albania as opposed to the towns they'd seen on their trek from Corfu to Menidi at the end of November last year.

"All the better for that," Gerald added. "As long as we've got our bully beef and beer here, I don't mind."

"Quite right Gerry, you tell that miserable sod to just get on with it."

All three laughed as they headed to find the tented quarters just yards from the runway - if it could be called that, such were the flotilla of pretty hyacinths, daffodils and alpine flowers (no one knew the name of) pushing their way skyward across it. Initially, there was one car at the base which would be used for everything from carrying fuel to getting food. The car also served to as the sole bomb carrier when the Blenheims loaded up for a raid.

That first night at Paramythia, as the heavens opened over the landing area, The Bish held a 'welcome briefing' for all six crews who had arrived. Everyone knew that was code for a beer and a chat, before they got down to the action. Everyone felt optimistic and positive about this new place despite the fact, when Gerald popped his head out of the tent, the landing area seemed to have temporary streams flowing across it. The beer ensured a good night's sleep and when everyone was up and about the following day, it felt a fantastic place to be, despite what Gerald thought were primitive conditions, with the mountain brook near the runway being the home of everyone's ablutions and laundry room regardless of rank. Those first few days of cold water shaves meant the squadron members had little inclination to shave and for the first time Gerald had an itchy beard appearing on his face.

The wet morning runway didn't stay wet for long. Water ran off to the nearby brook and spring warmth dried the grassy surface quickly. The sheer granite cliffs of the Pindus mountains to one side ensured a supply of cascading water, even when no one wanted it. This was a wild and remote place where there were reputed to be bears and wolves on the prowl, but it was a place where the men of 211 Squadron felt safe from attack.

Paramythia Landing Ground. Supplies being brought by Blenheim Bomber. Credit: Papa Spiro Monasterios who retains original image at Church of Saint Prokopios, Kavos, Corfu.

The nights were cold and the days were full of extraordinary beauty in this hidden Greek valley. As the moon rose on those first few nights at Paramythia, Gerald wrote a letter home to Lizzie and one to Susan. The content of the letters was almost identical, except of course for the words of love which accompanied the letter to Susan.

H.Q. B.A.F.G.
Athens

Nigel Davies-Williams

My dearest Sue,

We have now moved away from Athens, I cannot tell you where, but surely this place is the most beautiful place on earth. The colours in this verdant place are all the colours you might find shining from the most beautiful diamond ring on earth. There are golds, shades of amethyst and magenta and at night the moon takes me to you. I imagine looking up at the moon and you looking back from beside the river at Henley. Then I look to the photograph you sent to me and I am walking with you on a summer's day or a moonlit night. The photograph keeps me safe and one day it will sit, pride of place, in our very own home. Oh, yes, and thinking of rings, I shall buy for you the very best of rings, that is my solemn promise.

I now have a beard of sorts but I intend to rectify that tomorrow. Shaving is a task here in the cold water of a mountain stream but a scratchy face is ten times worse and I cannot stand it any longer. The next time you see me, you will never know I had a beard. I do not know when that will be and it seems such a long long time since we saw each other but time will go quickly and I will see you again as soon as I can.

I do have some company here. What is that I hear you say? I have a friend, (well he's Tommy Wisdom's friend really!) who sometimes sneaks to my bed and keeps me warm on chilly nights, but there's no need to worry. He is called Blenheim Mark IV and he's an adorable pooch. He arrived in the camp one day and Tommy adopted him as the mascot for the squadron. He could smell the food on the go in the tent where they cook. He likes his food and comfort. A bit like us all. Thinking of food, I went shooting the other day for some alternatives to our Bully Beef and Meat and Veg tins.. We dammed the mountain stream and made a pond to go swimming in. Seems the ducks liked it as well as they flocked in for a paddle from the swamp nearby, so we fancied our chances at some different lunch, but I found out I'm a rubbish shot.

Anyway, I am doing fine and I hope you are fine too. Don't work too hard in those jobs of yours either.

I am doing what I can to shorten this damn war, so the sooner it is over, the sooner we can be together.

By the way, you won't know me when you see me. I'm turning into the colour of my leather belt slowly and my skin feels like it as well. Many kisses to you,
Your Gerald.
xxx

Credit: Wings Over Olympus. T.H. Wisdom. Blenheim MkIV, the dog at Paramythia.

John D'Albiac and General Wavell paid a visit to Paramythia in the first few days of 211 Squadron's arrival there to see how they had settled. They would take the mail from the men back to Athens, and so Gerald was happy that his letters would soon be on their way to Britain. John D'Albiac brought the best of news with him and told everyone that the crew of Blenheim L1487, which had been shot down well over a month before, were now PoWs, so there was a sense of relief that Bobby Campbell, Apple and John Beharrel weren't dead as everyone thought they surely were.

John D'Albiac and Archibald Wavell settled into a meeting with The Bish and as soon as they had departed, The Bish called the men together.

"I have good news gentlemen, not only are your letters headed back to Blighty, but Hurricanes are headed our way and should be with us by the 18th. Flight Lieutenant Jimmie Kettlewell *[1]* of 80 Squadron has gone back to Athens to test fly the new arrivals as and when they come. Three cheers for 80 Squadron!"

Of course, there was still work to do from Paramythia in the short time left without modern fighter cover. 211 Squadron had been accompanied at Paramythia by Wellingtons and Gloster Gladiator fighters were based at nearby Yanina, just a few miles east of them, for air support during bombing raids. The Bish continued, "Yanina, our sister airbase has had it hard for a couple of days, the It is have hit seven Glosters and a wagon there. We can't have that gentlemen, can we?"

Everyone nodded in agreement, hanging on The Bish's every word.

"Tomorrow at ten sharp, with a detachment of Blenheims from 84 along with 14 Gladiators, we will head for targets north of Tepelenë and we'll give the Itis a proper bashing. Tommy... "

"Yes, Skip" answered Tommy Wisdom.

"You can ride shotgun with Gerry, Arthur and me. Give a good write up of us giving the wops a trouncing."

Everyone laughed and once again there were cheers, but their hearts were in their mouths when a big raid was on. It was usually met with a show of force from the enemy.

The morning of Thursday 13th February came around too quickly and no one slept that well before they headed off into the blue and towards the front in Epirus. As The Bish took off, just to his side he had Gerald and behind him, sat in the plane's well, between Gerald and Arthur was Tommy Wisdom looking hot and uncomfortable in his Irvin suit. The Bish circled Paramythia base to wait for the others to get airborne, and as he did so the Blenheim coughed and spluttered as if the engines were going to give up the ghost. He looked at The Bish who glowered at the controls shouting, "Come on you bitch, come on."

The worried frown on The Bish's face did nothing for Tommy's confidence and he became even more hot under the collar at the thought of a two-minute flight followed by plummeting to earth at great speed, but within seconds the engines seemed to roar into life and The Bish gave a thumbs up.

Gerald had seen it all before, but all the same gave the photograph in his pocket a reassuring pat.

The immense force flew north through mountainous passes and over Agryrokaston, where Gerald gave a firm thumbs down to all to indicate the plane was now over enemy territory.

"We've crossed the River Styx chaps, have we?"

"The River What?" Gerald retorted.

"He's a heathen Tommy ol' man," The Bish crackled as a back puff of smoke exploded to the port of the plane.

"They've spotted us." Gerald nodded and then thought about what The Bish had said."Heathen Skip?"

"He's lacking a certain educational je ne sais quoi." The Bish pointed out to Tommy.

"Gerry, my man, the river Kalamos below, I do believe in Greek mythology is THE legendary River Styx. It is the very river that forms the boundary between Earth and the Underworld, you know, the river over which Charon ferried the souls of the dead... so I mentioned it as we'd plainly entered enemy territory. Simple when you know your classics ol' chap."

Another black puff of smoke to the starboard, this time even closer. The plane shuddered a little at the shock wave.

"... goodness!... which is where we are now over."

"Gotcha Tommy. Thank you all for the lesson in Ancient Greek culture."

Gerald was keen eyed and soon spotted a couple of enemy fighters, Fiat G 50 Freccias. The planes were escort to an archaic and out of date Italian reconnaissance two-seater biplane, a Lynx Meridionali Ro.37. They had met the enemy by accident.

Tommy Wisdom chirped up. "Will they have a go at us? I mean, there's lots of us and just a couple of them."

Tracer bullets whisking their way past Gerald answered the question. Tommy Wisdom clung on behind. He could only watch as further back down the fuselage of the Blenheim, Arthur Geary fired away relentlessly. "Jesus, Gerry ol' boy, that last one was close."

"We've had it closer, haven't we Skip." Gerald laughed through the crackling intercom as he watched the Italian fighters heading away. The overwhelming force before them and being chased by four Glosters had been enough to make their minds up pretty sharply.

"Sure have." The Bish proclaimed knowingly. "We're not there yet chaps and they'll have radioed up front we're on our way, so eyes open wide. There'll be more to come, for sure."

Another ten minutes passed and the fleet of Blenheims and Glosters were over their intended targets, a mountain ridge to the north-west of Tepelenë where Intelligence Officer Willie had informed everyone at the briefing, the Italians were planning an offensive. Gerald looked down. There was certainly lots of movement on the ground with trucks pulling heavy equipment up mountain roads.

As usual, The Bish Boys were first in and first to drop their bombs. Bombs which most of the time they'd had to head off to Menidi to load up with first, as there was insufficient storage at Paramythia.

Gerry had, as usual, almost gone into a trance-like state, peering down the sighting apparatus which he used expertly. As he looked down, gun flashes of bright reds, oranges and yellows sparked up silently, followed by those black puffs of innocent, yet deadly, looking clouds all around.

Gerald deftly moved his right hand on the bomb release gear and once again pronounced, "Bombs gone!"

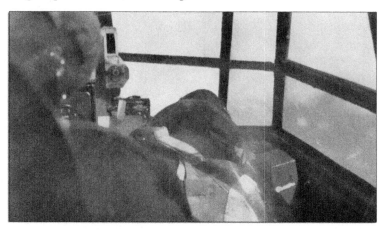

Credit: Wings Over Olympus. T.H. Wisdom. The Bish to the left and Gerry looking through the bomb aimer over Tepelenë.

"How exciting!" shouted Tommy Wisdom, looking through the plexiglass at the ground below. "I can see the fleecy white puffs of the bombs going off, Gerry. You've hit some stuff down there. There are huge spurts of earth. I can't quite make it out, but I can see movement. Yes, moving specks. Yes... yes it is... it's Itis on the run."

Gerald almost didn't want to hear that there may be people on the receiving end of his attacks.

<'They've got families like me! Poor chaps!">

Then it began. Explosions all around. The ack-ack was thick and fast.

The Bish took evasive action. "Coming around. Jobs a good one chaps. Let's head home." he crackled as the plane shook repeatedly, with shells bursting all around.

Then Gerald saw them. "Fighters!" he shouted at the top of his voice. "Bloody everywhere."

Arthur Geary had sprung into action and his machine gun hammered away, rattling the plane with every bullet leaving the hot barrel of the .303 inch Vickers VGO machine gun.

Pilot Officer Arthur Geary's position as Air Gunner and Wireless Operator atop a Blenheim at Paramythia.

Credit: Papa Spiro Monasterios who retains original image at Church of Saint Prokopios, Kavos, Corfu.

The sky was once again full of Freccias and Macchis. The Bish had been right, the first lot had radioed back and now they were almost being ambushed.

Gerald looked to the starboard and a little behind. "Buck's got one on his tail, Arthur."

"Never mind the one we've got coming up the rear Gerry."

The Vickers rattled more, as did the guns from the other Blenheims.

"Keep tight!" urged The Bish. "Keep tight."

The tight formation of the Squadron was doing its job and the Italians were loath to come in too close but as Gerald looked out to the side to see L8541 with Buck at the helm, machine gunfire ripped through the aircraft and debris flew off from underneath.

"Buck's hit!" blurted Gerald. "He's not down though."

Beside them, Buck's gunner was pounding away at the Macchi 200 which had done the damage.

"Where the hell are the Glosters, chaps?" The Bish shouted.

"We lost them when we went through the cloud over Tepelenë!" shouted Gerald. "No idea where they are now."

"That's a bummer." The Bish responded as someone's bullets hit one of the Macchis behind. The Macchi tumbled to the snowy mountains with a trail of black smoke in its wake.

The Blenheims headed for cloud cover. "I think we lost them."

Buck crackled in over the radio. "Buck limping home!"

"Good show, Buck! Good show!" The Bish riposted. "Let's get back, reload and get ready for round two later."

It was a short run back to Paramythia and everyone was thankful for its closeness now, particularly Buck who was flying a heavily damaged plane with its fuselage, wings and underneath looking decidedly ropey and ready to come apart at any moment. As it was, he landed the plane with one wheel and the crew of L8541 survived their ordeal.

Later the same afternoon, Gerald was out again over Bousi in Albania. Tommy Wisdom on this occasion, after a brief training session from Gerald, acted as bomb-aimer. The Blenheims of 211 Squadron once again had good fortune, but of the other squadrons involved that day, three planes were lost. [2]

As they sat and chatted that night in the mess tent at Paramythia, Tommy Wisdom said to Gerald, "Do you know how close we came to death today, Gerry ol' man. I could bloody well see the hooded head of the pilot of the Macchi. I saw him fire and I could bloody well smell the bullet which hit our engine nacelle. Bits flew everywhere, but the engine carried on turning. That's how close it was. That's how close we came to…"

"Don't even say it. Don't say it." Gerald said, patting his tunic pocket where the photograph of him and Susan was. "I have my lucky charm and she keeps me safe. I'm sure that's true."

"The photograph?" Tommy Wisdom smiled. "Glad you like it."

"All thanks to you Tommy, my best pal. All thanks to you."

*

Now 211 Squadron was closer to the front and despite the hidden location of Paramythia, a lone enemy fighter might find them, after all Yanina had been attacked by the Italians, so Paramythia might soon come into the firing line.

The Bish had been pushing for the Hurricanes he had been

promised to arrive, and on 18 February six Hurricanes from 80 Squadron roared their way down the Valley of Fairy Tales, to the delight of everyone.

Now they had some proper fighter protection. The delight showed on the faces of all.

Credit: Wings Over Olympus. T.H. Wisdom. The Six Hurricanes as they arrive at Paramythia. 18 February 1941

Author's Note

[1] George Victor Wildeman 'Jimmie' Kettlewell (1916 - 2007) eventually became Wing Commander Kettlewell. He was an RAF Gloster Gladiator fighting ace serving in North Africa and Greece. During the middle of February 80 Squadron's Gladiators continued to operate from Yanina while the Gladiators of 21 Mira moved up to Paramythia and here on 17 February they were joined by 80 Squadron's six new Hurricanes, led by Flight Lieutenant Kettlewell, and by four 30 Squadron Blenheims.

[2] p. 82 Air War for Yugoslavia, Greece and Crete. (See reference page)

Chapter Twenty-eight

'Read All About It!'

Blenheims and Glosters and eventually Hurricanes were in and out of Paramythia every day and often they were in a bad state of repair, or as Tommy Wisdom once felt, they needed a good service and so based with everyone at any air base were a veritable army of RAF mechanics and service specialists. They were the ones Gerald trusted to get the planes airworthy after any mission they'd been on. In short, the men who flew the planes trusted the men on the ground with their lives, every day of the week. The men servicing the planes of 211 Squadron rarely came into direct contact with the enemy, but that wouldn't always be the case.

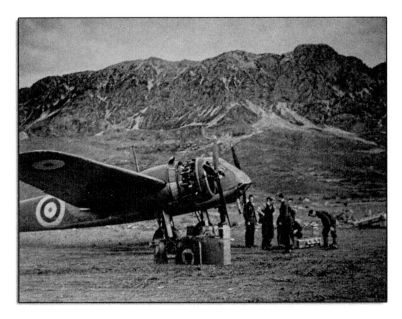

Blenheim L1434 being serviced at Paramythia.
Credit: Papa Spiro Monasterios who keeps original image at Church of
Saint Prokopios, Kavos, Corfu.

Daily briefings and de-briefings at Paramythia were once again called
by three bursts on the Lewis gun and when the familiar sound came,
everyone headed for the Ops tent. The Bish led the briefings as he was
station commander and Pat Pattle, the South African air ace led the
briefings for the Hurricane crews of 80 Squadron. Whilst The Bish
talked abut the targets for the upcoming raid, Pat Pattle told everyone
how they tactically would seek to defend everyone from attack by
Italian fighters.

Amid all of this was Embros, the liaison officer and interpreter who
was in touch regularly via the field telephone with his own H.Q., and
he would often be the one relating how the raids had gone via
intelligence on the ground.

Gerald listened to Embros with eagerness. Embros reported back
with some accuracy, the reality on the ground.

"Reports are coming in that since our raids, their troops on the
ground have moved forward and prisoners have been taken,"

There were great cheers in the Ops tent.

"There is mores gentlemens. Much more. We have entirely wiped out the offensive being undertaken by the 53rd Sforzesca Division.[1] It seems they are no more… "

More cheers.

"But there are still other divisions in those mountains."

"Then we shall see them off too. Good show, gents. Good show." The Bish said as he congratulated the surrounding men. "With the Hurri-buses now here in The Valley of Fairy Tales, we shall be unstoppable. As long as they get used to flying through that damn cloud in the mountains."

"G-F, dear man, we are here to defend your bombers 100%. No cloud is going to deviate our plans. We shall see you chaps to the target. We shall see you drop your bombs and then we shall see you get safely away. Not until then shall we seek to have some fun with the Italians. I can promise you that."

Pat was always sincere and always on the number with the tactics he proposed. Everyone listened to him with confidence, knowing he was the exact man for the job.

*

As February progressed, the raids on Tepelenë and surrounding areas continued with a renewed vigour. The Bish Boys now emboldened by their fast and powerful escort Hurricanes from 80 Squadron.

Embros made it known that *"at the sight of the Hurricane mans, one man in Italian plane has but one job… that is to tell the others to bale out before they are shots down."*

Everyone had laughed at this comment, but it was becoming a truth. On Thursday 20 February the Germans had come onto the scene, saying they wanted to have a role as mediator in the Greco-Italian war, but the Greeks had refused. The same day, to show no-one wanted German interference, the RAF and the Greeks put up a tremendous show of force and had sent 51 planes of all types to the war zone in Epirus. Some planes had dropped much needed supplies to the Greek troops on the ground and others had continued on to bomb the strategic positions of the Italians both inland and on the coast. Gerald had never seen such a huge armada of planes. The Italians sent in their monoplanes but the Hurri-buses, as The Bish called them, were too fast and too nimble for the Italian fighters to deal with.

Gerald and Arthur Geary had sat down with Tommy Wisdom later that day in the mess and told him the story of the raid.

"A G.50 came for us, " Arthur Geary began, "and in a flash a Hurricane just shot it off our wing tip."

"You should have seen it go down!" Gerald said excitedly. "Seen nothing like it. Before, we'd have been mince meat once the Iti got behind us."

"It simply rolled over, went on fire and dived into the mountain. It was wizard."

"Unbelievable. I can't help but think of the pilot though, Arthur. Would have preferred it had the blighter got out."

"He was probably dead, anyway. Those shells wrecked his bus good and proper."

Tommy Wisdom was always writing notes. "The Hurricanes got four Italian planes in quick succession, so I'm told."

"Possibly more" added Gerald.

"I'm told that even the Gladiators got involved in the action, shooting down another four."

"Think that's right." added in Arthur Geary.

"Yes," responded Gerald, "and don't forget, Embros told us the Greeks got another four. So twelve in all today. Wow, that's some going."

"They'll be running out of planes soon, Tommy!"

Tommy Wisdom didn't always go out on raids but reported successes with a renewed eagerness, having seen the loss now being taken by the Italians. On Thursday 27 February The Bish Boys were back raiding Valona. They loved the protection the super fast Hurricanes gave to them. It gave them a new confidence in the air. Tommy Wisdom knew instinctively it was The Bish Boys who would bring back the good news, so he waited in the mess to interview them when they got back. He wasn't disappointed as he sat with his reporter's notebook in his hand.

Earlier that day, he'd counted twelve Blenheims out and twelve back, along with their escort of six Hurricanes. The call of 'all planes safe' was reassuring to everyone, including Tommy Wisdom as he sat waiting for the crews to return. As the war progressed it seemed to be heard less frequently. The first people Tommy made for to chat about the day's events was Gerald and Arthur. Tommy and Gerald were firm friends after Tommy had managed to secure a copy of the photograph for Gerald and they spent much time together talking about life after the war. That's what kept them going.

"I'm going to drive in the countryside in that MG of mine and take in the sunshine of England's green and pleasant land with Susan." Gerald had told Tommy just a few days after their arrival at Paramythia. "Then I'm going to take her to Wales to meet my family in Shotton. Wales is a more green and more pleasant land than England," he said, winking at Tommy Wisdom.

"With mountains as bleak as here." Tommy retorted.

"But we have to get this bloody war done first, hey?"

They'd both agreed the war impeded life but it had to be done. "If we don't beat the Itis here, you can be sure the Huns will invade Britain," Gerald said.

"You're not wrong Gerry ol' chap. This front here keeps them on their toes, but I can see within weeks they'll be tumbling down. The Itis are doing a rubbish job and my ears on the ground in the news agencies tell me the Germans are getting fed up of it. They have plans afoot, dear Gerry."

"G-F did say. He said, after Metaxas went, things might alter. I suppose we'll have to wait and see."

Squadron Leader Tommy Wisdom was not only a press reporter, but he was an RAF officer as well and now a practised bomb-aimer in his own right. Tommy often had a beer or two waiting for Gerald and Arthur when they returned from raids, and the 27th February was no different. Everyone knew Tommy was with them to report on the war and everyone wanted the folks back home to know they were doing well, so telling Tommy what they'd seen or experienced was a way of indirectly speaking to the folks back home about the actions they were involved in on the Greek front, even though it didn't mention names, it was a reassuring read.

"How did Valona go, gentlemen?"

"Like clockwork, Tommy. Like clockwork." Gerald gave a thumbs up as he sipped his beer in the tent.

"I'll interview the Hurricane pilots as well and a few of the others to get a story together, but I want the Blenheim bomber view first."

"I had a grandstand view of the whole affair," Arthur Geary said, pulling his chair closer to the table. " It was lovely bombing, with direct hits all over the aerodrome and other buildings."

"Why that's a compliment, thanks Arthur dear chap," Gerald patted Arthur on the back. Happy for that to go in the paper.... And it was your gunnery which kept us up there, remember?"

Arthur Geary nodded. "A large formation of CR 42s took off to intercept us. One got on my tail, so I put a burst into him, and he fell away. Then two Hurricanes appeared in a flash, and… well, he just fell to pieces."

"Saw them myself, Tommy. Amazing planes. Amazing."

Tommy Wisdom nodded, writing furiously as the men spoke.

"So," went on Arthur Geary, "the Hurricanes wheeled and proceeded to deal with the others. The sky was full of crashing aircraft…"

"Yep, and they were all enemy," chipped in Gerald."

"The Hurricanes shot down seven, all of them in flames, and two others evidently got so fuddled with what was going on that they collided and went down too. We had a most pleasant tour home, and the scenery looked more lovely than ever." [2]

The next day, Friday there was an even bigger tally for scores against the Italians, and when Tommy Wisdom interviewed the Hurricane and Gladiator pilots of 80 and 112 Squadrons, they reported shooting down *"at least 27 Italians."*

As Gerald and Arthur sat with Tommy Wisdom for a beer on the Friday night, the two clinked glasses and revelled in the successes of the past few days.

Tommy looked at his notes before him. "I'm going to have a headline *[3]* which reads something like RAF shoots down 26 in Albania."

"From what I hear, it could be more?"

"We'll keep it at an even number. The powers that be don't like too much exaggeration."

"You do it all the time, Tommy!" Arthur Geary laughed.

Tommy Wisdom ignored the remark. "Then follow it up with the story… It is officially announced from Athens that RAF fighters on patrol … er … that's you lot… with the Hurricanes and Glosters. "

Everyone smiled.

"… yes… fighters patrol over the southern Albanian front, shot down 26 enemy aircraft, in a battle against considerable odds. Sound wonderful chaps?"

"Sounds great. Should put the Itis on the back foot." Gerald added. "The reality is, the Hurricanes and Glosters allowed us to get to the target, Valona… er, the runway and, without a fuss, I might add. By that I mean no enemy fighters having a direct go at our Blenheims at all."

"Made such a difference," Arthur chipped in. "I saw the difference by the amount of ammo I used. A rather relaxing time was had by us all considering what we've had to put up with in recent weeks."

*

It was St. David's Day when Gerald and Arthur sat down with Jimmie Kettlewell and Pat Pattle in the mess and bought them a drink by way of thanks for the difference they had made to their lives. Gerald had been out to pick one of the wild daffodils growing everywhere in the area.

"Dydd Gŵyl Dewi Hapus!" Gerald said, raising his glass to the table.

"What language is that young man, huh?" asked Pat in his thick South African drawl.

"Like my daffodil chaps? It's St. David's Day today, the first of March. The Patron saint of Wales he is. We sport a daffodil or a leek in Wales on this day. Done it since I was a little spec of a lad in school."

"So what's it mean then?... what you said in that weird language!"

"Happy Saint David's Day, chaps," Gerald raised his glass again.

"Bloody Welsh!" joked Jimmie. "They're only good for singing."

"Give us a song then Gerry?" Arthur butted in as he laughed away with the others.

"You'll laugh on the other side of your faces chaps when us Welsh get together as a bunch! We'll choir you out. Anyway, you've got a Welshman in YOUR squadron chaps."

"Who's that then?" Pat exclaimed.

"Who's that? I met him over in Egypt. Dahl is his name. Pilot Officer Roald Dahl."

"Roald who?" expressed Pat.

"The tall guy. The one who crashed in the Gladiator when some bugger sent him to the wrong place."

"Ah, yes, lanky legs Dahl." Jimmie replied. "Not seen him in an age! As far as I know, the poor bugger is still laid up in hospital across the Med."

And that was as far as the conversation went. No one had time to wonder about the injured, or the dead, for that matter. Keeping oneself and crew mates around them alive in this horrendous situation was all anyone thought about.

*

* * *

On Monday 3 March 1941 a great earthquake hit the Greek town of Larissa, where the RAF had a base. It was unaffected by the quake but in the city 10,000 people were left homeless and hundreds had been killed. Old men, women and children alike had been slain by falling masonry. Most young men were at the front and so escaped the tragedy.

The Bish was madder than Gerald had every seen him. "What's up, Skip?" he asked.

"You know about the quake in Larissa?"

"Sure do."

"Rescuers in the place have been pulling at rubble and stones with their bare hands to get to the trapped and injured of the city… so what do the bloody wops do?"

Gerald didn't have time to answer.

"They launch bombing raids on the place. I mean, it's already in ruins because of the earthquake. Damn bastards they are."

Gerald's face was enough. He was horrified at this despicable act.

"What's the action we take then boss?"

"I've spoken with Pat and Jimmie. They've already gone out to intercept any more of the buggers coming in."

"Get the Lewis gun fired. We're joining them to bomb the aerodromes to stop the bastards doing it again."

Over the next two days, 211 Squadron did exactly that. This was to lead to the first loss of a Hurricane and the loss of Pat Pattle's wingman, the 23-year-old Australian Nigel Cullen. [4] On 4 March, Cullen was in his Hurricane, Hurricane V7288, escorting The Bish Boys and their group of Blenheims near Himarë over southern Albania. Gerald had released his bombs over five Italian warships, as had the other Blenheims, and they were all on their way home. As Pat had said, once the Blenheims had done their job, they would go 'looking for fun,' so the Hurricanes left Gerald and the others to head back to Paramythia. The Hurricanes, all in pairs, met Italian fighters. Whilst Pat was engaged with one Italian plane another surprised Cullen and his was hit, crashing down near Himarë in southern Albania.

Back at base everyone was shocked to learn of the death of Cullen whom everyone knew as The Ape. Pat Pattle blamed himself.

"I should have seen it! I should have seen it!" he exclaimed as he knocked back several whiskies that night.

No one blamed him, of course. This was the destiny of war.

The men of 211 Squadron realised for the first time that the Hurricanes were not as invincible as they had first thought. No one said or mentioned this, of course, but it gave the flyers of 211 Squadron a jolt of reality once again.

Author's Note

[1] *The 53rd Sforzesca Division was a mountain Infantry Division of the Italian Army, newly arrived in Tepelenë.*

[2] *Conversation based on first hand account as described on page 147 Wings Over Olympus. T.H. Wisdom. (1942)*

[3] *The story was reported across the British Press. Here's a sample:*

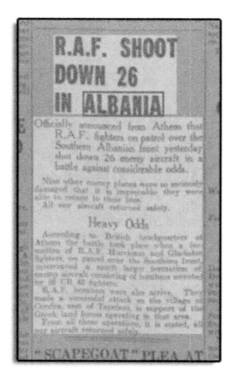

The Dundee Courier of 1st March 1941.

[4] *Richard Nigel Cullen, DFC (5 June 1917 – 4 March 1941) 80 Squadron. Awarded a DFC for his actions of 28th February 1941 in shooting down 5*

Italian planes who were attacking 211 and other squadrons during the Greco-Italian War.

Chapter Twenty-nine

'Death of the C.O.'

Back home in Shotton, Lizzie and Francis read the papers avidly. They knew Gerald was on the front line in Greece and were pleased to read of the successes of the RAF there. A letter from Gerald had dropped on the mat and they were relieved to see his handwriting.

"He's okay." Lizzie had shouted as they read the letter from him. "He's 23 on the 7th. Can't believe where time has gone."

"Me neither Lizzie! All we know right now is that he was well when he wrote the letter," said Francis with some optimism in his tone.

"We have to keep our hopes up he is fine. That's the best thing we can do. God willing, he will survive this and come home. I've sent him a card for his birthday but no idea if it'll get there."

"It will. They're pretty good, you know. Pretty good."

"I miss him. It's been such a long time since we've seen him."

*

A hundred or more miles away, Susan Hall heard the post drop through the letterbox at Wargrave Road in Henley. At once, she knew it was Gerald's handwriting.

That afternoon Susan was off to work at The Horns, but first she had her Home Guard Duty with the Upper Thames Patrol to perform. It seemed a lifetime ago that she was sitting on the river with Gerald. In the precious hour she had before she left the house for the day, she wandered across to the garage of the house. She took Gerald's letter with her and opened it whilst sitting in his racing green MG, which he had left there for safekeeping whilst he was away. The touch of the ox-blood leather seats, the smell of the car and all the little bits and pieces left lying around in the car reminded her of Gerald. She lovingly touched the car as if feeling for Gerald's presence.

Susan was sitting in the passenger seat of the car and her hand eventually made its way to the one place she knew he would have touched last in the car. The steering wheel.

She remembered Gerald getting out of the car the previous September.

"I'll get someone to bring my motor to you if you'll see your way to looking after the old girl, will you?" he'd said as the two sat in the car. "I shall be back to claim it... and you!" he added at the end.

Susan remembered the kiss in the gloom of the garage. The warm touch of Gerald's hand on her face seemed to remain with her still.

Susan had looked up at Gerald and as their eyes met, she'd laughed. "Lipstick on your face again. That's not a good look for an aspiring officer in the RAF is it now," she said, wiping his face with the handkerchief from her pocket.

"Can I have that?" Gerald asked as she went to put the handkerchief away.

"This old hanky? You want it?"

"It's you and it smells of you. Can I take it with me? Always good to hold it when you're not there."

"If you must."

"I insist!" Gerald had said, taking the lipstick covered handkerchief.

"One thing then, it needs a proper pair of lips on it! " Susan remembered herself saying as she kissed the handkerchief, leaving an impression of her full, red lips on it.

"That'll be the best thing ever."

Gerald had placed the handkerchief into his tunic pocket and the two had stayed in the car for what seemed hours. Now she was sitting there all alone, just with memories and hopes.

She looked at the letter and read it out loud, as if Gerald was there talking to her. She could see his face plain and clear before her. It was as good as she could hope for there and then. She prayed Gerald would return to her when this was all over. She wasn't hopeful, though. People were coming into The Horns every week nowadays telling her they'd lost someone or they knew of someone who'd lost someone in the war.

<'Don't let it be Gerald. Don't let it be Gerald.'>

* * *

*

In the heat of war, Gerald had forgotten about the handkerchief as the lost photograph had concentrated his mind to the one object he treasured most, which he now had again in his possession. Many months before, he'd placed the lipstick stained handkerchief into the canvas pouch which held his .38 Enfield Revolver, which he'd never used in anger. He hoped he never would. The gun was a last resort if he fell into enemy hands, so the handkerchief lay untouched and forgotten, more often than not, left in the Blenheim as he did not need to carry the revolver back and forth every time he went on a mission.

Gerald had forgotten it was around the time of his birthday when the two cards arrived from Britain. One from Lizzie and family; the other from Susan was a postcard with a drawing of The Horns on it. The cards lifted his heart so much, especially the picture of The Horns where he'd spent so many happy times.

As March progressed, the briefings came thick and fast, as did the rumours of an impending German advance, but no one took it seriously. The shufti-kites weren't reporting any German movements anywhere to the north, but there was one Italian gun placement in the hills not far away which was causing havoc to the Greek soldiers on the ground. The information had come in from Alan - Flight Lieutenant Godfrey, who'd had seven days leave and gone to the Greek front to see what the situation was, making his way there by any means he could. When he arrived back at Paramythia, after an exhausting donkey ride in places, he pleaded with The Bish to go on a mission to bomb the Italian gun emplacements.

To set the mission in motion, an impromptu briefing was held outside over lunch and a glass or two of ouzo brought in by the Greeks to thank the RAF for their efforts on 28th February.

Credit: Wings Over Olympus. Outdoor Briefing over lunch. (Left to right) Constantine John Manussis - aka 'Embros' (partially hidden), Pilot Officer Gerald Davies, Squadron Leader James Richmond Gordon-Finlayson - The Bish, Flying Officer Alexander James Muir Fabian aka 'Curly' and next to him Flight Lieutenant Alan Godfrey.

The following day Gerald and the others raided the area pointed out by Alan Godfrey and Embros reported back from the Greek commander on the ground that the Italian gunnery battery was no more.

But it wasn't the Italians who should have worried the men at Paramythia.

*

On March 2nd 1941 Churchill had sent British Foreign Secretary Anthony Eden to Greece to enter talks with the Greek Government and King George II about the impending German threat. The Germans were now building up their forces in nearby Romania and Bulgaria. From previous experience everyone knew about the German tactic of Blitzkrieg and no one could afford to ignore their presence so close to a country where there was a pitiful presence of forces to deter them from attack.

Embros fed back to the people on the ground at Paramythia that some reinforcements had been agreed, but he felt it might be 'too little and too late.'

"Just when the Italians are on the verge of capitulation and we had the chance to reach the coast at Valona," Embros told The Bish, "we might be hemmed in elsewhere."

"Not good, not good!" The Bish ruminated as he rubbed his brow. "But we shall push on and get your forces to the coast, hey!"

The non-stop bombing push for Gerald carried on through March as mounting concerns about German intentions grew in everyone's hearts. As Gerald sat at yet another briefing, he thought about his and the squadron's future.

<'We are pushed to the limit fighting the Italians. Fighting the Germans might push us beyond the limit.'>

*

There was some good news on the horizon though, at least for one member of 211 Squadron. The Bish found out he had been awarded the Distinguished Service Order. [1] This was the first to be awarded to anyone in this theatre of war, so everyone was granted some time back in Athens to celebrate.

Gerald loved Athens. It felt so far from the war. So peaceful and now in March it was warmer than ever. Pretty flowers were everywhere and trees were in new leaf. He wandered the streets of the capital with several others and paid a visit to the marvellous Acropolis.

He thought of all the things Giorgios had taught him about Greece and wandered if he ever might want to leave this beautiful country. The thought even came to him he might invite Susan over to the country and suggest this might be a place they could eventually live. A place of permanent Spring.

At night, everyone ended up at Zonars for a planned celebration of The Bish's DSO.

Gerald was reminded of the night of Potato Jones' birthday and the aftermath of that event which saw Keeper - Dennis Barrett fatally injured and The Bish himself with a broken leg which he still hobbled from, despite having his plaster off some weeks ago. Despite these bad memories of Athens from the previous New Year's Eve, everyone set about enjoying themselves. After all, as Gerald commented to Arthur, "This isn't Maxim's, this is Zonars, so the bad luck of that place is not here."

"Good shout, Gerry lad!" Arthur Geary replied, as he sloshed down his first beer of the night. "We shall enjoy ourselves."

"Yes, you shall" The Bish had walked in to the conversation. "Eat, drink and be merry for tomorrow we... " The Bish stopped. "Well, we know the last word and we have no intention of that."

The Bish banged his unlit pipe on the table and announced all drinks were courtesy of him adding 'within reason' to everyone's merriment.

"We shall surely lose him now he is DSO," Gerald whispered to Arthur. "He's an outstanding leader of us lads."

"I hope not. I hope not, but I fear you may be right."

"Think I might be. I've seen it before. He'll be posted for sure."

"Then I wonder who might come in his place?"

"I don't know, but it'll be a whole new start. I'm not sure it'll be good, especially with what we know about the Huns massing up north."

"Then all we can hope is that G-F stays, hey?"

*

In the days which followed, Gerald and Arthur's assumptions had been right and The Bish was promoted to Wing Commander. He left the squadron on 19 March and little did they know that a night raid on Valona on 13th March had been his last raid carried out with the squadron. The Bish would now to lead the newly formed Eastern Wing of the RAF in Greece.

At the time James Gordon-Finlayson left the squadron, Gerald and Arthur had flown over 70 operations as a team with him. Gerald was saddened at his departure but knew all good things ended.

The new boss of 211 Squadron was announced immediately and as from 22 March 1941, the new C.O. was to be Squadron Leader Richard Nedwill, a New Zealander and a distinguished flyer of Gloster Gladiators having seen action with 112 Squadron.

By coincidence, at 7.30am, that Saturday, the Italians found the location of the airfield at Paramythia and three fighters had strafed the place before quickly heading off as the Greek army protecting the base fired away at them.

Gerald chatted with Arthur as they moved their quarters away from the airfield.

"They'll be back for sure. They know we are here now. We have to be ready next time - we need an early warning system or something.

We've been struggling with communications since we've been here, Arthur."

"I know, Gerry lad. I know. And, yes, there is a good chance they'll be back today, but there's bugger-all we can do about it now. The new boss is coming later and all we can hope is that he's got enough upstairs to give us the lowdown on what we do next."

"Let's hope so. Our planes are sitting ducks here. Sitting ducks!"

Richard Nedwill flew into Paramythia not long afterwards in his Gladiator to find the men moving tents and supplies hundreds of yards away against the side of the valley wall where they would be more protected. He immediately mucked in and afterwards gathered the men for their first briefing.

"Dat was some introduction chaps! Some introduction to life at Paramythia! Tough times are ahead, you know," he began, with an accent which sounded like he was a New Zealander from Belfast, "but de Bish tells me you men are like old boots. "

Everyone laughed at the comment.

"I've been through it myself and I know. I grew up in a tough Irish farming family…"

<'So that's why he sounds like that.'>

"They moved via Australia to New Zealand in 1910, to farm sheep. Then they had me, their first little Antipodean child."

More laughs.

"My bugger of a father tried to get me to do the same. I mean, be a sheep farmer like him. He wanted me to move sheep an' shit around the hills of Christchurch. He even sent me off for agricultural training, but I thought *'bugger that for a game of soldiers - what the hell am I doing with my life?'…* to cut a long story, sort of short, I joined the RAF in 1934. Cut my teeth in so many planes, I've forgotten the names of most of them."

The assembled personnel nodded.

"One thing is for certain though, the effort we put in here will surely delay or even stop any invasion of Britain, so what we do is of vital importance to everyone… here and in Blighty. The hun is on our doorstep everywhere, nowhere more so than here in Greece. I know and from what de Bish tells me, you are all stoked up for action and ready to give them a thorough pasting."

The men cheered.

"Long and short of it is though, you guys know the territory here, so I'll be guided by your experience to start with and we'll see how it goes, hey?"

First impression was that this man was a winner.

"First things first though," Nedwill finished with, "… we have to ensure we are better protected and have more advanced warnings of any attacks, so I've already set I motion with the Greek authorities, via Embros, for better communications with their forces further north. That'll give us a few minutes to get our planes up in the air in the event of attack. I know communications are terrible here and this situation has to alter and today."

<'This man is going to be just fine!'>

The prediction by Gerald that another attack would take place came to fruition at 2.30pm. Once again there was no warning, when 18 Italian Macchi C.200 Saetta planes arrived at low altitude travelling at over 250 m.p.h. The first anyone knew was when they opened up with their Breda-SAFAT machine guns, sat in pairs at the front of the aircraft.

Several of the ground crew were caught in the open and dived into ready-made protection trenches. Others, like Gerald and Arthur who'd been stood by their Blenheim had a split second to dive for the deep ruts made by their own planes in wetter times.

After the first wave had come through, Gerald and Arthur ran for better cover against rocks, under some olive trees down by the mountain stream. As Gerald looked back, he could already see one Blenheim on fire. The Greeks had been quick to return fire, but the Macchis were so swift and manoeuvrable through the air, they had little chance of getting a hit.

The second wave came in and strafed the ground with exploding bullets, hitting two more Blenheims and a Wellington. All were firmly ablaze and the Wellington exploded violently from bombs recently loaded up for a raid later that day.

As quickly as they had arrived the Italian fighters were gone, leaving tents full of holes, flight kits riddled with bullets. All in all, four planes were destroyed in the raid, but everyone thanked their lucky stars no one was killed or injured.

The new C.O. was out and about at a pace.

"Any kites not hit let's get dem rolling! NOW!" he shouted. "Fighters after the raiders and bombers regroup to Menidi."

*

* * *

Gerald was once again looking down at the peaceful royal palace as he landed at Menidi. Everyone from 211 was safe and back on old territory, whilst those on the ground at Paramythia had stayed there in great danger, the raids continuing by the Italians. Gerald was reminded of the good and bad times here and thought of the people he'd lost so far in this terrible war.

On the Monday night, Gerald sat in the old mess with Arthur and they both quietly sipped a few beers.

"Do you think we'll ever get out of this alive?"

"Your guess is as good as mine, dear chap. As good as mine. If I'm honest, I think this will be the place we spend our last days in, unless that photo of yours keeps our luck riding high. You still have it, don't you?"

"Right here!" Gerald produced the photograph and kissed it, before placing it back in his tunic pocket.

"You keep that photograph safe then ol' chap. Keep it safe. Even I think it might be charmed now. Let's hope it's charmed enough to get us back to Blighty, hey?"

*

Early on Wednesday 26th March, the C.O. Richard Nedwill ordered a general return to Paramythia as *'defences had been stepped up,'* which hopefully made the place safe enough to return to. Richard Nedwill said he would follow along in his Gloster Gladiator.

Gerald and Arthur were brewing a cup of tea on a camp stove when they heard his plane returning. They both looked up to the sun as they heard strange engine noises from the plane, which seemed to be in a terminal dive.

"Pull up, you bugger" shouted Gerald. Others were shouting the same.

The Gladiator seemed to be out of control, diving towards the ground, as if controlled by some crazed pilot on a suicide mission

"Is he trying to kill himself?" Arthur said, looking puzzled.

"Jesus, yes, he's had it!" Gerald's enamel tea cup fell from his grasp. "The last one I know who did that was Dahl..."

"Who?"

They both watched with horror. What else could they do?

"You know, Pilot Officer Roald Dahl of 80. He hit the ground hard in one of those last September in the desert close to Fouka. Poor bugger is still in hospital, so Pat… or was it Jimmie who said."

"If the C.O. recovers from this one, he's bloody immortal."

At that very moment the biplane hit the ground with an awful crunch of metal, the propeller flaring off to the side like an out-of-control jackie-jumper on Bonfire night. In the split second following, the fuel in the plane exploded, sending shards of metal everywhere and a black plume of smoke skyward. Those nearest ran to the scene, as did Gerald and Arthur.

Someone shouted.

"He's here. He's gone! He's dead!"

Gerald looked across and the mangled body of Squadron Leader Richard Nedwill, [2] the C.O. of 211 Squadron for just four days, had been thrown clear in the explosion and was contorted in ways even Gerald had never imagined. Next to him lay the number of his doomed aircraft, still in one piece from a part of the fuselage of the Gladiator - N5910. The rest of the wreckage burned away just a few yards away.

This was death as close up as it got for most of the men in the RAF.

Gerald stood there, shocked.

"Shit, shit, shit!" Arthur exclaimed. "Shit, he's gone."

"Do you think he tried to kill himself, Arthur?"

"Dunno. It looked odd to me."

"The stress of war does funny things to people, hey? Funny things."

"Poor chap. Jesus. Poor chap. Did he have a wife and family?"

"No idea. I hardly knew him."

"I don't want to die Gerry ol' man."

Gerald could see the tears in Arthur's eyes. "Me neither. Me neither. None of us do. I feel like I'm losing my soul in this place. Chipped away with every friend I lose."

Gerald took a deep breath and sighed. Tears filled his eyes and the two patted each other on the arm.

Author's Note

[1] *25th March 1941 - James Richmond Gordon-Finlayson (The Bish), is awarded the Distinguished Service Order.*

The KING has been graciously pleased to approve the following awards in recognition of gallantry displayed in flying operations against the enemy:

This officer has completed over 100 operational sorties both by day and night. Throughout these operations, most of which have been carried out under exceptionally difficult conditions, he has displayed outstanding leadership and skill and, by his splendid example of courage and determination, has contributed materially to the successes achieved by his squadron.

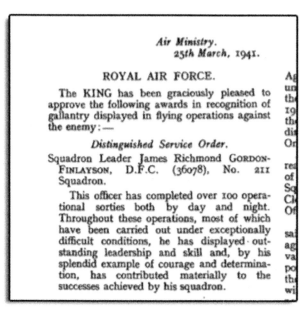

Air Ministry.
25th March, 1941.

ROYAL AIR FORCE.

The KING has been graciously pleased to approve the following awards in recognition of gallantry displayed in flying operations against the enemy:—

Distinguished Service Order.

Squadron Leader James Richmond GORDON-FINLAYSON, D.F.C. (36078), No. 211 Squadron.

This officer has completed over 100 operational sorties both by day and night. Throughout these operations, most of which have been carried out under exceptionally difficult conditions, he has displayed · outstanding leadership and skill and, by his splendid example of courage and determination, has contributed materially to the successes achieved by his squadron.

London Gazette No 35116 - 25 Mar 1941

[2] Squadron Leader Richard John Courtney Nedwill A.F.C. (1913 - 1941)
   Squadron Leader Nedwill AFC died in a Gladiator accident at Paramythia on 26th March 1941. He was posted from 112 Squadron just four days before to command 211 Squadron at Paramythia. He is buried at Phaleron War Cemetery, Athens, Greece.
   Following his death, he was awarded the Air Force Cross:

* * *

THE LONDON GAZETTE, 1 APRIL, 1941 1903

ing combat, Flight Lieutenant
wn a Junkers and a Messer-
a cannon shell burst in his
vering him with petrol, setting
ire, and slightly wounding his
spite this, he continued to
Messerschmitt at a low level
nition was expended. He then
s aircraft. Throughout the
officer displayed outstanding
courage in the face of greatly
rs of enemy forces.

w DUNCAN (103203), South
ce, No. 1 Squadron.

ebruary, 1941, this officer was
rry out an offensive recon-
mpanied by another aircraft.
an advanced landing ground
aircraft was damaged and
iceable. He immediately took
aircraft and flew on, alone,
100 miles to his objective,
ne gunned the aerodrome, set
mail plane and blew up its
days earlier, during an attack
aerodrome, his commanding

Air Ministry,
1st April, 1941.

ROYAL AIR FORCE.

The KING has been graciously pleased to
approve the following awards :—

Air Force Cross.

Wing Commander Reginald Bryson WARDMAN
(29028).

Acting Wing Commander Francis Stanhope
HOMERSHAM, D.C.M., M.M. (19114).

Acting Wing Commander Peter Rodriquez MAY
(28048).

Acting Wing Commander Godfrey Cathbar
O'DONNELL, D.F.C. (04150).

Squadron Leader Cyril Carlile HODDER
(34124).

Squadron Leader Richard John Courtney
NEDWILL (34169).

Squadron Leader Mervyn Hugh RHYS (33012).

Squadron Leader Henry de Clifford Anthony
WOODHOUSE (34189).

Acting Squadron Leader Douglas George
ALLISON (70010), Reserve of Air Force
Officers.

London Gazette No 35124 - 1 April 1941.

The citation read:

'This officer has been employed as a flying instructor at No.4 Service Flying Training School for over two years, and is at present in charge of advanced training. He is a most capable pilot and an excellent exponent of the art of front gun attack. By his perseverance and hard work he has produced excellent results. Squadron Leader Nedwill has completed over 1,000 hours instructional flying.'

He was remembered as an alumnus of his old college - Canterbury Agricultural College Magazine No. 66 (Nov 1941).

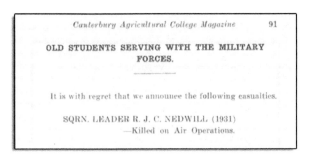

Canterbury Agricultural College Magazine 91

OLD STUDENTS SERVING WITH THE MILITARY
FORCES.

It is with regret that we announce the following casualties.

SQRN. LEADER R. J. C. NEDWILL (1931)
—Killed on Air Operations.

Chapter Thirty

'Two Men, a Boy and a Flying Hearse'

Over in Yugoslavia, the people had had enough, and the day after the death of Squadron Leader Nedwill, a revolution was afoot in the capital Belgrade. A Royal Yugoslav Army Air Force General called Dušan Simović, a pro-British Serbian-nationalist, had rid the country of Prince Paul Karađorđević to put seventeen-year-old King Peter II on the throne - Paul was a first cousin of Peter's father, Alexander I. It was a complicated situation but a situation which saw the people of Yugoslavia ready to fight against the Axis powers. The people of Belgrade fervently waved British and French flags on the streets in celebration of the coup, but this would be a short-lived celebration and within a week many of those celebrants would be dead through the Luftwaffe mercilessly bombing Belgrade and killing almost 4,000 of its citizens.

The reality of the Balkan situation would change the course of the war for Gerald and 211 Squadron. The men of 211 Squadron knew it was only a matter of time before the Germans made their push into Greece.

Back at Paramythia, The Bish was elsewhere and the new C.O. was dead but there was one wonderful piece of news in the day following, Flight Lieutenant Graham Danson 'Potato' Jones DFC, was made temporary commanding officer of 211 Squadron. Potato knew the squadron and its tactics inside out. Everyone was made up for him.

During Potato Jones' first briefing, Willie the Intelligence Officer informed everyone about what he knew about the Germans. And what he said was chilling.

"The Germans already have in the region of a thousand planes in the Balkans. Their air superiority is unquestionable and they are within easy striking distance of us now. That's not even mentioning their capabilities on the ground. Truth is they have a ground force which could crush any of the current opposition in its path. The Greeks cannot hope to hold them and, if what we think is going to happen... happens, then our only tactic could be delay, whilst we do our best to get the hell out of here. To conclude, we have to be extra careful wherever and whenever we go into action. It's the wops today, but tomorrow, or in a few days, it WILL be the huns. It could be both at once."

The briefing of the day was also attended by the other squadrons there. 84 Blenheim Squadron also had a new leader, he was Squadron Leader Hubert Jones, [1] whom everyone knew as 'Jonah Jones.' Jonah was a close friend of Tommy Wisdom from the Bafflers days and made everyone laugh with his comment, when he started his part of the briefing.

"We certainly have a fight on our hands, gentlemen," he began. "... looks like it's going to be a pleasant little show. All the wops in the world and half the Jerries, versus two men, a boy and a flying hearse."

Jonah was referring to the dangerously low resources the RAF had at their disposal, and Jonah Jones' succinct appraisal of the situation said it all. At this time the RAF in Greece had only 12 aircraft serviceable and many of these were the outdated and cumbersome Blenheims. Faced with a new enemy with the most vicious and up-to-date war machine on the planet, the coming battle would be a fight they might not win this time.

The briefing ended in silent contemplation as prayers were said for Squadron Leader Nedwill, who's funeral was due to take place on Friday 28th March.

By chance on that Friday, the Italians were unusually quiet. There'd been lots of warnings of air raids which never materialised. As usual, the best place for any of the squadrons was airborne and Paramythia was now a little stronger with the arrival of 113 Squadron to bolster the strength of 211 and 84 Squadrons. Several times that day, Gerald bombed the Italian fleet as it sailed down the Adriatic, close to the Yugoslav border. One Blenheim had been lost that day but everyone felt they had achieved some success making two direct hits on cruisers which were later fully sunk by the Royal Navy.

At 6pm that evening a big funeral for Squadron Leader Nedwill paraded through the streets of Paramythia and the poor unfortunate 27-year-old was laid to rest at Paramythia village church, with full military honours and the usual three gun salute.

Gerald wondered how long he could go on riding his luck, despite the lucky mascot in his tunic pocket.

*

Fortunes alter quickly in war and April would see that change. Adolf Hitler saw the Yugoslav coup, which had overthrown Prince Paul's pro-Axis government, as a personal insult. As a result, on 27 March 1941, he had called his top military advisors together to discuss the situation. From this meeting came Führer Directive number 25, which Adolf Hitler saw the planning of what the Germans called 'The April War.' The war began with some venom on 6 April 1941 with a blitzkrieg invasion of Yugoslavia.

Potato Jones brought the men together that evening at Paramythia to discuss tactics and strategies for dealing with this new menace.

Embros began by telling those present, "Our Government has announced today that the Nazis will be at our borders withins 24 hours and after that who knows whats."

Potato Jones also gave a stark warning to the men.

"And I've also heard The Germans are announcing on the radio that they will kill every British man they find on Greek soil, so now we know gentlemen, now we know. Keep those sidearms, or whatever some of you have in your kites close to you at all times, and if you are unfortunate enough to get shot down and you survive, there'll be no surrendering to the Nazi."

Gerald nodded and thought about his revolver in his plane. It was time to make sure he had it with him all the time.

Potato Jones went on, "This afternoon I heard that a Junkers 88 [2] shufti-kite was shot down over Patras by Flying Officer Pete Dowding of 33 Squadron. Tells us the reality of our situation. The Huns were taking a shufti at the defences of Athens. It's coming boys! It's coming!"

Potato Jones wasn't wrong, as when darkness fell a mass bombing raid by the Germans took place on the port of Athens at Piraeus. The fires created a glow in the skies visible for many miles. Gerald in the meantime had headed in the darkness to his Blenheim and had searched out his gun which he brought back to the tent with him.

"Just in case Arthur," he said, pulling the gun from the canvas holster with a handkerchief attached to the end of the barrel.

"What the hell's that?" Arthur said. "Looks like ready prepared surrender flag!" He laughed.

"Bloody hell, Arthur. I'd forgotten about that. It's Susan's."

"So now you've got the photo and a dirty hanky of Susan's. Our luck should be all in ol' man."

Gerald looked at the imprint of her lips in the flickering oil lamp. "See, she's there, Arthur. She kissed it for me before I left. They're her lips."

Gerald showed the handkerchief to Arthur.

"Nice! All I got from home was a comb and some Brylcreem."

Gerald looked at the lips as he lay down on his camp bed and kissed them. "Goodnight sweetheart. Goodnight."

*

News came to the squadron that a permanent new C.O. had been appointed. Someone called Tony Irvine had been promoted to Squadron Leader on 1st March and would be heading to lead 211 Squadron soon.

Buck Buchannan had some reservations about the new C.O. and, over a beer, shared what he knew with Arthur and Gerald.

"The new C.O., will be with you, so you need to know a few things gents," Buck had begun. "He's been over in North Africa since June of '40 at Port Sudan with 14 and Wellesleys."

"Those awful things!"

"Yep."

"So what's the issue?" Asked Gerald.

"No issue really…"

"No?"

"Well, there was some trouble of a sort. Don't get me wrong, Tony Irvine is experienced but I'm not sure he's the best decision maker, gents?"

Gerald and Arthur both breathed heavily together.

"There was something about tactics and a low level dusk attack on an Iti fuel dump. Nine Welleseys were involved, and Tony's oppo gave clear and concise instructions as to how the raid should be executed and the result was a very successful raid with not one loss."

"So what happened then?"

"Old Tony Irvine, has a mind of his own and wanted to do something different. Mid June last year it was when Irvine set out for a place called Massawa again. It was NOT an authorised sortie. The bugger broke the rules."

"Why?"

"Just because he had the mind to see how useful a broad daylight, yes broad daylight dive-bombing raid would be."

"And was it?" asked Arthur.

"They took two planes, so I heard, when they shouldn't have done. Well, Tony Irvine got back in one piece, but the guy who he persuaded to fly with him, a Reggie [3] someone or other, copped it out there. No one ever saw him again, and they didn't find any trace of his plane either.

"So didn't they court-marshall him?"

"What in these days of pilot shortages? No. They posted him to 113 Squadron... er ... so they got him out of the way."

Gerald looked worried. "And now he's with us. I suppose everyone is allowed to make mistakes."

Buck nodded. "Pretty worrying though, hey? Poor decision making does no one any good."

*

News updates about the German advance were almost non existent in the days to follow. Communications seemed to have gone down everywhere, and even Embros was struggling to find out what was going on. As a result, the base at Paramythia was almost paralysed as no one, not even the new C.O., knew where they should be raiding. His orders were to take down the camp and prepare to evacuate.

The air raids by the Germans intensified across Greece and Gerald and the other men slept in an old derelict house not far from the base, as most of the equipment had been loaded and ready to go.

"We'll be away from here Easter Friday. There is no way we can stem the tide of this advance." Potato Jones announced with some conviction, but as Easter Friday came, the boys of 211 Squadron were told they had to wait at least another twenty-four hours before leaving. Some bright spark at Greece H.Q., wanted the British forces to remain until the very last minute to check the German advance. The theory being this would give others a chance to evacuate the country. That included the King of Yugoslavia, who had sped south to avoid the

German occupation of his country.

*

Back home in Shotton it was Easter Friday, 11th April. Lizzie, Francis and their children had headed to Rivertown Congregational church as they always did on Good Friday. They'd met with Frank and Edith, and everyone had prayed for the safety of Gerald while he was away.

The radio was reporting a huge German advance on the Yugoslav-Greek border.

Lizzie squeezed her eyes and said a little private prayer for Gerald, hoping he was well away from any areas of trouble. Little did she know he was right on the front line.

*

Susan Hall paraded with the Upper Thames Patrol as the Davies family, whom she'd never met, were in church. She had listened to the radio, which was full of talk about the German intentions in Greece. She couldn't talk to anyone about how she felt, and she really wanted to express her concerns for Gerald's safety, but everyone was in the same situation and no one would listen, anyway.

*

In those days leading up to Easter weekend of April 1941, Squadron Leader Potato Jones had been called to H.Q., and once again the Squadron was to get a new commanding officer. The twenty-seven-year-old Squadron Leader Tony Irvine, originally a Birkenhead lad, led his first raid on advancing German forces with Gerald and Arthur. It was an eye-opener for everyone concerned and a bit of a wobble for the squadron.

The de-briefing had seen concerned faces. No one had seen so much armour on the move in one place, even with the huge North African experience most of them had.

"We were so lucky to have the Hurri-buses with us," Gerald commented quietly to Arthur, "otherwise it would have been curtains for us all."

The Hurricane squadrons were out in force trying to stem the tide of the German advance into Greece, and as the country increasingly came under attack from the Germans, British RAF units were diverted to Greece. At the forefront was 80 Squadron and on the twelfth of April they were rejoined once again by Pilot Officer Roald Dahl who had been declared fit to fly again and had flown in his new and newly acquired Hurricane to Eleusis, near Athens, where the Germans had already arrived with their killer 109s. The bullet holes everywhere and damaged aircraft on the ground were testament to that.

One of the ground crew had commented to him, "We'll be overrun by Krauts soon son, millions of 'em there are. You'll see and we ain't got nowhere to go... 'cept the sea. It'll be Dunkirk all over again, son. One tip sonny, if one of those 109s gets on your arse end, you're done for. Don't let the bastards get behind you!"

This would be a baptism of fire for him, but he was yet to face the worst.

Further north in Greece 211 Squadron still lay waiting for news about what their orders would be and on that Easter Saturday night, Gerald once again sat with several of the men from the squadron, all concerned as to whether they might be evacuated or whether they might have to undertake a few more missions to the front to tackle the invaders.

Gerald sat down and wrote a letter to Lizzie. "It's a just-in-case letter," he anguished to Arthur.

"Just in case what?"

"Just in case!" Was all he repeated.

Gerald sealed the letter into an envelope and settled down to sleep and placed the photograph of him and Susan onto a loose stone near his bed so he could see it and fall asleep looking at Susan's face. His revolver with the lipstick stained handkerchief lay alongside it.

Author's Note

[1] Squadron Leader Hubert Douglas Jones, the C.O. of 84 Squadron. Killed in action on 18 April 1941 aged 27 years. The Blenheim he was piloting whilst attacking German troops in the Larissa area of Greece was shot down by two Messerschmitt Bf 110's. Squadron Leader Jones managed to put the stricken aircraft down onto the sea but all the crew were killed when the aircraft was further strafed in the sea by Messerschmitt Bf 109's. Local residents buried the crew in the Greek village of Keramidi. Now buried at Phaleron War Cemetery, Athens. (Quote from Squadron Leader Jones courtesy of Wings Over Olympus p. 171)

[2] Shot down at 3pm on 6th April 1941 by Flying Officer Dowding as it approached Athens. Dowding saw the plane and pursued it over the Gulf of Corinth in his Hurricane. The two planes exchanged fire and Dowding's plane was hit but not badly damaged. Dowding continued to fire and the German plane crashed into the sea off Patras. On board was Unteroffizier Fritz Dreyer and two of his crew. All were killed.

[3] Pilot Officer Reginald Patrick Blennerhassett Plunkett. 14 Squadron RAF Killed in Action 14th June 1940 flying Wellesley K7743. Aged 23 years.

No known grave - memorialised at Panel 9. Runnymede Memorial.

Chapter Thirty-one

'Easter Sunday'

It was Easter Sunday, 13th April 1941.

Lizzie, Francis and the three children had gone to Riverside Church on the Main Street in Shotton, as they always did on this day. They'd spoken to Frank and Edith who were there, and things seemed to be going well between the family. Since Gerald had gone missing back in late November, there seemed to be a bond between them.

"We have to have a united front for Gerald's sake" Lizzie had commented after the telegram of November. All had agreed.

That morning, they sang hymns and said prayers for all families with troops fighting away.

*

Gerald and Arthur breakfasted at first light. It was just a cup of tea with tinned bacon and eggs before they had a shave. The rations were running low, as everyone had expected to have left by now. Worse still, to a man, everyone was nervous about the day ahead and what might be before them. Someone mentioned it was Easter Sunday, but no one said any prayers out loud. One or two had said, 'Where is bloody God in all of this?' Others whispered prayers to themselves, to whoever was above, to keep them safe that day.

No one had time to think about God, anyway. Everyone's thoughts were for survival, and they had been for some time now. Gone were the good old days of Ismailia and Athens, before them was the reality of a dirty and intensifying war.

Gerald found one of the ground crew, Jimmy Riddle. He trusted Jim and knew he would do as he was asked, besides which Jim was from the same county as him in Wales. He gave him the letter addressed to Lizzie Davies at 6 Ashfield Road, Shotton.

"If I don't get back, make sure it's posted for me Jim."

"Will do, sir" he replied. "Good luck later. It's hell out there I hear."

Gerald smiled. "We'll give them hell back, Jim."

There was one tent remaining at Paramythia, and that was where the radio was based. Inside was the Cipher Officer Flying Officer Alexander Fabian, who everyone knew as 'Curly' - he was listening out, as usual for any orders coming through from H.Q.

Gerald heard Curly's frantic shout…

"Troops and M.T. on the road north of Lake Ochrida. No fighter escort available to us gents!"

"Arthur!" shouted Gerald. "Come on, we're on the move."

"The Yugoslavs have been routed and the Huns are coming hell for leather south." Curly shouted again.

They rushed around gathering their bits and pieces and were soon airborne with six other planes, but poor weather blocked their path and they soon returned.

The Blenheims were refuelled from four-gallon tins of petrol which a plane had delivered earlier and everyone waited nervously for the orders to head off again. All the planes were loaded with a mixture of 250lb and fragmentation bombs.

At twenty to four in the afternoon, Squadron Leader Irvine gave the order to head off again. The sun had come out and the day had transformed into a beautiful Spring day.

"A good to be alive day," Gerald joked as he climbed into the Blenheim and sat at the controls. "A bit of a concern we have no fighter escort with us though, hey?"

Squadron Leader Irvine sighed. "Well, we can't have everything, can we Gerry? We need to get out there and confront the hun!"

"Without fighter protection, it could be a dice with death sir?"

"Nonsense, we'll be all right. We'll be just fine." He seemed to be reassuring himself. "In you lot, I know I have a wealth of experience I can rely on. I'm sure there won't be much opposition out there. The Huns have got more to do with their time than look for some old clapped out Blenheims."

"Fingers crossed, sir."

Tony Irvine nodded in agreement and went on, " Besides which, even I had no say so today in this operation. The boys from H.Q. want a shufti at what's going on."

Gerald almost didn't hear the last remark of Tony Irvine as he felt in his pocket for THAT photograph, to realise he'd left it on the stone near his temporary sleeping arrangements.

"Shit!" he exclaimed.

"What's that, Gerry? You saw something?"

"No... er... no, nothing Skip. Nothing."

Gerald's face said it all. Gerald fumbled for with his revolver and removed it from the canvas holster.

"Not going to shoot me are you, ol' man." Tony Irvine said, looking worried at the sight of the gun.

Gerald laughed. "Definitely not, just need my handkerchief."

Gerald pulled the handkerchief free and re-holstered the gun. He looked at the lipstick mark and touched it to his face.

Tony Irvine must have thought he was wiping his nose, but Gerald had kissed the lipstick and breathed the smell of Susan deeply in.

He sighed. <'A new lucky mascot for me. Thank goodness!'>

Gerald placed the handkerchief down between his thighs and smiled to himself. He was safe now, despite his misgivings about Tony Irvine, who was flying them towards an enemy who would outnumber them massively. He hoped against hope they would not meet too much opposition. Arthur Geary was oblivious to anything and remained unusually quiet in his usual position as gunner, watching the skies avidly for bandits.

As the six aircraft had left the approaching purple shadows of Paramythia, there were some temporary newcomers hitching a ride, at the behest of John D'Albiac. Wing Commander Paddy Coote and Squadron Leader Les Cryer had come from Western Wing Headquarters in Athens, to get first-hand information about the German movements into Greece and it was they who were responsible for ordering the raid, with not one Hurricane or even a Gloster Gladiator in sight to protect them.

The formation of six Blenheims, noisily rumbled their way north.

Gerald and crew were leading in L8478.

In L4819 were Herby, Paddy, Jock and the Wing Commander.

L1434 contained Buck, Les Cryer and George Pattison.

L8449 was flown by Peggy O'Neil, with Godfrey and Jack Wainhouse

L8664 was piloted by Tommy Thompson, with Pete Hogarth and the oldest member of the squadron at 38, Wilf Arscott.

Bringing up the rear was L1539 flown by Andy Bryce with Pongo Waring and Jimmy James.

Initially, they flew through the azure skies of a perfect Greek afternoon, but ahead there was broken cloud over the mountains and the Monastir Gap, which they knew the Germans were flooding through.

Gerald was happier now he'd seen the handkerchief and then touched it now and then for reassurance. He tried to put to the back of his mind that he'd forgotten the photograph, but the thought niggled him from time to time, so he chatted freely with Tony Irvine to try to forget about the photograph.

"So, how do you find this old bird then, Gerry?"

"The Blenheim… well… er… yes… The Blenheim… what a great flyer, with a remarkable and reliable engine. You know, I've been in one of these kites which kept on flying, despite losing half its bodywork… and an engine too, so I suppose I would say that the old bird is a workhorse of a machine without a doubt… er… but…"

"There's always a but hey." Tony Irvine smiled.

"Er… yes… I suppose it's a like comparing a racehorse with a cart horse, if I'm honest. I mean, it gets the job done, but it's a lot slower and it's no war horse is it?"

"We can but hope that after this the powers that be will see sense and get us upgraded, hey Gerry?"

Gerald was feeling more despondent than ever, having forgotten his mascot photograph. He said it as it was. "I could name a few now who've gone down in this flying hearse - not my words… those of Jonah the other day. The Messerschmitt Bf 109 is our biggest threat I am told, so let's hope, without our fighters, we don't meet any today."

Tony Irvine nodded. "Well, I'll keep my fingers crossed for us. I'm optimistic by nature you know. Take the fight to the enemy and surprise them when they least expect it. That's what I say."

"Let's hope we surprise them, Skip. If we meet 109s, I think we're in for some heavy trouble. A thousand planes Willie said the Jerries have at their disposal. That's a lot more than we've ever seen."

"A thousand?"

"So I'm told."

"Well, they won't all be up at once and in the same place will they, hey?"

"Four or five, or even two 109s might be enough to see us off."

Tony Irvine said nothing.

"You know what Skip, I'll be astounded if any of us get away with it in this damn war. There's a sort of inevitability about it all. We all say, if it's our day to go, then so be it, but we'll go down fighting."

"We've all lost someone."

"Yep. It's very sad when you lose your pals, I mean Nedwill was only here four days. FOUR damn days, poor soul. The odds are stacked against us, but we always do our best... life and the war goes on, hey?"

Squadron Leader Irvine tried not to show how nervous he was, but inside he was terrified. Even to him, the Germans and the northern frontier of Greece were an unknown quantity. He thought about his response, then smiled. "That's the ticket, Gerry. Keep the pecker up!"

The squadron flew on, parachutes strapped on and uniform ties neatly done up. Only the British would wear a necktie on a bombing run!

Gerald shouted back to Arthur. "You're quiet, Arth?"

"Concentrating Gerry, lad. Concentrating! Besides, I don't want to move much, I might knock a valve out."

He laughed over the intercom and said no more.

*

The German high command was afraid that British bombers based in Greece, if allowed to remain there unchecked, would bomb the Romanian oil fields which were the only supply of oil the Germans possessed on the Eastern front. This would halt the proposed Operation Barbarossa[1] in its tracks. So, on the ground somewhere ahead of the Blenheims, in the Florina area of the mountainous Macedonia in northern Greece, Field Marshal Wilhelm List, commanded the German 12th Army in the invasion of Greece - Operation Marita. To rid Greece of the British. To bypass the fortified Metaxas line to the north-east of Greece, the Germans had two points of easy access to Greece, one was at Mt. Belles and the other weak spot was the Monastir pass. If this area fell to the Germans, the Greek army in Albania would be surrounded and forced to capitulate.

In charge of the German offensive at Monastir Pass was General der Panzertruppe Georg Stumme, a 55-year-old veteran of the First World War and now commander of the 9th Panzer Corps and the elite SS

Adolf Hitler Regiment.

No one had any idea, just how big his forces were, but before the Blenheims was an approaching blitzkrieg, the likes of which had only been seen when the low-countries and France were invaded not that many months before. It was an immense force of men and machines which totally outmatched the Greek defending forces. Salonika had already fallen to the Germans, Yugoslavia had capitulated, and all the gains made by the Greeks in their advances towards Valona and Durazzo were now at risk. The Greeks' only option was to pull back from Albania to stop their men being encircled by the German advance. It was clear to all, Greece was going to be occupied. It was just a matter of how much time this would take.

John D'Albiac knew 211 Squadron was the only RAF unit with anywhere near like the experience and capability to tackle and slow down such an invasion and to help British and allied forces led by a colossus of a man with the nickname 'Jumbo' - General Henry Maitland Wilson. His forces were the only ones now on the ground who had any chance of doing anything to slow down the German invasion, but they needed air support from 211 Squadron. Time was fast approaching when they would all confront the forces of the German 12th Army - an altogether different and unknown proposition.

The six Blenheims of 211 Squadron flew through the partially cloud covered steep crags of the mountains which they knew so well and over which they'd flown so many missions before. Everyone knew the dangers and were quite aware that ice and foul weather had seen off many a plane. It was only in December they had lost The Airedale, Pilot Officer Jerdein and Pickers, because of atrocious weather in these same mountain ranges.

They flew on at 7,000 feet, which gave them some 1500 feet of clearance from the rocks below. They were divided into two flights with A-Flight leading in a V formation and B-Flight astern in the same formation.

At the front of A-Flight was L8478 with Gerald on board and flying either side, but slightly behind to form the V were Blenheims L4819 and L1434. B-Flight were astern with L8449 leading and L8604 and L1539 once again forming the V.

"Approaching target area!" announced Gerald. "Eyes open, gents."

The planes dropped out of low cloud and into clear skies.

*

* * *

Ahead and as yet unseen by any of the Blenheim crews, were three Messerschmitt 109E-4 fighters from 6 Staffel/Jagdgeschwader 27. *[2]* The planes were protecting the advancing German 12th Army on the ground from any potential air attack.   The lead Messerschmitt was piloted by Hauptmann Hans-Joachim Gerlach.   All the pilots in the formation had seen action in the Battle of Britain and were experienced in air-to-air combat.   None of the German pilots had seen the RAF formation either.

*

As Gerald looked down at the roads below, they were crawling with German soldiers, tanks and military vehicles of every kind. More than he'd ever seen in his life before.

"Jesus gents. Below at ten o'clock."

It was the 9th Panzer Corps and the elite SS Adolf Hitler Regiment. Transport lorries, tanks and heavy artillery galore being pulled along the road; pouring through the Monastir Gap towards Kozani. Australian and Greek troops were fighting a losing battle below and were quickly withdrawing towards Mt. Olympus.

"Let's give them hell" Squadron Leader Irvine shouted as the six Blenheims headed for the massed German armies on the move.

The squadron knew the exact routine and, going down twice and low over the roads below them, crammed with German armaments, they delivered their bomb loads within the space of a minute.   The German troops fired at them with any gun they could lay their hands on but none of the Blenheims were hit.

"We're away lads" shouted Gerald, knowing that the bomb bays were empty.   He'd seen the bombs fall in and around the troop movements, but the drop didn't seem to have made much difference. There would be no machine gun fire as this was to be reserved for any potential attack from the air.

They could do no more now.

"Paddy Coote and Les Cryer will have seen what they need to see," shouted Tony Irvine. "Let's head home chaps."

It was two minutes past four in the afternoon of Easter Sunday as the squadron turned to port.

<'The best words spoken all day by the new C.O.'>

Then he saw them.

Three of them in formation and approaching at breakneck speed. Messerschmitt 109s.

"Bandits at six o'clock below!" shouted Gerald with some force down the intercom. Everyone heard it and took evasive action. The cumbersome Blenheims had no chance of outrunning the approaching Messerschmitt 109s who could easily fly 100 m.p.h. faster.

"Heading west into the sun! Defensive box formation! Emergency Nine Boost Lever"

"Gotcha Leader."

The Bristol Mercury 840hp engines would be supercharged on all the planes as a result, giving them some extra emergency power.

All six planes headed at speed for the heavily wooded and rocky sided valley. The winding rough valley road which led towards the village of Alona, was as close as Gerald had ever seen the ground at the speed they were going at. In the fuselage Arthur Geary waited to pound away with the machine gun and Gerald watched as a burst of fire came past from a pursuing 109. They were still too far away though, to be accurate. No more shots were fired.

It was more than a worry. Each of the 109s was capable of firing 60 rounds of high explosive armour-piercing cannon rounds, at over 400 rounds a minute. That wasn't the only extent of their firepower. The 109s were each equipped with two 7.9mm machine guns mounted in the engine nacelle. These guns could fire over a thousand rounds per minute.

At three minutes past four the six Blenheims almost took the red roof tiles off houses in the village of Alona. Villagers below, tending to their crops and animals, stopped what they were doing to look at the spectacle. Those inside the homes raced out to see what was going on, some ducking with fright as the planes sped past. No one had seen planes this close before. They cheered for the RAF and hissed and spat as the swastika laden 109s went by, closing in on the planes of 211 Squadron.

The Blenheims stuck to their plan and headed into the sun. Gerald and the others knew it was their only option in such a circumstance.

Gerald was looking for cloud too. Cloud was safety.

At four minutes past four, the six Blenheims were now climbing to gain height as they headed further down the valley, passing the village of Vigla, sweeping right towards the hamlet of Pisoderi towards Lake Prespa.

"Hold formation chaps!"

Gerald and crew led in L8478 and all remained in close 'box' formation. All were still safe but their futures looking precarious, as the 109s closed in to select their targets.

*

It had almost turned five past four on Easter Sunday afternoon. In Shotton it was two hours earlier, 2.04pm, and Lizzie was walking back home along Chester Road. Leaving Francis at home to read yesterday's newspapers, she'd just walked the three children Cliff, Vince and Ruby to the Rivertown Church Sunday school and was returning home for a pleasant cup of tea without the children. She looked forward to that on a Sunday afternoon. It gave her chance to have five minutes to herself and prepare sandwiches for an early afternoon tea when the children got back. She'd learned from experience they were always hungry after Sunday School was over. It was a pleasant sunny afternoon and at last spring seemed to have arrived. Things felt good but she always worried about Gerald and the newspaper reports she'd briefly looked at yesterday told a story of a battle just where Gerald was.

Francis had bought two newspapers on the Saturday, the Daily Mirror and The Daily Herald. By the time Lizzie was walking back from Sunday school he'd read the papers from front to back and from back to front over the past day or so. The front pages of both newspapers carried headlines about the war in the north of Greece.

Right at that moment in Henley, Susan Hall was helping her parents plant vegetables in the garden of their Thames riverside home. People passed by on the river. It was the first chance anyone had had that year of getting out on the river when it wasn't cold and people were taking advantage of the warmth now in the air.

Susan watched as the odd boat went by, some people waved as she dug away at the soil to make a bed for the potting plants her father had nurtured over the past few weeks. She waved back.

She saw one or two couples rowing on the river and thought about those heady days of last summer when she'd been on the river with Gerald. Reminders of Gerald were everywhere. She looked across to the open garage where she could see Gerald's beloved MG just waiting for the moment he got back. As Susan dug away at the garden she dreamed of those future drives in the countryside, drinks at The

Horns or boat rides with Hobbs.

She wondered when she would hear from Gerald again after the last letter just a few days ago.

*

It was now five past four in northern Greece.

The rock slopes surrounding the village of Antartiko had new and noisy visitors, as the three Messerschmitt 109E-4 fighters came into range behind the squadron.

"Jesus, they're close." Arthur Geary shouted. Bursts of gunfire followed from one of the Blenheims behind. Arthur Geary didn't have a shot with his single Vickers GO .303 inch machine gun in the rear turret. The others from the squadron were behind and in his line of fire.

"At 800 yards, Gerry."

"Gotcha Arthur."

Then they heard it and saw the 20mm cannon bursts from the wings of the 109s. Tracer bullets whizzed past them, but they were not hit. Behind them, they heard the other Blenheims hammering away with their turret machine guns.

The leader of the three 109s, Hauptmann Gerlach, once again grasped the trigger on the control stick of his Messerschmitt and fired a burst of tracer to sight the Blenheim L8449 flown by Flying Officer Godfrey. Almost immediately, with the plane in his sights, Gerlach fired off a burst of armour piercing cannon round, hitting the Blenheim.

Gerald heard Godfrey's shout over the intercom.

"Jesus, boys. Going down. Crew dead."

Arthur Geary chirped up. "He's brolly'd! Plane's gone down on fire."

"Godfrey? Christ! He's only at 300 feet!"

Then another burst of cannon came. This time it hit Blenheim L8604 piloted by Tommy Thompson. The intercom was silent.

Both L8449 and L8604 [3] crashed to the ground in flames near the village of Karia (Karies) as Gerald, Tony and Arthur looked on horrified and helpless. Two of the six Blenheims were now gone and those remaining were in the fight of their lives.

*

* * *

Back home, Lizzie walked in and talked with Francis.

"Stop reading those damn papers, Francis. They're doing no one any good."

"Look, Lizzie, it says here that the RAF in northern Greece is battering Hitler's Panzers. Damn Nazis. That's our Gerald doing his bit."

"I don't want to hear Francis, you know that. If he's involved in that battle, you can be sure he's being fired at himself. Who knows what's going on? It's a worry all the time. All I want to do is hear that he's safe."

"You will, you will. Now let's have that nice cup of tea you promised before you walked up the road with the children."

Back near Lake Pespa in northern Greece, Gerald looked at his watch; it had just turned six minutes past four. He knew Lizzie's routine and knew she'd just be arriving home, having taken the children to Sunday school. Thoughts whisked through his head of times at Rivertown Sunday School and prizes he'd achieved there. He remembered how chuffed everyone was to see his name in the local newspapers. He was a far cry from all of that now.

Gerald broke to port and headed east, followed by L4819 with Herby, Paddy and Jock on board. The other two Blenheims broke to the starboard with 109s close in. It was too late for L1539 and its crew, Andy Bryce, Pongo (Arthur Waring) and Jimmy. The 109 behind had closed in and strafed the plane, killing Andy and Pongo outright. Jimmy James [4], pulled back the escape hatch and just baled out in time before the plane hit the ground and exploded, as it hit marshy ground to the south-west of the village of Mikrolimni on the shoreline of Lake Prespa.

The rear V formation of Blenheims was now gone and the 109s concentrated on the remaining three aircraft.

The radio crackled in. It was Buck in L1434. [5] "I'm hit chaps. Everyone else gone. Not looking good. Gonna try to pancake it down on the lake. There's still enough control. If I don't make it, say my goodbyes to… "

There was nothing more. Buck and his crew were gone. They skimmed into the shallow waters at the south end of Little Lake Prespa, just over the invisible border into Albania.

Gerald gripped the handkerchief given him by Susan tight between his knees. "Come on, come on!" he shouted. "We have to get to cloud cover."

Inside, he prayed away like mad. Now the salty taste of fear Czech Pilot Sergeant Josef František had told him about at Northolt all that time ago, dripped down his face.

Arthur Geary rattled his machine gun at the 109, closing in fast. He now had a clear line of fire.

Another minute had gone by and the two remaining Blenheims were now dicing with death in the skies of northern Greece. L8478 and L4819, each being pursued by a much more powerful Messerschmitt 109. In those Blenheims were six terrified young men, all doing their utmost, working hard to stay alive, against overwhelming odds. Gerald, at 23 wasn't the youngest, that was Herby piloting the other plane. The oldest in the planes were Gerald's friend Arthur Geary and Paddy Coote, who were both 31.

"We have no option but to head east otherwise we're sitting ducks open over the lake!" Gerald shouted as he weaved the Blenheim around to head back into the mountains followed by L4819.

"Sun's not good!"

Gerald remembered the words of Josef František as they repeated in his head.

<'Beware of the gun in the sun. Beware of the gun in the sun!'>

It was too late, the fatal error had been forced by the Germans. Gerald shouted as he saw the sun behind them. "Lights us up like a proper target. We need those damn clouds."

Gerlach pressed his cannon to fire, but he had used up all his ammunition, as had the other 109 pilots in bringing down the first four Blenheims. The 109s accelerated forward; they would need to be nearer to use their machine guns

"Climbing to 4,000!" shouted Herby, as he sent the Blenheim into a steep climb to avoid the tops of the mountains. Then a burst of machine gun fire came from the 109 behind him.

"He's hit!" Arthur Geary announced with more panic in his voice than Gerald had ever heard. Tony Irvine was eerily quiet, as if frozen in the moment.

Smoke and fire poured from Herby's Blenheim and it fell uncontrolled towards the village of Trigonon.

"They're baling out!" [6] Arthur cracked. "They're hell of a low! Shit. Not good."

Gerald saw none of it and headed away alone. Arthur Geary still fired away from his turret. Gerald felt thankful he had Arthur close.

* * *

*

It was now almost ten past four on Easter Sunday afternoon. Back in Lizzie's house the tea was brewing and at Henley-on-Thames, Susan Hall had also settled down for a pleasant drink of tea with some biscuits on the lawn as she and her parents watched people passing along the river. The first flies of the season had appeared on the water and skipped back and to, with the fish jumping out for a tasty meal now and then. It was an idyllic scene at any stretch of the imagination.

In both the Shotton and Henley households, Gerald was never far from their minds.

*

Gerald had climbed up to almost 6000 feet, aiming for beautiful billowing clouds ahead.

"All we can hope for is they're low on ammo. Looks like they're out of cannon, so we might be in luck," he shouted to the frozen Tony Irvine. Arthur Geary was replacing the last feed of bullets into his gun.

Behind and closing, the leader of the Messerschmitts, Hauptmann Hans-Joachim Gerlach, said on the radio, "Dieser gehört mir!" *'This one is mine.'*

He pulled the trigger to to operate the 7.9mm machine guns in the engine nacelle. A short burst and Blenheim L8478 was hit. As Gerald looked out to the right and left, he saw both engines instantly on fire and shedding metal everywhere. One prop shaft had gone completely. This wasn't anything like crash-landing at Lefkimmi anymore, this was much worse. The controls were completely useless, and the plane was going into free-fall.

Gerald shouted to Arthur, but there was nothing. Arthur was dead, hit directly with one of the bullets. He'd have known little about it. His body was now slumped against the radio equipment he'd used so efficiently over the years. As Gerald looked to his right, Tony Irvine was also hit and unconscious, blood pouring from every orifice on his head.

The outdated Blenheim had met its match.

Gerald looked down and saw blood coming from his chest. He'd had no idea he'd been hit. Whatever had hit him was painless, and he couldn't move at all. He grasped the lipstick, kissed handkerchief and held it to his face. Everything seemed in slow motion. Gerald sang the Squadron song…

"Everybody's Doin' It, Doin' It…
  Early in the morning, at the break of dawning,
  See all the Blenheims, lined in a row,
  See the flight mechanic, turning little handles,
  Chuff, chuff, chuff, and away we go.
  Two Eleven's shaking 'em, shaking 'em, shaking 'em,
  Two Eleven's shaking 'em, shaking 'em, shaking 'em…"

Gerald, the lad from the backstreets of Shotton, who'd made officer in the RAF, drifted into a time when he was on the Thames with Susan and everything went black.

Hauptmann Hans-Joachim Gerlach watched the out of control L8478 *[7]* hurtle towards the ground near the small hamlet of Vigla in northern Greece. The plane burst into flames upon impact. Hauptmann Hans-Joachim Gerlach looked up to the heavens as he banked away with the other 109s.

"Das ist Krieg. Es tut mir leid, meine Kameraden."
'This is war. I am sorry, my comrades.'
He felt no pleasure at seeing his flying compatriots die.
Not one of the six aircraft who had left Paramythia that day had survived.

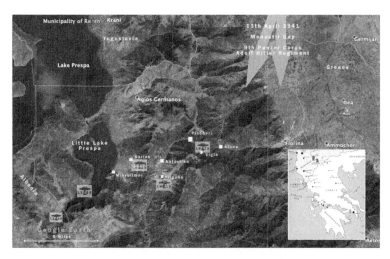

Image: Google Earth. Map of the hills surrounding the lakes at Prespa and

locations where the six Blenheim aircraft crashed. Inset is the map of Greece.

Alternative Ending to Gerald's Life and Comment by Author

In 1983 an Edward Nourse *[8]* spoke to eyewitnesses to the incident in 1983. One eyewitness was a man called Kias Filkos a villager in the area where the six planes crashed.

This is what he said.

'One Blenheim had crash-landed in a farmer's field after jettisoning its bombs, found unexploded on the mountainside. One of the crew had baled out but at low-level and his body was found impaled on the branches of the trees. One of the crew was alive but was trapped in the front cockpit. He was shouting for help and was firing his pistol in the air. There was a small fire and he was burning from the waist down. He died before they could get him out. The two airmen were buried in an unmarked grave about a hundred metres from the crash. A bomb was found in this aircraft. Two pairs of fleece-lined boots were found and bits of uniform and a parachute. All the crew were officers.'

Note *[6]* below suggests the plane was L4819, but from the witness information given, it also suggests this was Gerald and his crew in L8478, but there is no way to confirm this either way. However, L8478 Blenheim was the only one which contained ALL RAF officers. The other Blenheims contained a mixture of ranks.

It beggars belief that people who fought in the war should have suffered so badly, but they did.

I almost didn't include this report as part of the book, such were the disturbing circumstances of the crash, as witnessed by Kias Filkos. So, when I wrote about Gerald's death, I altered the circumstances, so you the reader, could make your own mind up about this.   It seems the truth of this matter is that the crew   of L8478 probably died from what they feared most - FIRE and being burned alive.

The truth of this matter is much more shocking.

Author's Note

[1] Operation Barbarossa (commenced 22 June 1941) - Nazi Germany's ideological goal to conquer the western Soviet Union and repopulate it with Germans.

[2] The Luftwaffe Messerschmitt 109E-4 Pilots:

Feldwebel Herbert Krenz - killed in action in the Western Desert - September I, 1942

Unteroffizier Fritz Gromotka - survived the war, dying in 1981 of old age.

Shot down 27 planes during the war..

Hauptmann Hans-Joachim Gerlach - was shot down the next day (14 April 1941). He baled out and spent the rest of the war as a PoW.

[3] Blenheims L8449 and L8604 crashed near the village of Karies in Northern Greece. Whilst there is no trace of where one of the Blenheims crashed, there is a gouged crash crater in corn fields there which, as a mark of respect, has been left undisturbed by local farmers to this day. Flight Lieutenant Alan Godfrey, whilst drifting down on his parachute, was witness to the events which followed.

[4] Sergeant James, the pilot, baled out at but was at a low altitude. He hit the ground heavily and as a result he broke his ankle.

[5] L1434. An unconfirmed report states that Flight Lieutenant Lindsay Basil Buchanan (Buck) and Squadron Leader Leslie Edward Cryer died of their injuries in a local hospital. The air gunner, Sergeant George Pattison DFM, died outright in the aircraft and is commemorated on the war memorial at Barnard Castle. In 1992, the wreckage of L1434 was discovered in Mikro Prespa (Little Lake Prespa) and the remains recovered by the Greek authorities. An engine and part of a wing now form a display at the Hellenic Air Force Museum, Acharnes north of Athens.

[6] L4819 - Crashes near Trigonon in northern Greece. Before crashing all bale out but only one parachute is seen to partially open partially as the unfortunate crew member plummets into the woods there. All aboard are killed.

[7] Villagers buried the bodies of airmen they found in the churchyards of Karia and Akritas. There is a plaque on the gate at the church in Karie which was erected by 211 Squadron at a later date. It reads:

'To commemorate the air action in this area on the 13th April 1941 in which 16 aircrew of No. 211 (B) Squadron RAF gave their lives in the defence of Greece. Our sincere thanks to the Priest and villagers of Karie who found and interred several of these aircrew in this churchyard.'

The whole of this incident is described in some detail in 'Fly Past' November 1983.

The combat reports of the pilots who shot down the Blenheims, were traced, and the full story revealed.

[8] In May 1983 Edward Nourse who had become interested in the story, visited the area and spoke with eye witnesses who remembered seeing the Blenheims being shot down, hence there is such a comprehensive account available - see page 242 Blenheim Over The Balkans.

Tragedy was to come to the two survivors who baled out. Sergeant Jimmy

James was killed two days later and Flying Officer Godfrey died on 7 August 1946 in a mid-air collision over North Wales.

Chapter Thirty-two

'Godfrey's Tale'

The twelve Hurricanes operating in Greece were increasingly struggling to hold back the flood of German planes coming across the border from the north. Alone, Pilot Officer Dahl had been dealing with a huge of armada German bombers attacking shipping at Chalcis in eastern Greece on Easter Sunday. It was his first ever foray into battle in the Hurricane. His eight Brownings had fired away and he'd taken enough metal off the engine of a Junkers 88 bomber to send it on its way to the ground below, its crew all baling safely.

*

At Paramythia, the ground crew had waited and waited for the return of the six Blenheims, but in the end everyone agreed they must be lost. King Peter of Yugoslavia had arrived at the base on the instructions of the British and was whisked away to the relative safety of Menidi in Athens in L8533, the only flyable Blenheim available. Even so, this aircraft had been well shot-up. The place where the turret should have been was boarded up with a piece of plywood as the turret had been lost in combat.

The presumed death of everyone in the squadron was a shocking event and the airfield at Paramythia was hastily packed away by the ground crew remaining. The swastika from the German Embassy which had been hung by Buck outside his tent was now safely tucked in a bag to head its way with the rest of the ground crew to Menidi.

Knowing the Germans might be on their way soon, the ground crew at Paramythia destroyed papers and several fires were lit. Any piece of paper which they couldn't remove from the site was burned.

The process of clearing Paramythia took a couple of days and as everyone drove away with the supplies, the wind got up and there was one thing blowing across the deserted grass runway in the Valley of Fairy Tales - the picture of Gerald and Susan.

*

A few days after the tragic events of Easter Sunday, Tommy Wisdom was in Athens and had been told one of the crew had survived and was in hospital. He headed over to the hospital Athens and couldn't believe his eyes. There, all bandaged up, was Flight Lieutenant Alan Clement Godfrey.

Notebook in hand, Tommy asked what had happened. *[1]*

"We had run out of cloud. We went on towards the target. Then Me 109s were reported - I don't know how many. We were ordered to dive. Next thing the cockpit was a mass of flames. As they blazed up in my face, I tore the hatch back and jumped. We were at about 300 feet then - my parachute opened just as I hit the ground. I noticed that there were three aircraft in the air - all in flames. My crew was dead. Sergeant James had baled out too - he was hurt. We saw one aircraft - it was Tommy's' I think - dive into the lake. We saw the two remaining aircraft going away to the East. A 109 was on the tail of each. No one knows what happened to them."

"Jesus, Godfrey. That's one hell of a time you've had. So they're all dead then, apart from you and Jimmy James?

"We buried our friends - those we could find - and struggled back the 150 miles to Larissa, on foot, on mule-back and finally, in a Greek lorry."

"My mate, happy-go-lucky Gerry? Arthur? The others in the plane?"

"Don't know Tommy. We didn't bury them, if that's what you mean. So, it was, yes, er... the Tuesday, yes the 15th, *then we both - Sergeant James and myself - got a lift in the rear seats of two Lysanders that were going south. We had just taken off and were over the edge of the aerodrome when 109s appeared and shot both down. Sergeant James was killed; I lost two fingers - an explosive bullet - and the two pilots got away with scratches."*

"Poor Jimmy James." Tommy Wisdom's head sank. "Such bad luck. Such bad luck."

"What you going to do with those notes Tommy ol' chap?" Godfrey said pointing at Tommy Wisdom's full notepad.

"Don't know. Bad news like this won't make the press."

"So it shouldn't."

"The last communique I wrote for the BUP was that we were mercilessly bombing the Huns in the Monastir Gap. That'll probably be in the papers this week back home. First casualty of war here?"

"What's that, Tommy?"

"The truth."

"Always the case."

"So what you gong to do with all that information?"

"Well, for the papers, we'll say that the Expeditionary Force in Greece is pulling out. Of course, the Germans are already reporting that they have inflicted heavy casualties on the enemy. We will report what they are saying, but there will always be a hint of scepticism added. I mean, the Germans won't be telling the truth, will they?"

They both laughed.

"So as regards my notepad. It's like a tribute to 211 Squadron and I am of a mind to write a book about these heroes in Greece like you Godfrey."

"Why, that's a compliment."

"The story of the men of the RAF in Greece will be lost in the bigger picture when this country falls as it will in a few days. You mark my words. The swastika we stole from the German Embassy will be replaced by thousands more. So, these notes will be put into a book. A tribute to you and the others."

"Most of us have different wings nowadays, Tommy, hey? The Blenheim wings which flew over Mt. Olympus are now but shadows of history."

Great sentiments, Godfrey. By jove, you've given me the title. Wings Over Olympus."

*

A week to the day after Gerald lost his life, the Germans were battling for the city of Athens itself and British forces were pouring out of the country by any means possible. Dog fights between the Hurricanes of 80 Squadron and the overwhelming forces of the Luftwaffe were watched by the citizens of the city in terror. They watched as four Hurricanes met their end over the city, including the Hurricane flown by the South African Pat Pattle.

Pilot Officer Roald Dahl avoided any gremlins taking hold of his plane that day and became the famous author everyone now knows him to be.

At 6pm on St. George's Day, Wednesday 23 April 1941, ten days after the tragic Easter Sunday raid by 211 Squadron, the Greek government unconditionally surrendered to the Germans and Greece fell under the occupation of the Nazis.

Author's Note
[1] Wings Over Olympus - page 183.

Chapter Thirty-three

'The RAF Writes'

In the days which followed Easter Sunday, telegrams were sent out to the families of the missing. Once again Lizzie read the news from the 'angel of death' who had called with the telegram to Frank and Edith's house in Ash Grove, Shotton.

It was the Missing Feared Killed telegram again. [1] This time the telegram said missing as the result of air operations on 13 April 1941. Everyone noticed it was more precise than before.

"Let's take it with a pinch of salt and wait, " Francis said.

Reluctantly, because of the previous information they'd had back in November, she agreed.

"No news is good news!" said Francis as he hugged Lizzie and made her feel a little better.

Francis was buying every national daily he could in the days when Greece was falling to the Germans and after it had fallen. It didn't look good, and no one had heard anything. Worse still, information of what loved ones were up to in the war was kept to an absolute minimum and there wasn't even anyone you could ask.

It was the last week of April when the postman pushed a letter through the door at 6 Ashfield Road.

Lizzie saw the writing. It was Gerald's! She avidly pulled open the envelope and headed to the back to read it to Francis, who was sat with an early morning cup of cocoa, in his ripped vest, with his trousers untidily unbuttoned at the waist.

"What's it say then love?" Francis enquired.

She read every last word from top to bottom without stopping.

H.Q. B.A.F.G.
Athens
Greece

12th April 1941

Dearest Aunt Lizzie, Uncle Francis and all,
I should have addressed this to 'Dear Mother,' as Lizzie, you have been like a mother to me.
I have given this letter to my friend Jim Riddle to post, as events here are moving at such a rapid rate and we are involved in some very heavy stuff to the north in Greece. I told Jim to post it, should I fail to return from one of the many raids I go on daily. I do not complain about my war duty. You can take comfort from the fact I have done that duty to the best of my ability and have done my piece to end this horrible war. You can and should hope on for a few weeks that I am not dead, but, regretfully there will come a time when you may have to accept the worst could have happened to me. If that is the case, I shall follow in the footsteps of the brave of the RAF who have lost their lives before me, of that you can be assured.
I understand that getting such a letter may dispirit you all, but you must only think of me in the best ways. Think of me telling my unfunny jokes or taking the children to play on the banks of the Dee to give you five minutes peace. Think of me the Christmas before last, when the children were so pleased with the books I got them for Christmas. Think of me the day I got my commission. My officer photograph looks so good in the parlour at number 6. Look at me each day and I will look back at you through that photograph. Keep it there until posterity runs out for you all and I will say hello to you every day of your lives.
It will be difficult for you and everyone, that I know. In that I include Frank. In his own way he did what he thought was right and I shall not take any blame with me to wherever I go. All and everyone are forgiven. All I ask is that you live on for me and smile when you look at my photograph.
Be proud of me. No man could do more than I have done. My soul sits on the wings of a Blenheim and my heart with the people I know.
My dear Aunt Lizzie, you are a woman of such courage yourself. You have faced your own disappointments and reversals of fortune, that I know. I admire you for the way you have faced up to things and

I have learned so much from you, so for that I am grateful. It was you who encouraged my learning and you who was always positive when I was down. You helped me through the death of my mother and gave me a faith in myself to tackle the future with confidence.

You must take strength from my death, if you don't, my death will have been in vain and what spirit remains in you will be weakened beyond repair. Keep strong and keep the faith. When you pray at Rivertown, then you must pray for a good life for yourself ahead. My sacrifice in war will see us together again one day - I firmly believe that.

Fighting for Britain and what she stands for as a country is written through my entire being. The freedoms, the justice, the peace, the civilisation which we hold so dear and take for granted, those monsters in Germany and Italy want to take away from us. For the sake of our future generations I have taken this fight on, in my own small way, so all can be free from tyranny. If you think nothing else of me, then do think those thoughts, as when at some future date, we have won this war, you can toast me and say, 'he did his bit, he did his bit!'

Once again I thank you all for what you have done for me dear Aunt Lizzie and Uncle Francis. Be proud of your achievements and think of the sacrifices of all who, after the war is over, should go on and ally against all who try to impose their tyrannical views on us. Evil things are sent to try us all the time and good people must stand up to it, otherwise evil wins.

Lastly, I know you will worry about how I might have died, but I lost my fear of death a long time ago, such are the experiences I have been through in war. The men I have been alongside are the bravest I have ever known and all have confronted fear with fortitude, courage and resolve. I have done likewise and fear is long gone from me. So, you must not lament my passing.

Live on for me! If you live on in tranquillity and liberty, then losing my life at 23 will not have been in vain.

With much love for all time.

Gerald

xxx

Lizzie fell back into the chair and wept. No words came from her mouth. She held the letter as if her life depended on it.

The door knocked within ten minutes. Francis answered and brought Frank and Edith through to the back, where he saw a tearful

Lizzie.

"I've had a letter Lizzie - a follow-up from the telegram, I believe."

Lizzie still held Gerald's letter. "So have we."

"From?"

"From Gerald." She handed the letter to Frank. "He's dead for sure."

Frank handed his letter to Lizzie. "This came through he post today from Greece. Gerald is missing."

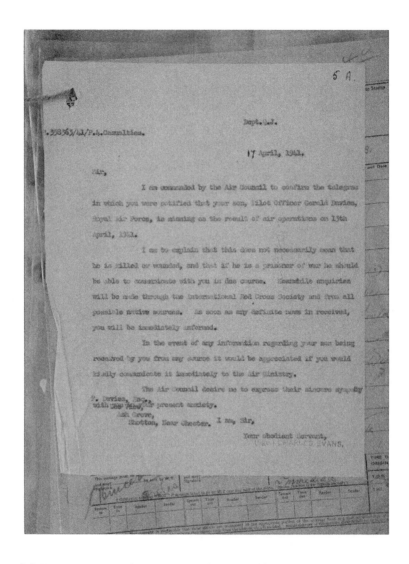

[1] Letter courtesy of Kostas Kavvadias - see Chapter re Author's visit to Corfu. Provided by Greek Authorities in Athens in 2020.

Lizzie and Frank read the letters they now held.

"There's still hope" Francis said as he looked at the letter from the RAF, "I mean, when you look at that it says he's just missing."

Frank added in, "And in Gerald's letter he actually says *'You can and should hope on for a few weeks that I am not dead,'* there you are you see. He's had to put this letter together, knowing he's off to battle, they all do it... and he's saying nice things. He'll be making his way back or he's a PoW. You wait and see"

Edith nodded in agreement. It was all she could do. She was unusually quiet.

"I think he's gone." Lizzie sobbed away. "He's gone."

"Gerald says himself we have to be hopeful. I mean, it's only a couple of weeks since he's gone missing, so we have to keep our hopes up for him."

Nothing could console Lizzie. She rocked backwards and forwards her chair mouthing the words *'We'll meet again, don't know where don't know when.'*

No one knew what to say to her.

Francis mumbled on, trying to help. "Perhaps it's a mistake. They made a mistake when he was lost in Greece before. He came back then. He came back then. I said he would as well."

Lizzie still sang away quietly. Francis' eyes were full of tears, as were Frank and Edith's. Everyone felt as if they had just been knifed in the chest. Crestfallen and broken.

Edith broke the silence. "I'll get the kettle on and make a nice cup of tea for us all."

"Good idea, Ede, " Frank replied through a sniffly nose.

Lizzie stopped singing and through her tears said, "There's no sugar or milk in Edith. Get my purse and go up the road for some. It's on the sideboard with the ration books."

Edith and Frank headed out.

Lizzie got up and wandered to the tiny backyard of the two up two down. Francis followed.

"He had a photo taken here, you know. I can see him now in his smart Pilot Officer's uniform. Beautiful boy. Beautiful boy."

"He's not gone, Lizzie. Not gone. Just away at the moment."

"He's gone. I know it."

*

Many weeks later, in the early evening, the door of The Horns at Crazies Hill swung open and in walked Tommy Wisdom. He looked straight across to the bar to where Susan Hall was standing.

"They told me I'd find you here," he said. "Recognise you from your photograph."

Tommy Wisdom walked up to the bar, shook hands with Susan Hall and introduced himself.

"I promised Gerry I would find you."

"Find me?"

Tommy looked at the landlady, Mrs Edith Burrough, who was standing not a couple of yards away. "Do you have a private place at the back or something?"

Edith Burrough knew what Tommy Wisdom was there for and immediately showed him and Susan to a back room. Susan looked around nervously. The landlady closed the door and went to the bar to get a brandy as she heard shrieks coming from the room in the back. [2]

*

None of the Davies family heard anything more for months until Frank got a second letter from the RAF in early June.

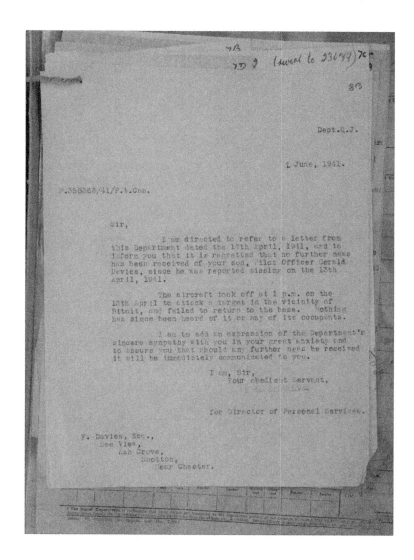

Letter courtesy of Kostas Kavvadias - see Chapter re Author's visit to Corfu. Provided by Greek Authorities in Athens in 2020.

Frank immediately told Lizzie, but the contents only confirmed what she already knew.

A further letter followed in August 1941.

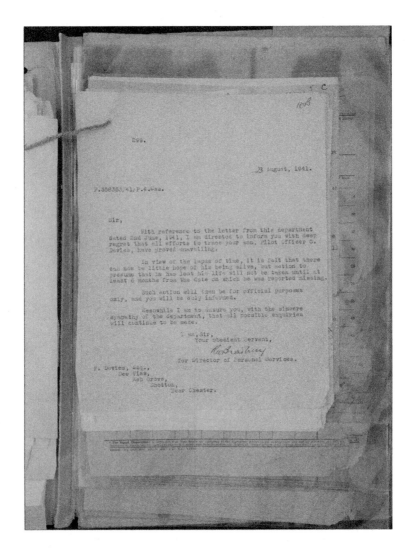

Letter courtesy of Kostas Kavvadias - see Chapter re: Author's visit to Corfu. Provided by Greek Authorities in Athens in 2020.

By this time Lizzie was sure in her mind that Gerald was dead and that all hope was gone. If anyone ever asked about him after that she referred to him as 'Missing Over Greece.' Somewhere inside she thought and hoped he might live amongst the hills there. Inside though, she knew the truth.

Lizzie had always treasured the Victorian penny Gerald had been given by Miss Jones at Shotton Central School in 1934. She went to the clock, ticking on the mantlepiece, where she'd kept it safely for years.

"This was Gerald's 'good-luck' charm, you know. Give him by his nice teacher Miss Jones, when Frank made him leave school all those years ago."

"I remember," Francis said, looking sad.

"Didn't bring him much luck though, did it?"

"Well, I'm not sure" Francis smiled. "He was heading up the ladder in the RAF. He was doing better than any of us have ever done in our family. When you're confronted with danger every day of your life, your luck is bound to run out. Perhaps Gerald had used every bit of luck in that coin and it just ran out. His legacy to us all will be the man and boy we knew. His bravery and his loyalty, his legacy to the country. Of that we can be proud and we should be proud."

*

Later that year Lizzie walked to the banks of the River Dee with Francis. She remembered the Heinkel chased by the Spitfires and thought of Gerald, whose favourite place in the world was the quietness of the side of the river. The two had taken flowers with them and both walked up to the Hawarden Bridge, looking up towards Chester. Lizzie threw the autumn coloured chrysanthemums into the tide and watched as the flowers headed away from her with the flow of the river, just as Gerald's life had flowed away.

"One last thing to throw in…" Lizzie pulled the Victorian coin from her pocket. "Perhaps in ten thousand years, someone will find this coin and hold it in their hand. They will never know the reason the coin got there, but we shall know for ever what the coin symbolises."

With that, she threw the coin from the bridge.

"Goodbye, Gerald. Goodbye."

*

The Missing Research Section part of the Air Ministry Casualty Branch, which investigated, monitored and reported on the status of missing aircraft and airmen, subsequently published the following information regarding the crews of 211 Squadron in 1945. Nothing about this was passed on to the Davies family in Shotton.

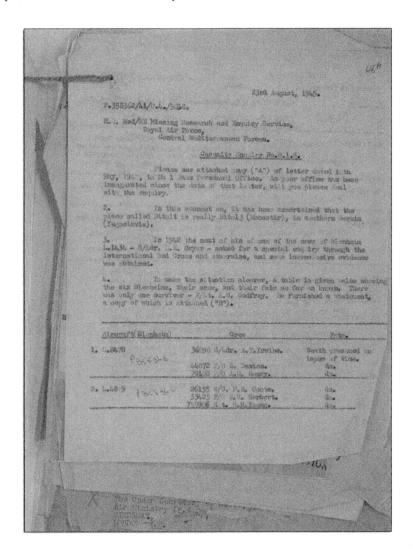

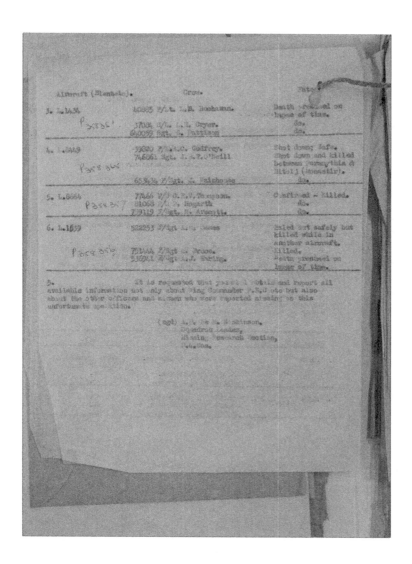

Information courtesy of Kostas Kavvadias - see Chapter re Author's visit to Corfu. Provided by Greek Authorities in Athens in 2020.

Presumption of death enabled a death certificate to be issued; personal belongings could then be sent to the next of kin, along with any monies due.

*

* * *

Many facts came to light in the late seventies when the brother of
Sergeant Andy Bryce, (Blenheim L1539) attempted to find out where
his bother was buried. The result was that the graves of some of the
airmen who had been laid to rest in northern Greece were now
established. This meant the remains could be repatriated to Phaleron
War Cemetery near Athens.

The report below suggests the crew of L8478, Gerald's crew, were re-
buried at Phaleron in 1945 but that their exact identities were not
known so they were buried together in an unmarked grave. Plot 4,
Row D. Grave 13.

Image: Courtesy CWGC

No one thought to inform the Davies family of this in 1945.

Following further discoveries of information in 1981, the remains in
the above grave were recorded as those of Gerald and his crew. In June
1981, a permanent Italian Marble headstone was placed over the grave
to mark the final resting place of Gerald, Arthur and Tony.

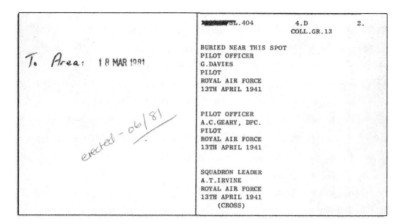

Image: Courtesy CWGC

All three had been mentioned on the Alamein Memorial, but with this recent information they now have a permanent resting place at Phaleron War Cemetery *[3]* in Athens.

DAVIES, Pilot Offr. GERALD, 44072. R.A.F.
211 Sqdn. 13th April, 1941. Age 24. Son of
Francis and Elizabeth Mary Davies; stepson of
Edith Mary Davies, of Shotton, Cheshire. Coll.
grave. 4. D. 13.

Common wealth War Graves Commission: Grave of Pilot Officer 440720

Gerald Davies, Gerald Plot 4. Row D. Grave 13 - with Pilot Officer Arthur Geary DFC and Squadron Leader Anthony Irvine.

Lizzie Davies died on 16 May 1970 and Francis Davies died on 5 February 1982.

Frank Davies died on 11 July 1951 and his second wife, Edith Davies, died on 2 Aug 1972

None were told any of this information.

Author's Note

[1] *On 14 April 1941 the remaining members of 211 Squadron informed Bomber Command, the Air Ministry and the RAF Records Office the aircraft and crew were missing.*

Telegrams, along with a follow-up letter from the Commanding Officer, were sent to the next of kin of each crew member advising them he was 'missing as the result of air operations on 13 April 1941.'

[2] *It is believed the full name of Susan Hall was Suzanne M.G. Hall, born in 1919. In 1939 she was a clerical shipping officer. Ancestry records show she married a Charles Banks in Henley in 1943.*

[3] *Phaleron War Cemetery lies six kilometres to the South-East of Athens, at the boundary between old Phaleron district and Kalamaki district. It is on the coast road from Athens to Vouliaghmeni, 5 kilometres west of the international airport.*

Chapter Thirty-four

'The Picture on The Wall'
A Story Which Had To Be Written - The Author's Tale

The pale lime green wooden door at 6 Ashfield Road, Shotton, had been painted with stolen Shotton steelworks' paint. Every door in the street was the same, apart from one of two which were black, but even then, this colour was a steelworks' shade. This was one perk of being an employee there. I knocked, my usual two slow taps followed by three faster taps with a final hard tap. This was the code. I waited for the door to open. It was eerily quiet, a morning fog coming off the River Dee, only a few hundred yards away, was just lifting as a steam train, one of the last going along the Holyhead to Chester line, pounded its way past not thirty yards away, further adding to the smog. A purple Ford Anglia estate idled no more than three yards away, its purple fumes mixing into the soup of smells pervading the day.

The door opened excruciatingly slowly. Someone made an eerie creaking noise to mimic the opening of the door.

The old gentleman opened the door, well he seemed old to me at eight years old.

"You Rang!"

"Grandad!" I shouted, looking a little concerned. He was stern faced and stood tall mimicking Lurch from The Addams Family, which had recently began broadcasting weekly on British television. I turned around and waved at the Ford Anglia. Dad was flicked his ash from the window. He took one last drag on his cigarette, then he peeled away down the street, disappearing quickly into the fog. All that was left was the noise of the car as it headed away.

Mum had got a job as a cook in the local school and dad was dropping me off to be looked after for the day. I'd complained of stomach ache to get a day off school and, despite feeling completely well, I had feigned sickness by holding my stomach and complaining for long enough about the pain.

"Go through, Hoss. The Cartwright brothers are in the back." Grandad had flipped a switch and was now acting out Bonanza. He blew on the ends of his fingers, held like a smoking gun, and ushered me in as if at gunpoint. The Cartwright brothers was code for 'Nana's in the back.'

I walked through, passing the familiar dark walnut sideboard on top of which was a large carriage clock presented to my Grandad for his long service at what was now called the steelworks. On top of the clock was a khaki forage cap sporting a badge of the Cheshire regiment all polished and new.

I went through to the back and there was my Nana, Lizzie Davies, sat in front of the Yorkshire grate which was blazing away, making the room cosy and warm. She held a toasting fork to the fire with a piece of thickly cut white bread speared on it, browning away. The smell was wonderful. Fire seemed to fill the room and everyone had glowing faces, like a scene from Joe Gargery's blacksmith's shop and I felt like Pip just sitting contented with my life there.

Thought you might want something to eat to help your stomach along." She winked at me. Grandad followed in. "He's a fool, that Grandad of yours. A complete fool."

"Hey! Less of the fool, ol' girl. Just keeping the lad happy."

It was my turn to smile now as thickly buttered toast arrived on a plate and I sat in the old spindle back chair next to the grate.

The year was 1965 and this was a time, when, as a child, I used to visit my Nana and Grandad's humble abode in the back streets of Shotton pretty regularly. Sometimes playing unwell to get there on a school day but mostly on a weekend or during school holiday time. Shotton in Flintshire is a little known area on the north-east coast of North Wales, nestling grimly against the canalised River Dee and was the place where my mother had grown up. This River Dee, unlike its royal counterpart in Scotland, was, for the most part of the twentieth century, the lifeblood flowing to the heavily industrialised communities along its estuary. The river brought the industry and brought many families, including my own, to the area because working in the growing iron, then steel industry, meant regular wages and food on the table.

The Hawarden Bridge John Summers' Steelworks at Shotton was formerly opened in 1896 and thereafter generations of people worked on the site until February 1980, which turned out to be the most disastrous day in Shotton's history, when 6,000 jobs were lost. This remains the biggest single job loss on one day in British history.

Nana finished making some toast for Grandad and I sat with a book and read quietly. I was just happy not to be in school. Nana and Grandad were both people I loved dearly as a child, and I always wanted to be there. They had very little in worldly goods but their life was happy although they had been through some very hard times. Their house was no great mansion, just a terrace you might imagine you'd now see in Coronation Street on the television, two up two down, still with its original outside toilet which they had used until, with local authority grants in the sixties, this altered and they had a new extension with a toilet and kitchen area in 1964. Before this, the toilet hadn't been one of those modern fangled flushing ones, but it was a dirt toilet, with a wooden door in a boundary wall from which the yuck could be collected.   I can remember them being made up with this new chic arrival to improve their lives.   They had not complained before this event and would have readily carried on as before because they were proud people.

A tour of the house would take less than 30 seconds for a fit child, as I was in the sixties. The main danger in the house for anyone was the lethally steep stairs to the two tiny bedrooms. Goodness knows how they had reared three children in the house.

Then there was the parlour.

This was the 'posh' room of the house and a treasure chest of many things. This is where Nana and Grandad - Lizzie and Francis, kept all their posh stuff and they called it the 'special room.' The parlour was generally off bounds for me as a child with boundless energy and liable to knock things over, but I passed through it every time I visited the house. There was no option, as going via the parlour was the only way to the back living room from the street.

The parlour was a strange and mysterious room. A dark room, not because of some evil force but for the fact the curtains were always drawn, come day or night. Warmth, or should I say heat-loss, was a factor in those days of drafty doors and windows , so heavy curtains kept the heat where it was supposed to be.

I was never told I could not enter the parlour when staying at the house, but no one ever did, so I just followed the house rules. When I got to go in the special room and spend time there, sometimes because Nana looked for something in the depths of the walnut sideboard as I stood in the background, I used to cast my eyes around in awe but I never got to spend much more than a few minutes in the room in the whole of my childhood days.

The parlour was no different to most similar rooms of the period. There were water colours of Chester on the wall, chiming clocks tucked away in side areas, large vases in which I never saw flowers and a large old screen with some fantastic black and white Japanese floral design on it.

I suppose because the room was darkened and mostly unused, it always intrigued me as a child.

Nana and Grandad had married at the height of the roaring twenties and had lived in the same house ever since. I also learned that before they were married they'd lived with Grandad's parents at 31 Ash Grove, only fifty yards away at the end of the street. Although Granddad's parents Frank and Elizabeth had long since passed away, the house was still occupied by someone I knew as Aunty Edie who had married Francis Davies, my great grandfather after his wife Elizabeth had passed away.

My mother was one of four children born to Francis and Elizabeth Davies in March 1933, she was the youngest. A fourth child named Virginia was born in 1945 but didn't survive more than a day.

My mother told me she had a happy and pleasant childhood in and around the back streets close to the smoky steelworks and she had great recollections of the Second World War as it affected Shotton. She recalled seeing the glowing fires of bombing raids by the Luftwaffe on Liverpool, a short distance away as the crow flies, and remembered wave after wave of German aeroplanes as they passed overhead en route to that destination to off load their deadly cargo. She recalled the military uniforms of the time and their abundance in the area because everyone knew someone with a member of the family who was in one of the armed forces.

As a child, I loved my comics and books; all of which were replete with stories about the great campaigns, fantastic machines and heroes of the Second World War. Then there were the Airfix models of every conceivable type of craft from the war and I can remember avidly constructing and painting those models, not really understanding what it may have been like to be involved in warfare. Then there were the war games we all played as children. No one wanted to be a German or a Japanese soldier, we all wanted to be commandos or characters we'd seen on television such as Douglas Bader the great pilot or John Wayne landing on the shores of Iwo Jima. This was a time when Brian Inglis presented highlights of the Second World War in the programme 'All Our Yesterdays' which we all used to watch on a Sunday. All of those black and white portrayals of the allies moving forward to victory together with the original 'Mr Cholomendy Warner' narration are still vivid in my mind and we played them out on the streets every day as children.

These events of the Second World War were not too distant away in the sixties and many houses still carried the psychological scars, in addition to various bits and pieces of war memorabilia which hung around everywhere. Nana and Grandad's house was no different and the 'special room' of 6 Ashfield Road contained a variety of artefacts from a bygone era.

Grandad had worked slavishly for decades in the rolling mill, where the hot steel plates were cooled down with copious amounts of water. For five days a week and sometimes more over this period, he would get soaked in water and the result was severe arthritis in his body but it was his toes I noticed most as a child. It was impossible not to notice, as the uppers of his house shoes were cut away to give room for his bent toes to move.

It was not an unusual occurrence for Grandad to play war with me. He would march up and down the cramped back room with the fire-poker over his shoulder, as if he had a rifle and was on parade. Sometimes he would put on the old army cap he got from the parlour and shout 'Attention!' He would stand bolt upright with his rifle (poker!) shouldered.

It was on that foggy day in 1965 when I found out something I never knew before.

"This was me during the war, son," he said. "Captain Francis Davies, Cheshire Regiment reporting for duty."

The cap badge said 'Cheshire Regiment.' He was telling the truth. He then went into his usual silly act of pretending to lunge forward as if with a bayonetted rifle shouting "Halt, who goes there."

I'd seen it before many times and shouted, "me Grandad."

Nana shouted, "You boys and war."

I was at an age where I wanted to know more. "So, what did you do during the war Grandad?"

"Home Guard son. This is my Home Guard cap. I was with the Cheshires. Our duty was to guard the river and the factory from the invading Germans."

"The Germans invaded?"

"No... but they might have done but for the likes of us guarding the river. You've seen the pill-boxes on the banks?"

I had even climbed on the concrete structures placed strategically along the canalised part of the River Dee, just next to the steelworks.

"Well, I spent the war doing things like that. Too old to fight and anyway I was in a reserved occupation at the steel works."

"Reserved... what does that mean?"

"They needed steel for all things... tanks, planes, shells, bullets... you name it, we made the steel. "

I nodded as if I knew what it was all about. War to me was jumping around with my school friends and making silly noises shouting "You're dead, I got you" to replies of "I'm not a German anyway, so I'm not dead."

This was the first time I can recall seeing the faces of Nana and Grandad alter when they talked of the war. Grandad then walked me into the parlour. An official visit.

Nana followed.

In that dark parlour, Nana drew the curtains back a little. More light came into the room. Probably the reason I recall this memory so much. I'd never seen it so light other than momentarily when the door was opened. Grandad approached the wooden carriage clock and doffed his forage cap, placing it back into the position it had occupied for years, since the clock had arrived. Badge facing into the room.

Grandad was just about to speak when Nana spoke, pointing to a large vase painted with ornate flowers in greens, whites and golds. The vase had an image of King George V.

"This'll be yours one day," she said, caressing the vase as if it held some importance I had no idea about.

At eight years old, possession of some old vase wasn't uppermost in my thoughts. I really didn't want that vase but politely offered a "thanks Nana."

Grandad laughed. "He doesn't want an old pot Lizzie."

"He might do one day."

"Here's what I want to show you, lad."

Granddad pointed to a photograph which took pride of place above the heavy wooden sideboard. It was in a brown wooden frame and was artificially coloured in pastel shades, with a misted oval fading out from the centre. The object of the photograph was a young man who looked no more than twenty years old. His face and upper chest were the only parts of the person on view, but it was obvious even at eight years old, it was a person in uniform. The uniform colour was a gun-barrel, grey-blue and the upper part of the tunic contained what looked like out-spread wings. The person wore what we would now recognise as a Royal Air Force cap. Of course I didn't know then, but I now realise that I was looking at a photograph of a young RAF officer.

Grandad just stopped and looked at the photograph. Nana came alongside and griped his arm and put her hand on my head.

"Who's that?" I asked innocently. Followed quickly by, "was he in the war?"

"Uncle Gerald, that is. It's our Gerald."

"Uncle Gerald?"

"Yes, he WAS your uncle."

This was the first time I'd even heard I had an Uncle Gerald.

"Was he killed in the war?"

I'd never seen Nana and Grandad look so sad. They glanced at each other, teary eyed.

It was Nana who spoke first. "We're not sure for certain, but he went missing somewhere over Greece in the war!"

"He was with the RAF in Greece in 1941..." Grandad reached out, took the photograph from the wall and held it. He looked closely at it and touched the face of Gerald. "He just never returned home and they never told us any more. This was 'The War' and news about loved ones...well...it... "

"It was awful, awful news for us. Beautiful, smart young man he was. A pilot officer he was. Proud of him we were."

Nana cried.

Grandad put the picture back on the wall and put his arm around Nana. "It's all right Lizzie." He looked at me. "It's still upsetting for us. Very upsetting!"

Nana looked at me. "He was doing his job and just never came home. We got the message that they could only presume he was dead. No Gerald! No funeral! No nothing!"

We sat down in the parlour, something I'd never done before. This was definitely a day of firsts.

"We loved him lots, our son..."

Grandad shook his head, "Lizzie… no. We can't call him…"

"I can AND we shall." Nana looked at me. "Uncle Gerald was really bright and intelligent. He made a success of working in school and then he went to work at the steelworks, but he knew he could make a success elsewhere and he got a career in the RAF. Proud of him we were. An officer."

"We were."

"He would have gone a long way in life. He would. A life tragically cut short." Nana stared into the distance. "Fond, fond memories. Lovely boy."

Nana got up and walked to the one of the drawers in the sideboard, which she opened. She brought out a newspaper cutting.

"He went missing before you know and turned up alive. It gave us hope when he went missing the second time, but days turned into weeks and turned into years and he never came home."

Nana showed me the newspaper cutting. A picture of Uncle Gerald and a girl called Susan.

"He was going to marry her!" Tears flowed again. 'But he never came back."

"You don't have to do this Lizzie."

"I do. It's good for me."

She placed the newspaper cutting in my hand and read it out loud to me.

"PRESS "POPPED QUESTION

This is Susan Hall, the girl who received a proposal of marriage via the newspapers. The young man is now Pilot-Officer Gerald Davies, on service in Greece, the sender of the proposal. He was explaining to a reporter that the reason he got lost on a bombing trip was that he had left his mascot – a picture of Miss Hall – behind. No, it wasn't his wife, but . . . . 'you can tell her I am going to marry her after this job is over. She doesn't know it yet, but this goes as a proposal'."

Nana sobbed more. Grandad did his best to hold back the tears, but his eyes were full and watery too. The conversation ended there. This was too much for them.

They sent me off to Mona Jeffs' shop, with a penny and a brand new half-penny, taken from the top of a tin of polish, with the instructions to get an ounce of sweets. Mona was the very fat lady who used to sit in the shop around the corner, no more than ten yards from the bottom of the railway footbridge which led across the line towards the steelworks.

As I walked to Mona's, I realised why the front parlour was so special. It was kept for the memory of Gerald. A shrine, but at eight years old I never understood this and never took my questioning further. I suppose I was satisfied I knew who the person in the photograph was and, as far as I was concerned, he was no different to any of my other uncles except for the fact I never got to see him or meet him in my life. I went back into the back room of the house but from then onwards I looked at the image of the man in the RAF uniform in a different light.

Nana and Grandad didn't drive, so I waited until dad picked me up and headed home and thought no more of the day.

Nana died in 1970 and Grandad passed away some twelve years later. Both went to their graves without knowing anything further about what had really happened to Gerald and why he hadn't come home from the war. The photograph on the wall disappeared and the house in Shotton was sold and as for THAT vase I've no idea where it went either.

My questions developed to 'Where's he now?' and such like questions. I suppose it is here that this absolutely fantastic story began to unravel itself.

*

I never questioned my mother until I was much older about who uncle Gerald was and then one day, after Grandad had died she was going through a box of things she'd had from the house when she came across the newspaper cutting I'd seen all the years before.

"I recognise that," I said instantly.

Mum nodded longingly at the photograph. Tears came to her eyes. "Uncle Gerald."

"I know. Nana and Granddad told me about him years ago."

"You never told me you knew of him."

"I was shown that cutting from the paper years ago and the picture on the wall in the house… was that of Uncle Gerald."

"He was a lovely man. Tall and handsome. He used to buy me toys and books for Christmas and spoilt me rotten."

She showed me a book, almost falling apart. *'Every Girl's Storybook.'*

* * *

"He got me that for Christmas in 1939."

I took the book and opened it. Sure enough, on the inside cover was the first time I had ever seen Gerald's handwriting.

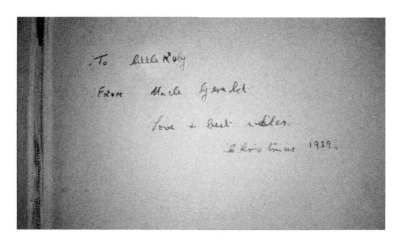

Mum went on, "I always sat on his knee when he was at the house and got lots of cuddles."

"Was he at your house a lot?"

"He lived at my Grandad and Aunty Edie's just along the road, but he was always at ours. ALWAYS. He hated Aunty Edie. She was vile to him."

I knew who Aunty Edie was. I had even met her when I was young and went to Nana and Grandad's in Shotton. She was a fat grey haired woman who we used to visit occasionally in a house a few yards away from their house. She was always sitting in a rocking chair in a dark house which smelled of urine and made no attempt to welcome us. I'd heard my Nana say once as we'd left the house, "I'm never coming here again. Ungrateful so and so. She'll die in her own filth one day. I don't know why I do this. The ungrateful... I'd better stop and shut my mouth now."

Nana never swore, but she nearly did this day, stopping just short of using even worse expletives I think, although I probably think the 'f' would have been fat or frosty or flamer. Nana liked the word flamer, so yes, that would have been it.

Nana had cooked a full Sunday dinner for Edie. She plated it all up, knife, fork, condiments, the lot on a tray made in school by Gerald in a woodwork lesson long ago. She even placed a cup of tea on the tray, sugared with four spoons as Edie liked it. Then Nana quickly headed down the road before it got cold to get it to Edie. She knew what she was like. Edie was not in the least bit grateful. A series of favours had turned into expectation. But the comment she made on the day was the straw that broke the camel's back.

As her twenty stone frame sat in a chair creaking under her weight, he venom poured forth. "Where've you been 'til now. You're late, Lizzie. Frank always said you were lazy. I don't want that now. I've had my dinner. Made my own."

Lizzie left the tray and the meal. She placed it down in disgust.

She never went to the house again and never got that precious tray back.

After Nana and Grandad had died, I spoke with my mum about Gerald many times over the years, fascinated about this person who had gone missing in Greece with no one having a clue what had happened to him. Mum repeated endlessly the story about how she could remember running to him as a child and being picked up into his arms for a cuddle. She remembers his smart uniform distinctly and the revolver he carried in a holster at his side. She repeated the story that Uncle Gerald never forgot about her or her brothers at Christmas and when he appeared he always brought them gifts.

There were a million more questions I should have asked, but I didn't.

The years rolled by and because I no longer passed that photograph on the wall the whole affair disappeared into the depths of my psyche but it did not fade into oblivion altogether.

'He went missing over Greece' hung disturbingly in my mind for many a year.

As a child I never really understood the meaning of the phrase. What did missing mean? Did it mean that Gerald might still be alive somewhere else? Did it mean that he may be in Greece, still living his life? I was not sure what to think as a child, but for sure these words had sown the seeds of something which would haunt me for years until a point came when I would have to do something about it!

But what would the catalyst be to take action!

Then in the mid-1980's I read Roald Dahl's autobiography called Going Solo. Dahl had joined the RAF in 1938 and had ended up in 1941 in Greece as a Hurricane Pilot. In his book Dahl mentions he believed he was only one of five pilots to make it out of Greece and two to make it from Crete afterwards; (*p 197/198*) so began my quest to find out what had happened to Uncle Gerald. All this in the days before the internet was fully established.

Pictured above in 1945 are members of the Rivertown Congregational Church at Shotton, during VE Celebrations. Elizabeth Davies, grandmother to the author, is sat stern-faced at the very front, in the light coloured clothing.

* * *

Pictured above at other VE celebrations in Shotton, Flintshire, outside what is now the Central Hotel, is the author's mother Ruby Davies (dark hair, just below the little boy being held) and below her, wearing a tie with a light jacket, is her brother Clifford Davies. Once again neither are smiling.

Much was sacrificed by many during the Second World War and many families mourned their losses with little cause to celebrate as the war ended, knowing loved ones would never return home.

Losing Gerald Davies gave no cause to celebrate for the Davies family of Shotton and the legacy of his loss reverberates through time to this day.

Chapter Thirty-five

'Corfu 2020'

Syd Lawrence came back to Shotton after the war and performed at the Vaughan Hall, a famous venue for big bands and dancing in the post war days. Perhaps he wondered what had happened to the young Pilot Officer Gerald Davies whom he'd met in Ismailia, but in the days of peace, there would have been no way of finding out. What is certain is that Gerald's sister Ruby danced with her future husband there to Syd Lawrence before he became famous.

Small world!

*

By the late-nineties I had spoken with Don Clark, whom I owe much for helping me with my research into my uncle, Gerald Davies. He was and is the architect behind the 211 Squadron website and sent me much information to get me going, including notes put together by his father Sergeant Cyril Frederick Robert 'Nobby' Clark who had been with 211 Squadron. I intensified my research and managed to get hold of Gerald's Service Record from RAF Innsworth in Gloucestershire.

Don Clark had also told me about Squadron Leader Tommy Wisdom, who had written a book in 1942 about the exploits of 211 Squadron. He told me the book was out of print but that there was at least one photograph of my uncle in the book called Wings Over Olympus.

There was only one place to go. I knew of a place not too far from my home, in the picturesque Dee Valley - Llangollen. From the outside, the place looked like any other cafe but upstairs the place was cavernous and full to the brim with books. This was Maxine's Second Hand Books and a treasure trove of old and out of print books lay inside. Question was, would I find what I was looking for?

It was a Saturday morning, the 27 November 1999 when I went along. I wasn't a stranger to Maxine's. I'd been before to have a quick nose around but had never had occasion to buy anything. This time I was on a mission to find Tommy Wisdom's out of print book, written in 1942. Remember, these were the days before you could search online for a book like this. This was a physical search of the most unorganised and uncatalogued book shop you might ever go in.

Three hours later I was exhausted from searching and headed out of the shop along a huge line of piled up books I hadn't searched. I flipped up the top books just in case and to my surprise, almost the last book I turned over had a copy of Tommy Wisdom's book underneath. The needle in the haystack had been found.

I quickly flicked through the book and there he was, on a photographic plate, opposite page 165, my Uncle Gerald. Standing next to The Bish. Of course, I had no idea who any of these people were and what the story was the book might reveal.

First thing I did was to email Don Clark in Australia to tell him I'd found the book. Don was so helpful and sent through many other snippets of information over the next months. He also put me in touch with people who might know more.

I write everything down. It's just an old habit I have from the days I was a police officer, so I know it was 5.20 pm on Sunday 19 March 2000 when I spoke to James Dunnet, the author of Blenheim Over The Balkans. What a lovely man he was! Sadly, he passed away in March 2013, but I was happy I'd had the chance to speak with him about 211 Squadron operations and his memories of that time in the Second World War. He told me all about The Bish, how he'd been part of the airmen who had ferried Blenheims over to North Africa in 1940. He had remained in the RAF until 1966, when he'd retired as Flight Lieutenant after 27 years' service.

James Dunnet had been due to fly in the Easter Sunday raid in Blenheim L4819 flown by Herby - Flying Officer Richard Vivian Herbert but at the last minute Wing Commander Paddy Coote had told him to stand down as he wanted to go instead to see for himself the situation in the north of Greece. So James Dunnet was one hell of a lucky guy and I felt privileged to talk with him.

In those last months of 1999 and into the new millennium, I put information on various websites to ask whether anyone might have any more information about Gerald and this is how I came to be in touch with a person who is now my good friend, Kostas Kavvadias who lives in Lefkimmi, Corfu.

Kostas rang me late one evening on 9th May 2001, telling me he had more information for me and informed me there were people still alive who recalled Gerald, The Bish and Arthur Geary crashing in Lefkimmi on 24 November 1940. The crash when the crew of the aircraft survived.

Getting to know Kostas Kavvadias in Corfu meant I could begin to write this story so much more comprehensively and with some closure for our family. Over the years my career got in the way and I was not able to get to Corfu, but in October 2020, I flew to Corfu, amidst the pandemic. Luckily, I was able to leave the country and Corfu was open to visitors.

My stay was short, but at last I met Kostas, whom I'd spoken to on the phone many times.

"We are friends through time. Your uncle, he brings us together and it is good," he said as we shook hands for the first time.

At 10.30am on 10th October, Kostas took me to see his friend Papa Spiro Monasterios who resided at the Church of St. Prokopios in Kavos.

Image: Nigel Davies-Williams. Church of St. Prokopios, Kavos.

Papa Spiro, a smart man in his 70's spoke some broken English but Kostas ably translated everything for me.

"We have a surprise for you!" Kostas insisted.

I wondered what on earth it could be?

"We have parts of your uncle's plane here."

"You do!"

"Yes. Yes."

Around the back of the church was a large storeroom which Papa Spiro unlocked. Inside the room was a veritable treasure trove of bits and pieces from the Second World War. Crashed aircraft parts, photographs of servicemen who'd visited since the war and spoken with Papa Spiro, letters from the same in English... you name it, if it had any connection with the war on Corfu it was stored there.

Image: Nigel Davies-Williams. Storeroom with Papa Spiro Monasterios, Church of St. Prokopios, Kavos.

Papa Spiro was a genial man. He'd not been a priest all of his life, he'd been a tram driver in Athens and he flew aeroplanes. Yes, he was a pilot as well. This was a man of many means. I already knew of course Kostas had a vast knowledge of the war and he was also an accomplished aviation artist in his own right, painting images for the boxes of plastic model kits for Airfix and Revell. His artwork was second to none.

Then the conversation began as Papa Spiro shifted boxes away from the top of a glass cabinet.

"There are parts in here which were taken from your uncle's plane." Kostas revealed as Papa Spiro rooted away. "Yes, the prop shaft is here with other smaller bits and pieces."

Image: Nigel Davies-Williams. Papa Spiro Monasterios and Kostas Kavvadias in storeroom at Church of St. Prokopios, Kavos.

Papa Spiro beckoned me over. "See. Look here."

He pointed to the glass cabinet. "The compass. Your uncle." He was nodding vigorously.

He spoke to Kostas in Greek. "Papa Spiro says that here in the cupboard, is the compass for your uncle's plane which crash landed at Lefkimmi back in 1940."

I looked across but could hardly see anything, there were so many other things in the way. "He will get it for you to see."

I waited as Papa Spiro extracted the compass from under the glass. He brought it over to me. "Look is here." Papa Spiro said in broken English.

It was difficult to see in the poor light of the storeroom. "Can I take it outside to look please?" I asked.

"Of course, of course."

I walked out into the bright morning sunlight of Corfu and looked into the compass.

Image: Nigel Davies-Williams. Compass from Blenheim L8511.

The sight before me was unbelievable and brought a tear to my eye. I had never met my uncle, and now I was looking at an object he would have stared into so many times. I held the heavy object and looked at it with awe and wonderment.

"It is yours. You keep. You take home." Papa Spiro said.

"No, I just can't," I said. "It has been here for so long."

Papa Spiro and Kostas spoke together in Greek.

"We want you to have it." Kostas said. "It belongs with you and it needs to go home. You can take your uncle home with you now for the first time."

More tears came to my eyes.

"I will look after it and I shall make sure it gets a good home." I replied, shaking hands with both men but still fixated on the compass.

Image: Nigel Davies-Williams. Papa Spiro Monasterios and Kostas Kavvadias present the author with the compass from Blenheim L8511 at the Church of St. Prokopios, Kavos - 10ᵗʰ October 2020.

I showed Papa Spiro and Kostas images I had on my phone of Gerald Davies. Images neither had ever seen before.

"Look like you." Papa Spiro said. "Same face and ears."

We all laughed.

"We go now and we take you to see where the plane came down."

Kostas said. "This is now a revelation to me," he went on. "I have never known the exact place where the plane of Finlayson comes down, so you follow us."

*

I followed Papa Spiro in my hire car as we headed for Meliki and then into the extremely narrow streets of Lefkimmi, where often one car could just get through, never mind two cars pass. The place was old and quaint, with little sign of modern interference. I supposed it had altered little since the war, so anything I saw, I am sure my Uncle Gerald would have seen.

At the far end of Lefkimmi, we turned off down a sharp right onto a poor dirt road. If I thought the road was poor there it got even worse as we headed through huge areas with bamboo either side followed by some open grass fields, then through the tightest of olive groves and back through bamboo which touched the car on both sides as I went through.

I thought about Gerald coming back along this road with the infamous Spiro Amerikanos, in his Dodge all those years ago. The ride must have been ten times worse with the deep ruts and potholes. My Citroen was just about getting through.

Eventually we came to a clearing with the Ionian Sea in front. Nothing else. It was spectacular.

To the right was a white building and we parked up close by.

There were two fishermen who bid us 'good morning' as they walked by.

"It is here." Papa Spiro said. "Right here."

He pointed to a white building with a cross on its roof at the far end and once again spoke to Kostas in Greek.

"This is the Church of St. Mary. It is only opened once a year for a service on the 23 August. The feast of St. Mary, but Papa Spiro tell me that during the war it was a different place. This is where the man with the gun who held your uncle at gunpoint was staying. He was guard to this area for the Corfiots to stop any invasion. What one man could do with a gun... yes, we don't know, but here he was."

Image: Nigel Davies-Williams. Church of St. Mary on the seashore at Lefkimmi. Only this half would have been seen by Gerald and crew in 1940..

"So, as I was saying, we hold your uncle up at gunpoint." Kostas laughed. "We couldn't be too careful. The Italians crashed here too, you know."

"What was the name of the man who held him at gunpoint?" I asked curiously.

"His name was Fokion Halikiopoulos. His brother was Spiro Amerikanos, the man with the big car on Corfu. They called him to come and get them to take them to Corfu Town. It was a big event. Lots of Corfiots came to see. They had seen the crippled aircraft coming to crash lands. They party after you know."

"So I heard."

"Yes, we likes the British. They do so much to help us during the war. Not so much the drunks in Kavos though sometimes."

We both laughed.

Papa Spiro then beckoned us toward the seashore.

"It is here they crash." He pointed to the narrowest of beaches I had ever seen.

I looked down the line of the shore with the mountains of northern Greece and far off Albania in the distance.

"Here!"

"Yes, here."

Image: Nigel Davies-Williams. The shoreline at Lefkimmi where The Bish put down the crippled Blenheim L8511 on 24 November 1940. All three crew walked away uninjured.

Kostas spoke Greek again with Papa Spiro.

"The area was used to make salt at the time of the war, so was flatter and more open. They would have seen this from the air, but there were ditches to drain the water away which they had to avoid, so the beach was the only option. Lots of people would have been working in the fields, and more people would surely come to see. No wonder they said there were hundreds of people to greet them."

We wondered more down the beach and I looked at the achievement of safely bringing down a plane without wrecking it completely.

"These were exceptional people" I said to Kostas and Papa Spiro. "None of us know what they went through in these days. None of us. If I didn't think my uncle and all those men were heroes before, then I do now!"

"The people of this island are so grateful to the British and Americans who helped to save our island. The servicemen who crashed here, yes there were others, were greeted like heroes... once Fokion had put his gun down of course."

We both laughed again.

It had been such a humbling experience to be in Corfu, and I did so many other things there in my brief visit. I was treated like a hero myself by the people I met, especially Papa Spiro, Kostas and his family - with whom I shared a wonderful night's hospitality in the centre of Lefkimmi. I now understood what Corfiot hospitality meant and felt I'd walked at least a few yards in my Uncle Gerald's shoes. The bit I experienced felt good but was always tinged with sadness at what my uncle went through. I'd touched down on Ryanair at Corfu airport and he'd pancaked it into the Ionian Sea.

The difference between me and him was now eighty years wide AND I was going to fly back without an Me 109 on my tail.

Chapter Thirty-six

'From The Author'

The story of Gerald Davies is based on true events founded in historical research. A complete reference guide to the sources of this research you can see in reference section of this book. The remarkable events in this story actually happened.

I have tried to be historically accurate where possible but for the sake of continuity I have had to fill in the blanks with a storyline, although even then, I have followed, as much as possible historical events. The King's visit to Henley in 1940, is one such example.

Conversations in the book are taken from my extensive research of contemporary accounts, the research of other texts on this subject, and family recollections of those who knew the brave men and women mentioned in this book. Instances described in the book are either as close as I could possibly make them given the research conducted or, in the case of conversations, they are included to add some drama to a situation - based around known circumstances and facts. Not that any of the drama in conversations would have been any more dramatic than any of the crews of Bomber or Fighter Command went through during the Second World War. They faced hell every time they went out, and none of us today can imagine the horrors they would have faced every day of their lives. Lives cut tragically short in too many instances.

This story does not claim to be a comprehensive history of 211 Squadron or operations of other RAF Squadrons mentioned in the book at various times, either at home or in North Africa or Greece. The book is not aimed at 'history purists' either. It is an attempt to focus on the everyday trials and tribulations of war and the history behind people who went to war and never came back. Their known exploits are recalled in this book; added to this, I have tried to be as accurate as possible using Gerald Davies' own RAF Service Record and other records and newspapers available for research. I have used records from many sources to piece together as accurate a story as possible about Gerald's movements both in Great Britain and when he was away. There will be omissions and forgive me if there are some inaccuracies. These are not intended and no intention whatsoever is made in the book to claim complete accuracy as regards crew and flight lists. I have done my best to tell the full life story of my uncle, Gerald Davies.

He was a brave man and received no recognition or honours for his deeds.

His two crew companions, 'The Bish' - James Gordon Finlayson became DSO and DFC. On 29 December 1942, he was also awarded the Greek Distinguished Flying Cross.

Pilot Officer Arthur Geary [1] also received the DFC posthumously.

I have always wondered why Gerald Davies received no honours, despite being on those missions when both of his comrades deservedly received DFCs. He displayed nothing but loyalty of service and bravery on more occasions than even related in this work.

In some ways it matters not, this work to write his story is testament to the man and his life and I hope it stands as a permanent memorial to him and his bravery in perpetuity.

*

The Bish - Squadron Leader James Richmond Gordon-Finlayson was born on 19th August 1914 to General Sir Robert Gordon-Finlayson and his wife, Lady Mary Gordon-Finlayson. The Bish survived the war and rose to the rank of Air-Vice Marshall in the RAF. He retired in 1963 and died in 1990 (3 March) at the grand old age of 85.

Squadron Leader Thomas 'Tommy' Henry Wisdom (1907 - 1972), the author of Wings Over Olympus, also survived the war, going back to live in Sussex. He was a racing driver and motoring journalist with the Daily Herald before he joined the RAF Volunteer Reserve for the war. He came first twice at the Le Mans 24 hours race - 1950 & 1952, such was his motoring prowess. He competed in the Monte Carlo Rally 23 times.

Image: Tommy Wisdom doing what he loved best.

Author's Note

[1] Arthur Geary DFC

The KING has been graciously pleased to approve the following awards in recognition of gallantry and devotion to duty in the execution of air operations:

13 March 1942 - Awarded with effect from 21 March 1941 - Distinguished Flying Cross

This officer has completed 62 sorties, of which 38 were carried out within 42 days. He has acted as a rear gunner in his Commanding Officer's aircraft for six months, and his keen observation and clear reports on the numerous manoeuvres of enemy aircraft have undoubtedly helped to save our own

aircraft on many occasions. He has assisted in beating off enemy fighters on 16 occasions. His courage and devotion to duty have been exemplary.
Courtesy: London Gazette

Epilogue

'Gerald's Easter Sunday 1941 Poem'

For Gerald and the brave men of 211 Squadron…

You were born during the First War. You died for our freedom in the Second.

Your life was tough, losing your mother was rough, then the RAF beckoned.

You went away with a joyful heart, content you had chosen the right avenue.

It was a path to glory, pain and death, but trod it you did, responsibly and true.

For the music you never heard, the Beatles, Buddy Holly, perhaps The Who?

For the wife and children, you never had; who could never miss you.

For the walks you never went on, and for the family you never came back to,

We lived our lives and got on from day to day, but no one ever forgot you.

One Easter Sunday, 1941 it was, in a land far away, where holiday jets now fly,

You lost those days of future, because you flew for all of us in that fearful sky.

To me, you were but a picture on a wall but to others, you were someone so tall,

In your officer's uniform. Proudly you served, but in the end you lost it all.

In Athens you now lie. There, almost forgotten, a name on a white piece of stone,

With others from 211 who lost their lives in '40 and '41. You were not alone.

Lost were men, with names people once shouted with love; or hugged tight,

As they let them go to a foreign land far away, to join this gruesome fight.

So here we remember those shouted names; shouts which will never come again.

Gerry! Arthur! Herby! Paddy! Jock! Buck! Cryer! George! ... all running to a plane.

Irvine! Peggy! Godfrey! Tommy! Pete! Wilf! Andy! Pongo! Jimmy! and Jack!

Remember them at every sunset, for they're never coming back.

Nigel Davies-Williams
13th April 2021

Post Script

'A Meeting with Ian Carter'

Just when you think you've seen it all, someone gets in touch and tells you they have something to show you. So it was, on an overcast and rainy Sunday, the 12th September 2021 a very special visitor came to my home in North Wales, all the way from County Durham.

Ian Carter has a very special interest in the history of 211 Squadron. He typed up and transformed the handwritten notes of James Dunnet which became the book Blenheim Over The Balkans. In Chapter XXIX of the book, entitled 'Last Words,' Ian can be seen with the battered wreckage of Blenheim L1434 recently recovered from Lake Mikro Prespa at the Hellenic Air Force Museum, Acharnes near Athens. What I was not aware of was Ian Carter had in his possession part of the wreckage of aircraft, Blenheim L8478 in which 'Uncle Gerald' along with Squadron Leader Antony Thorburn Irvine and Pilot Officer Arthur Geary DFC died. This was recovered by Edward Nourse in May 1983 (see Chapter 31) and he subsequently gave it to Ian Carter.

It's a sobering moment when you look upon a tangled piece of metal measuring no more than 24"x 18" and think to yourself, *'this was part of the plane in which my uncle met such a harrowing end.'*

Images: The author, holding the compass from Corfu crashed Blenheim L8511 (on 23rd November 1940) and Ian Carter with the tangled piece of starboard wing from Blenheim L8478 which was shot down in Northern Greece on 13th April 1941. Ian Carter is also pictured looking at the compass at the home of the author. The other images are of the starboard wing wreckage and inset is the plate showing the date of manufacture of the aircraft - 24th April 1939. This was the first time these two items from aircraft in which Gerald Davies had flown were reunited.

The author and Ian Carter still retain these precious items of wreckage but both agree they should be preserved for posterity, to commemorate the heroic deeds of the brave men who perished to preserve our freedoms.

References

Sources and References

1. The History of the Cheshire Regiment in the Great War by Colonel Arthur Crookenden (ISBN-13: 978-1845741402) W.H.Evans Sons & Co. Ltd, 1939
2. Wings Over Olympus (Allen & Unwin -1942) T.H. Wisdom
3. War Cabinet Minutes September to December 1940 - National Archives Documents
4. Diggers and Greeks: The Australian Campaigns in Greece and Crete (2010) Maria Hill (ISBN-13: 978-1742230146)
5. Archifau Gogledd Ddwyrain Cymru (Rhuthun) / North East Wales Archives (Ruthin)
6. Crown Copyright: 211 Squadron Badge - Reproduced with the permission of the Controller of Her Britannic Majesty's Stationery Office.
7. Air War for Yugoslavia, Greece and Crete 1940—41 of Shores, Cull & Malizia in 1987
8. Spirit of the Blue: A Fighter Pilot's Story: Peter Ayerst - A Fighter Pilot's Story Paperback –Illustrated, 21 Oct 2005 - ISBN-13: 978-0750935395 - ISBN-10: 0750935391
9. Charles Darwin 1871 - The Descent of Man
10. Britain's Wonderful Air Force (Odhams - 1940) - Air Commodore P.F. M. Fellowes.
11. Going Solo - Roald Dahl, (1986) ISBN: 978-1-405-93753-5
12. Ebenezer Howard, 1902 Edition - Garden Cities of Tomorrow
13. The Blenheim Society - www.blenheimsociety.com

14. D Clark 211 Squadron RAF website: www.211squadron.org
15. Epitaph For A Squadron: James Robert Gordon-Finlayson DSO DFC
16. Blenheim Over the Balkans (Pentland Books - 2001) James Dunnet
    - A special mention to Ian Carter who supported the writing of this book and who helped with much information.
17. The Colossus of Maroussi by Henry Miller (1941)   ISBN-10: 0141980540
18. 'January 22nd, Missolonghi' - by George Gordon - Lord Byron (1824)
19. New York Times (3 Jan 1990) Obituary: Evangelos Averoff, Ex-Official of Greece And a Politician, 79
20. www.levantineheritage.com - the Blacklers Resident in Greece
21. Aviation News (12-25 Oct 1990) The Greyhounds. No. 211 Squadron, Royal Air Force by Andrew Thomas
22. The London Gazette - Air Operations in Greece 1940 - 1941 p.205. (pub: 7 January 1947)
23. North East Wales Archives (Ruthin) Collections & Public Service (North Wales Hospital Records)
24. Diary of a Disaster: British Aid to Greece, 1940-1941 (1986) - Robin Higham Kansas State University
25. Commonwealth War Graves Commission
26. 211 Squadron RAF - Greece - An Observer's Notes & Recollections. C.F.R. Clark (1998) (Copy 8 of 10)
27. Fly Past Magazine - November 1983. The Lost Squadron. J.B. Dunnet.
28. Canterbury (New Zealand) Agricultural College Magazine No. 66 (Pub: Nov 1941)
29. Air Enthusiast (Sixteen) - The RAF in Greece 1940/41,   Eric Bevington-Smith, 1981.
30. Parade Middle East Weekly - Volume III No 33, 29 March 1941
31. Wikipedia - Various Fact Checks
32. US National Library of Medicine
33. London Gazette:
    - 20 June 1916
    - 20 Sept 1940
    - 29 Oct 1940
    - 7 January 1941

- 11 February 1941
- 25 March 1941
- 1 April 1941
- 13 March 1942

34. Illustrated London News - 3 August 1940.
35. British Newspaper Archive
36. Imperial War Museum - Images and Information
37. Tatler Magazine - 13th November 1940

My thanks also to Ancestry® and Findmypast® for the wealth of information I found from these sites which is included throughout this book.

Printed in Great Britain
by Amazon